# CHILDREN OF DUNE

*Books by Frank Herbert*
*published by New English Library:*

DUNE
DUNE MESSIAH
CHILDREN OF DUNE
GOD EMPEROR OF DUNE
HERETICS OF DUNE
DIRECT DESCENT
THE DRAGON IN THE SEA
THE EYES OF HEISENBERG
THE GODMAKERS
THE GREEN BRAIN
THE HEAVEN MAKERS
THE SANTAROGA BARRIER
WHIPPING STAR
THE WHITE PLAGUE
THE WORLDS OF FRANK HERBERT

THE HOME COMPUTER HANDBOOK
(with Max Barnard)

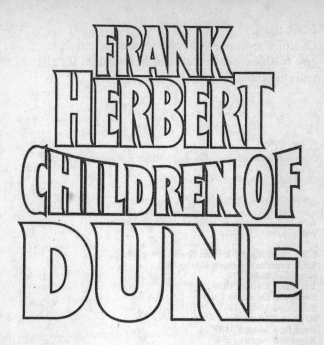

# FRANK HERBERT
# CHILDREN OF DUNE

NEW ENGLISH LIBRARY

FOR BEV:
Out of the wonderful commitment of our love
and to share her beauty and her wisdom for she
truly inspired this book.

First published in Great Britain by Victor Gollancz Ltd, in 1976

Copyright © by Frank Herbert 1976

NEL Open Market Edition September 1977
NEL Paperback Edition March 1978
Reprinted May 1979
Reprinted January 1980
Reprinted December 1980
Reprinted March 1981
Reprinted September 1981
Reprinted January 1982
Reprinted August 1983
Reprinted May 1984
Reprinted October 1984
Reprinted March 1985

NEL Books are published by
New English Library,
Mill Road, Dunton Green, Sevenoaks, Kent.
Editorial office: 47 Bedford Square, London WC1B 3DP.

Made and printed in Great Britain by
Hunt Barnard Printing Ltd, Aylesbury, Bucks.

0 450 03427 5

*Muad'Dib's teachings have become the playground of scholastics, of the superstitious and the corrupt. He taught a balanced way of life, a philosophy with which a human can meet problems arising from an ever-changing universe. He said humankind is still evolving, in a process which will never end. He said this evolution moves on changing principles which are known only to eternity. How can corrupted reasoning play with such an essence?*

> — Words of the Mentat
> Duncan Idaho

A spot of light appeared on the deep red rug which covered the raw rock of the cave floor. The light glowed without apparent source, having its existence only on the red fabric surface woven of spice-fiber. A questing circle about two centimeters in diameter, it moved erratically – now elongated, now an oval. Encountering the deep green side of a bed, it leaped upward, folded itself across the bed's surface.

Beneath the green covering lay a child with rusty hair, face still round with baby fat, a generous mouth – a figure lacking the lean sparseness of Fremen tradition, but not as water-fat as an off-worlder. As the light passed across closed eyelids, the small figure stirred. The light winked out.

Now there was only the sound of even breathing and, faint behind it, a reassuring drip-drip-drip of water collecting in a catchbasin from the windstill far above the cave.

Again the light appeared in the chamber – slightly larger, a few lumens brighter. This time there was a suggestion of source and movement to it: a hooded figure filled the arched doorway at the chamber's edge and the light originated there. Once more the light flowed around the chamber, testing, questing. There was a sense of menace in it, a restless dissatisfaction. It avoided the sleeping child, paused on the gridded air inlet at an upper corner, probed a bulge in the green and gold wall hangings which softened the enclosing rock.

Presently the light winked out. The hooded figure moved with a betraying swish of fabric, took up a station at one side of the arched doorway. Anyone aware of the routine here in Sietch Tabr would have suspected at once that this must be Stilgar,

5

Naib of the Sietch, guardian of the orphaned twins who would one day take up the mantle of their father, Paul Muad'Dib. Stilgar often made night inspections of the twins' quarters, always going first to the chamber where Ghanima slept and ending here in the adjoining room, where he could reassure himself that Leto was not threatened.

*I'm an old fool*, Stilgar thought.

He fingered the cold surface of the light projector before restoring it to the loop in his belt sash. The projector irritated him even while he depended upon it. The thing was a subtle instrument of the Imperium, a device to detect the presence of large living bodies. It had shown only the sleeping children in the royal bedchambers.

Stilgar knew his thoughts and emotions were like the light. He could not still a restless inner projection. Some greater power controlled *that* movement. It projected him into this moment where he sensed the accumulated peril. Here lay the magnet for dreams of grandeur throughout the known universe. Here lay temporal riches, secular authority and that most powerful of all mystic talismans: the divine authenticity of Muad'Dib's religious bequest. In these twins – Leto and his sister Ghanima – an awesome power focused. While they lived, Muad'Dib, though dead, lived in them.

These were not merely nine-year-old children; they were a natural force, objects of veneration and fear. They were the children of Paul Atreides, who had become Muad'Dib, the Mahdi of all the Fremen. Muad'Dib had ignited an explosion of humanity; Fremen had spread from this planet in a jihad, carrying their fervor across the human universe in a wave of religious government whose scope and ubiquitous authority had left its mark on every planet.

*Yet these children of Muad'Dib are flesh and blood*, Stilgar thought. *Two simple thrusts of my knife would still their hearts. Their water would return to the tribe.*

His wayward mind fell into turmoil at such a thought.

*To kill Muad'Dib's children!*

But the years had made him wise in introspection. Stilgar knew the origin of such a terrible thought. It came from the left hand of the damned, not from the right hand of the blessed. The *ayat* and *burhan* of Life held few mysteries for him. Once he'd been proud to think of himself as Fremen, to think of the desert as a friend, to name his planet Dune in his thoughts and not Arrakis, as it was marked on all the Imperial star charts.

*How simple things were when our Messiah was only a dream*, he thought. *By finding our Mahdi we loosed upon the universe countless messianic dreams. Every people subjugated by the jihad now dreams of a leader to come.*

Stilgar glanced into the darkened bedchamber.

*If my knife liberated all of those people, would they make a messiah of me?*

Leto could be heard stirring restlessly in his bed.

Stilgar sighed. He had never known the Atreides grandfather whose name this child had taken. But many said the moral strength of Muad'Dib had come from that source. Would that terrifying quality of *rightness* skip a generation now? Stilgar found himself unable to answer this question.

He thought: *Sietch Tabr is mine. I rule here. I am a Naib of the Fremen. Without me there would have been no Muad'Dib. These twins, now . . . through Chani, their mother and my kinswoman, my blood flows in their veins. I am there with Muad'Dib and Chani and all the others. What have we done to our universe?*

Stilgar could not explain why such thoughts came to him in the night and why they made him feel so guilty. He crouched within his hooded robe. Reality was not at all like the dream. The Friendly Desert, which once had spread from pole to pole, was reduced to half its former size. The mythic paradise of spreading greenery filled him with dismay. It was not like the dream. And as his planet changed, he knew he had changed. He had become a far more subtle person than the one-time sietch chieftain. He was aware now of many things – of statecraft and profound consequences in the smallest decisions. Yet he felt his knowledge and subtlety as a thin veneer covering an iron core of simpler, more deterministic awareness. And that older core called out to him, pleaded with him for a return to cleaner values.

The morning sounds of the sietch began intruding upon his thoughts. People were beginning to move about in the cavern. He felt a breeze against his cheeks: people were going out through the doorseals into the predawn darkness. The breeze spoke of carelessness as it spoke of the time. Warren dwellers no longer maintained the tight water discipline of the old days. Why should they, when rain had been recorded on this planet, when clouds were seen, when eight Fremen had been inundated and killed by a flash flood in a wadi? Until that event, the word *drowned* had not existed in the language of Dune. But this was no longer Dune; this was Arrakis . . . and it was the morning of an eventful day.

7

He thought: *Jessica, mother of Muad'Dib was grandmother of these royal twins, returns to our planet today. Why does she end her self-imposed exile at this time? Why does she leave the softness and security of Caladan for the dangers of Arrakis?*

And there were other worries: Would she sense Stilgar's doubts? She was a Bene Gesserit witch, graduate of the Sisterhood's deepest training, and a Reverend Mother in her own right. Such females were acute and they were dangerous. Would she order him to fall upon his own knife as the Umma-Protector of Liet-Kynes had been ordered?

*Would I obey her?* he wondered.

He could not answer that question, but now he thought about Liet-Kynes, the planetologist who had first dreamed of transforming the planetwide desert of Dune into the human-supportive green planet which it was becoming. Liet-Kynes had been Chani's father. Without him there would have been no dream, no Chani, no royal twins. The workings of this fragile chain dismayed Stilgar.

*How have we met in this place?* he asked himself. *How have we combined? For what purpose? Is it my duty to end it all, to shatter that great combination?*

Stilgar admitted the terrible urging within him now. He could make that choice, denying love and family to do what a Naib must do on occasion: make a deadly decision for the good of the tribe. By one view, such a murder represented ultimate betrayal and atrocity. *To kill mere children!* Yet they were not mere children. They had eaten melange, had shared in the sietch orgy, had probed the desert for sandtrout and played the other games of Fremen children . . . And they sat in the Royal Council. Children of such tender years, yet wise enough to sit in the Council. They might be children in flesh, but they were ancient in experience, born with a totality of genetic memory, a terrifying awareness which set their Aunt Alia and themselves apart from all other living humans.

Many times in many nights had Stilgar found his mind circling this *difference* shared by the twins and their aunt; many times had he been awakened from sleep by these torments, coming here to the twins' bedchambers with his dreams unfinished. Now his doubts came to focus. Failure to make a decision was in itself a decision – he knew this. These twins and their aunt had awakened in the womb, knowing there all of the memories passed on to them by their ancestors. Spice addiction had done this, spice addiction of the mothers – the Lady Jessica and Chani. The Lady

8

Jessica had borne a son, Muad'Dib, before her addiction. Alia had come after the addiction. That was clear in retrospect. The countless generations of selective breeding directed by the Bene Gesserits had achieved Muad'Dib, but nowhere in the Sisterhood's plans had they allowed for melange. Oh, they knew about this possibility, but they feared it and called it *Abomination*. That was the most dismaying fact. Abomination. They must possess reasons for such a judgment. And if they said Alia was an Abomination, then that must apply equally to the twins, because Chani, too, had been addicted, her body saturated with spice, and her genes had somehow complemented those of Muad'Dib.

Stilgar's thoughts moved in ferment. There could be no doubt these twins went beyond their father. But in which direction? The boy spoke of an ability to *be* his father – and had proved it. Even as an infant, Leto had revealed memories which only Muad'Dib should have known. Were there other ancestors waiting in that vast spectrum of memories – ancestors whose beliefs and habits created unspeakable dangers for living humans?

Abominations, the holy witches of the Bene Gesserit said. Yet the Sisterhood coveted the genophase of these children. The witches wanted sperm and ovum without the disturbing flesh which carried them. Was that why the Lady Jessica returned at this time? She had broken with the Sisterhood to support her Ducal mate, but rumor said she had returned to the Bene Gesserit ways.

*I could end all of these dreams,* Stilgar thought. *How simple it would be.*

And yet again he wondered at himself that he could contemplate such a choice. Were Muad'Dib's twins responsible for the reality which obliterated the dreams of others? No. They were merely the lens through which light poured to reveal new shapes in the universe.

In torment, his mind reverted to primary Fremen beliefs, and he thought: *God's command comes; so seek not to hasten it. God's it is to show the way; and some do swerve from it.*

It was the religion of Muad'Dib which upset Stilgar most. Why did they make a god of Muad'Dib? Why deify a man known to be flesh? Muad'Dib's *Golden Elixir of Life* had created a bureaucratic monster which sat astride human affairs. Government and religion united, and breaking a law became sin. A smell of blasphemy arose like smoke around any questioning of governmental edicts. The guilt of rebellion invoked hellfire and self-righteous judgments.

9

Yet it was men who created these governmental edicts.

Stilgar shook his head sadly, not seeing the attendants who had moved into the Royal Antechamber for their morning duties.

He fingered the crysknife at his waist, thinking of the past it symbolized, thinking that more than once he had sympathized with rebels whose abortive uprisings had been crushed by his own orders. Confusion washed through his mind and he wished he knew how to obliterate it, returning to the simplicities represented by the knife. But the universe would not turn backward. It was a great engine projected upon the grey void of nonexistence. His knife, if it brought the deaths of the twins, would only reverberate against that void, weaving new complexities to echo through human history, creating new surges of chaos, inviting humankind to attempt other forms of order and disorder.

Stilgar sighed, growing aware of the movements around him. Yes, these attendants represented a kind of order which was bound around Muad'Dib's twins. They moved from one moment to the next, meeting whatever necessities occurred there. *Best to emulate them*, Stilgar told himself. *Best meet what comes when it comes.*

*I am an attendant yet*, he told himself. *And my master is God the Merciful, the Compassionate.* And he quoted to himself: '*Surely, We have put on their necks fetters up to the chin, so their heads are raised; and We have put before them a barrier and behind them a barrier; and We have covered them, so they do not see.*'

Thus was it written in the old Fremen religion.

Stilgar nodded to himself.

To *see*, to anticipate the next moment as Muad'Dib had done with his awesome visions of the future, added a counter-force to human affairs. It created new places for decisions. To be unfettered, yes, that might well indicate a whim of God. Another complexity beyond ordinary human reach.

Stilgar removed his hand from the knife. His fingers tingled with remembrance of it. But the blade which once had glistened in a sandworm's gaping mouth remained in its sheath. Stilgar knew he would not draw this blade now to kill the twins. He had reached a decision. Better to retain that one old virtue which he still cherished: loyalty. Better the complexities one thought he knew than the complexities which defied understanding. Better the now than the future of a dream. The bitter taste in his mouth told Stilgar how empty and revolting some dreams could be.

*No! No more dreams!*

CHALLENGE: '*Have you seen The Preacher?*'
RESPONSE: '*I have seen a sandworm.*'
CHALLENGE: '*What about that sandworm?*'
RESPONSE: '*It gives us the air we breathe.*'
CHALLENGE: '*Then why do we destroy its land?*'
RESPONSE: '*Because Shai-Hulud* [sandworm deified] *orders it.*'

– Riddles of Arrakis
by Harq al-Ada

As was the Fremen custom, the Atreides twins arose an hour before dawn. They yawned and stretched in secret unison in their adjoining chambers, feeling the activity of the cave-warren around them. They could hear attendants in the antechamber preparing breakfast, a simple gruel with dates and nuts blended in liquid skimmed from partially fermented spice. There were glowglobes in the antechamber and a soft yellow light entered through the open archways of the bedchambers. The twins dressed swiftly in the soft light, each hearing the other nearby. As they had agreed, they donned stillsuits against the desert's parching winds.

Presently the royal pair met in the antechamber, noting the sudden stillness of the attendants. Leto, it was observed, wore a black-edged tan cape over his stillsuit's gray slickness. His sister wore a green cape. The neck of each cape was held by a clasp in the form of an Atreides hawk – gold with red jewels for eyes.

Seeing this finery, Harah, who was one of Stilgar's wives, said: 'I see you have dressed to honor your grandmother.' Leto picked up his breakfast bowl before looking at Harah's dark and wind-creased face. He shook his head. Then: 'How do you know it's not ourselves we honor?'

Harah met his taunting stare without flinching, said: 'My eyes are just as blue as yours!'

Ghanima laughed aloud. Harah was always an adept at the Fremen challenge-game. In one sentence, she had said: 'Don't taunt me, boy. You may be royalty, but we both bear the stigma of melange addiction – eyes without whites. What Fremen needs more finery or more honor than that?'

Leto smiled, shook his head ruefully. 'Harah, my love, if you were but younger and not already Stilgar's, I'd make you my own.'

Harah accepted the small victory easily, signaling the other

11

attendants to continue preparing the chambers for this day's important activities. 'Eat your breakfasts,' she said. 'You'll need the energy today.'

'Then you agree that we're not too fine for our grandmother?' Ghanima asked, speaking around a mouthful of gruel.

'Don't fear her, Ghani,' Harah said.

Leto gulped a mouthful of gruel, sent a probing stare at Harah. The woman was infernally folk-wise, seeing through the game of finery so quickly. 'Will she believe we fear her?' Leto asked.

'Like as not,' Harah said. 'She was our Reverend Mother, remember. I know her ways.'

'How was Alia dressed?' Ghanima asked.

'I've not seen her.' Harah spoke shortly, turning away.

Leto and Ghanima exchanged a look of shared secrets, bent quickly to their breakfast. Presently they went out into the great central passage.

Ghanima spoke in one of the ancient languages they shared in genetic memory: 'So today we have a grandmother.'

'It bothers Alia greatly,' Leto said.

'Who likes to give up such authority?' Ghanima asked.

Leto laughed softly, an oddly adult sound from flesh so young. 'It's more than that.'

'Will her mother's eyes observe what we have observed?'

'And why not?' Leto asked.

'Yes . . . That could be what Alia fears.'

'Who knows Abomination better than Abomination?' Leto asked.

'We could be wrong, you know,' Ghanima said.

'But we're not.' And he quoted from the Bene Gesserit Azhar Book: 'It is with reason and terrible experience that we call the pre-born *Abomination*. For who knows what lost and damned persona out of our evil past may take over the living flesh?'

'I know the history of it,' Ghanima said. 'But if that's true, why don't we suffer from this inner assault?'

'Perhaps our parents stand guard within us,' Leto said.

'Then why not guardians for Alia as well?'

'I don't know. It could be because one of her parents remains among the living. It could be simply that we are still young and strong. Perhaps when we're older and more cynical . . .'

'We must take great care with this grandmother,' Ghanima said.

'And not discuss this Preacher who wanders our planet speaking heresy?'

12

'You don't really think he's our father!'

'I make no judgment on it, but Alia fears him.'

Ghanima shook her head sharply. 'I don't believe this Abomination nonsense!'

'You've just as many memories as I have,' Leto said. 'You can believe what you want to believe.'

'You think it's because we haven't dared the spice trance and Alia has,' Ghanima said.

'That's exactly what I think.'

They fell silent, moving out into the flow of people in the central passage. It was cool in Sietch Tabr, but the stillsuits were warm and the twins kept their condenser hoods thrown back from their red hair. Their faces betrayed the stamp of shared genes: generous mouths, widely set eyes of spice addict blue-on-blue.

Leto was first to note the approach of their Aunt Alia.

'Here she comes now,' he said, shifting to Atreides battle language as a warning.

Ghanima nodded to her aunt as Alia stopped in front of them, said: 'A *spoil of war* greets her illustrious relative.' Using the same Chakobsa language, Ghanima emphasized the meaning of her own name – *Spoil of War*.

'You see, Beloved Aunt,' Leto said, 'we prepare ourselves for today's encounter with your mother.'

Alia, the one person in the teeming royal household who harbored not the faintest surprise at adult behavior from these children, glared from one to the other. Then: 'Hold your tongues, both of you!'

Alia's bronze hair was pulled back into two golden water rings. Her oval face held a frown, the wide mouth with its downturned hint of self-indulgence was held in a tight line. Worry wrinkles fanned the corners of her blue-on-blue eyes.

'I've warned both of you how to behave today,' Alia said. 'You know the reasons as well as I.'

'We know your reasons, but you may not know ours,' Ghanima said.

'Ghani!' Alia growled.

Leto glared at his aunt, said: 'Today of all days, we will not pretend to be simpering infants!'

'No one wants you to simper,' Alia said. 'But we think it unwise for you to provoke dangerous thoughts in my mother. Irulan agrees with me. Who knows what role the Lady Jessica will choose? She is, after all, Bene Gesserit.'

13

Leto shook his head, wondering: *Why does Alia not see what we suspect? Is she too far gone?* And he made special note of the subtle gene-markers on Alia's face which betrayed the presence of her maternal grandfather. The Baron Vladimir Harkonnen had not been a pleasant person. At this observation, Leto felt the vague stirrings of his own disquiet, thinking: *My own ancestor, too.*

He said: 'The Lady Jessica was trained to rule.'

Ghanima nodded. 'Why does she choose this time to come back?'

Alia scowled. Then: 'Is it possible she merely wants to see her grandchildren?'

Ghanima thought: *That's what you hope, my dear aunt. But it's damned well not likely.*

'She cannot rule here,' Alia said. 'She has Caladan. That should be enough.'

Ghanima spoke placatingly: 'When our father went into the desert to die, he left you as Regent. He . . .'

'Have you any complaint?' Alia demanded.

'It was a reasonable choice,' Leto said, following his sister's lead. 'You were the one person who knew what it was like to be born as we were born.'

'It's rumored that my mother has returned to the Sisterhood,' Alia said, 'and you both know what the Bene Gesserit think about . . .'

'Abomination,' Leto said.

'Yes!' Alia bit the word off.

'Once a witch, always a witch – so it's said,' Ghanima said.

*Sister, you play a dangerous game,* Leto thought, but he followed her lead, saying: 'Our grandmother was a woman of greater simplicity than others of her kind. You share her memories, Alia; surely you must know what to expect.'

'Simplicity!' Alia said, shaking her head, looking around her at the thronged passage, then back to the twins. 'If my mother were less complex, neither of you would be here – nor I. I would have been her firstborn and none of this . . . ' A shrug, half shudder, moved her shoulders. 'I warn you two, be very careful what you do today.' Alia looked up. 'Here comes my guard.'

'And you still don't think it safe for us to accompany you to the spaceport?' Leto asked.

'Wait here,' Alia said. 'I'll bring her back.'

Leto exchanged a look with his sister, said: 'You've told us many times that the memories we hold from those who've passed

14

before us lack a certain usefulness until we've experienced enough with our own flesh to make them reality. My sister and I believe this. We anticipate dangerous changes with the arrival of our grandmother.'

'Don't stop believing that,' Alia said. She turned away to be enclosed by her guards and they moved swiftly down the passage toward the State Entrance where ornithopters awaited them.

Ghanima wiped a tear from her right eye.

'Water for the dead?' Leto whispered, taking his sister's arm.

Ghanima drew in a deep, sighing breath, thinking of how she had observed her aunt, using the way she knew best from her own accumulation of ancestral experiences. 'Spice trance did it?' she asked, knowing what Leto would say.

'Do you have a better suggestion?'

'For the sake of argument, why didn't our father . . . or even our grandmother succumb?'

He studied her for a moment. Then: 'You know the answer as well as I do. They had secure personalities by the time they came to Arrakis. The spice trance – well . . . ' He shrugged. 'They weren't born into this world already possessed of their ancestors. Alia, though . . . '

'Why didn't she believe the Bene Gesserit warnings?' Ghanima chewed her lower lip. 'Alia had the same information to draw upon that we do.'

'They already were calling her Abomination,' Leto said. 'Don't you find it tempting to find out if you're stronger than all of those . . . '

'No, I don't!' Ghanima looked away from her brother's probing stare, shuddered. She had only to consult her genetic memories and the Sisterhood's warnings took on vivid shape. The pre-born observably tended to become adults of nasty habits. And the likely cause . . . Again she shuddered.

'Pity we don't have a few pre-born in our ancestry,' Leto said.

'Perhaps we do.'

'But we'd . . . Ahh, yes, the old unanswered question. Do we really have open access to every ancestor's total file of experiences?'

From his own inner turmoil, Leto knew how this conversation must be disturbing his sister. They'd considered this question many times, always without conclusion. He said: 'We must delay and delay and delay every time she urges the trance upon us. Extreme caution with a spice overdose; that's our best course.'

'An overdose would have to be pretty large,' Ghanima said.

15

'Our tolerance is probably high,' he agreed. 'Look how much Alia requires.'

'I pity her,' Ghanima said. 'The lure of it must've been subtle and insidious, creeping up on her until . . . '

'She's a victim, yes,' Leto said. 'Abomination.'

'We could be wrong.'

'True.'

'I always wonder,' Ghanima mused, 'if the next ancestral memory I seek will be the one which . . . '

'The past is no farther away than your pillow,' Leto said.

'We must make the opportunity to discuss this with our grandmother.'

'So her memory within me urges,' Leto said.

Ghanima met his gaze. Then: 'Too much knowledge never makes for simple decisions.'

> *The sietch at the desert's rim*
> *Was Liet's, was Kynes's,*
> *Was Stilgar's, was Muad'Dib's*
> *And, once more, was Stilgar's,*
> *The Naibs one by one sleep in the sand,*
> *But the sietch endures.*
>
> — from a Fremen song

Alia felt her heart pounding as she walked away from the twins. For a few pulsing seconds, she had felt herself near compulsion to stay with them and beg their help. What a foolish weakness! Memory of it sent a warning stillness through Alia. Would these twins dare practice prescience? The path which had engulfed their father must lure them – spice trance with its visions of the future wavering like gauze blown on a fickle wind.

*Why cannot I see the future?* Alia wondered. *Much as I try, why does it elude me?*

The twins must be made to try, she told herself. They could be lured into it. They had the curiosity of children and it was linked to memories which traversed millennia.

*Just as I have*, Alia thought.

Her guards opened the moisture seals at the State Entrance of the sietch, stood aside as she emerged onto the landing lip where the ornithopters waited. There was a wind from the desert blowing dust across the sky, but the day was bright. Emerging from the glowglobes of the sietch into the daylight sent her thoughts outward.

Why was the Lady Jessica returning at this moment? Had stories been carried to Caladan, stories of how the Regency was ...

'We must hurry, My Lady,' one of her guards said, raising his voice above the wind sounds.

Alia allowed herself to be helped into her ornithopter and secured the safety harness, but her thoughts went leaping ahead.

*Why now?*

As the ornithopter's wings dipped and the craft went skidding into the air, she felt the pomp and power of her position as physical things – but they were fragile, oh, how fragile!

Why now, when her plans were not completed?

The dust mists drifted, lifting, and she could see the bright sunlight upon the changing landscape of the planet: broad reaches of green vegetation where parched earth had once dominated.

*Without a vision of the future, I could fail. Oh, what magic I could perform if only I could see as Paul saw! Not for me the bitterness which prescient visions brought.*

A tormenting hunger shuddered through her and she wished she could put aside the power. Oh, to be as others were – blind in that safest of all blindnesses, living only the hypnoidal half-life into which birth-shock precipitated most humans. But no! She had been born an Atreides, victim of that eons-deep awareness inflicted by her mother's spice addiction.

*Why does my mother return today?*

Gurney Halleck would be with her – ever the devoted servant, the hired killer of ugly mien, loyal and straightforward, a musician who played murder with a sliptip, or entertained with equal ease upon his nine-string baliset. Some said he'd become her mother's lover. That would be a thing to ferret out; it might prove a most valuable leverage.

The wish to be as others were left her.

*Leto must be lured into the spice trance.*

She recalled asking the boy how he would deal with Gurney Halleck. And Leto, sensing undercurrents in her question, had said Halleck was loyal 'to a fault,' adding: 'He adored . . . my father.'

She'd noted the small hesitation. Leto had almost said 'me'

17

instead of 'my father'. Yes, it was hard at times to separate the genetic memory from the chord of living flesh. Gurney Halleck would not make that separation easier for Leto.

A harsh smile touched Alia's lips.

Gurney had chosen to return to Caladan with the Lady Jessica after Paul's death. His return would tangle many things. Coming back to Arrakis, he would add his own complexities to the existing lines. He had served Paul's father – and thus the succession went: Leto I to Paul to Leto II. And out of the Bene Gesserit breeding program: Jessica to Alia to Granima – a branching line. Gurney, adding to the confusion of identities, might prove valuable.

*What would he do if he discovered we carry the blood of Harkonnens, the Harkonnens he hates so bitterly?*

The smile on Alia's lips became introspective. The twins were, after all, children. They were like children with countless parents, whose memories belonged both to others and to self. They would stand at the lip of Sietch Tabr and watch the track of their grandmother's ship landing in the Arrakeen Basin. That burning mark of a ship's passage visible on the sky – would it make Jessica's arrival more real for her grandchildren?

*My mother will ask me about their training*, Alia thought. *Do I mix* prana-bindu *disciplines with a judicious hand? And I will tell her that they train themselves – just as I did. I will quote her grandson to her: 'Among the responsibilities of command is the necessity to punish . . . but only when the victim demands it.'*

It came to Alia then that if she could only focus the Lady Jessica's attention sharply enough onto the twins, others might escape a closer inspection.

Such a thing could be done. Leto was very like Paul. And why not? He could be Paul whenever he chose. Even Ghanima possessed this shattering ability.

*Just as I can be my mother or any of the others who've shared their lives with us.*

She veered away from this thought, staring out at the passing landscape of the Shield Wall. Then: *How was it to leave the warm safety of water-rich Caladan and return to Arrakis, to this desert planet where her Duke was murdered and her son died a martyr?*

Why did the Lady Jessica come back at this time?

Alia found no answer – nothing certain. She could share another's ego-awareness, but when experiences went their separate ways, then motives diverged as well. The stuff of decisions lay in the private actions taken by individuals. For the pre-born, the *many-born* Atreides, this remained the paramount reality, in itself another kind of birth: it was the absolute separation of living, breathing flesh when that flesh left the womb which had afflicted it with multiple awareness.

Alia saw nothing strange in loving and hating her mother simultaneously. It was a necessity, a required balance without room for guilt or blame. Where could loving or hating stop? Was one to blame the Bene Gesserit because they set the Lady Jessica upon a certain course? Guilt and blame grew diffuse when memory covered millennia. The Sisterhood had only been seeking to breed a Kwisatz Haderach: the male counterpart of a fully developed Reverend Mother . . . and more – a human of superior sensitivity and awareness, the Kwisatz Haderach who could be many places simultaneously. And the Lady Jessica, merely a pawn in that breeding program, had the bad taste to fall in love with the breeding partner to whom she had been assigned. Responsive to her beloved Duke's wishes, she produced a son instead of the daughter which the Sisterhood had commanded as the firstborn.

*Leaving me to be born after she became addicted to the spice! And now they don't want me. Now they fear me! With good reason . . .*

They'd achieved Paul, their Kwisatz Haderach, one lifetime too early – a minor miscalculation in a plan that extended. And now they had another problem: the Abomination, who carried the precious genes they'd sought for so many generations.

Alia felt a shadow pass across her, glanced upward. Her escort was assuming the high guard position preparatory to landing. She shook her head in wonderment at her wandering thoughts. What good was served by calling up old lifetimes and rubbing their mistakes together? This was a new lifetime.

Duncan Idaho had put his mentat awareness to the question of why Jessica returned at this time, evaluating the problem in the human-computer fashion which was his gift. He said she returned to take over the twins for the Sisterhood. The twins, too, carried those precious genes. Duncan could well be right. That might be enough to take the Lady Jessica out of her self-imposed seclusion on Caladan. If the Sisterhood commanded . . . Well, why else would she come back to the scenes of so much that must be shatteringly painful to her?

'We shall see,' Alia muttered.

She felt the ornithopter touch down on the roof of her Keep, a positive and jarring punctuation which filled her with grim anticipation.

melange (me'-lange *also* ma,lanj) *n-s, origin uncertain* (*thought to derive from ancient Terran Franzh*) : *a. mixture of spices ; b. spice of Arrakis* (*Dune*) *with geriatric properties first noted by Yanshuph Ashkoko, royal chemist in reign of Shakkad the Wise ; Arrakeen melange, found only in deepest desert sands of Arrakis, linked to prophetic visions of Paul Muad'Dib* (*Atreides*), *first Fremen Mahdi ; also employed by Spacing Guild Navigators and the Bene Gesserit.*

– Dictionary Royal
fifth edition

The two big cats came over the rock ridge in the dawn light, loping easily. They were not really into the passionate hunt as yet, merely looking over their territory. They were called Laza tigers, a special breed brought here to the planet Salusa Secundus almost eight thousand years past. Genetic manipulation of the ancient Terran stock had erased some of the original tiger features and refined other elements. The fangs remained long. Their faces were wide, eyes alert and intelligent. The paws were enlarged to give them support on uneven terrain and their sheathed claws could extend some ten centimeters, sharpened at the ends into razor tips by abrasive compression of the sheath. Their coats were a flat and even tan which made them almost invisible against sand.

They differed in another way from their ancestors: servo-stimulators had been implanted in their brains while they were cubs. The stimulators made them pawns of whoever possessed the transmitter.

It was cold and as the cats paused to scan the terrain, their breath made fog on the air. Around them lay a region of Salusa Secundus left sere and barren, a place which harbored a scant few sandtrout smuggled from Arrakis and kept precariously alive in the dream that the melange monopoly might be broken. Where the cats stood, the landscape was marked by tan rocks and a scattering of sparse bushes, silvery green in the long shadows of the morning sun.

With only the slightest movement the cats grew suddenly alert.

Their eyes turned slowly left, then their heads turned. Far down in the scarred land two children struggled up a dry wash, hand in hand. The children appeared to be of an age, perhaps nine or ten standard years. They were red-haired and wore stillsuits partly covered by rich white bourkas which bore all around the hem and at the forehead the hawk crest of the House Atreides worked in flame-jewel threads. As they walked, the children chattered happily and their voices carried clearly to the hunting cats. The Laza tigers knew this game; they had played it before, but they remained quiescent, awaiting the triggering of the chase signal in their servo-stimulators.

Now a man appeared on the ridgetop behind the cats. He stopped and surveyed the scene: cats, children. The man wore a Sardaukar working uniform in gray and black with insignia of a Levenbrech, aide to a Bashar. A harness passed behind his neck and under his arms to carry the servo-transmitter in a thin package against his chest where the keys could be reached easily by either hand.

The cats did not turn at his approach. They knew this man by sound and smell. He scrambled down to stop two paces from the cats, mopped his forehead. The air was cold, but this was hot work. Again his pale eyes surveyed the scene: cats, children. He pushed a damp strand of blond hair back under his black working helmet, touched the implanted microphone in his throat.

'The cats have them in sight.'

The answering voice came to him through receivers implanted behind each ear. 'We see them.'

'This time?' the Levenbrech asked.

'Will they do it without a chase command?' the voice countered.

'They're ready,' the Levenbrech said.

'Very well. Let us see if four conditioning sessions will be enough.'

'Tell me when you're ready.'

'Any time.'

'Now, then,' the Levenbrech said.

He touched a red key on the right hand side of his servo-transmitter, first releasing a bar which shielded the key. Now the cats stood without any transmitted restraints. He held his hand over a black key below the red one, ready to stop the animals should they turn on him. But they took no notice of him, crouched, and began working their way down the ridge toward the children. Their great paws slid out in smooth gliding motions.

The Levenbrech squatted to observe, knowing that somewhere around him a hidden transeye carried this entire scene to a secret monitor within the Keep where his Prince lived.

Presently the cats began to lope, then to run.

The children, intent on climbing through the rocky terrain, still had not seen their peril. One of them laughed, a high and piping sound in the clear air. The other child stumbled and, recovering balance, turned and saw the cats. The child pointed. 'Look!'

Both children stopped and stared at the interesting intrusion into their lives. They were still standing when the Laza tigers hit them, one cat to each child. The children died with a casual abruptness, necks broken swiftly. The cats began to feed.

'Shall I recall them?' the Levenbrech asked.

'Let them finish. They did well. I knew they would; this pair is superb.'

'Best I've ever seen,' the Levenbrech agreed.

'Very good, then. Transport is being sent for you. We will sign off now.'

The Levenbrech stood and stretched. He refrained from looking directly off to the high ground on his left where a telltale glitter had revealed the location of the transeye, which had relayed his fine performance to his Bashar far away in the green lands of the Capitol. The Levenbrech smiled. There would be a promotion for this day's work. Already he could feel a Bator's insignia at his neck – and someday, Burseg . . . Even, one day, Bashar. People who served well in the corps of Farad'n, grandson of the late Shaddam IV, earned rich promotions. One day, when the Prince was seated on his rightful throne, there would be even greater promotions. A Bashar's rank might not be the end of it. There were Baronies and Earldoms to be had on the many worlds of this realm . . . once the twin Atreides were removed.

*The Fremen must return to his original faith, to his genius in forming human communities; he must return to the past, where that lesson of survival was learned in the struggle with Arrakis. The only business of the Fremen should be that of opening his soul to the inner teachings. The worlds of the Imperium, the Landsraad and the CHOAM Confederacy have no message to give him. They will only rob him of his soul.*

— The Preacher at Arrakeen

All around the Lady Jessica, reaching far out into the dun flatness of the landing plain upon which her transport rested, crackling and sighing after its dive from space, stood an ocean of humanity. She estimated half a million people were there and perhaps only a third of them pilgrims. They stood in awesome silence, attention fixed on the transport's exit platform, whose shadowy hatchway concealed her and her party.

It lacked two hours until noon, but already the air above that throng reflected a dusty shimmering in promise of the day's heat.

Jessica touched her silver-flecked copper hair where it framed her oval face beneath the aba hood of a Reverend Mother. She knew she did not look her best after the long trip, and the black of the aba was not her best color. But she had worn this garment here before. The significance of the aba robe would not be lost upon the Fremen. She sighed. Space travel did not agree with her, and there'd been that added burden of memories – the other trip from Caladan to Arrakis when her Duke had been forced into this fief against his better judgment.

Slowly, probing with her Bene Gesserit-trained ability to detect significant minutiae, she scanned the sea of people. There were stillsuit hoods of dull gray, garments of Fremen from the deep desert; there were white-robed pilgrims with penitence marks on their shoulders; there were scattered pockets of rich merchants, hoodless in light clothing to flaunt their disdain for water loss in Arrakeen's parching air . . , and there was the delegation from the Society of the Faithful, green robed and heavily hooded, standing aloof within the sanctity of their own group.

Only when she lifted her gaze from the crowd did the scene take on any similarity to that which had greeted her upon her arrival with her beloved Duke. How long ago had that been? *More than twenty years.* She did not like to think of those intervening heartbeats. Time lay within her like a dead weight, and it was as though her years away from this planet had never been.

*Once more into the dragon's mouth*, she thought.

Here, upon this plain, her son had wrestled the Imperium from the late Shaddam IV. A convulsion of history had imprinted this place into men's minds and beliefs.

She heard the restless stirrings of the entourage behind her and again she sighed. They must wait for Alia, who had been delayed. Alia's party could be seen now approaching from the far edge of the throng, creating a human wave as a wedge of Royal Guards opened a passage.

Jessica scanned the landscape once more. Many differences submitted to her searching stare. A prayer balcony had been added to the landing field's control tower. And visible far off to the left across the plain stood the awesome pile of plasteel which Paul had built as his fortress – his 'sietch above the sand'. It was the largest integrated single construction ever to rise from the hand of man. Entire cities could have been housed within its walls and room to spare. Now it housed the most powerful governing force in the Imperium, Alia's 'Society of the Faithful', which she had built upon her brother's body.

*That place must go*, Jessica thought.

Alia's delegation had reached the foot of the exit ramp and stood there expectantly. Jessica recognized Stilgar's craggy features. And God forfend! There stood the Princess Irulan hiding her savagery in that seductive body with its cap of golden hair exposed by a vagrant breeze. Irulan seemed not to have aged a day; it was an affront. And there, at the point of the wedge, was Alia, her features impudently youthful, her eyes staring upward into the hatchway's shadows. Jessica's mouth drew into a straight line and she scanned her daughter's face. A leaden sensation pulsed through Jessica's body and she heard the surf of her own life within her ears. The rumors were true! Horrible! Horrible! Alia had fallen into the forbidden way. The evidence was there for the initiate to read. *Abomination!*

In the few moments it took her to recover, Jessica realized how much she had hoped to find the rumors false.

*What of the twins?* she asked herself. *Are they lost, too?*

Slowly, as befitted the mother of a god, Jessica moved out of the shadows and onto the lip of the ramp. Her entourage remained behind as instructed. These next few moments were the crucial ones. Jessica stood alone in full view of the throng. She heard Gurney Halleck cough nervously behind her. Gurney had objected: *'Not even a shield on you? Gods below, woman! You're insane!'*

But among Gurney's most valuable features was a core of obedience. He would say his piece and then he would obey. Now he obeyed.

The human sea emitted a sound like the hiss of a giant sandworm as Jessica emerged. She raised her arms in the benedictory to which the priesthood had conditioned the Imperium. With significant pockets of tardiness, but still like one giant organism, the people sank to their knees. Even the official party complied.

Jessica had marked out the places of delay, and she knew that other eyes behind her and among her agents in the throng had memorized a temporary map with which to seek out the tardy.

As Jessica remained with her arms upraised, Gurney and his men emerged. They moved swiftly past her down the ramp, ignoring the official party's startled looks, joining the agents who identified themselves by handsign. Quickly they fanned out through the human sea, leaping knots of kneeling figures, dashing through narrow lanes. A few of their targets saw the danger and tried to flee. They were the easiest: a thrown knife, a garrotte loop and the runners went down. Others were herded out of the press, hands bound, feet hobbled.

Through it all, Jessica stood with arms outstretched, blessing by her presence, keeping the throng subservient. She read the signs of spreading rumors though, and knew the dominant one because it had been planted: *'The Reverend Mother returns to weed out the slackers. Bless the mother of our Lord!'*

When it was over – a few dead bodies sprawled on the sand, captives removed to holding pens beneath the landing tower – Jessica lowered her arms. Perhaps three minutes had elapsed. She knew there was little likelihood Gurney and his men had taken any of the ringleaders, the ones who posed the most potent threat. They would be the alert and sensitive ones. But the captives would contain some interesting fish as well as the usual culls and dullards.

Jessica lowered her arms and, cheering, the people surged to their feet.

As though nothing untoward had happened, Jessica walked alone down the ramp, avoiding her daughter, singling out Stilgar for concentrated attention. The black beard which fanned out across the neck of his stillsuit hood like a wild delta contained flecks of gray, but his eyes carried that same whiteless intensity they'd presented to her on their first encounter in the desert.

Stilgar knew what had just occurred, and approved. Here stood a true Fremen Naib, a leader of men and capable of bloody decisions. His first words were completely in character.

'Welcome home, My Lady. It's always a pleasure to see direct and effective action.'

Jessica allowed herself a tiny smile. 'Close the port, Stil. No one leaves until we've questioned those we took.'

'It's already done, My Lady,' Stilgar said. 'Gurney's man and I planned this together.'

'Those were your men, then, the ones who helped.'

'Some of them, My Lady.'

She read the hidden reservations, nodded. 'You studied me pretty well in those days, Stil.'

'As you once were at pains to tell me, My Lady, one observes the survivors and learns from them.'

Alia stepped forward then and Stilgar stood aside while Jessica confronted her daughter.

Knowing there was no way to hide what she had learned, Jessica did not even try concealment. Alia could read the minutiae when she needed, could read as well as any adept of the Sisterhood. She would already know by Jessica's behavior what had been seen and interpreted. They were enemies for whom the word *mortal* touched only the surface.

Alia chose anger as the easiest and most proper reaction.

'How dare you plan an action such as this without consulting me?' she demanded, pushing her face close to Jessica's.

Jessica spoke mildly: 'As you've just heard, Gurney didn't even let me in on the whole plan. It was thought . . .'

'And you, Stilgar!' Alia said, rounding on him. 'To whom are *you* loyal?'

'My oath is to Muad'Dib's children,' Stilgar said, speaking stiffly. 'We have removed a threat to them.'

'And why doesn't that fill you with joy . . . daughter?' Jessica asked.

Alia blinked, glanced once at her mother, suppressed the inner tempest, and even managed a straight-toothed smile. 'I *am* filled with joy . . . mother,' she said. And to her own surprise, Alia found that she *was* happy, experiencing a terrible delight that it was all out in the open at last between herself and her mother. The moment she had dreaded was past and the power balance had not really been changed. 'We will discuss this in more detail at a more convenient time,' Alia said, speaking both to her mother and Stilgar.

'But of course,' Jessica said, turning with a movement of dismissal to face the Princess Irulan.

For a few brief heartbeats, Jessica and the Princess stood silently studying each other — two Bene Gesserits who had broken with the Sisterhood for the same reason: love, ,, both of them for love of men who now were dead. This Princess had loved Paul in vain, becoming his wife but not his mate. And now she lived only for the children given to Paul by his Fremen concubine, Chani.

Jessica spoke first: 'Where are my grandchildren?'

'At Sietch Tabr.'

'Too dangerous for them here; I understand.'

Irulan permitted herself a faint nod. She had observed the interchange between Jessica and Alia, but put upon it an interpretation for which Alia had prepared her. *'Jessica has returned to the Sisterhood and we both know they have plans for Paul's children.'* Irulan had never been the most accomplished adept in the Bene Gesserit — valuable more for the fact that she was a daughter of Shaddam IV than for any other reason; often too proud to exert herself in extending her capabilities. Now she chose sides with an abruptness which did no credit to her training.

'Really, Jessica,' Irulan said, 'the Royal Council should have been consulted. It was wrong of you to work only through — '

'Am I to believe none of you trust Stilgar?' Jessica asked.

Irulan possessed the wit to realize there could be no answer to such a question. She was glad that the priestly delegates, unable to contain their impatience any longer, pressed forward. She exchanged a glance with Alia, thinking: *Jessica's as haughty and certain of herself as ever!* A Bene Gesserit axiom arose unbidden in her mind, though: *'The haughty do but build castle walls behind which they try to hide their doubts and fears.'* Could that be true of Jessica? Surely not. Then it must be a pose. But for what purpose? The question disturbed Irulan.

The priests were noisy in their possession of Muad'Dib's mother. Some only touched her arms, but most bowed low and spoke greetings. At last the leaders of the delegation then took their turn with the Most Holy Reverend Mother, accepting the ordained role — 'The first shall be last' — with practiced smiles, telling her that the official Lustration ceremony awaited her at the Keep, Paul's old fortress-stronghold.

Jessica studied the pair, finding them repellent. One was called Javid, a young man of surly features and round cheeks, shadowed eyes which could not hide the suspicions lurking in their depths.

The other was Zebataleph, second son of a Naib she'd known in her Fremen days, as he was quick to remind her. He was easily classified; jollity linked with ruthlessness, a thin face with blond beard, an air about him of secret excitements and powerful knowledge. Javid she judged far more dangerous of the two, a man of private counsel, simultaneously magnetic and – she could find no other word – *repellent*. She found his accents strange, full of old Fremen pronunciations, as though he'd come from some isolated pocket of his people.

'Tell me, Javid,' she said, 'whence come you?'

'I am but a simple Fremen of the desert,' he said, every syllable giving the lie to the statement.

Zebataleph intruded with an offensive deference, almost mocking: 'We have much to discuss of the old days, My Lady. I was one of the first, you know, to recognize the holy nature of your son's mission.'

'But you weren't one of his Fedaykin,' she said.

'No, My Lady. I possessed a more philosophic bent; I studied for the priesthood.'

*And insured the preservation of your skin*, she thought.

Javid said: 'They await us at the Keep, My Lady.'

Again she found the strangeness of his accent an open question demanding an answer. 'Who awaits us?' she asked.

'The Convocation of the Faith, all those who keep bright the name and the deeds of your holy son,' Javid said.

Jessica glanced around her, saw Alia smiling at Javid, asked: 'Is this man one of your appointees, daughter?'

Alia nodded. 'A man destined for great deeds.'

But Jessica saw that Javid had no pleasure in this attention, marked him for Gurney's special study. And there came Gurney with five trusted men, signaling that they had the suspicious laggards under interrogation. He walked with the rolling stride of a powerful man, glance flicking left, right, all around, every muscle flowing through the relaxed alertness she had taught him out of the Bene Gesserit *prana-bindu* manual. He was an ugly lump of trained reflexes, a killer, and altogether terrifying to some, but Jessica loved him and prized him above all other living men. The scar of an inkvine whip ripped along his jaw, giving him a sinister appearance, but a smile softened his face as he saw Stilgar.

'Well done, Stil,' he said. And they gripped arms in the Fremen fashion.

'The Lustration,' Javid said, touching Jessica's arm.

Jessica drew back, chose her words carefully in the controlled power of Voice, her tone and delivery calculated for a precise emotional effect upon Javid and Zebataleph: 'I returned to Dune to see my grandchildren. Must we take time for this priestly nonsense?'

Zebataleph reacted with shock, his mouth dropping open, eyes alarmed, glancing about at those who had heard. The eyes marked each listener. *Priestly nonsense!* What effect would such words have, coming from the mother of their messiah?

Javid, however, confirmed Jessica's assessment. His mouth hardened, then smiled. The eyes did not smile, nor did they waver to mark the listeners. Javid already knew each member of this party. He had an earshot map of those who would be watched with special care from this point onward. Only seconds later, Javid stopped smiling with an abruptness which said he knew how he had betrayed himself. Javid had not failed to do his homework: he knew the observational powers possessed by the Lady Jessica. A short, jerking nod of his head acknowledged those powers.

In a lightning flash of mentation, Jessica weighed the necessities. A subtle hand signal to Gurney would bring Javid's death. It could be done here for effect, or in quiet later, and be made to appear an accident.

She thought: *When we try to conceal our innermost drives, the entire being screams betrayal.* Bene Gesserit training turned upon this revelation – raising the adepts above it and teaching them to read the open flesh of others. She saw Javid's intelligence as valuable, a temporary weight in the balance. If he could be won over, he could be the link she needed, the line into the Arrakeen priesthood. And he was Alia's man.

Jessica said: 'My official party must remain small. We have room for one addition, however. Javid, you will join us. Zebataleph, I am sorry. And, Javid . . . I will attend this – this ceremony – if you insist.'

Javid allowed himself a deep breath and a low-voiced 'As Muad'Dib's mother commands.' He glanced to Alia, to Zebataleph, back to Jessica. 'It pains me to delay the reunion with your grandchildren, but there are, ahhh, reasons of state . . . '

Jessica thought: *Good. He's a businessman above all else. Once we've determined the proper coinage, we'll buy him.* And she found herself enjoying the fact that he insisted on his precious ceremony. This little victory would give him power with his fellows, and they both knew it. Accepting his Lustration could be a down payment on later services.

'I presume you've arranged transportation,' she said.

> *I give you the desert chameleon, whose ability to blend itself into the background tells you all you need to know about the roots of ecology and the foundations of a personal identity.*
>
> — Book of Diatribes
> from the Hayt Chronicle

Leto sat playing a small baliset which had been sent to him on his fifth birthday by that consummate artist of the instrument, Gurney Halleck. In four years of practice, Leto had achieved a certain fluency, although the two bass side strings still gave him trouble. He had found the baliset soothing, however, for particular feelings of upset – a fact which had not escaped Ghanima. He sat now in twilight on a rock shelf at the southernmost extremity of the craggy outcropping which sheltered Sietch Tabr. Softly he strummed the baliset.

Ghanima stood behind him, her small figure radiating protest. She had not wanted to come here into the open after learning from Stilgar that their grandmother was delayed in Arrakeen. She particularly objected to coming here with nightfall near. Attempting to hurry her brother, she asked: 'Well, what is it?'

For answer, he began another tune.

For the first time since accepting the gift, Leto felt intensely aware that this baliset had originated with a master craftsman on Caladan. He possessed inherited memories which could inflict him with profound nostalgia for that beautiful planet where House Atreides had ruled. Leto had but to relax his inner barriers in the presence of this music and he would hear memories from those times when Gurney had employed the baliset to beguile his friend and charge, Paul Atreides. With the baliset sounding in his own hands, Leto felt himself more and more dominated by his father's psychical presence. Still he played, relating more strongly to the instrument with every second that passed. He sensed the absolute idealized summation within himself which *knew* how to play this baliset, though nine-year-old muscles had not yet been conditioned to that inner awareness.

Ghanima tapped her foot impatiently, unaware that she

matched the rhythm of her brother's playing.

Setting his mouth in a grimace of concentration, Leto broke from the familiar music and tried a song more ancient than any even Gurney had played. It had been old when Fremen migrated to their fifth planet. The words echoed a Zensunni theme, and he heard them in his memory while his fingers elicited a faltering version of the tune.

> 'Nature's beauteous form
> Contains a lovely essence
> Called by some – decay.
> By this lovely presence
> New life finds its way.
> Tears shed silently
> Are but water of the soul :
> They bring new life
> To the pain of being –
> A separation from that seeing
> Which death makes whole.'

Ghanima spoke behind him as he strummed the final note. 'There's a mucky old song. Why that one?'

'Because it fits.'

'Will you play it for Gurney?'

'Perhaps.'

'He'll call it moody nonsense.'

'I know.'

Leto peered back over his shoulder at Ghanima. There was no surprise in him that she knew the song and its lyrics, but he felt a sudden onset of awe at the singleness of their twinned lives. One of them could die and yet remain alive in the other's consciousness, every shared memory intact; they were that close. He found himself frightened by the timeless web of that closeness, broke his gaze away from her. The web contained gaps, he knew. His fear arose from the newest of those gaps. He felt their lives beginning to separate and wondered: *How can I tell her of this thing which has happened only to me?*

He peered out over the desert, seeing the deep shadows behind the barachans – those high, crescent-shaped migratory dunes which moved like waves around Arrakis. This was *Kedem*, the inner desert, and its dunes were rarely marked these days by the irregularities of a giant worm's progress. Sunset drew bloody streaks over the dunes, imparting a fiery light to the shadow edges. A hawk falling from the crimson sky captured his awareness as it captured a rock partridge in flight.

31

Directly beneath him on the desert floor plants grew in a profusion of greens, watered by a qanat which flowed partly in the open, partly in covered tunnels. The water came from giant windtrap collectors behind him on the highest point of rock. The green flag of the Atreides flew openly there.

*Water and green.*

The new symbols of Arrakis: water and green.

A diamond-shaped oasis of planted dunes spread beneath his high perch, focusing his attention into sharp Fremen awareness. The bell call of a nightbird came from the cliff below him, and it amplified the sensation that he lived this moment out of a wild past.

*Nous avons changé tout cela,* he thought, falling easily into one of the ancient tongues which he and Ghanima employed in private. '*We have altered all of that.*' He sighed. *Oublier je ne puis.* '*I cannot forget.*'

Beyond the oasis, he could see in this failing light the land Fremen called 'The Emptiness' – the land where nothing grows, the land never fertile. Water and the great ecological plan were changing that. There were places now on Arrakis where one could see the plush green velvet of forested hills. Forests on Arrakis! Some in the new generation found it difficult to imagine dunes beneath those undulant green hills. To such young eyes there was no shock value in seeing the flat foliage of rain trees. But Leto found himself thinking now in the Old Fremen manner, wary of change, fearful in the presence of the new.

He said: 'The children tell me they seldom find sandtrout here near the surface anymore.'

'What's that supposed to indicate?' Ghanima asked. There was petulance in her tone.

'Things are beginning to change very swiftly,' he said.

Again the bird chimed in the cliff, and night fell upon the desert as the hawk had fallen upon the partridge. Night often subjected him to an assault of memories – all of those inner lives clamoring for their moment. Ghanima didn't object to this phenomenon in quite the way he did. She knew his disquiet, though, and he felt her hand touch his shoulder in sympathy.

He struck an angry chord from the baliset.

How could he tell her what was happening to him?

Within his head were wars, uncounted lives parceling out their ancient memories: violent accidents, love's languor, the colors of many places and many faces . . . the buried sorrows and leaping joys of multitudes. He heard elegies to springs on planets which no longer existed, green dances and firelight, wails and halloos, a harvest of conversations without number.

Their assault was hardest to bear at nightfall in the open.

'Shouldn't we be going in?' she asked.

He shook his head, and she felt the movement, realizing at last that his troubles went deeper than she had suspected.

*Why do I so often greet the night out here?* he asked himself. He did not feel Ghanima withdraw her hand.

'You know why you torment yourself this way,' she said.

He heard the gentle chiding in her voice. Yes, he knew. The answer lay there in his awareness, obvious: *Because that great known-unknown within moves me like a wave.* He felt the cresting of his past as though he rode a surfboard. He had his father's time-spread memories of prescience superimposed upon everything else, yet he wanted all of those pasts. He wanted them. And they were so very dangerous. He knew that completely now with this new thing which he would have to tell Ghanima.

The desert was beginning to glow under the rising light of First Moon. He stared out at the false immobility of sand furls reaching into infinity. To his left, in the near distance, lay The Attendant, a rock outcropping which sandblast winds had reduced to a low, sinuous shape like a dark worm striking through the dunes. Someday the rock beneath him would be cut down to such a shape and Sietch Tabr would be no more, except in the memories of someone like himself. He did not doubt that there would be somone like himself.

'Why're you staring at The Attendant?' Ghanima asked.

He shrugged. In defiance of their guardians' orders, he and Ghanima often went to The Attendant. They had discovered a secret hiding place there, and Leto knew now why that place lured them.

Beneath him, its distance foreshortened by darkness, an open stretch of qanat gleamed in moonlight; its surface rippled with movements of predator fish which Fremen always planted in their stored water to keep out the sandtrout.

'I stand between fish and worm,' he murmured.

'What?'

He repeated it louder.

She put a hand to her mouth, beginning to suspect the thing which moved him. Her father had acted thus; she had but to peer inward and compare.

Leto shuddered. Memories which fastened him to places his flesh had never known presented him with answers to questions

33

he had not asked. He saw relationships and unfolding events against a gigantic inner screen. The sandworm of Dune would not cross water; water poisoned it. Yet water had been known here in prehistoric times. White gypsum pans attested to bygone lakes and seas. Wells, deep-drilled, found water which sandtrout sealed off. As clearly as if he'd witnessed the events, he saw what had happened on this planet and it filled him with foreboding for the cataclysmic changes which human intervention was bringing.

His voice barely above a whisper, he said: 'I know what happened, Ghanima.'

She bent close to him. 'Yes?'

'The sandtrout . . .'

He fell silent and she wondered why he kept referring to the haploid phase of the planet's giant sandworm, but she dared not prod him.

'The sandtrout,' he repeated, 'was introduced here from some other place. This was a wet planet then. They proliferated beyond the capability of existing ecosystems to deal with them. Sandtrout encysted the available free water, made this a desert planet . . . and they did it to survive. In a planet sufficiently dry, they could move to their sandworm phase.'

'The sandtrout?' She shook her head, not doubting him, but unwilling to search those depths where he gathered such information. And she thought: *Sandtrout?* Many times in this flesh and other had she played the childhood game, poling for sandtrout, teasing them into a thin glove membrane before taking them to the deathstill for their water. It was difficult to think of this mindless little creature as a shaper of enormous events.

Leto nodded to himself. Fremen had always known to plant predator fish in their water cisterns. The haploid sandtrout actively resisted great accumulations of water near the planet's surface; predators swam in that qanat below him. Their sandworm vector could handle small amounts of water – the amounts held in cellular bondage by human flesh, for example. But confronted by large bodies of water, their chemical factories went wild, exploded in the death-transformation which produced the dangerous melange concentrate, the ultimate awareness drug employed in a diluted fraction for the sietch orgy. That pure concentrate had taken Paul Muad'Dib through the walls of Time, deep into the well of dissolution which no other male had ever dared.

Ghanima sensed her brother trembling where he sat in front

34

of her. 'What have you done?' she demanded.

But he would not leave his own train of revelation. 'Fewer sandtrout – the ecological transformation of the planet . . . '

'They resist it, of course,' she said, and now she began to understand the fear in his voice, drawn into this thing against her will.

'When the sandtrout go, so do all the worms,' he said. 'The tribes must be warned.'

'No more spice,' she said.

Words merely touched high points of the system danger which they both saw hanging over human intrusion into Dune's ancient relationships.

'It's the thing Alia knows,' he said. 'It's why she gloats.'

'How can you be sure of that?'

'I'm sure.'

Now she knew for certain what disturbed him, and she felt the knowledge chill her.

'The tribes won't believe us if she denies it,' he said.

His statement went to the primary problem of their existence: What Fremen expected wisdom from a nine-year-old? Alia, growing farther and farther from her own inner sharing each day, played upon this.

'We must convince Stilgar,' Ghanima said.

As one, their heads turned and they stared out over the moon-lit desert. It was a different place now, changed by just a few moments of awareness. Human interplay with that environment had never been more apparent to them. They felt themselves as integral parts of a dynamic system held in delicately balanced order. The new outlook involved a real change of consciousness which flooded them with observations. As Liet-Kynes had said, the universe was a place of constant conversation between animal populations. The haploid sandtrout had spoken to them as human animals.

'The tribes would understand a threat to water,' Leto said.

'But it's a threat to more than water. It's a – ' She fell silent, understanding the deeper meaning of his words. Water was the ultimate power symbol on Arrakis. At their roots, Fremen re-mained special-application animals, desert survivors, governance experts under conditions of stress. And as water became plentiful, a strange symbol transfer came over them even while they under-stood the old necessities.

'You mean a threat to power,' she corrected him.

'Of course.'

'But will they believe us?'

'If they see it happening, if they see the imbalance.'

'Balance,' she said, and repeated her father's words from long ago: 'It's what distinguishes a people from a mob.'

Her words called up their father in him and he said: 'Economics versus beauty – a story older than Sheba.' He sighed, looked over his shoulder at her. 'I'm beginning to have prescient dreams, Ghani.'

A sharp gasp escaped her.

He said: 'When Stilgar told us our grandmother was delayed – I already knew that moment. Now my other dreams are suspect.'

'Leto . . . ' She shook her head, eyes damp. 'It came later for our father. Don't you think it might be –'

'I've dreamed myself enclosed in armor and racing across the dunes,' he said. 'And I've been to Jacurutu.'

'Jacu<sub>r</sub> . . ' She cleared her throat. 'That old myth!'

'A real place. Ghani! I must find this man they call The Preacher. I must find him and question him.'

'You think he's . . . our father?'

'Ask yourself that question.'

'It'd be just like him,' she agreed, 'but . . <sub>r</sub>'

'I don't like the things I know I'll do,' he said. 'For the first time in my life I understand my father.'

She felt excluded from his thoughts, said: 'The Preacher's probably just an old mystic.'

'I pray for that,' he whispered. 'Oh, how I pray for that!' He rocked forward, got to his feet. The baliset hummed in his hand as he moved. 'Would that he were only Gabriel without a horn.' He stared silently at the moonlit desert.

She turned to look where he looked, saw the foxfire glow of rotting vegetation at the edge of the sietch plantings, then the clean blending into lines of dunes. That was a living place out there. Even when the desert slept, something remained awake in it. She sensed that wakefulness, hearing animals below her drinking at the qanat. Leto's revelation had transformed the night: this was a living moment, a time to discover regularities within perpetual change, an instant in which to feel that long movement from their Terranic past, all of it encapsulated in her memories.

'Why Jacurutu?' she asked, and the flatness of her tone shattered the mood.

'Why . . . I don't know. When Stilgar first told us how they killed the people there and made the place tabu, I thought . . .

36

what you thought. But danger comes from there now . . . and The Preacher.'

She didn't respond, didn't demand that he share more of his prescient dreams with her, and she knew how much this told him of her terror. That way led to Abomination and they both knew it. The word hung unspoken between them as he turned and led the way back over the rocks to the sietch entrance. *Abomination.*

> *The Universe is God's. It is one thing, a wholeness against which all separations may be identified. Transient life, even that self-aware and reasoning life which we call sentient, holds only fragile trusteeship on any portion of the wholeness.*
>
> – Commentaries from the C.E.T.
> (Commission of Ecumenical Translators)

Halleck used hand signals to convey the actual message while speaking aloud of other matters. He didn't like the small ante-room the priests had assigned for this report, knowing it would be crawling with spy devices. Let them try to break the tiny hand signals, though. The Atreides had used this means of communication for centuries without anyone the wiser.

Night had fallen outside, but the room had no windows, depending upon glowglobes at the upper corners.

'Many of those we took were Alia's people,' Halleck signaled, watching Jessica's face as he spoke aloud, telling her the interrogation still continued.

'It was as you anticipated then,' Jessica replied, her fingers winking. She nodded and spoke an open reply: 'I'll expect a full report when you're satisfied, Gurney.'

'Of course, My Lady,' he said, and his fingers continued: 'There is another thing, quite disturbing. Under the deep drugs, some of our captives talked of Jacurutu and, as they spoke the name, they died.'

'A conditioned heart-stopper?' Jessica's fingers asked. And she said: 'Have you released any of the captives?'

'A few, My Lady – the more obvious culls.' And his fingers darted: 'We suspect a heart-compulsion but are not yet certain. The autopsies aren't completed. I thought you hould know about this thing of Jacurutu, however, and came immediately.'

'My Duke and I always thought Jacurutu an interesting legend

37

probably based on fact,' Jessica's fingers said, and she ignored the usual tug of sorrow as she spoke of her long-dead love.

'Do you have orders?' Halleck asked, speaking aloud.

Jessica answered in kind, telling him to return to the landing field and report when he had positive information, but her fingers conveyed another message: 'Resume contact with your friends among the smugglers. If Jacurutu exists, they'll support themselves by selling spice. There'd be no other market for them except the smugglers.'

Halleck bowed his head briefly while his fingers said: 'I've already set this course in motion, My Lady.' And because he could not ignore the training of a lifetime, added: 'Be very careful in this place. Alia is your enemy and most of the priesthood belongs to her.'

'Not Javid,' Jessica's fingers responded. 'He hates the Atreides. I doubt anyone but an adept could detect it, but I'm positive of it. He conspires and Alia doesn't know of it.'

'I'm assigning additional guards to your person,' Halleck said, speaking aloud, avoiding the light spark of displeasure which Jessica's eyes betrayed. 'There are dangers, I'm certain. Will you spend the night here?'

'We'll go later to Sietch Tabr,' she said and hesitated, on the point of telling him not to send more guards, but she held her silence. Gurney's instincts were to be trusted. More than one Atreides had learned this, both to his pleasure and his sorrow. 'I have one more meeting – with the Master of Novitiates this time,' she said. 'That's the last one and I'll be happily shut of this place.'

*And I beheld another beast coming up out of the sand; and he had two horns like a lamb, but his mouth was fanged and fiery as the dragon and his body shimmered and burned with great heat while it did hiss like the serpent.*

– Revised Orange Catholic Bible

He called himself *The Preacher*, and there had come to be an awesome fear among many on Arrakis that he might be Muad'Dib returned from the desert, not dead at all. Muad'Dib could be alive; for who had seen his body? For that matter, who saw any body that the desert took? But still – Muad'Dib? Points of comparison could be made, although no one from the old days came forward and said: 'Yes, I see that this is Muad'Dib, I know him.'

Still . . . Like Muad'Dib. The Preacher was blind, his eye sockets black and scarred in a way that could have been done by a stone burner. And his voice conveyed that crackling penetration, that same compelling force which demanded a response from deep within you. Many remarked this. He was lean, this Preacher, his leathery face seamed, his hair grizzled. But the deep desert did that to many people. You had only to look about you and see this proven. And there was another fact for contention: The Preacher was led by a young Fremen, a lad without known sietch who said, when questioned, that he worked for hire. It was argued that Muad'Dib, knowing the future, had not needed such a guide except at the very end, when his grief overcame him. But he'd needed a guide then; everyone knew it.

The Preacher had appeared one winter morning in the streets of Arrakeen, a brown and ridge-veined hand on the shoulder of his young guide. The lad, who gave his name as Assan Tariq, moved through the flint-smelling dust of the early swarming, leading his charge with the practiced agility of the warren-born, never once losing contact.

It was observed that the blind man wore a traditional bourka over a stillsuit which bore the mark about it of those once made only in the sietch caves of the deepest desert. It wasn't like the shabby suits being turned out these days. The nose tube which captured moisture from his breath for the recycling layers beneath the bourka was wrapped in braid, and it was the black vine braid so seldom seen anymore. The suit's mask across the lower half of his face carried green patches etched by the blown sand. All in all, this Preacher was a figure from Dune's past.

Many among the early crowds of that winter day had noted his passage. After all, a blind Fremen remained a rarity. Fremen Law still consigned the blind to Shai-Hulud. The wording of the Law, although it was less honored in these modern, water-soft times, remained unchanged from the earliest days. The blind were a gift to Shai-Hulud. They were to be exposed in the open *bled* for the great worms to devour. When it was done – and there were stories which got back to the cities – it was always done out where the largest worms still ruled, those called Old Men of the Desert. A blind Fremen, then, was a curiosity, and people paused to watch the passing of this odd pair.

The lad appeared about fourteen standard, one of the new breed who wore modified stillsuits; it left the face open to the moisture-robbing air. He had slender features, the all-blue spice-tinted eyes, a nubbin nose, and that innocuous look of innocence which so often masks cynical knowledge in the young. In contrast, the blind man was a reminder of times almost forgotten — long in stride and with a wiriness that spoke of many years on the sand with only his feet or a captive worm to carry him. He held his head in that stiff-necked rigidity which some of the blind cannot put off. The hooded head moved only when he cocked an ear at an interesting sound.

Through the day's gathering crowds the strange pair came, arriving at last on the steps which led up like terraced hectares to the escarpment which was Alia's Temple, a fitting companion to Paul's Keep. Up the steps The Preacher went until he and his young guide came to the third landing, where pilgrims of the Hajj awaited the morning opening of those gigantic doors above them. They were doors large enough to have admitted an entire cathedral from one of the ancient religions. Passing through them was said to reduce a pilgrim's soul to *motedom*, sufficiently small that it could pass through the eye of a needle and enter heaven.

At the edge of the third landing The Preacher turned, and it was as though he looked about him, seeing with his empty eye sockets the foppish city dwellers, some of them Fremen, with garments which simulated stillsuits but were only decorative fabrics, *seeing* the eager pilgrims fresh off the Guild space transports and awaiting that first step on the devotion which would ensure them a place in paradise.

The landing was a noisy place: there were Mahdi Spirit Cultists in green robes and carrying live hawks trained to screech a 'call to heaven'. Food was being offered for sale, the voices shouting in competitive stridence: there was the Dune Tarot with its booklets of commentaries imprinted on shigawire. One vendor had exotic bits of cloth 'guaranteed to have been touched by Muad'Dib himself!' Another had vials of water 'certified to have come from Sietch Tabr, where Muad'Dib lived'. Through it all there were conversations in a hundred or more dialects of Galach interspersed with harsh gutturals and squeaks of *outrine* languages which were gathered under the Holy Imperium. Face Dancers and little people from the suspected artisan planets of the Tleilaxu bounced and gyrated through the throng in bright clothing. There were lean faces and fat, water-rich faces. The susurration of nervous feet came from the gritty plasteel which formed the wide steps,

And occasionally a keening voice would rise out of the cacophony in prayer — 'Mua-a-a-ad'Dib! Mua-a-ad'Dib! Greet my soul's entreaty! You, who are God's anointed, greet my soul! Mua-a-a-ad'Dib!'

Nearby among the pilgrims, two mummers played for a few coins, reciting the lines of the currently popular 'Disputation of Armistead and Leandgrah'.

The Preacher cocked his head to listen.

The mummers were middle-aged city men with bored voices. At a word of command, the young guide described them for The Preacher. They were garbed in loose robes, not even deigning to simulate stillsuits on their water-rich bodies. Assan Tariq thought this amusing, but The Preacher reprimanded him.

The mummer who played the part of Leandgrah was just concluding his oration: 'Bah! The universe can be grasped only by the sentient hand. That hand is what drives your precious brain, and it drives everything else that derives from the brain. You see what you have created, you *become* sentient, only after the hand has done its work!'

A scattering of applause greeted his performance.

The Preacher sniffed and his nostrils recorded the rich odors of this place: uncapped esters of poorly adjusted stillsuits, masking musks of diverse origin, the common flinty dust, exhalations of uncounted exotic diets and aromas of rare incense which already had been ignited within Alia's Temple and now drifted down over the steps in cleverly directed currents. The Preacher's thoughts were mirrored on his face as he absorbed his surroundings: *We have come to this, we Fremen!*

A sudden diversion rippled through the crowd on the landing. Sand Dancers had come into the plaza at the foot of the steps, half a hundred of them tethered to each other by elacca ropes. They obviously had been dancing thus for days, seeking a state of ecstasy. Foam dribbled from their mouths as they jerked and stamped to their secret music. A full third of them dangled unconscious from the ropes, tugged back and forth by the others like dolls on strings. One of these dolls had come awake, though, and the crowd apparently knew what to expect.

'I have *see-ee-een!*' the newly awakened dancer shrieked. 'I have *see-ee-een!*' Hè resisted the pull of the other dancers, darted his wild gaze right and left. 'Where this city is, there will be only sand! I have *see-ee-een!*'

A great swelling laugh went up from the onlookers. Even the new pilgrims joined it.

This was too much for The Preacher. He raised both arms and roared in a voice which surely had commanded worm riders: '*Silence!*' The entire throng in the plaza went still at that battle cry.

The Preacher pointed a thin hand toward the dancers, and the illusion that he actually saw them was uncanny. 'Did you not hear that man? Blasphemers and idolaters! All of you! The religion of Muad'Dib is not Muad'Dib. He spurns it as he spurns you! Sand will cover this place. Sand will cover you.'

Saying this, he dropped his arms, put a hand on his young guide's shoulder, and commanded: 'Take me from this place.'

Perhaps it was The Preacher's choice of words: *He spurns it as he spurns you!* Perhaps it was his tone, certainly something more than human, a vocality trained surely in the arts of the Bene Gesserit Voice which commanded by mere nuances of subtle inflection. Perhaps it was only the inherent mysticism of this place where Muad'Dib had lived and walked and ruled. Someone called out from the landing, shouting at The Preacher's receding back in a voice which trembled with religious awe: 'Is that Muad'Dib come back to us?'

The Preacher stopped, reached into the purse beneath his bourka, and removed an object which only those nearby recognized. It was a desert-mummified human hand, one of the planet's jokes on mortality which occasionally turned up in the sand and were universally regarded as communications from Shai-Hulud. The hand had been dessicated into a tight fist which ended in white bone scarred by sandblast winds.

'I bring the Hand of God, and that is all I bring!' The Preacher shouted. 'I speak for the Hand of God. I am The Preacher.'

Some took him to mean that the hand was Muad'Dib's, but others fastened on that commanding presence and the terrible voice – and that was how Arrakis came to know his name. But it was not the last time his voice was heard.

*It is commonly reported, my dear Georad, that there exists great natural virtue in the melange experience. Perhaps this is true. There remains within me, however, profound doubts that every use of melange always brings virtue. Meseems that certain persons have corrupted the use of melange in defiance of God. In the words of the Ecumenon, they have disfigured the soul. They skim the surface of melange and believe thereby to attain grace. They deride their fellows, do great harm to godliness, and they distort the meaning of abundant gift maliciously, surely a mutilation beyond the power of man to restore. To be truly at one with the virtue of the spice, uncorrupted in all ways, full of goodly honor, a man must permit his deeds and his words to agree. When your actions describe a system of evil consequences, you should be judged by those consequences and not by your explanations. It is thus that we should judge Muad'Dib.*

— **The Pedant Heresy**

It was a small room tinged with the odor of ozone and reduced to a shadowy grayness by dimmed glowglobes and the metallic blue light of a single transeye monitoring screen. The screen was about a meter wide and only two-thirds of a meter in height. It revealed in remote detail a barren, rocky valley with two Laza tigers feeding on the bloody remnants of a recent kill. On the hillside above the tigers could be seen a slender man in Sardaukar working uniform, Levenbrech insignia at his collar. He wore a servo-control keyboard against his chest.

One veriform suspensor chair faced the screen, occupied by a fair-haired woman of indeterminate age. She had a heart-shaped face and slender hands which gripped the chair arms as she watched. The fullness of a white robe trimmed in gold concealed her figure. A pace to her right stood a blocky man dressed in the bronze and gold uniform of a Bashar Aide in the old Imperial Sardaukar. His graying hair had been closely cropped over square, emotionless features.

The woman coughed, said: 'It went as you predicted, Tyekanik.'

'Assuredly, Princess,' the Bashar Aide said, his voice hoarse.

She smiled at the tension in his voice, asked: 'Tell me, Tyekanik, how will my son like the sound of Emperor Farad'n I?'

'The title suits him, Princess.'

'That was not my question.'

43

'He might not approve some of the things done to gain him that, ahh, title.'

'Then again . . . ' She turned, peered up through the gloom at him. 'You served my father well. It was not your fault that he lost the throne to the Atreides. But surely the sting of that loss must be felt as keenly by you as by any –'

'Does the Princess Wensicia have some special task for me?' Tyekanik asked. His voice remained hoarse, but there was a sharp edge to it now.

'You have a bad habit of interrupting me,' she said.

Now he smiled, displaying thick teeth which glistened in the light from the screen. 'At times you remind me of your father,' he said. 'Always these circumlocutions before a request for a delicate . . . ahh, assignment.'

She jerked her gaze away from him to conceal anger, asked: 'Do you really think those Lazas will put my son on the throne?'

'It's distinctly possible, Princess. You must admit that the bastard get of Paul Atreides would be no more than juicy morsels for those two. And with those twins gone . . . ' He shrugged.

'The grandson of Shaddam IV becomes the logical successor,' she said. 'That is if we can remove the objections of the Fremen, the Landsraad and CHOAM, not to mention any surviving Atreides who might –'

'Javid assures me that his people can take care of Alia quite easily. I do not count the Lady Jessica as an Atreides. Who else remains?'

'Landsraad and CHOAM will go where the profit goes,' she said, 'but what of the Fremen?'

'We'll drown them in their Muad'Dib's religion!'

'Easier said than done, my dear Tyekanik.'

'I see,' he said. 'We're back to the old argument.'

'House Corrino has done worse things to gain power,' she said.

'But to embrace this . . . this Mahdi's religion!'

'My son respects you,' she said.

'Princess, I long for the day when House Corrino returns to its rightful seat of power. So does every remaining Sardaukar here on Salusa. But if you –'

'Tyekanik! This is the planet Salusa *Secundus*. Do not fall into the lazy ways which spread through our Imperium. Full name, complete title – attention to every detail. Those attributes will send the Atreides lifeblood into the sands of Arrakis. Every detail, Tyekanik!'

He knew what she was doing with this attack. It was part of

44

the shifty trickiness she'd learned from her sister, Irulan. But he felt himself losing ground.

'Do you hear me, Tyekanik?'

'I hear, Princess.'

'I want you to embrace this Muad'Dib religion,' she said.

'Princess, I would walk into fire for you, but this . . . '

'That is an order, Tyekanik!'

He swallowed, stared into the screen. The Laza tigers had finished feeding and now lay on the sand completing their toilet, long tongues moving across their forepaws.

'An *order*, Tyekanik – do you understand me?'

'I hear and obey, Princess.' His voice did not change tone.

She sighed. 'Ohh, if my father were only alive . . . '

'Yes, Princess.'

'Don't mock me, Tyekanik. I know how distasteful this is to you. But if you set the example . . . '

'He may not follow, Princess.'

'He'll follow.' She pointed at the screen. 'It occurs to me that the Levenbrech out there could be a problem.'

'A problem? How is that?'

'How many people know this thing of the tigers?'

'That Levenbrech who is their trainer . . . one transport pilot, you, and of course . . . ' He tapped his own chest.

'What about the buyers?'

'They know nothing. What is it you fear, Princess?'

'My son is, well, sensitive.'

'Sardaukar do not reveal secrets,' he said.

'Neither do dead men.' She reached forward and depressed a red key beneath the lighted screen.

Immediately the Laza tigers raised their heads. They got to their feet and looked up the hill at the Levenbrech. Moving as one, they turned and began a scrambling run up the hillside.

Appearing calm at first, the Levenbrech depressed a key on his console. His movements were assured but, as the cats continued their dash toward him, he became more frenzied, pressing the key harder and harder. A look of startled awareness came over his features and his hand jerked toward the working knife at his waist. The movement came too late. A raking claw hit his chest and sent him sprawling. As he fell, the other tiger took his neck in one great-fanged bite and shook him. His spine snapped.

'Attention to detail,' the Princess said. She turned, stiffened as Tyekanik drew his knife. But he presented the blade to her, handle foremost.

45

'Perhaps you'd like to use my knife to attend to another detail,' he said.

'Put that back in its sheath and don't act the fool!' she raged. 'Sometimes, Tyekanik, you try me to the –'

'That was a good man out there, Princess. One of my best.'

'One of *my* best,' she corrected him.

He drew a deep, trembling breath, sheathed his knife. 'And what of my transport pilot?'

'This will be ascribed to an accident,' she said. 'You will advise him to employ the utmost caution when he brings those tigers back to us. And of course, when he has delivered our pets to Javid's people on the transport . . .' She looked at his knife.

'Is that an order, Princess?'

'It is.'

'Shall I, then, fall on my knife, or will you take care of that, ahhh, detail?'

She spoke with a false calm, her voice heavy: 'Tyekanik, were I not absolutely convinced that you *would* fall on your knife at my command, you would not be standing here beside me – armed.'

He swallowed, stared at the screen. The tigers once more were feeding.

She refused to look at the scene, continued to stare at Tyekanik as she said: 'You will, as well, tell our buyers not to bring us any more matched pairs of children who fit the necessary description.'

'As you command, Princess.'

'Don't use that tone with me, Tyekanik.'

'Yes, Princess.'

Her lips drew into a straight line. Then: 'How many more of those paired costumes do we have?'

'Six sets of the robes, complete with stillsuits and the sand shoes, all with the Atreides insignia worked into them.'

'Fabrics as rich as the ones on that pair?' she nodded toward the screen.

'Fit for royalty, Princess.'

'Attention to detail,' she said. 'The garments will be dispatched to Arrakis as gifts for our royal cousins. They will be gifts from my son, do you understand me, Tyekanik?'

'Completely, Princess.'

'Have him inscribe a suitable note. It should say that he sends these few paltry garments as tokens of his devotion to House Atreides. Something on that order.'

'And the occasion?'

'There must be a birthday or holy‚day or something, Tyekanik. I leave that to you. I trust you, my friend.'

He stared at her silently.

Her face hardened. 'Surely you must know that? Who else can I trust since the death of my husband?'

He shrugged, thinking how closely she emulated the spider. It would not do to get on intimate terms with her, as he now suspected his Levenbrech had done.

'And Tyekanik,' she said, 'one more detail.'

'Yes, Princess.'

'My son is being trained to rule. There will come a time when he must grasp the sword in his own hands. You will know when that moment arrives. I'll wish to be informed immediately.'

'As you command, Princess.'

She leaned back, peered knowingly at Tyekanik. 'You do not approve of me, I know that. It is unimportant to me as long as you remember the lesson of the Levenbrech.'

'He was very good with animals, but disposable; yes, Princess.'

'That is not what I mean!'

'It isn't? Then . . . I don't understand.'

'An army,' she said, 'is composed of disposable, completely replaceable parts. That is the lesson of the Levenbrech.'

'Replaceable parts,' he said. 'Including the supreme command?'

'Without the supreme command there is seldom a reason for an army, Tyekanik. That is why you will immediately embrace this Mahdi religion and, at the same time, begin the campaign to convert my son.'

'At once, Princess. I presume you don't want me to stint his education in the other martial arts at the expense of his, ahh, religion?'

She pushed herself out of the chair, strode around him, paused at the door, and spoke without looking back. 'Someday you will try my patience once too often, Tyekanik.' With that, she let herself out.

*Either we abandon the long-honored Theory of Relativity, or we cease to believe that we can engage in continued accurate prediction of the future. Indeed, knowing the future raises a host of questions which cannot be answered under conventional assumptions unless one first projects an Observer outside of Time and, second, nullifies all movement. If you accept the Theory of Relativity, it can be shown that Time and the Observer must stand still in relationship to each other or inaccuracies will intervene. This would seem to say that it is impossible to engage in accurate prediction of the future. How, then, do we explain the continued seeking after this visionary goal by respected scientists? How, then, do we explain Muad'Dib?*

> – Lectures on Prescience
> By Harq al-Ada

'I must tell you something,' Jessica said, 'even though I know my telling will remind you of many experiences from our mutual past, and that this will place you in jeopardy.'

She paused to see how Ghanima was taking this.

They sat alone, just the two of them, occupying low cushions in a chamber of Sietch Tabr. It had required considerable skill to maneuver this meeting, and Jessica was not at all certain that she had been alone in the maneuvering. Ghanima had seemed to anticipate and augment every step.

It was almost two hours after daylight, and the excitements of greeting and all of the recognitions were past. Jessica forced her pulse back to a steady pace and focused her attention into this rock-walled room with its dark hangings and yellow cushions. To meet the accumulated tensions, she found herself for the first time in years recalling the Litany Against Fear from the Bene Gesserit rite.

*'I must not fear. Fear is the mind-killer. Fear is the little-death that brings total obliteration. I will face my fear. I will permit it to pass over me and through me. And when it has gone past I will turn the inner eye to see its path. Where the fear has gone there will be nothing. Only I will remain.'*

She did this silently and took a deep, calming breath.

'It helps at times,' Ghanima said. 'The Litany, I mean.'

Jessica closed her eyes to hide the shock of this insight. It had been a long time since anyone had been able to read her that intimately. The realization was disconcerting, especially when it was ignited by an intellect which hid behind a mask of childhood.

Having faced her fear, though Jessica opened her eyes and knew the source of turmoil: *I fear for my grandchildren.* Neither of these children betrayed the stigmata of Abomination which Alia flaunted, although Leto showed every sign of some terrifying concealment. It was for that reason he'd been deftly excluded from this meeting.

On impulse, Jessica put aside her ingrained emotional masks, knowing them to be of little use here, barriers to communication. Not since those loving moments with her Duke had she lowered these barriers, and she found the action both relief and pain. There remained facts which no curse or prayer or litany could wash from existence. Flight would not leave such facts behind. They could not be ignored. Elements of Paul's vision had been rearranged and the times had caught up with his children. They were a magnet in the void; evil and all the sad misuses of power collected around them.

Ghanima, watching the play of emotions across her grandmother's face, marveled that Jessica had let down her controls.

With catching movements of their heads remarkably synchronized, both turned, eyes met, and they stared deeply, probingly at each other. Thoughts without spoken words passed between them.

Jessica: *I wish you to see my fear.*

Ghanima: *Now I know you love me.*

It was a swift moment of utter trust.

Jessica said: 'When your father was but a boy, I brought a Reverend Mother to Caladan to test him.'

Ghanima nodded. The memory of it was extremely vivid.

'We Bene Gesserits were always cautious to make sure that the children we raised were human and not animal. One cannot always tell by exterior appearances.'

'It's the way you were trained,' Ghanima said, and the memory flooded into her mind: that old Bene Gesserit, Gaius Helen Mohiam. She'd come to Castle Caladan with her poisoned gom jabbar and her box of burning pain. Paul's hand (Ghanima's own hand in the shared memory) screamed with the agony of that box while the old woman talked calmly of immediate death if the hand were withdrawn from the pain. And there had been no doubt of the death in that needle held ready against the child's neck while the aged voice droned its rationale:

'You've heard of animals chewing off a leg to escape a trap. There's an animal kind of trick. A human would remain in the trap, endure the pain, feigning death that he might kill the trapper and remove a threat to his kind.'

Ghanima shook her head against the remembered pain. The burning! The burning! Paul had imagined his skin curling black on that agonized hand within the box, flesh crisping and dropping away until only charred bones remained. And it had been a trick – the hand unharmed. But sweat stood out on Ghanima's forehead at the memory.

'Of course you remember this in a way that I cannot,' Jessica said.

For a moment, memory-driven, Ghanima saw her grandmother in a different light: what this woman might do out of the driving necessities of that early conditioning in the Bene Gesserit schools! It raised new questions about Jessica's return to Arrakis.

'It would be stupid to repeat such a test on you or your brother,' Jessica said. 'You already know the way it went. I must assume you are human, that you will not misuse your inherited powers.'

'But you don't make that assumption at all,' Ghanima said.

Jessica blinked, realized that the barriers had been creeping back in place, dropped them once more. She asked: 'Will you believe my love for you?'

'Yes.' Ghanima raised a hand as Jessica started to speak. 'But that love wouldn't stop you from destroying us. Oh, I know the reasoning: "Better the animal-human die than it re-create itself." And that's especially true if the animal-human bears the name Atreides.'

'You at least are human,' Jessica blurted. 'I trust my instinct on this.'

Ghanima saw the truth in this, said: 'But you're not sure of Leto.'

'I'm not.'

'Abomination?'

Jessica could only nod.

Ghanima said: 'Not yet, at least. We both know the danger of it, though. We can see the way of it in Alia.'

Jessica cupped her hands over her eyes, thought: *Even love can't protect us from unwanted facts.* And she knew then that she still loved her daughter, crying out silently against fate: *Alia! Oh, Alia! I am sorry for my part in your destruction.*

Ghanima cleared her throat loudly.

Jessica lowered her hands, thought: *I may mourn my poor daughter, but there are other necessities now.* She said: 'So you've recognized what happened to Alia.'

'Leto and I watched it happen. We were powerless to prevent it, although we discussed many possibilities.'

'You're sure that your brother is free of this curse?'

'I'm sure.'

The quiet assurance in that statement could not be denied. Jessica found herself accepting it. Then: 'How is it you've escaped?'

Ghanima explained the theory upon which she and Leto had settled, that their avoiding of the spice trance while Alia entered it often made the difference. She went on to reveal his dreams and the plans they'd discussed – even Jacurutu.

Jessica nodded. 'Alia is an Atreides, though, and that poses enormous problems.'

Ghanima fell silent before the sudden realization that Jessica still mourned her Duke as though his death had been but yesterday, that she would guard his name and memory against all threats. Personal memories from the Duke's own lifetime fled through Ghanima's awareness to reinforce this assessment, to soften it with understanding.

'Now,' Jessica said, voice brisk, 'what about this Preacher? I heard some disquieting reports yesterday after that damnable Lustration.'

Ghanima shrugged. 'He could be –'

'Paul?'

'Yes, but we haven't seen him to examine.'

'Javid laughs at the rumors,' Jessica said.

Ghanima hesitated. Then: 'Do you trust this Javid?'

A grim smile touched Jessica's lips. 'No more than you do.'

'Leto says Javid laughs at the wrong things,' Ghanima said.

'So much for Javid's laughter,' Jessica said. 'But do you actually entertain the notion that my son is still alive, that he has returned in this guise?'

'We say it's possible. And Leto . . . ' Ghanima found her mouth suddenly dry, remembered fears clutching her breast. She forced herself to overcome them, recounted Leto's other revelations of prescient dreams.

Jessica moved her head from side to side as though wounded.

Ghanima said: 'Leto says he must find this Preacher and make sure.'

'Yes . . . Of course. I should never have left here. It was cowardly of me.'

'Why do you blame yourself? You had reached a limit. I know that. Leto knows it. Even Alia may know it.'

51

Jessica put a hand to her own throat, rubbed it briefly. Then: 'Yes, the problem of Alia.'

'She works a strange attraction on Leto,' Ghanima said. 'That's why I helped you meet alone with me. He agrees that she is beyond hope, but still he finds ways to be with her and . . . study her. And . . . it's very disturbing. When I try to talk against this, he falls asleep. He –'

'Is she drugging him?'

'No-o-o.' Ghanima shook her head. 'But he has this odd empathy for her. And . . . in his sleep, he often mutters *Jacurutu*.'

'That again!' And Jessica found herself recounting Gurney's report about the conspirators exposed at the landing field.

'I sometimes fear Alia wants Leto to seek out Jacurutu,' Ghanima said. 'And I always thought it only a legend. You know it, of course.'

Jessica shuddered. 'Terrible story. Terrible.'

'What must we do?' Ghanima asked. 'I fear to search all of my memories, all of my lives . . .'

'Ghani! I warn you against that. You mustn't risk –'

'It may happen even if I don't risk it. How do we know what really happened to Alia?'

'No! You could be spared that . . . that *possession*.' She ground the word out. 'Well . . . Jacurutu, is it? I've sent Gurney to find the place – if it exists.'

'But how can he . . . Oh! Of course: the smugglers.'

Jessica found herself silenced by this further example of how Ghanima's mind worked in concert with what must be an inner awareness of others. *Of me!* How truly strange it was, Jessica thought, that this young flesh could carry all of Paul's memories, at least until the moment of Paul's spermal separation from his own past. It was an invasion of privacy against which something primal in Jessica rebelled. Momentarily she felt herself sinking into the absolute and unswerving Bene Gesserit judgment: *Abomination!* But there was a sweetness about this child, a willingness to sacrifice for her brother, which could not be denied.

*We are one life reaching out into a dark future,* Jessica thought. *We are one blood.* And she girded herself to accept the events which she and Gurney Halleck had set in motion. Leto must be separated from his sister, must be trained as the Sisterhood insisted.

*I hear the wind blowing across the desert and I see the moons of a winter night rising like great ships in the void. To them I make my vow : I will be resolute and make an art of government ; I will balance my inherited past and become a perfect storehouse of my relic memories. And I will be known for kindliness more than for knowledge. My face will shine down the corridors of time for as long. as humans exist.*

> – Leto's Vow
> After Harq al-Ada

When she had been quite young, Alia Atreides had practiced for hours in the *prana-bindu* trance, trying to strengthen her own private personality against the onslaught of *all those others*. She knew the problem – melange could not be escaped in a sietch warren. It infested everything: food, water, air, even the fabrics against which she cried at night. Very early she recognized the uses of the sietch orgy where the tribe drank the death-water of a worm. In the orgy, Fremen released the accumulated pressures of their own genetic memories, and they denied those memories. She saw her companions being temporarily possessed in the orgy.

For her, there was no such release, no denial. She had possessed full consciousness long before birth. With that consciousness came a cataclysmic awareness of her circumstances: womb-locked into intense, inescapable contact with the personae of all her ancestors and of those identities death-transmitted in spice-*tau* to the Lady Jessica. Before birth, Alia had contained every bit of the knowledge required in a Bene Gesserit Reverend Mother – plus much, much more from *all those others*.

In that knowledge lay recognition of a terrible reality – Abomination. The totality of that knowledge weakened her. The pre-born did not escape. Still she'd fought against the more terrifying of her ancestors, winning for a time a Pyrrhic victory which had lasted through childhood. She'd known a private personality, but it had no immunity against casual intrusions from those who lived their reflected lives through her.

*Thus will I be one day*, she thought. This thought chilled her. To walk and dissemble through the life of a child from her own loins, intruding, grasping at consciousness to add a quantum of experience.

Fear stalked her childhood. It persisted into puberty. She had fought it, never asking for help. Who would understand the help she required? Not her mother, who could never quite drive away that specter of Bene Gesserit judgment: the pre-born were Abomination.

There had come that night when her brother walked alone into the desert seeking death, giving himself to Shai-Hulud as blind Fremen were supposed to do. Within the month, Alia had been married to Paul's swordmaster, Duncan Idaho, a mentat brought back from the dead by the arts of the Tleilaxu. Her mother fled back to Caladan. Paul's twins were Alia's legal charge.

And she controlled the Regency.

Pressures of responsibility had driven the old fears away and she had been wide open to the inner lives, demanding their advice, plunging into spice trance in search of guiding visions.

The crisis came on a day like many others in the spring month of Laab, a clear morning at Muad'Dib's Keep with a cold wind blowing down from the pole. Alia still wore the yellow for mourning, the color of the sterile sun. More and more these past few weeks she'd been denying the inner voice of her mother, who tended to sneer at preparation for the coming Holy Days to be centered on the Temple.

The inner-awareness of Jessica faded, faded . . . sinking away at last with a faceless demand that Alia would be better occupied working on the Atreides Law. New lives began to clamor for their moment of consciousness. Alia felt that she had opened a bottomless pit, and faces arose out of it like a swarm of locusts, until she came at last to focus on one who was like a beast: the old Baron Harkonnen. In terrified outrage she had screamed out against all of that inner clamor, winning a temporary silence.

On this morning, Alia took her pre-breakfast walk through the Keep's roof garden. In a new attempt to win the inner battle, she tried to hold her entire awareness within Choda's admonition to the Zensunni:

'*Leaving the ladder, one may fall upward!*'

But morning's glow along the cliffs of the Shield Wall kept distracting her. Plantings of resilient fuzz-grass filled the garden's pathways. When she looked away from the Shield Wall she saw dew on the grass, the catch of all the moisture which had passed here in the night. It reflected her own passage as of a multitude.

That multitude made her giddy. Each reflection carried the imprint of a face from the inner multitude.

She tried to focus her mind on what the grass implied. The presence of plentiful dew told her how far the ecological transformation had progressed on Arrakis. The climate of these northern latitudes was growing warmer; atmospheric carbon dioxide was on the increase. She reminded herself how many new hectares would be put under green plants in the coming year – and it required thirty-seven thousand cubic feet of water to irrigate just one hectare.

Despite every attempt at mundane thoughts, she could not drive away the sharklike circling of all those others within her.

She put her hands to her forehead and pressed.

Her temple guards had brought her a prisoner to judge at sunset the previous day: one Essas Paymon, a dark little man ostensibly in the pay of a House Minor, the Nebiros, who traded in holy artifacts and small manufactured items for decoration. Actually Paymon was known to be a CHOAM spy whose task was to assess the yearly spice crop. Alia had been on the point of sending him into the dungeons when he'd protested loudly 'the injustice of the Atreides'. That could have brought him an immediate sentence of death on the hanging tripod, but Alia had been caught by his boldness. She'd spoken sternly from her Throne of Judgment, trying to frighten him into revealing more than he'd already told her inquisitors.

'Why are our spice crops of such interest to the Combine Honnete?' she'd demanded. 'Tell us and we may spare you.'

'I only collect something for which there is a market,' Paymon said. 'I know nothing of what is done with my harvest.'

'And for this petty profit you interfere with our royal plans?' Alia demanded.

'Royalty never considers that we might have plans, too,' he countered.

Alia, captivated by his desperate audacity, said: 'Essas Paymon, will you work for me?'

At this a grin whitened his dark face, and he said: 'You were about to obliterate me without a qualm. What is my new value that you should suddenly make a market for it?'

'You've a simple and practical value,' she said. 'You're bold and you're for hire to the highest bidder. I can bid higher than any other in the Empire.'

At which, he named a remarkable sum which he required for his services, but Alia laughed and countered with a figure she considered more reasonable and undoubtedly far more than he'd ever before received. She added: 'And, of course, I throw in the gift of your life upon which, I presume, you place an even more inordinate value.'

'A bargain!' Paymon cried and, at a signal from Alia, was led

55

away by her priestly Master of Appointments, Ziarenko Javid.

Less than an hour later, as Alia prepared to leave the Judgment Hall, Javid came hurrying to report that Paymon had been overheard to mutter the fateful lines from the Orange Catholic Bible: '*Maleficos non patieris vivere.*'

'Thou shalt not suffer a witch to live,' Alia translated. So that was his gratitude! He was one of those who plotted against her very life! In a flush of rage such as she'd never before experienced, she ordered Paymon's immediate execution, sending his body to the Temple deathstill where his water, at least, would be of some value in the priestly coffers.

And all night long Paymon's dark face haunted her.

She tried all of her tricks against this persistent, accusing image, reciting the *Bu Ji* from the Fremen Book of Kreos: 'Nothing occurs! Nothing occurs!' But Paymon took her through a wearing night into this giddy new day, where she could see that his face had joined those in the jeweled reflections from the dew.

A female guard called her to breakfast from the roof door behind a low hedge of mimosa. Alia sighed. She felt small choice between hells: the outcry within her mind or the outcry from her attendants – all were pointless voices, but persistent in their demands, hourglass noises that she would like to silence with the edge of a knife.

Ignoring the guard, Alia stared across the roof garden toward the Shield Wall. A *bahada* had left its broad outwash like a detrital fan upon the sheltered floor of her domain. The delta of sand spread out before her gaze, outlined by the morning sun. It came to her that an uninitiated eye might see that broad fan as evidence of a river's flow, but it was no more than the place where her brother had shattered the Shield Wall with the Atreides Family atomics, opening a path from the desert for the sandworms which had carried his Fremen troops to shocking victory over his Imperial predecessor, Shaddam IV. Now a broad qanat flowed with water on the Shield Wall's far side to block off sandworm intrusions. Sandworms would not cross open water; it poisoned them.

*Would that I had such a barrier within my mind*, she thought.

The thought increased her giddy sensation of being separated from reality.

*Sandworms! Sandworms!*

Her memory presented a collection of sandworm images: mighty Shai-Hulud, the demiurge of the Fremen, deadly beast of the desert's depths whose outpourings included the priceless spice. How odd it was, this sandworm, to grow from a flat and leathery sandtrout, she thought. They were like the flocking multitude within her awareness. The sandtrout, when linked edge to edge against the planet's bedrock, formed living cisterns; they held back the water that their sandworm vector might live. Alia could feel the analogy: some of *those others* within her mind held back dangerous forces which could destroy her.

Again the guard called her to breakfast, a note of impatience apparent.

Angrily Alia turned, waved a dismissal signal.

The guard obeyed, but the roof door slammed.

At the sound of the slamming door, Alia felt herself caught by everything she had attempted to deny. The other lives welled up within her like a hideous tide. Each demanding life pressed its face against her vision centers – a cloud of faces. Some presented mange-spotted skin, other were callous and full of sooty shadows; there were mouths like moist lozenges. The pressure of the swarm washed over her in a current which demanded that she float free and plunge into them.

'No,' she whispered. 'No . . . no . . . no . . .'

She would have collapsed onto the path but for a bench beside her which accepted her sagging body. She tried to sit, could not, stretched out on the cold plasteel, still whispering denial.

The tide continued to rise within her.

She felt attuned to the slightest show of attention, aware of the risk, but alert for every exclamation from those guarded mouths which clamored within her. They were a cacophony of demand for her attention: '*Me! Me!*' '*No, me!*' And she knew that if she once gave her attention, gave it completely, she would be lost. To behold one face out of the multitude and follow the voice of that face would be to be held by that egocentrism which shared her existence.

'Prescience does this to you,' a voice whispered.

She covered her ears with her hands, thinking: *I'm not prescient! The trance doesn't work for me!*

But the voice persisted: '*It might work, if you had help.*'

'No . . . no,' she whispered.

Other voices wove around her mind: 'I, Agamemnon, your ancestor, demand audience!'

'No . . . no.' She pressed her hands against her ears until the flesh answered her with pain.

An insane cackle within her head asked: 'What has become of Ovid? Simple. He's John Bartlett's ibid!'

57

The names were meaningless in her extremity. She wanted to scream against them and against all the other voices but could not find her own voice.

Her guard, sent back to the roof by senior attendants, peered once more from the doorway behind the mimosa, saw Alia on the bench, spoke to a companion: 'Ahhh, she is resting. You noted that she didn't sleep well last night. It is good for her to take the *zaha*, the morning siesta.'

Alia did not hear her guard. Her awareness was caught by shrieks of singing: 'Merry old birds are we, hurrah!' the voices echoed against the inside of her skull and she thought: *I'm going insane. I'm losing my mind.*

Her feet made feeble fleeing motions against the bench. She felt that if she could only command her body to run, she might escape. She had to escape lest any part of that inner tide sweep her into silence, forever contaminating her soul. But her body would not obey. The mightiest forces in the Imperial universe would obey her slightest whim, but her body would not.

An inner voice chuckled. Then: 'From one viewpoint, child, each incident of creation represents a catastrophe.' It was a basso voice which rumbled against her eyes, and again that chuckle as though deriding its own pontification. 'My dear child, I will help you, but you must help me in return.'

Against the swelling background clamor behind that basso voice, Alia spoke through chattering teeth: 'Who . . . who . . . '

A face formed itself upon her awareness. It was a smiling face of such fatness that it could have been a baby's except for the glittering eagerness of the eyes. She tried to pull back, but achieved only a longer view which included the body attached to that face. The body was grossly, immensely fat, clothed in a robe which revealed by subtle bulges beneath it that this fat had required the support of portable suspensors.

'You see,' the basso voice rumbled, 'it is only your maternal grandfather. You know me. I was the Baron Vladimir Harkonnen.'

'You're . . . you're dead!' she gasped.

'But, of course, my dear! *Most* of us within you are dead. But none of the others are really willing to help you. They don't understand you.'

'Go away,' she pleaded. 'Oh, please go away.'

'But you need help, granddaughter,' the Baron's voice argued.

*How remarkable he looks*, she thought, watching the projection of the Baron against her closed eyelids.

'I'm willing to help you,' the Baron wheedled. 'The others in here would only fight to take over your entire consciousness. Any one of them would try to drive you out. But me . . . I want only a little corner of my own.'

Again the other lives within her lifted their clamor. The tide once more threatened to engulf her and she heard her mother's voice screeching. And Alia thought: *She's not dead.*

'Shut up!' the Baron commanded.

Alia felt her own desires reinforcing that command, making it felt throughout her awareness.

Inner silence washed through her like a cool bath and she felt her hammering heart begin slowing to its normal pace. Soothingly the Baron's voice intruded: 'You see? Together, we're invincible. You help me and I help you.'

'What . . . what do you want?' she whispered.

A pensive look came over the fat face against her closed eyelids. 'Ahhh, my darling granddaughter,' he said, 'I wish only a few simple pleasures. Give me but an occasional moment of contact with your senses. No one else need ever know. Let me feel but a small corner of your life when, for example, you are enfolded in the arms of your lover. Is that not a small price to ask?'

'Y-yes.'

'Good, good,' the Baron chortled. 'In return, my darling granddaughter, I can serve you in many ways. I can advise you, help you with my counsel. You will be invincible within and without. You will sweep away all opposition. History will forget your brother and cherish you. The future will be yours.'

'You . . . won't let . . . the . . . the others take over?'

'They cannot stand against us! Singly we can be overcome, but together we command. I will demonstrate. Listen.'

And the Baron fell silent, withdrawing his image, his inner presence. Not one memory, face, or voice of the other lives intruded.

Alia allowed herself a trembling sigh.

Accompanying that sigh came a thought. It forced itself into her awareness as though it were her own, but she sensed silent voices behind it.

*The old Baron was evil. He murdered your father. He would've killed you and Paul. He tried to and failed.*

The Baron's voice came to her without a face: 'Of course I would've killed you. Didn't you stand in my way? But that argument is ended. You've won it, child! You're the new truth.'

59

She felt herself nodding and her cheek moved scratchingly against the harsh surface of the bench.

His words were reasonable, she thought. A Bene Gesserit precept reinforced the reasonable character of his words: '*The purpose of argument is to change the nature of truth.*'

*Yes . . . that was the way the Bene Gesserit would have it.*

'Precisely!' the Baron said. 'And I am dead while you are alive. I have only a fragile existence. I'm a mere memory-self within you. I am yours to command. And how little I ask in return for the profound advice which is mine to deliver.'

'What do you advise me to do now?' she asked, testing.

'You're worried about the judgment you gave last night,' he said. 'You wonder if Paymon's words were reported truthfully. Perhaps Javid saw in this Paymon a threat to his position of trust. Is this not the doubt which assails you?'

'Y-yes.'

'And your doubt is based on acute observation, is it not? Javid behaves with increasing intimacy toward your person. Even Duncan has noted it, hasn't he?'

'You know he has.'

'Very well, then. Take Javid for your lover and – '

'No!'

'You worry about Duncan? But your husband is a mentat mystic. He cannot be touched or harmed by activities of the flesh. Have you not felt sometimes how distant he is from you?'

'B-but he . . .'

'Duncan's mentat part would understand should he ever have need to know the device you employed in destroying Javid.'

'Destroy . . .'

'Certainly! Dangerous tools may be used, but they should be cast aside when they grow too dangerous.'

'Then . . . why should . . . I mean . . .'

'Ahhh, you precious dunce! Because of the value contained in the lesson.'

'I don't understand.'

'Values, my dear grandchild, depend for their acceptance upon their success. Javid's obedience must be unconditional, his acceptance of your authority absolute, and his – '

'The morality of this *lesson* escapes – '

'Don't be dense, grandchild! Morality must always be based on practicality. Render unto Caesar and all that nonsense. A victory is useless unless it reflects your deepest wishes. Is it not true that you have admired Javid's manliness?'

Alia swallowed, hating the admission, but forced to it by her complete nakedness before the inner-watcher. 'Ye-es.'

'Good!' How jovial the word sounded within her head. 'Now we begin to understand each other. When you have him helpless, then, in your bed, convinced that you are *his* thrall, you will ask him about Paymon. Do it jokingly: a rich laugh between you. And when he admits the deception, you will slip a crysknife between his ribs. Ahhh, the flow of blood can add so much to your satis – '

'No,' she whispered, her mouth dry with horror. 'No ,,, no ... no ...'

'Then I will do it for you,' the Baron argued. 'It must be done; you admit that. If you but set up the conditions, I will assume temporary sway over ...'

'No!'

'Your fear is so transparent, granddaughter. My sway of your senses cannot be else but temporary. There are others, now, who could mimic you to a perfection that ... But you know this. With me, ahhh, people would spy out my presence immediately. You know the Fremen Law for those possessed. You'd be slain out of hand. Yes – even you. And you know I do not want *that* to happen. I'll take care of Javid for you and, once it's done, I'll step aside. You need only ...'

'How is this good advice?'

'It rids you of a dangerous tool. And, child, it sets up the working relationship between us, a relationship which can only teach you well about future judgments which – '

'Teach me?'

'Naturally!'

Alia put her hands over her eyes, trying to think, knowing that any thought might be known to this presence within her, that a thought might originate with that presence and be taken as her own.

'You worry yourself needlessly,' the Baron wheedled. 'This Paymon fellow, now, was – '

'What I did was wrong! I was tired and acted hastily, I should've sought confirmation of – '

'You did right! Your judgments cannot be based on any such foolish abstract as that Atreides notion of equality. That's what kept you sleepless, not Paymon's death. You made a good decision! He was another dangerous tool. You acted to maintain order in your society. Now there's a good reason for judgments, not this *justice* nonsense! There's no such thing as equal justice

61

anywhere. It's unsettling to a society when you try to achieve such a false balance.'

Alia felt pleasure at this defense of her judgment against Paymon, but shocked at the amoral concept behind the argument. 'Equal justice was an Atreides . . . was . . . ' She took her hands from her eyes, but kept her eyes closed.

'All of your priestly judges should be admonished about this error,' the Baron argued. 'Decisions must be weighed only as to their merit in maintaining an orderly society. Past civilizations without number have foundered on the rocks of equal justice. Such foolishness destroys the natural hierarchies which are far more important. Any individual takes on significance only in his relationship to your total society. Unless that society be ordered in logical steps, no one can find a place in it – not the lowliest or the highest. Come, come, grandchild! You must be the stern mother of your people. It's your duty to maintain order.'

'Everything Paul did was to . . . '

'Your brother's dead, a failure!'

'So are you!'

'True . . . but with me it was an accident beyond my designing. Come now, let us take care of this Javid as I have outlined for you.'

She felt her body grow warm at the thought, spoke quickly: 'I must think about it.' And she thought: *If it's done, it'll be only to put Javid in his place. No need to kill him for that. And the fool might just give himself away . . . in my bed.*

'To whom do you talk, My Lady?' a voice asked.

For a confused moment, Alia thought this another intrusion by those clamorous multitudes within, but recognition of the voice opened her eyes. Ziarenka Valefor, chief of Alia's guardian amazons, stood beside the bench, a worried frown on her weathered Fremen features.

'I speak to my inner voices,' Alia said, sitting up on the bench. She felt refreshed, buoyed up by the silencing of that distracting inner clamor.

'Your inner voices, My Lady. Yes.' Ziarenka's eyes glistened at this information. Everyone knew the Holy Alia drew upon inner resources available to no other person.

'Bring Javid to my quarters,' Alia said. 'There's a serious matter I must discuss with him.'

'To your quarters, My Lady?'

'Yes! To my private chamber.'

'As My Lady commands.' The guard turned to obey.

'One moment,' Alia said. 'Has Master Idaho already gone to Sietch Tabr?'

'Yes, My Lady. He left before dawn as you instructed. Do you wish me to send for . . .'

'No. I will manage this myself. And Zia, no one must know that Javid is being brought to me. Do it yourself. This is a very serious matter.'

The guard touched the crysknife at her waist. 'My Lady, is there a threat to —'

'Yes, there's a threat, and Javid may be at the heart of it.'

'Ohhh, My Lady, perhaps I should not bring —'

'Zia! Do you think me incapable of handling such a one?'

A lupine smile touched the guard's mouth. 'Forgive me, My Lady. I will bring him to your private chamber at once, but . . , with My Lady's permission, I will mount guard outside your door.'

'You only,' Alia said.

'Yes, My Lady. I go at once.'

Alia nodded to herself, watching Ziarenka's retreating back. Javid was not loved among her guards, then. Another mark against him. But he was still valuable — very valuable. He was her key to Jacurutu and with that place, well . . .

'Perhaps you were right, Baron,' she whispered.

'You see!' the voice within her chortled. 'Ahhh, this will be a pleasant service to you, child, and it's only the beginning . . .'

> *These are illusions of popular history which a successful religion must promote : Evil men never prosper ; only the brave deserve the fair ; honesty is the best policy ; actions speak louder than words ; virtue always triumphs ; a good deed is its own reward ; any bad human can be reformed ; religious talismans protect one from demon possession ; only females understand the ancient mysteries ; the rich are doomed to unhappiness . . .*
>
> — From the Instruction Manual:
> Missionaria Protectiva

'I am called Muriz,' the leathery Fremen said.

He sat on cavern rock in the glow of a spice lamp whose fluttering light revealed damp walls and dark holes which were passages from this place. Sounds of dripping water could be heard down one of those passages and, although water sounds were essential to the Fremen paradise, the six bound men facing Muriz took no pleasure from the rhythmic dripping. There was the musty smell of a deathstill in the chamber.

A youth of perhaps fourteen standard years came out of the passage and stood at Muriz's left hand. An unsheathed crysknife reflected pale yellow from the spice lamp as the youth lifted the blade and pointed it briefly at each of the bound men.

With a gesture toward the youth, Muriz said: 'This is my son, Assan Tariq, who is to undergo his test of manhood.'

Muriz cleared his throat, stared once at each of the six captives. They sat in a loose semicircle across from him, tightly restrained with spice-fiber ropes which held their legs crossed, their hands behind them. The bindings terminated in a tight noose at each man's throat. Their stillsuits had been cut away at the neck.

The bound men stared back at Muriz without flinching. Two of them wore loose off-world garments which marked them as wealthy residents of an Arrakeen city. These two had skin which was smoother, lighter than that of their companions, whose sere features and bony frames marked them as desert-born.

Muriz resembled the desert dwellers, but his eyes were more deeply sunken, whiteless pits which not even the glow of the spice lamp touched. His son appeared an unformed copy of the man, with a flatness of face which did not quite hide the turmoil boiling within him.

'Among the Cast Out we have a special test for manhood,' Muriz said. 'One day my son will be a judge in Shuloch. We must know that he can act as he must. Our judges cannot forget Jacurutu and one day of despair. Kralizec, the Typhoon Struggle, lives in our hearts.' It was all spoken with the flat intonation of ritual.

One of the soft-featured city dwellers across from Muriz stirred, said: 'You do wrong to threaten us and bind us captive. We came peacefully on *umma*.'

Muriz nodded. 'You came in search of a personal religious awakening? Good. You shall have that awakening.'

The soft-featured man said: 'If we –'

Beside him a darker desert Fremen snapped. 'Be silent, fool! These are the water stealers. These are the ones we thought we'd wiped out.'

'That old story,' the soft-featured captive said.

'Jacurutu is more than a story,' Muriz said. Once more he gestured to his son. 'I have presented Assan Tariq. I am *arifa* in

64

this place, your only judge. My son, too, will be trained to detect demons. The old ways are best.'

'That's why we came into the deep desert,' the soft-featured man protested. 'We chose the old way, wandering in –'

'With paid guides,' Muriz said, gesturing to the darker captives. 'You would buy your way into heaven?' Muriz glanced up at his son. 'Assan, are you prepared?'

'I have reflected long upon that night when men came and murdered our people,' Assan said. His voice projected an uneasy straining. 'They owe us water.'

'Your father gives you six of them,' Muriz said. 'Their water is ours. Their shades are yours, your guardians forevermore. Their shades will warn you of demons. They will be your slaves when you cross over into the *alam al-mythal*. What do you say, my son?'

'I thank my father,' Assan said. He took a short step forward. 'I accept manhood among the Cast Out. This water is our water.'

As he finished speaking, the youth crossed to the captives. Starting on the left, he gripped the man's hair and drove the crysknife up under the chin into the brain. It was skillfully done to spill the minimum blood. Only the one soft-featured city Fremen protested, squalling as the youth grabbed his hair. The others spat at Assan Tariq in the old way, saying by this: '*See how little I value my water when it is taken by animals!*'

When it was done, Muriz clapped his hands once. Attendants came and began removing the bodies, taking them to the death-still where they could be rendered for their water.

Muriz arose, looked at his son who stood breathing deeply, watching the attendants remove the bodies. 'Now you are a man,' Muriz said. 'The water of our enemies will feed slaves. And, my son . . .'

Assan Tariq turned an alert and pouncing look upon his father. The youth's lips were drawn back in a tight smile.

'The Preacher must not know of this,' Muriz said.

'I understand, father.'

'You did it well,' Muriz said. 'Those who stumble upon Shuloch must not survive.'

'As you say, father.'

'You are trusted with important duties,' Muriz said. 'I am proud of you.'

*A sophisticated human can become primitive. What this really means is that the human's way of life changes. Old values change, become linked to the landscape with its plants and animals. This new existence requires a working knowledge of those multiples and cross-linked events usually referred to as nature. It requires a measure of respect for the inertial power within such natural systems. When a human gains this working knowledge and respect, that is called 'being primitive'. The converse, of course, is equally true : the primitive can become sophisticated, but not without accepting dreadful psychological damage.*

> – The Leto Commentary
> After Harq al-Ada

'How can we be sure?' Ghanima asked. 'This is very dangerous.'

'We've tested it before,' Leto argued.

'It may not be the same this time. What if –'

'It's the only way open to us,' Leto said. 'You agree we can't go the way of the spice.'

Ghanima sighed. She did not like this thrust and parry of words, but knew the necessity which pressed her brother. She also knew the fearful source of their own reluctance. They had but to look at Alia and know the perils of that inner world.

'Well?' Leto asked.

Again she sighed.

They sat cross-legged in one of their private places, a narrow opening from the cave to the cliff where often their mother and father had watched the sun set over the *bled*. It was two hours past the evening meal, a time when the twins were expected to exercise their bodies and their minds. They had chosen to flex their minds.

'I will try it alone if you refuse to help,' Leto said.

Ghanima looked away from him toward the black hangings of the moisture seals which guarded this opening in the rock. Leto continued to stare out over the desert.

They had been speaking for some time in a language so ancient that even its name remained unknown in these times. The language gave their thoughts a privacy which no other human could penetrate. Even Alia, who avoided the intricacies of her inner world, lacked the mental linkages which would allow her to grasp any more than an occasional word.

Leto inhaled deeply, taking in the distinctive furry odor of a

66

Fremen cavern-sietch which persisted in the windless alcove. The murmurous hubbub of the sietch and its damp heat were absent here, and both felt this as a relief.

'I agree we need guidance,' Ghanima said. 'But if we –'

'Ghani! We need more than guidance. We need protection.'

'Perhaps there is no protection.' She looked directly at her brother, met that gaze in his eyes like the waiting watchfulness of a predator. His eyes belied the placidity of his features.

'We must escape possession,' Leto said. He used the special infinitive of the ancient language, a form strictly neutral in voice and tense but profoundly active in its implications.

Ghanima correctly interpreted his argument.

'Mohw'pwium d'mi hish pash moh'm ka,' she intoned. *The capture of my soul is the capture of a thousand souls.*

'Much more than that,' he countered.

'Knowing the dangers, you persist.' She made it a statement, not a question.

'Wabun 'k wabunat!' he said. *Rising, thou risest!*

He felt his choice as an obvious necessity. Doing this thing, it were best done actively. They must wind the past into the present and allow it to unreel into their future.

'Muriyat,' she conceded, her voice low. *It must be done lovingly.*

'Of course.' He waved a hand to encompass total acceptance. 'Then we will consult as our parents did.'

Ghanima remained silent, tried to swallow past a lump in her throat. Instinctively she glanced south toward the great open *erg* which was showing a dim gray pattern of dunes in the last of the day's light. In that direction her father had gone on his last walk into the desert.

Leto stared downward over the cliff edge at the green of the sietch oasis. All was dusk down there, but he knew its shapes and colors; blossoms of copper, gold, red, yellow, rust, and russet spread right out to the rock markers which outlined the extent of the qanat-watered plantings. Beyond the rock markers stretched a stinking band of dead Arrakeen life, killed by foreign plants and too much water, now forming a barrier against the desert.

Presently Ghanima said: 'I am ready. Let us begin.'

'Yes, damn all!' He reached out, touched her arm to soften the exclamation, said 'Please, Ghani . . . Sing that song. It makes this easier for me.'

Ghanima hitched herself closer to him, circled his waist with her left arm. She drew in two deep breaths, cleared her throat, and began singing in a clear piping voice the words her mother had so often sung for their father:

> 'Here I redeem the pledge thou gavest;
> I pour sweet water upon thee.
> Life shall prevail in this windless place:
> My love, thou shalt live in a palace,
> Thy enemies shall fall to emptiness.
> We travel this path together
> Which love has traced for thee.
> Surely well do I show the way
> For my love is thy palace . . . '

Her voice fell into the desert silence which even a whisper might despoil, and Leto felt himself sinking, sinking – becoming the father whose memories spread like an overlayer in the genes of his immediate past.

*For this brief space, I must be Paul*, he told himself. *This is not Ghani beside me; it is my beloved Chani, whose wise counsel has saved us both many a time.*

For her part, Ghanima had slipped into the persona-memory of her mother with frightening ease, as she had known she would. How much easier this was for the female – and how much more dangerous.

In a voice turned suddenly husky, Ghanima said: 'Look there, beloved!' First Moon had risen and, against its cold light, they saw an arc of orange fire falling upward into space. The transport which had brought the Lady Jessica, laden now with spice, was returning to its mother-cluster in orbit.

The keenest of remembrances ran through Leto then, bringing memories like bright bell-sounds. For a flickering instant he was another Leto – Jessica's Duke. Necessity pushed those memories aside, but not before he felt the piercing of the love and the pain.

*I must be Paul*, he reminded himself.

The transformation came over him with a frightening duality, as though Leto were a dark screen against which his father was projected. He felt both his own flesh and his father's, and the flickering differences threatened to overcome him.

'Help me, father,' he whispered.

The flickering disturbance passed and now there was another imprint upon his awareness, while his own identity as Leto stood at one side as an observer.

'My last vision has not yet come to pass,' he said, and the voice was Paul's. He turned to Ghanima. 'You know what I saw.'

She touched his cheek with her right hand. 'Did you walk into the desert to die, beloved? Is that what you did?'

'It may be that I did, but that vision . . . Would that not be reason enough to stay alive?'

'But blind?' she asked.

'Even so.'

'Where can you go?'

He took a deep, shuddering breath. 'Jacurutu.'

'Beloved!' Tears began flowing down her cheeks.

'Muad'Dib, the hero, must be destroyed utterly,' he said. 'Otherwise this child cannot bring us back from chaos.'

'The Golden Path,' she said. 'It is not a good vision.'

'It's the only possible vision.'

'Alia has failed, then . . . '

'Utterly. You see the record of it.'

'Your mother has returned too late.' She nodded and it was Chani's wise expression on the childish face of Ghanima. 'Could there not be another vision? Perhaps if – '

'No, beloved. Not yet. This child cannot peer into the future yet and return safely.'

Again a shuddering breath disturbed his body, and Leto-observer felt the deep longing of his father to live once more in vital flesh, to make living decisions and . . . How desperate the need to unmake past mistakes!

'Father!' Leto called, and it was as though he shouted echoingly within his own skull.

It was a profound act of will which Leto felt then: the slow, clinging withdrawal of his father's internal presence, the release of senses and muscles.

'Beloved,' Chani's voice whispered beside him, and the withdrawal slowed. 'What is happening?'

'Don't go yet,' Leto said, and it was his own voice, rasping and uncertain, still his own. Then: 'Chani, you must tell us: How do we avoid . . . what has happened to Alia?'

It was Paul-within who answered him, though, with words which fell upon his inner ear, halting and with long pauses: 'There is no certainty. You . . . saw . . . what almost . . . happened . . . with . . . me.'

'But Alia . . . '

'The damned Baron has her!'

Leto felt his throat burning with dryness. 'Is he . . . have I . . . '

'He's in you . . . but ₁ . . I . . . we cannot ₁ . ₁ sometimes we sense . ₁ . each other, but you ₓ . ₁'

'Can you not read my thoughts?' Leto asked. 'Would you know then if . . . he . . .'

'Sometimes I can feel your thoughts ₓ . . but I . ₁ . we live only through ₁ . ₁ the . . . reflection of . . . your awareness. Your memory creates us. The danger . ₁ . it is a precise memory. And . . . those of us . . . those of us who loved power . . . and gathered it at . . . any price . . . those can be . ₓ . more precise.'

'Stronger?' Leto whispered.

'Stronger.'

'I know your vision,' Leto said. 'Rather than let him have me, I'll become you.'

'Not that!'

Leto nodded to himself, sensing the enormous will-force his father had required to withdraw, recognizing the consequences of failure. *Any* possession reduced the possessed to Abomination. The recognition gave him a renewed sense of strength, and he felt his own body with abnormal acuteness and a deeply drawn awareness of past mistakes: his own and those of his ancestors. It was the uncertainties which weakened – he saw this now. For an instant, temptation warred with fear within him. This flesh possessed the ability to transform melange into a vision of the future. With the spice, he could breathe the future, shatter Time's veils. He found the temptation difficult to shed, clasped his hands and sank into the *prana-bindu* awareness. His flesh negated the temptation. His flesh wore the deep knowledge learned in blood by Paul. Those who sought the future hoped to gain the winning gamble on tomorrow's race. Instead they found themselves trapped into a lifetime whose every heartbeat and anguished wail was known. Paul's final vision had shown the precarious way out of that trap, and Leto knew now that he had no other choice but to follow that way₁

'The joy of living, its beauty is all bound up in the fact that life can surprise you,' he said.

A soft voice whispered in his ear. 'I've always known that beauty.'

Leto turned his head, stared into Ghanima's eyes which glistened in the bright moonlight. He saw Chani looking back at him. 'Mother,' he said, 'you must withdraw.'

'Ahhh, the temptation!' she said, and kissed him.

He pushed her away. 'Would you take your daughter's life?' he demanded.

'It's so easy . . . so foolishly easy,' she said.

Leto, feeling panic begin to grip him, remembered what an effort of will his father's persona-within had required to abandon the flesh. Was Ghanima lost in that observer-world where he had watched and listened, learning what he had required from his father?

'I will despise you, mother,' he said.

'Others won't despise me,' she said. 'Be my beloved.'

'If I do . . . you know what you both will become,' he said. 'My father will despise you.'

'Never!'

'I will!'

The sound was jerked out of his throat without his volition and it carried all the old overtones of Voice which Paul had learned from his witch mother.

'Don't say it,' she moaned.

'I will despise you!'

'Please . . . please don't say it.'

Leto rubbed his throat, feeling the muscles become once more his own. 'He will despise you. He will turn his back on you. He will go into the desert again.'

'No . . . no . . .'

She shook her head from side to side.

'You must leave, mother,' he said.

'No . . . no . . .' But the voice lacked its original force.

Leto watched his sister's face. How the muscles twitched! Emotions fled across the flesh at the turmoil within her.

'Leave,' he whispered. 'Leave.'

'No-o-o-o . . .'

He gripped her arm, felt the tremors which pulsed through her muscles, the nerves twitching. She writhed, tried to pull away, but he held tightly to her arm, whispering: 'Leave . . . leave . . .'

And all the time, Leto berated himself for talking Ghani into this *parent game* which once they'd played often, but she had lately resisted. It was true that the female had more weakness in that inner assault, he realized. There lay the origin of the Bene Gesserit fear.

Hours passed and still Ghanima's body trembled and twitched with the inner battle, but now his sister's voice joined the argument. He heard her talking to that imago within the pleading.

'Mother . . . please – ' And once: 'You've seen Alia! Will you become another Alia?'

At last Ghanima leaned against him, whispered: 'She has accepted it. She's gone.'

He stroked her head. 'Ghani, I'm sorry. I'm sorry. I'll never ask you to do that again. I was selfish. Forgive me.'

'There's nothing to forgive,' she said, and her voice came panting as though after great physical exertion. 'We've learned much that we needed to know.'

'She spoke to you of many things,' he said. 'We'll share it later when –'

'No! We'll do it now. You were right.'

'My Golden Path?'

'Your damned Golden Path!'

'Logic's useless unless it's armed with essential data,' he said. 'But I –'

'Grandmother came back to guide our education and to see if we'd been . . . contaminated.'

'That's what Duncan says. There's nothing new in –'

'Prime computation,' she agreed, her voice strengthening. She pulled away from him, looked out at the desert which lay in a predawn hush. This battle , , . this knowledge, had cost them a night. The Royal Guard beyond the moisture seal must have had much to explain. Leto had charged that nothing disturb them.

'People often learn subtlety as they age,' Leto said. 'What is it we're learning with all of this agedness to draw upon?'

'The universe as we see it is never quite the exact physical universe,' she said. 'We mustn't perceive this grandmother just as a grandmother.'

'That'd be dangerous,' he agreed. 'But my ques—'

'There's something beyond subtlety,' she said. 'We must have a place in our awareness to perceive what we can't preconceive. That's why . . . my mother spoke to me often of Jessica. At the last, when we were both reconciled to the inner exchange, she said many things.' Ghanima sighed.

'We *know* she's our grandmother,' he said. 'You were with her for hours yesterday. Is that why –'

'If we allow it, our *knowing* will determine how we react to her,' Ghanima said. 'That's what my mother kept warning me. She quoted our grandmother once and – ' Ghanima touched his arm. ' – I heard the echo of it within me in our grandmother's voice.'

'Warning you,' Leto said. He found his thoughts disturbing. Was nothing in this world dependable?

'Most deadly errors arise from obsolete assumptions,
said. 'That's what my mother kept quoting.'

'That's pure Bene Gesserit.'

'If . . . if Jessica has gone back to the Sisterhood comple

'That'd be very dangerous to us,' he said, complet
thought. 'We carry the blood of their Kwisatz Haderach
male Bene Gesserit.'

'They won't abandon that search,' she said, 'but they
abandon us. Our grandmother could be the instrument.'

'There's another way,' he said.

'Yes – the two of us . . . mated. But they know what recessive
might complicate that pairing.'

'It's a gamble they must've discussed.'

'And with our grandmother, at that. I don't like that way.'

'Nor I.'

'Still, it's not the first time a royal line has tried to . . .'

'It repels me,' he said, shuddering.

She felt the movement, fell silent.

'Power,' he said.

And in that strange alchemy of their similarities she knew
where his thoughts had been. 'The power of the Kwisatz
Haderach must fail,' she agreed.

'Used in their way,' he said.

In that instant, day came to the desert beyond their vantage
point. They sensed the heat beginning. Colors leaped forth from
the plantings beneath the cliff. Gray-green leaves sent spiked
shadows along the ground. The low moaning light of Dune's
silvery sun revealed the verdant oasis full of golden and purple
shadows in the well of the sheltering cliffs.

Leto stood, stretched.

'The Golden Path, then,' Ghanima said, and she spoke as
much to herself as to him, knowing how their father's last vision
met and melted into Leto's dreams.

Something brushed against the moisture seals behind them
and voices could be heard murmuring there.

Leto reverted to the ancient language they used for privacy:
'L'ii ani howr samis sm'kwi owr samit sut.'

That was where the decision lodged itself in their awareness.
Literally: *We will accompany each other into deathliness, though
only one may return to report it.*

Ghanima stood then and, together, they returned through the
moisture seals to the sietch, where the guards roused themselves
and fell in behind as the twins headed toward their own quarters.

The throngs parted before them with a difference on this morning, exchanging glances with the guards. Spending the night alone above the desert was an old Fremen custom for the holy sages. All the Umma had practiced this form of vigil. Paul Muad-'Dib had done it . . . and Alia. Now the royal twins had begun.

Leto noted the difference, mentioned it to Ghanima.

'They don't know what we've decided for them,' she said. 'They don't really know.'

Still in the private language, he said: 'It requires the most fortuitous beginning.'

Ghanima hesitated a moment to form her thoughts. Then: 'In that time, mourning for the sibling, it must be exactly real — even to the making of the tomb. The heart must follow the sleep lest there be no awakening.'

In the ancient tongue it was an extremely convoluted statement, employing a pronominal object separated from the infinitive. It was a syntax which allowed each set of internal phrases to turn upon itself, becoming several different meanings, all definite and quite distinct but subtly interrelated. In part, what she had said was that they risked death with Leto's plan and, real or simulated, it made no difference. The resultant change would be like death, literally: 'funeral murder'. And there was an added meaning to the whole which pointed accusatively at whoever *survived* to report, that is: *act out the living part*. Any misstep there would negate the entire plan, and Leto's Golden Path would become a dead end.

'Extremely delicate,' Leto agreed. He parted the hangings for them as they entered their own anteroom.

Activity among their attendants paused only for a heartbeat as the twins crossed to the arched passage which led into the quarters assigned to the Lady Jessica.

'You are not Osiris,' Ghanima reminded him.

'Nor will I try to be.'

Ghanima took his arm to stop him. 'Alia darsatay haunus m'smow,' she warned.

Leto stared into his sister's eyes. Indeed, Alia's actions did give off a foul smell which their grandmother must have noted. He smiled appreciatively at Ghanima. She had mixed the ancient tongue with Fremen superstition to call up a most basic tribal omen. *M'smow*, the foul odor of a summer night, was the harbinger of death at the hands of demons. And Isis had been the demon-goddess of death to the people whose tongue they now spoke.

74

'We Atreides have a reputation for audacity to maintain,' he said.

'So we'll *take* what we need,' she said.

'It's that or become petitioners before our own Regency,' he said. 'Alia would enjoy that.'

'But our plan . . . ' She let it trail off.

*Our plan*, he thought. She shared it completely now. He said: 'I think of our plan as the toil of the shaduf.'

Ghanima glanced back at the anteroom through which they'd passed, smelling the furry odors of morning with their sense of eternal beginning. She liked the way Leto had employed their private language. *Toil of the shaduf.* It was a pledge. He'd called their plan agricultural work of a very menial kind: fertilizing, irrigating, weeding, transplanting, pruning – yet with the Fremen implication that this labor occurred simultaneously in Another World where it symbolized cultivating the richness of the soul.

Ghanima studied her brother as they hesitated here in the rock passage. It had grown increasingly obvious to her that he was pleading on two levels: one, for the Golden Path of his vision and their father's, and two, that she allow him free reign to carry out the extremely dangerous myth-creation which the plan generated. This frightened her. Was there more to his private vision that he had not shared? Could he see himself as the potentially deified figure to lead humankind into a rebirth – like father, like son? The cult of Muad'Dib had turned sour, fermenting in Alia's mismanagement and the unbridled license of a military priesthood which rode the Fremen power. Leto wanted regeneration.

*He's hiding something from me*, she realized.

She reviewed what he had told her of his dream. It held such iridescent reality that he might walk around for hours afterwards in a daze. The dream never varied, he said.

*I am on sand in bright yellow daylight, yet there is no sun. Then I realize that I am the sun. My light shines out as a Golden Path. When I realize this, I move out of myself. I turn, expecting to see myself as the sun. But I am not the sun; I am a stick figure, a child's drawing with zigzag lightning lines for eyes, stick legs and stick arms. There is a scepter in my left hand, and it's a real scepter – much more detailed in its reality than the stick figure which holds it. The scepter moves, and this terrifies me. As it moves, I feel myself awaken, yet I know I'm still dreaming. I realize then that my skin is encased in something – an armor which moves as my skin moves. I cannot see this armor, but I feel it. My terror leaves me then, for this armor gives me the strength of ten thousand men.'*

As Ghanima stared at him, Leto tried to pull away, to continue their course toward Jessica's quarters. Ghanima resisted.

'This Golden Path could be no better than any other path,' she said.

Leto looked at the rock floor between them, feeling the strong return of Ghanima's doubts. 'I must do it,' he said.

'Alia is possessed,' she said. 'That could happen to us. It could already have happened and we might not know it.'

'No.' He shook his head, met her gaze. 'Alia resisted. That gave the powers within her their strength. By her own strength she was overcome. We've dared to search within, to seek out the old languages and the old knowledge. We're already amalgams of those lives within us. We don't resist; we ride with them. This was what I learned from our father last night. It's what I had to learn.'

'He said nothing of that within me.'

'You listened to our mother. It's what we – '

'And I almost lost.'

'Is she still strong within you?' Fear tightened his face.

'Yes . . . but now I think she guards me with her love. You were very good when you argued with her.' And Ghanima thought about the reflected mother-within, said: 'Our mother exists now for me in the *alam al-mythal* with the others, but she has tasted the fruit of hell. Now I can listen to her without fear. As to the others . . .'

'Yes,' he said. 'And I listened to my father, but I think I'm really following the counsel of the grandfather for whom I was named. Perhaps the name makes it easy.'

'Are you counseled to speak to our grandmother of the Golden Path?'

Leto waited while an attendant pressed past them with a basket-tray carrying the Lady Jessica's breakfast. A strong smell of spice filled the air as the attendant passed.

'She lives in us and in her own flesh,' Leto said. 'Her counsel can be consulted twice.'

'Not by me,' Ghanima protested. 'I'm not risking that again.'

'Then by me.'

'I thought we agreed that she's gone back to the Sisterhood.'

'Indeed. Bene Gesserit at her beginning, her own creature in the middle, and Bene Gesserit at the end. But remember that she, too, carries Harkonnen blood and is closer to it than we are, that

76

she has experienced a form of this inner sharing which we have.'

'A very shallow form,' Ghanima said. 'And you haven't answered my question.

'I don't think I'll mention the Golden Path.'

'I may.'

'Ghani!'

'We don't need any more Atreides gods! We need a space for some humanity!'

'Have I ever denied it?'

'No.' She took a deep breath and looked away from him. Attendants peered in at them from the anteroom, hearing the arguments by its tone but unable to understand the ancient words.

'We have to do it,' he said. 'If we fail to act, we might just as well fall upon our knives.' He used the Fremen form which carried the meaning of 'spill our water into the tribal cistern'.

Once more Ghanima looked at him. She was forced to agree. But she felt trapped within a construction of many walls. They both knew a day of reckoning lay across their path no matter what they did. Ghanima knew this with a certainty reinforced by the data garnered from those other memory-lives, but now she feared the strength which she gave those other psyches by using the data of their experiences. They lurked like harpies within her, shadow demons waiting in ambush.

Except for her mother, who had held the fleshly power and had renounced it. Ghanima still felt shaken by that inner struggle, knowing she would have lost but for Leto's persuasiveness.

Leto said his Golden Path led out of this trap. Except for the nagging realization that he withheld something from his vision, she could only accept his sincerity. He needed her fertile creativity to enrich the plan.

'We'll be tested,' he said, knowing where her doubts led.

'Not in the spice.'

'Perhaps even there. Surely, in the desert and in the Trial of Possession.'

'You never mentioned the Trial of Possession!' she accused. 'Is that part of your dream?'

He tried to swallow in a dry throat, cursed this betrayal. 'Yes.'

'Then we will be . . . possessed?'

'No.'

She thought about the Trial – that ancient Fremen examination whose ending most often brought hideous death. Then this plan had other complexities. It would take them onto an edge where a plunge to either side might not be countenanced by the human mind and that mind remain sane.

Knowing where her thoughts meandered, Leto said: 'Power attracts the psychotics. Always. That's what we have to avoid within ourselves.'

'You're sure we won't be ... possessed?'

'Not if we create the Golden Path.'

Still doubtful, she said: 'I'll not bear your children, Leto.'

He shook his head, suppressing the inner betrayals, lapsed into the royal-formal form of the ancient tongue: 'Sister mine, I love you more dearly than myself, but that is not the tender of my desires.'

'Very well, then let us return to another argument before we join our grandmother. A knife slipped into Alia might settle most of our problems.'

'If you believe that, you believe we can walk in mud and leave no tracks,' he said. 'Besides, when has Alia ever given anyone an opportunity?'

'There is talk about this Javid.'

'Does Duncan show any signs of growing horns?'

Ghanima shrugged. 'One poison, two poison.' It was the common label applied to the royal habit of cataloguing companions by their threat to your person, a mark of rulers everywhere.

'We must do it my way,' he said.

'The other way might be clearer.'

By her reply, he knew she had finally suppressed her doubts and come around to agreement with his plan. The realization brought him no happiness. He found himself looking at his own hands, wondering if the dirt would cling.

*This was Muad'Dib's achievement: He saw the subliminal reservoir of each individual as an unconscious bank of memories going back to the primal cell of our common genesis. Each of us, he said, can measure out his distance from the common origin. Seeing this and telling of it, he made the audacious leap of decision: Muad'Dib set himself the task of integrating genetic memory into ongoing evaluation. Thus did he break through Time's veils, making a single thing of the future and the past. That was Muad-'Dib's creation embodied in his son and his daughter.*

*— Testament of Arrakis*
*by Harq al-Ada*

Farad'n strode through the garden compound of his grandfather's royal palace, watching his shadow grow shorter as the sun of Salusa Secundus climbed toward noon. He had to stretch himself a bit to keep step with the tall Bashar who accompanied him.

'I have doubts, Tyekanik,' he said. 'Oh, there's no denying the attractions of a throne, but — ' He drew in a deep breath. ' — I have so many interests.'

Tyekanik, fresh from a savage argument with Farad'n's mother, glanced sidelong at the Prince, noting how the lad's flesh was firming as he approached his eighteenth birthday. There was less and less of Wensicia in him with each passing day and more and more of old Shaddam, who had preferred his private pursuits to the responsibilities of royalty. That was what had cost him the throne in the end, of course. He'd grown soft in the ways of command.

'You have to make a choice,' Tyekanik said. 'Oh, doubtless there'll be time for some of your interests, but . . . '

Farad'n chewed his lower lip. Duty held him here, but he felt frustrated. He would far rather have gone to the rock enclave where the sandtrout experiments were being conducted. Now *there* was a project with enormous potential: wrest the spice monopoly from the Atreides and anything might happen.

'You're sure these twins will be . . . eliminated?'

'Nothing absolutely certain, My Prince, but the prospects are good.'

Farad'n shrugged. Assassination remained a fact of royal life. The language was filled with the subtle permutations of ways to eliminate important personages. By a single word, one could

79

distinguish between poison in drink or poison in food. He presumed the elimination of the Atreides twins would be accomplished by a poison. It was not a pleasant thought. By all accounts the twins were a most interesting pair.

'Would we have to move to Arrakis?' Farad'n asked.

'It's the best choice, put us at the point of greatest pressure.' Farad'n appeared to be avoiding some question and Tyekanik wondered what it might be.

'I'm troubled, Tyekanik,' Farad'n said, speaking as they rounded a hedge corner and approached a fountain surrounded by giant black roses. Gardeners could be heard snipping beyond the hedges.

'Yes?' Tyekanik prompted.

'This, ah, religion which you've professed . . .'

'Nothing strange about that, My Prince,' Tyekanik said and hoped his voice remained firm. 'This religion speaks to the warrior in me. It's a fitting religion for a Sardaukar.' That, at least, was true.

'Yesss . . . But my mother seems so pleased by it.' *Damn Wensicia!* he thought. *She's made her son suspicious.*

'I care not what your mother thinks,' Tyekanik said. 'A man's religion is his own affair. Perhaps she sees something in this that may help to put you on the throne.'

'That was my thought,' Farad'n said.

*Ahhh, this is a sharp lad!* Tyekanik thought. He said: 'Look into the religion for yourself; you'll see at once why I chose it.'

'Still . . . Muad'Dib's preachings? He was an Atreides, after all.'

'I can only say that the ways of God are mysterious,' Tyekanik said.

'I see. Tell me, Tyek, why'd you ask me to walk with you just now? It's almost noon and usually you're off to someplace or other at my mother's command this time of day.'

Tyekanik stopped at a stone bench which looked upon the fountain and the giant roses beyond. The splashing water soothed him and he kept his attention upon it as he spoke. 'My Prince, I've done something which your mother may not like.' And he thought: *If he believes that, her damnable scheme will work.* Tyekanik almost hoped Wensicia's scheme would fail. *Bringing that damnable Preacher here. She was insane. And the cost!*

As Tyekanik remained silent, waiting, Farad'n asked: 'All right, Tyek, what've you done?'

'I've brought a practitioner of oneiromancy,' Tyekanik said.

Farad'n shot a sharp glance at his companion. Some of the older Sardaukar played the dream-interpretation game, had done so increasingly since their defeat by that 'Supreme Dreamer', Muad'Dib. Somewhere within their dreams, they reasoned, might lay a way back to power and glory. But Tyekanik had always eschewed this play.

'This doesn't sound like you, Tyek,' Farad'n said.

'Then I can only speak from my new religion,' he said, addressing the fountain. To speak of religion was, of course, why they'd risked bringing The Preacher here.

'Then speak from this religion,' Farad'n said.

'As My Prince commands.' He turned, looked at this youthful holder of all the dreams which now were distilled into the path which House Corrino would follow. 'Church and state, My Prince, even scientific reason and faith, and even more: progress and tradition – all of these are reconciled in the teachings of Muad'Dib. He taught that there are no intransigent opposites except in the beliefs of men and, sometimes, in their dreams. One discovers the future in the past, and both are part of a whole.'

In spite of doubts which he could not dispel, Farad'n found himself impressed by these words. He heard a note of reluctant sincerity in Tyekanik's voice, as though the man spoke against inner compulsions.

'And that's why you bring me this . . . this interpreter of dreams?'

'Yes, My Prince. Perhaps your dream penetrates Time. You win back your consciousness of your inner being when you recognize the universe as a coherent whole. Your dreams . . . well . . .'

'But I spoke idly of my dreams,' Farad'n protested. 'They are a curiosity, no more. I never once suspected that you . . .'

'My Prince, nothing you do can be unimportant.'

'That's very flattering, Tyek. Do you really believe this fellow can see into the heart of great mysteries?'

'I do, My Prince.'

'Then let my mother be displeased.'

'You will see him?'

'Of course – since you've brought him to displease my mother.'

*Does he mock me?* Tyekanik wondered. And he said: 'I must warn you that the old man wears a mask. It is an Ixian device which enables the sightless to see with their skin.'

'He is blind?'

'Yes, My Prince.'

81

'Does he know who I am?'

'I told him, My Prince.'

'Very well. Let us go to him.'

'If My Prince will wait a moment here, I will bring the man to him.'

Farad'n looked around the fountain garden, smiled. As good a place as any for this foolishness. 'Have you told him what I dreamed?'

'Only in general terms, My Prince. He will ask you for a personal accounting.'

'Oh, very well. I'll wait here. Bring the fellow.'

Farad'n turned his head, heard Tyekanik retire in haste. A gardener could be seen working just beyond the hedge, the top of a brown-capped head, the flashing of shears poking above the greenery. The movement was hypnotic.

*This dream business is nonsense*, Farad'n thought. *It was wrong of Tyek to do this without consulting me. Strange that Tyek should get religion at his age. And now it's dreams.*

Presently he heard footsteps behind him, Tyekanik's familiar positive stride and a more dragging gait. Farad'n turned, stared at the approaching dream interpreter. The Ixian mask was a black, gauzy affair which concealed the face from the forehead to below the chin. There were no eye slits in the mask. If one were to believe the Ixian boasts, the entire mask was a single eye.

Tyekanik stopped two paces from Farad'n, but the masked old man approached to less than a pace.

'The interpreter of dreams,' Tyekanik said.

Farad'n nodded.

The masked old man coughed in a remote grunting fashion, as though trying to bring something up from his stomach.

Farad'n was acutely conscious of a sour spice smell from the old man. It emanated from the long gray robe which covered his body.

'Is that mask truly a part of your flesh?' Farad'n asked, realizing he was trying to delay the subject of dreams.

'While I wear it,' the old man said, and his voice carried a bitter twang and just a suggestion of Fremen accent. 'Your dream,' he said. 'Tell me.'

Farad'n shrugged. *Why not?* That was why Tyek had brought the old man. Or was it? Doubts gripped Farad'n and he asked: 'Are you truly a practitioner of oneiromancy?'

'I have come to interpret your dream, Puissant Lord.'

Again Farad'n shrugged. This masked figure made him ner-

82

vous and he glanced at Tyekanik, who remained where he had stopped, arms folded, staring at the fountain.

'Your dream, then,' the old man pressed.

Farad'n inhaled deeply, began to relate the dream. It became easier to talk as he got fully into it. He told about the water flowing upward in the well, about the worlds which were atoms dancing in his head, about the snake which transformed itself into a sandworm and exploded in a cloud of dust. Telling about the snake, he was surprised to discover, required more effort. A terrible reluctance inhibited him and this made him angry as he spoke.

The old man remained impassive as Farad'n at last fell silent. The black gauze mask moved slightly to his breathing. Farad'n waited. The silence continued.

Presently Farad'n asked: 'Aren't you going to interpret my dream?'

'I have interpreted it,' he said, his voice seeming to come from a long distance.

'Well?' Farad'n heard his own voice squeaking, telling him the tension his dream had produced.

Still the old man remained impassively silent.

'Tell me, then!' The anger was obvious in his tone.

'I said I'd interpret,' the old man said. 'I did not agree to tell you my interpretation.'

Even Tyekanik was moved by this, dropping his arms into balled fists at his sides. 'What?' he grated.

'I did not say I'd reveal my interpretations,' the old man said.

'You wish more pay?' Farad'n asked.

'I did not ask pay when I was brought here.' A certain cold pride in the response softened Farad'n's anger. This was a brave old man, at any rate. He must know death could follow disobedience.

'Allow me, My Prince,' Tyekanik said as Farad'n started to speak. Then: 'Will you tell us why you won't reveal your interpretation?'

'Yes, My Lords. The dream tells me there would be no purpose in explaining these things.'

Farad'n could not contain himself. 'Are you saying I already know the meaning of my dream?'

'Perhaps you do, My Lord, but that is not my gist.'

Tyekanik moved up to stand beside Farad'n. Both glared at the old man. 'Explain yourself,' Tyekanik said.

'Indeed,' Farad'n said.

'If I were to speak of this dream, to explore these matters of water and dust, snakes and worms, to analyze the atoms which dance in your head as they do in mine – ahh, Puissant Lord, my words would only confuse you and you would insist upon misunderstanding.'

'Do you fear that your words might anger me?' Farad'n demanded.

'My Lord! You're already angry.'

'Is it that you don't trust us?' Tyekanik asked.

'That is very close to the mark, My Lord. I do not trust either of you and for the simple reason that you do not trust yourselves.'

'You walk dangerously close to the edge,' Tyekanik said, 'Men have been killed for behavior less abusive than yours.'

Farad'n nodded, said: 'Don't tempt us to anger.'

'The fatal consequences of Corrino anger are well known, My Lord of Salusa Secundus,' the old man said.

Tyekanik put a restraining hand on Farad'n's arm, asked: 'Are you trying to goad us into killing you?'

Farad'n had not thought of that, felt a chill now as he considered what such behavior might mean. Was this old man who called himself Preacher . . . was he more than he appeared? What might be the consequences of his death? Martyrs could be dangerous creations.

'I doubt that you'll kill me no matter what I say,' The Preacher said. 'I think you know my value, Bashar, and your Prince now suspects it.'

'You absolutely refuse to interpret his dream?' Tyekanik asked.

'I *have* interpreted it.'

'And you will not reveal what you see in it?'

'Do you blame me, My Lord?'

'How can you be valuable to me?' Farad'n asked.

The Preacher held out his right hand. 'If I but beckon with this hand, Duncan Idaho will come to me and he will obey me.'

'What idle boast is this?' Farad'n asked.

But Tyekanik shook his head, recalling his argument with Wensicia. He said: 'My Prince, it could be true. This Preacher has many followers on Dune.'

'Why didn't you tell me he was from that place?' Farad'n asked.

Before Tyekanik could answer, The Preacher addressed Farad'n: 'My Lord, you must not feel guilty about Arrakis. You are but a product of your times. This is a special pleading which any man may make when his guilts assail him.'

'Guilts!' Farad'n was outraged.

The Preacher only shrugged.

Oddly, this shifted Farad'n from outrage to amusement. He laughed, throwing his head back, drawing a startled glance from Tyekanik. Then: 'I like you, Preacher.'

'This gratifies me, Prince,' the old man said.

Suppressing a chuckle, Farad'n said: 'We'll find you an apartment here in the palace. You will be my official interpreter of dreams – even though you never give me a word of interpretation. And you can advise me about Dune. I have a great curiosity about that place.'

'This I cannot do, Prince.'

An edge of his anger returned. Farad'n glared at the black mask. 'And why not, pray tell?'

'My Prince,' Tyekanik said, again touching Farad'n's arm.

'What is it, Tyek?'

'We brought him here under bonded agreement with the Guild. He is to be returned to Dune.'

'I am summoned back to Arrakis,' The Preacher said.

'Who summons you?' Farad'n demanded.

'A power greater than thine, Prince.'

Farad'n shot a questioning glance at Tyekanik. 'Is he an Atreides spy?'

'Not likely, My Prince. Alia has put a price on his head.'

'If it's not the Atreides, then who summons you?' Farad'n asked, returning his attention to The Preacher.

'A power greater than the Atreides.'

A chuckle escaped Farad'n. This was only mystic nonsense. How could Tyek be fooled by such stuff? This Preacher had been *summoned* – most likely by a dream. Of what importance were dreams?

'This has been a waste of time, Tyek,' Farad'n said. 'Why did you subject me to this . . . this farce?'

'There is a double price here, My Prince,' Tyekanik said. 'This interpreter of dreams promised me to deliver Duncan Idaho as an agent of House Corrino. All he asked was to meet you and interpret your dream.' And Tyekanik added to himself: *Or so he told Wensicia!* New doubts assailed the Bashar.

'Why is my dream so important to you, old man?' Farad'n asked.

'Your dream tells me that great events move toward a logical conclusion,' The Preacher said. 'I must hasten my return.'

Mocking, Farad'n said: 'And you will remain inscrutable, giving me no advice.'

'Advice, Prince, is a dangerous commodity. But I will venture a few words which you may take as advice or in any other way which pleases you.'

'By all means,' Farad'n said.

The Preacher held his masked face rigidly confronting Farad'n. 'Governments may rise and fall for reasons which appear insignificant, Prince. What small events! An argument between two women . . . which way the wind blows on a certain day . . . a sneeze, a cough, the length of a garment or the chance collision of a fleck of sand and a courtier's eye. It is not always the majestic concerns of Imperial ministers which dictate the course of history, nor is it necessarily the pontifications of priests which move the hands of God.'

Farad'n found himself profoundly stirred by these words and could not explain his emotion.

Tyekanik, however, had focused on one phrase. Why did this Preacher speak of a garment? Tyekanik's mind focused on the Imperial costumes dispatched to the Atreides twins, the tigers trained to attack. Was this old man voicing a subtle warning? How much did he know?

'How is this advice?' Farad'n asked.

'If you would succeed,' The Preacher said, 'you must reduce your strategy to its point of application. Where does one apply strategy? At a particular place and with a particular people in mind. But even with the greatest concern for minutiae, some small detail with no significance attached to it will escape you. Can your strategy, Prince, be reduced to the ambitions of a regional governor's wife?'

His voice cold, Tyekanik interrupted: 'Why do you harp upon strategy, Preacher? What is it you think My Prince will have?'

'He is being led to desire a throne,' The Preacher said. 'I wish him good luck, but he will need much more than luck.'

'These are dangerous words,' Farad'n said. 'How is it you dare such words?'

'Ambitions tend to remain undisturbed by realities,' The Preacher said. 'I dare such words because you stand at a crossroad. You could become admirable. But now you are surrounded by those who do not seek moral justifications, by advisers who are strategy-oriented. You are young and strong and tough, but you lack a certain advanced training by which your character

86

might evolve. This is sad because you have weaknesses whose dimensions I have described.'

'What do you mean?' Tyekanik demanded.

'Have a care when you speak,' Farad'n said. 'What is this weakness?'

'You've given no thought to the kind of society you might prefer,' The Preacher said. 'You do not consider the hopes of your subjects. Even the form of the Imperium which you seek has little shape in your imaginings.' He turned his masked face toward Tyekanik. 'Your eye is upon the power, not upon its subtle uses and its perils. Your future is filled, thus, with manifest unknowns: with arguing women, with coughs and windy days. How can you create an epoch when you cannot see every detail? Your tough mind will not serve you. This is where you are weak.'

Farad'n studied the old man for a long space, wondering at the deeper issues implied by such thoughts, at the persistence of such discredited concepts. Morality! Social goals! These were myths to put beside belief in an upward movement of evolution.

Tyekanik said: 'We've had enough words. What of the price agreed upon, Preacher?'

'Duncan Idaho is yours,' The Preacher said. 'Have a care how you use him. He is a jewel beyond price.'

'Oh, we've a suitable mission for him,' Tyekanik said. He glanced at Farad'n. 'By your leave, My Prince?'

'Send him packing before I change my mind,' Farad'n said. Then, glaring at Tyekanik: 'I don't like the way you've used me, Tyek!'

'Forgive him, Prince,' The Preacher said. 'Your faithful Bashar does God's will without even knowing it.' Bowing, The Preacher departed, and Tyekanik hurried to see him away.

Farad'n watched the retreating backs, thought: *I must look into this religion which Tyek espouses.* And he smiled ruefully. *What a dream interpreter! But what matter? My dream was not an important thing.*

*And he saw a vision of armor. The armor was not his own skin;
it was stronger than plasteel. Nothing penetrated his armor – not
knife or poison or sand, not the dust of the desert or its dessicating
heat. In his right hand he carried the power to make the Coriolis
storm, to shake the earth and erode it into nothing. His eyes were
fixed upon the Golden Path and in his left hand he carried the
scepter of absolute mastery. And beyond the Golden Path, his eyes
looked into eternity which he knew to be the food of his soul and of
his everlasting flesh.*

> **- Heighia, My Brother's Dream
> from The Book of Ghanima**

'It'd be better for me never to become Emperor,' Leto said. 'Oh,
I don't imply that I've made my father's mistake and peered into
the future with a glass of spice. I say this thing out of selfishness.
My sister and I desperately need a time of freedom when we can
learn how to live with what we are.'

He fell silent, stared questioningly at the Lady Jessica. He'd
spoken his piece as he and Ghanima had agreed. Now what would
be their grandmother's response?

Jessica studied her grandson in the low light of glowglobes
which illuminated her quarters in Sietch Tabr. It was still early
morning of her second day here and she'd already had disturbing
reports that the twins had spent a night of vigil outside the sietch.
What were they doing? She had not slept well and she felt fatigue
acids demanding that she come down from the hyper-level which
had sustained her through all the demanding necessities since
that crucial performance at the spaceport. This was the sietch
of her nightmares – but outside, that was not the desert she
remembered. *Where have all the flowers come from?* And the air
around her felt too damp. Stillsuit discipline was lax among the
young.

'What are you, child, that you need time to learn about yourself?' she asked.

He shook his head gently, knowing it to be a bizarre gesture of
adulthood on a child's body, reminding himself that he must keep
this woman off balance. 'First, I am not a child. Oh . . . ' He
touched his chest. 'This is a child's body; no doubt of that. But *I*
am not a child.'

Jessica chewed her upper lip, disregarding what this betrayed.
Her Duke, so many years dead on this accursed planet, had

laughed at her when she did this. '*Your one unbridled response,*' he'd called that chewing of the lip. '*It tells me that you're disturbed, and I must kiss those lips to still their fluttering.*'

Now this grandson who bore the name of her Duke shocked her into heart-pounding stillness merely by smiling and saying: 'You are disturbed; I see it by the fluttering of those lips.'

It required the most profound discipline of her Bene Gesserit training to restore a semblance of calm. She managed: 'Do you taunt me?'

'Taunt you? Never. But I must make it clear to you how much we differ. Let me remind you of that sietch orgy so long ago when the Old Reverend Mother gave you her lives and her memories. She tuned herself to you and gave you that . . . that long chain of sausages, each one a person. You have them yet. So you know something of what Ghanima and I experience.'

'And Alia?' Jessica asked, testing him.

'Didn't you discuss that with Ghani?'

'I wish to discuss it with you.'

'Very well. Alia denied what she was and became that which she most feared. The *past-within* cannot be relegated to the unconscious. That is a dangerous course for any human, but for us who are pre-born, it is worse than death. And that is all I will say about Alia.'

'So you're not a child,' Jessica said.

'I'm millions of years old. That requires adjustments which humans have never before been called upon to make.'

Jessica nodded, calmer now, much more cautious than she'd been with Ghanima. And where was Ghanima? Why had Leto come here alone?

'Well, grandmother,' he said, 'are we Abominations or are we the hope of the Atreides?'

Jessica ignored the question. 'Where is your sister?'

'She distracts Alia to keep us from being disturbed. It is necessary. But Ghani would say nothing more to you than I've said. Didn't you observe that yesterday?'

'What I observed yesterday is my affair. Why do you prattle about Abomination?'

'Prattle? Don't give me your Bene Gesserit cant, grandmother. I'll feed it back to you, word for word, right out of your own memories. I want more than the fluttering of your lips.'

Jessica shook her head, feeling the coldness of this . . . person who carried her blood. The resources at his disposal daunted her. She tried to match his tone, asked: 'What do you know of my intentions?'

He sniffed. 'You needn't inquire whether I've made the mistake my father made. I've not looked outside our garden of time – at least not by seeking it out. Leave absolute knowledge of the future to those moments of *déjà vu* which any human may experience. I *know* the trap of prescience. My father's life tells me what I need to know about it. No, grandmother: to know the future absolutely is to be trapped into that future absolutely. It collapses time. Present becomes future. I require more freedom than that.'

Jessica felt her tongue twitch with unspoken words. How could she respond to him with something he didn't already know? This was monstrous! *He's mine! He's my beloved Leto!* This thought shocked her. Momentarily she wondered if the childish mask might not lapse into those dear features and resurrect . . . *No!*

Leto lowered his head, looked upward to study her. Yes, she could be maneuvered after all. He said: 'When you think of prescience, which I hope is rarely, you're probably no different from any other. Most people imagine how nice it would be to know tomorrow's quotation on the price of whale fur. Or whether a Harkonnen will once more govern their homeworld of Giedi Prime? But of course *we* know the Harkonnens without prescience, don't we, grandmother?'

She refused to rise to his baiting. Of course he would know about the cursed Harkonnen blood in his ancestry.

'Who is a Harkonnen?' he asked, goading. 'Who is Beast Rabban? Any one of us, eh? But I digress. I speak the popular myth of prescience: to *know* the future absolutely! All of it! What fortunes could be made – and lost – on such absolute knowledge, eh? The rabble believes this. They believe that if a little bit is good, more must be better. How excellent! And if you handed one of them the complete scenario of his life, the unvarying dialogue up to his moment of death – what a hellish gift that'd be. What utter boredom! Every living instant he'd be replaying what he knew absolutely. No deviation. He could anticipate every response, every utterance – over and over and over and over and over and . . .'

Leto shook his head. 'Ignorance has its advantages. A universe of surprises is what I pray for!'

It was a long speech and, as she listened, Jessica marveled at how his mannerisms, his intonations, echoed his father – her lost son. Even the ideas: these were things Paul might have said.

'You remind me of your father,' she said.

'Is that hurtful to you?'

'In a way, but it's reassuring to know he lives on in you.'

'How little you understand of how he lives on in me.'

Jessica found his tone flat but dripping bitterness. She lifted her chin to look directly at him.

'Or how your Duke lives in me,' Leto said. 'Grandmother, Ghanima is *you*! She's you to such an extent that your life holds not a single secret from her up to the instant you bore our father. And me! What a catalogue of fleshy recordings am I. There are moments when it is too much to bear. You come here to judge us? You come here to judge Alia? Better that we judge you!'

Jessica demanded answer of herself and found none. What was he doing? Why this emphasis on his difference? Did he court rejection? Had he reached Alia's condition -- Abomination?

'This disturbs you,' he said.

'It disturbs me,' She permitted herself a futile shrug. 'Yes, it disturbs me -- and for reasons you know full well. I'm sure you've reviewed my Bene Gesserit training. Ghanima admits it. I know Alia . . . did. You know the consequences of your *difference*.'

He peered upward at her with disturbing intensity. 'Almost, we did not take this tack with you,' he said, and there was a sense of her own fatigue in his voice. 'We know the fluttering of your lips as your lover knew them. Any bedchamber endearment your Duke whispered is ours to recall at will. You've accepted this intellectually, no doubt. But I warn you that intellectual acceptance is not enough. If any of us becomes Abomination -- it could be you within us who creates it! Or my father . . . or mother! Your Duke! Any one of you could possess us -- and the condition would be the same.'

Jessica felt a burning in her chest, dampness in her eyes. 'Leto . . . ' she managed, allowing herself to use his name at last. She found the pain less than she'd imagined it would be, forced herself to continue. 'What is it you want of me.'

'I would teach my grandmother.'

'Teach me what?'

'Last night, Ghani and I played the mother-father roles almost to our destruction, but we learned much. There are things one can know, given an awareness of condition. Actions can be predicted. Alia, now -- it's well nigh certainty that she's plotting to abduct you.'

Jessica blinked, shocked by the swift accusation. She knew

this trick well, had employed it many times: set a person up along one line of reasoning, then introduced the shocker from another line. She recovered with a sharp intake of breath.

'I know what Alia has been doing . . . what she *is*, but . . .'

'Grandmother, pity her. Use your heart as well as your intelligence. You've done that before. You pose a threat, and Alia wants the Imperium for her own – at least, the thing she has become wants this.'

'How do I know this isn't another Abomination speaking?'

He shrugged. 'That's where your heart comes in. Ghani and I know she fell. It isn't easy to adjust to the clamor of that inner multitude. Suppress their egos and they will come crowding back every time you invoke a memory. One day – ' He swallowed in a dry throat. ' – a strong one from that inner pack decides it's time to share the flesh.'

'And there's nothing you can do?' She asked the question although she feared the answer.

'We believe there is something . . . yes. We cannot succumb to the spice; that's paramount. And we must not suppress the past entirely. We must use it, make an amalgam of it. Finally we will mix them all into ourselves. We will no longer be our original selves – *but we will not be possessed.*'

'You speak of a plot to abduct me.'

'It's obvious. Wensicia is ambitious for her son. Alia is ambitious for herself, and . . .'

'Alia and Farad'n?'

'That's not indicated,' he said. 'But Alia and Wensicia run parallel courses right now. Wensicia has a sister in Alia's house. What simpler thing than a message to – '

'You know of such a message?'

'As though I'd seen it and read its every word.'

'But you've not seen such a message?'

'No need. I have only to know that the Atreides are all here together on Arrakis. All of the water in one cistern.' He gestured to encompass the planet.

'House Corrino wouldn't dare attack us here!'

'Alia would profit if they did.' A sneer in his voice provoked her.

'I won't be patronized by my own grandson!' she said.

'Then dammit, woman, stop thinking of me as your grandson! Think of me as your *Duke* Leto!' Tone and facial expression, even the abrupt hand gesture, were so exact that she fell silent in confusion.

In a dry, remote voice, Leto said: 'I tried to prepare you. Give me that, at least.'

'Why would Alia abduct me?'

'To blame it on House Corrino, of course.'

'I don't believe it. Even for her, this would be ᵥ . . . monstrous! Too dangerous! How could she do it without . . . I cannot believe this!'

'When it happens, you'll believe. Ahh, grandmother, Ghani and I have but to eavesdrop within ourselves and we *know*. It's simple self-preservation. How else can we even guess at the mistakes being made around us?'

'I do not for a minute accept that abduction is part of Alia's – '

'Gods below! How can you, a Bene Gesserit, be this dense? The whole Imperium suspects why you're here. Wensicia's propagandists are all prepared to discredit you. Alia can't wait for that to happen. If you go down, House Atreides could suffer a mortal blow.'

'What does the whole Imperium suspect?'

She measured out the words as coldly as possible, knowing she could not sway this *unchild* with any wile of Voice.

'The Lady Jessica plans to breed those twins together!' he rasped. 'That's what the Sisterhood wants. Incest!'

She blinked. 'Idle rumor.' She swallowed. 'The Bene Gesserits will not let such a rumor run wild in the Imperium. We still have some influence. Remember that.'

'Rumor? What rumor? You've certainly held your options open on interbreeding us.' He shook his head as she started to speak. 'Don't deny it. Let us pass puberty still living in the same household and *you* in that household, and your *influence* will be no more than a rag waved in the face of a sandworm.'

'Do you believe us to be such utter fools?' Jessica asked.

'Indeed I do. Your Sisterhood is nothing but a bunch of damn' fool old women who haven't thought beyond their precious breeding program! Ghani and I know the leverage they have. Do *you* think *us* fools?'

'Leverage?'

'They know you're a Harkonnen! It'll be in their breeding records: Jessica out of Tandidia Nerus by the Baron Vladimir Harkonnen. That record *accidentally* made public would pull your teeth to – '

'You think the Sisterhood would stoop to blackmail?'

'I *know* they would. Oh, they coated it sweetly. They told you to investigate the rumors about your daughter. They fed your curiosity and your fears. They invoked your sense of responsibility, made you feel guilty because you'd fled back to Caladan. And they offered you the prospect of *saving* your grandchildren.'

Jessica could only stare at him in silence. It was as though he'd eavesdropped on the emotional meetings with her Proctors from the Sisterhood. She felt completely subdued by his words, and now began to accept the possibility that he spoke the truth when he said Alia planned abduction.

'You see, grandmother, I have a difficult decision to make,' he said. 'Do I follow the Atreides mystique? Do I live for my subjects ; . . and die for them? Or do I choose another course – one which would permit me to live thousands of years?'

Jessica recoiled involuntarily. These words spoken so easily touched on a subject the Bene Gesserits made almost unthinkable. Many Reverend Mothers could choose that course . . . or try it. The manipulation of internal chemistry was available to initiates of the Sisterhood. But if one did it, sooner or later all would try it. There could be no concealing such an accumulation of ageless women. They knew for a certainty that this course would lead them to destruction. Shortlived humanity would turn upon them. No – it was unthinkable.

'I don't like the trend of your thoughts,' she said.

'You don't understand my thoughts,' he said. 'Ghani and I . . .' He shook his head. 'Alia had it in her grasp and threw it away.'

'Are you sure of that? I've already sent word to the Sisterhood that Alia practices the unthinkable. Look at her! She's not aged a day since last I . . .'

'Oh, that!' He dismissed Bene Gesserit body balance with a wave of his hand. 'I'm speaking of something else – a perfection of being far beyond anything humans have ever before achieved.'

Jessica remained silent, aghast at how easily he'd lifted her disclosure from her. He'd know surely that such a message represented a death sentence on Alia. And no matter how he changed the words, he could only be talking about committing the same offense. Didn't he know the peril of his words?

'You must explain,' she said finally.

'How?' he asked. 'Unless you understand that Time isn't what it appears. I can't even begin to explain. My father suspected it. He stood at the edge of realization, but fell back. Now it's up to Ghani and me.'

'I insist that you explain,' Jessica said and she fingered the poisoned needle she held beneath a fold of her robe. It was the gom jabbar, so deadly that the slightest prick of it killed within

seconds. And she thought: *They warned me I might have to use it.*
The thought sent the muscles of her arm trembling in waves
and she was thankful for the concealing robe.

'Very well,' he sighed. 'First, as to Time: there is no difference
between ten thousand years and one year; no difference between
one hundred thousand years and a heartbeat. No difference. That
is the first fact about Time. And the second fact: the entire universe with all of its Time is within me.'

'What nonsense is this?' she demanded.

'You see? You don't understand. I will try to explain in another way, then.' He raised his right hand to illustrate moving it
as he spoke. 'We go forward, we come back.'

'Those words explain nothing!'

'That is correct,' he said. 'There are things which words cannot explain. You must experience them without words. But you
are not prepared for such a venture, just as when you look at me
you do not see me.'

'But . . . I'm looking directly at you. Of course I see you!' She
glared at him. His words reflected knowledge of the Zensunni
Codex as she'd been taught it in the Bene Gesserit schools: play of
words to confuse one's understanding of philosophy.

'Some things occur beyond your control,' he said.

'How does that explain this . . . this *perfection* which is so far
beyond other human experiences?'

He nodded. 'If one delays old age or death by the use of melange
or by that learned adjustment of fleshly balance which you Bene
Gesserits so rightly fear, such a delay invokes only an illusion of
control. Whether one walks rapidly through the sietch or slowly,
one traverses the sietch. And that passage of time is experienced
internally.'

'Why do you bandy words this way? I cut my wisdom teeth
on such nonsense long before even your father was born.'

'But only the teeth grew,' he said.

'Words! Words!'

'Ahhh, you're very close!'

'Hah!'

'Grandmother?'

'Yes?'

He held his silence for a long space. Then: 'You see? You can
still respond as yourself.' He smiled at her. 'But you cannot see
past the shadows. I am here.' Again he smiled. 'My father came
very near to this. When he lived, he lived, but when he died, he
failed to die.'

95

'What're you saying?'

'Show me his body!'

'Do you think this Preacher . . .'

'Possible, but even so, that is not his body.'

'You've explained nothing,' she accused.

'Just as I warned you.'

'Then why . . .'

'You asked. You had to be shown. Now let us return to Alia and her plan of abduction for –'

'Are you planning the unthinkable?' she demanded, holding the poisonous gom jabbar at the ready beneath her robe.

'Will you be her executioner?' he asked, his voice deceptively mild. He pointed a finger at the hand beneath her robe. 'Do you think she'll permit you to use that? Or do you think I'd let you use it?'

Jessica found she could not swallow.

'In answer to your question,' he said, 'I do not plan the unthinkable. I am not that stupid. But I am shocked at you. You dare judge Alia. Of course she's broken the precious Bene Gesserit commandment! What'd you expect? You ran out on her, left her as queen here in all but name. All of that power! So you ran back to Caladan to nurse your wounds in Gurney's arms. Good enough. But who are you to judge Alia?'

'I tell you, I will not dis—'

'Oh, shut up!' He looked away from her in disgust. But his words had been uttered in that special Bene Gesserit way – the controlling *Voice*. It silenced her as though a hand had been clapped over her mouth. She thought: *Who'd know how to hit me with Voice better than this one?* It was a mitigating argument which eased her wounded feelings. As many times as she'd used Voice on others, she'd never expected to be susceptible to it . . . not ever again . . . not since the school days when . . .

He turned back to her. 'I'm sorry. I just happen to know how blindly you can be expected to react when –'

'Blindly? Me?' She was more outraged by this than she'd been by his exquisite use of Voice against her.

'You,' he said. 'Blindly. If you've any honesty left in you at all, you'll recognize your own reactions. I call your name and you say, "Yes?" I silence your tongue. I invoke all your Bene Gesserit myths. Look inward the way you were taught. That, at least, is something you can do for your –'

'How dare you! What do you know of . . .' Her voice trailed off. Of course he knew!

'Look inward, I say!' His voice was imperious.

Again, his voice enthralled her. She found her senses stilled, felt a quickening of breath. Just beyond awareness lurked a pounding heart, the panting of . . . Abruptly she realized that the quickened breath, the pounding heart, were not latent, not held at bay by her Bene Gesserit control. Eyes widening in shocked awareness, she felt her own flesh obeying other commands. Slowly she recovered her poise, but the realization remained. This *unchild* had been playing her like a fine instrument throughout their interview.

'Now you know how profoundly you were conditioned by your precious Bene Gesserits,' he said.

She could only nod. Her belief in words lay shattered. Leto had forced her to look her physical universe squarely in the face, and she'd come away shaken, her mind running with a new awareness. '*Show me his body!*' He'd shown her her own body as though it were newborn. Not since her earliest schooling days on Wallach, not since those terrifying days before the Duke's buyers came for her, not since then had she felt such trembling uncertainty about her next moments.

'You will allow yourself to be abducted,' Leto said.

'But –'

'I'm not asking for discussion on this point,' he said. 'You will allow it. Think of this as a command from your Duke. You'll see the purpose when it's done. You're going to confront a very interesting student.'

Leto stood, nodded. He said: 'Some actions have an end but no beginning; some begin but do not end. It all depends upon whether the observer is standing.' Turning, he left her chambers.

In the second anteroom, Leto met Ghanima hurrying into their private quarters. She stopped as she saw him, said; 'Alia's busy with the Convocation of the Faith.' She looked a question at the passage which led to Jessica's quarters.

'It worked,' Leto said.

*Atrocity is recognized as such by victim and perpetrator alike, by all who learn about it at whatever remove. Atrocity has no excuses, no mitigating argument. Atrocity never balances or rectifies the past. Atrocity merely arms the future for more atrocity. It is self-perpetuating upon itself – a barbarous form of incest. Whoever commits atrocity also commits those future atrocities thus bred.*

— The Apocrypha of Muad'Dib

Shortly after noon, when most of the pilgrims had wandered off to refresh themselves in whatever cooling shade and source of libation they could find. The Preacher entered the great square below Alia's Temple. He came on the arm of his surrogate eyes, young Assan Tariq. In a pocket beneath his flowing robe, The Preacher carried the black gauze mask he'd worn on Salusa Secundus. It amused him to think that the mask and the boy served the same purpose – disguise. While he needed surrogate eyes, doubts remained alive.

*Let the myth grow, but keep doubts alive,* he thought

No one must discover that the mask was merely cloth, not an Ixian artifact at all. His hand must not slip from Assan Tariq's bony shoulder. Let The Preacher once walk as the sighted despite his eyeless sockets, and all doubts would dissolve. The small hope he nursed would be dead. Each day he prayed for a change, something different over which he might stumble, but even Salusa Secundus had been a pebble, every aspect known. Nothing changed; nothing could be changed . . . yet.

Many people marked his passage past the shops and arcades, noting the way he turned his head from side to side, holding it centered on a doorway or a person. The movements of his head were not always blind-natural, and this added to the growing myth.

Alia watched from a concealed slit in the towering battlement of her temple. She searched that scarred visage far below for some sign – a sure sign of identity. Every rumor was reported to her. Each new one came with its thrill of fear.

She'd thought her order to take The Preacher captive would remain secret, but that, too, came back to her now as a rumor. Even among her guards, someone could not remain silent. She hoped now that the guards would follow her new orders and not take this robed mystery captive in a public place where it could be seen and reported.

It was dusty hot in the square. The Preacher's young guide had pulled the veil of his robe up around his nose, leaving only the dark eyes and a thin patch of forehead exposed. The veil bulged with the outline of a stillsuit's catchtube. This told Alia that they'd come in from the desert. Where did they hide out there?

The Preacher wore no veil protection from the searing air. He had even dropped the catchtube flap of his stillsuit. His face lay open to the sunlight and the heat shiverings which lifted off the square's paving blocks in visible waves.

At the Temple steps there stood a group of nine pilgrims making their departure obeisance. The shadowed edge of the square held perhaps fifty more persons, mostly pilgrims devoting themselves to various penances imposed by the priesthood. Among the onlookers could be seen messengers and a few merchants who'd not yet made enough sales to close up for the worst of the day's heat.

Watching from the open slit, Alia felt the drenching heat and knew herself to be caught between thinking and sensation, the way she'd often seen her brother caught. The temptation to consult within herself rang like an ominous humming in her head. The Baron was there: dutiful, but always ready to play upon her terrors when rational judgment failed and the things around her lost their sense of past, present, and future.

*What if that's Paul down there?* she asked herself.

'Nonsense!' the voice within her said.

But the reports of The Preacher's words could not be doubted. *Heresy!* It terrified her to think that Paul himself might bring down the structure built on his name.

*Why not?*

She thought of what she'd said in Council just that morning, turning viciously upon Irulan, who'd urged acceptance of the gift of clothing from House Corrino.

'All gifts to the twins will be examined thoroughly, just as always,' Irulan had argued.

'And when we find the gift harmless?' Alia had cried.

Somehow that had been the most frightening thing of all: to find that the gift carried no threat.

In the end they'd accepted the fine clothing and had gone on to the other issue: Was the Lady Jessica to be given a position on the Council? Alia had managed to delay a vote.

She thought of this as she stared down at The Preacher.

Things which happened to her Regency now were like the underside of that transformation they inflicted upon this planet. Dune had once symbolized the power of ultimate desert. That power dwindled physically, but the myth of its power grew apace. Only the ocean-desert remained, the great Mother Desert of the inner planet, with its rim of thorn bushes, which Fremen still called Queen of Night. Behind the thorn bushes arose soft green hills bending down to the sand. All the hills were man-made. Every last one of them had been planted by men who had labored like crawling insects. The green of those hills was almost overpowering to someone raised, as Alia had been, in the tradition of dun-shaded sand. In her mind, as in the minds of all Fremen, the ocean-desert still held Dune in a grip which would never relax. She had only to close her eyes and she would see that desert.

Open eyes at the desert edge saw now the verdant hills, marsh slime reaching out green pseudopods toward the sand – but the other desert remained as powerful as ever.

Alia shook her head, stared down at The Preacher.

He had mounted the first of the terraced steps below the Temple and turned to face the almost deserted square. Alia touched the button beside her window which would amplify voices from below. She felt a wave of self-pity, seeing herself held here in loneliness. Whom could she trust? She'd thought Stilgar remained reliable, but Stilgar had been infected by this blind man.

'You know how he counts?' Stilgar had asked her. 'I heard him counting coins as he paid his guide. It's very strange to my Fremen ears, and that's a terrible thing. He counts 'shuc, ishcai, qimsa, chuascu, picha, suçta, and so on. I've not heard counting like that since the old days in the desert.'

From this, Alia knew that Stilgar could not be sent to do the job which must be done. And she would have to be circumspect with her guards where the slightest emphasis from the Regency tended to be taken as absolute command.

What was he doing down there, this Preacher?

The surrounding marketplace beneath its protective balconies and arched arcades still presented a gaudy face: merchandise left on display with a few boys to watch over it. Some few merchants remained awake there sniffing for the spice-biscuit money of the back country or the jingle in a pilgrim's purse.

Alia studied The Preacher's back. He appeared poised for speech, but something withheld his voice.

*Why do I stand here watching that ruin in ancient flesh?* she asked herself. *That mortal wreckage down there cannot be the 'Vessel of magnificence' which once was my brother.*

Frustration bordering on anger filled her. How could she find out about The Preacher, find out for certain *without finding out?* She was trapped. She dared not reveal more than a passing curiosity about this heretic.

Irulan felt it. She'd lost her famous Bene Gesserit poise and screamed in Council: 'We've lost the power to think well of ourselves!'

Even Stilgar had been shocked.

Javid had brought them back to their senses: 'We don't have time for such nonsense!'

Javid was right. What did it matter how they thought of themselves? All that concerned them was holding onto the Imperial power.

But Irulan, recovering her poise, had been even more devastating: 'We've lost something vital, I tell you. When we lost it, we lost the ability to make good decisions. We fall upon decisions these days the way we fall upon an enemy – or wait and wait, which is a form of giving up, and we allow the decisions of others to move us. Have we forgotten that we were the ones who set this current flowing?'

And all over the question of whether to accept a gift from House Corrino.

*Irulan will have to be disposed of*, Alia decided.

What was that old man down there waiting for? He called himself a preacher. Why didn't he preach?

Irulan was wrong about our decision-making, Alia told herself. *I can still make proper decisions!* The person with life-and-death decisions to make must make decisions or remain caught in the pendulum. Paul had always said that stasis was the most dangerous of those things which were not natural. The only permanence was fluid. Change was all that mattered.

*I'll show them change!* Alia thought.

The Preacher raised his arms in benediction.

A few of those remaining in the square moved closer to him, and Alia noted the slowness of that movement. Yes, the rumors were out that The Preacher had aroused Alia's displeasure. She bent closer to the Ixian speaker beside her spy hole. The speaker brought her the murmurings of the people in the square, the sound of wind, the scratching of feet on sand.

'I bring you four messages!' The Preacher said.

His voice blared from Alia's speaker, and she turned down the volume.

'Each message is for a certain person,' The Preacher said. 'The first message is Alia, the suzerain of this place.' He pointed behind him toward her spy hole. 'I bring her a warning: You, who held the secret of duration in your loins, have sold your future for an empty purse!'

*How dare he?* Alia thought. But his words froze her.

'My second message,' The Preacher said, 'is for Stilgar, the Fremen Naib, who believes he can translate the power of the tribes into the power of the Imperium. My warning to you, Stilgar: The most dangerous of all creations is a rigid code of ethics. It will turn upon you and drive you into exile!

*He has gone too far!* Alia thought. *I must send the guards for him no matter the consequences.* But her hands remained at her sides.

The Preacher turned to face the Temple, climbed to the second step and once more whirled to face the square, all the time keeping his left hand upon the shoulder of his guide. He called out now: 'My third message is for the Princess Irulan. Princess! Humiliation is a thing which no person can forget. I warn you to flee!'

*What's he saying?* Alia asked herself. *We humiliated Irulan, but . . . Why does he warn her to flee? My decision was just made!* A thrill of fear shot through Alia. How did The Preacher know?

'My fourth message is for Duncan Idaho,' he shouted. 'Duncan! You were taught to believe that loyalty buys loyalty. Ohh, Duncan, do not believe in history, because history is impelled by whatever passes for money. Duncan! Take your horns and do what you know best how to do.'

Alia chewed the back of her right hand. *Horns!* She wanted to reach out and press the button which would summon guards, but her hand refused to move.

'Now I will preach to you,' The Preacher said. 'This is a sermon of the desert. I direct it to the ears of Muad'Dib's priest-hood, those who practice the ecumenism of the sword. Ohhh, you believers in manifest destiny! Know you not that manifest destiny has its demoniac side? You cry out that you find yourselves exalted merely to have lived in the blessed generations of Muad'-

Dib. I say to you that you have abandoned Muad'Dib. Holiness has replaced love in your religion! You court the vengeance of the desert!'

The Preacher lowered his head as though in prayer.

Alia felt herself shivering with awareness. Gods below! That voice! It had been cracked by years in the burning sands, but it could be the remnant of Paul's voice.

Once more The Preacher raised his head. His voice boomed out over the square where more people had begun to gather, attracted by this oddity out of the past.

'Thus it is written!' The Preacher shouted. 'They who pray for dew at the desert's edge shall bring forth the deluge! They shall not escape their fate through powers of reason! Reason arises from pride that a man may not know in this way when he has done evil.' He lowered his voice. 'It was said of Muad'Dib that he died of prescience, that knowledge of the future killed him and he passed from the universe of reality into the *alam al-mythal*. I say to you that this is the illusion of Maya. Such thoughts have no independent reality. They cannot go out from you and do real things: Muad-Dib said of himself that he possessed no Rihani magic with which to encipher the universe. Do not doubt him.'

Again The Preacher raised his arms, lifted his voice in a stentorian bellow: 'I warn the priesthood of Muad'Dib! The fire on the cliff shall burn you! They who learn the lesson of self-deception too well shall perish by that deception. The blood of a brother cannot be cleansed away!'

He had lowered his arms, found his young guide, and was leaving the square before Alia could break herself from the trembling immobility which had overcome her. Such fearless heresy! It must be Paul. She had to warn her guards. They dared not move against this *Preacher* openly. The evidence in the square below her confirmed this.

Despite the heresy, no one moved to stop the departing Preacher. No Temple guard leaped to pursue him. No pilgrim tried to stop him. That charismatic blind man! Everyone who saw or heard him felt his power, the reflection of divine talent.

In spite of the day's heat, Alia felt suddenly cold. She felt the thin edge of her grip on the Imperium as a physical thing. She gripped the edge of her spy hole window as though to hold her power, thinking of its fragility. The balance of Landsraad, CHOAM, and Fremen arms held the core of power, while Spacing Guild and Bene Gesserit dealt silently in the shadows.

The forbidden seepage of technological development which came from the edges of humankind's farthest migrations nibbled at the central power. Products permitted the Ixian and Tleilaxu factories could not relieve the pressure. And always in the wings there stood Farad'n of House Corrino, inheritor of Shaddam IV's titles and claims.

Without the Fremen, without House Atreides' monopoly on the geriatric spice, her grip would loosen. All the power would dissolve. She could feel it slipping from her right now. People heeded this Preacher. It would be dangerous to silence him; just as dangerous as it was to let him continue preaching such words as he'd shouted across her square today. She could see the first omens of her own defeat and the pattern of the problem stood out clearly in her mind. The Bene Gesserits had codified the problem:

'A large populace held in check by a small but powerful force is quite a common situation in our universe. And we know the major conditions wherein this large populace may turn upon its keepers –

'One: When they find a leader. This is the most volatile threat to the powerful; they must retain control of leaders.

'Two: When the populace recognizes its chains. Keep the populace blind and unquestioning.

'Three: When the populace perceives a hope of escape from bondage. They must never even believe that escape is possible!'

Alia shook her head, feeling her cheeks tremble with the force of movement. The signs were here in her populace. Every report she received from her spies throughout the Imperium reinforced her certain knowledge. Unceasing warfare of the Fremen Jihad left its mark everywhere. Wherever 'the ecumenism of the sword' had touched, people retained the attitude of a subject population: defensive, concealing, evasive. All manifestations of authority – and this meant essentially *religious* authority – became subject to resentment. Oh, pilgrims still came in their thronging millions, and some among them were probably devout. But for the most part, pilgrimage had other motivations than devotion. Most often it was a canny surety for the future. It emphasized obedience and gained a real form of power which was easily translated into wealth. The Hajji who returned from Arrakis came home to new authority, new social status. The Hajji could make profitable economic decisions which the planet-bound of his homeworld dared not challenge.

Alia knew the popular riddle: 'What do you see inside the

empty purse brought home from Dune?' And the answer: 'The eyes of Muad'Dib (fire diamonds).'

The traditional ways to counter growing unrest paraded themselves before Alia's awareness: people had to be taught that opposition was always punished and assistance to the ruler was always rewarded. Imperial forces must be shifted in random fashion. Major adjuncts to Imperial power had to be concealed. Every movement by which the Regency countered potential attack required delicate timing to keep the opposition off balance.

*Have I lost my sense of timing?* she wondered.

'What idle speculation is this?' a voice within her asked. She felt herself growing calmer. Yes, the Baron's plan was a good one. We eliminate the threat of the Lady Jessica and, at the same time, we discredit House Corrino. Yes.

The Preacher could be dealt with later. She understood his posture. The symbolism was clear. He was the ancient spirit of unbridled speculation, the spirit of heresy alive and functioning in her desert of orthodoxy. That was his strength. It didn't matter whether he was Paul . . . as long as that could be kept in doubt. But her Bene Gesserit knowledge told Alia that his strength would contain the key to his weakness.

*The Preacher has a flaw which we will find. I will have him spied upon, watched every moment. And if the opportunity arises, he will be discredited.*

> *I will not argue with the Fremen claims that they are divinely inspired to transmit a religious revelation. It is their concurrent claim to ideological revelation which inspires me to shower them with derision. Of course, they make the dual claim in the hope that it will strengthen their mandarinate and help them to endure in a universe which finds them increasingly oppressive. It is in the name of all those opposed people that I warn the Fremen : short-term expediency always fails in the long term.*
>
> – The Preacher at Arrakeen

Leto had come up in the night with Stilgar to the narrow ledge at the crest of the low rock outcropping which Sietch Tabr called The Attendant. Under the waning light of Second Moon, the ledge gave them a panoramic view – the Shield Wall with Mount Idaho to the north, the Great Flat to the south and rolling dunes eastward toward Habbanya Ridge. Winding dust, the aftermath of a storm, hid the southern horizon. Moonlight frosted the rim of the Shield Wall.

Stilgar had come against his will, joining the secretive venture finally because Leto aroused his curiosity. Why was it necessary to risk a sand crossing in the night? The lad had threatened to sneak away and make the journey alone if Stilgar refused. The way of it bothered him profoundly, though. Two such important targets alone in the night!

Leto squatted on the ledge facing south toward the flat. Occasionally he pounded his knee as though in frustration.

Stilgar waited. He was good at silent waiting, and stood two paces to one side of his charge, arms folded, his robe moving softly in the night breeze.

For Leto, the sand crossing represented a response to inner desperation, a need to seek a new alignment for his life in a silent conflict which Ghanima could no longer risk. He had maneuvered Stilgar into sharing the journey because there were things Stilgar had to know in preparation for the days ahead.

Again Leto pounded his knee. It was difficult to know a beginning! He felt, at times, like an extension of those countless other lives, all as real and immediate as his own. In the flow of those lives there was no ending, no accomplishment – only eternal beginning. They could be a mob, too, clamoring at him as though he were a single window through which each desired to peer. And there lay the peril which had destroyed Alia.

Leto stared outward at the moonlight silvering the storm remnants. Folds and overfolds of dunes spread across the flat: silica grit measured out by the winds, mounded into waves – pea sand, grit sand, pebbles. He felt himself caught in one of those poised moments just before dawn. Time pressed at him. It was already the month of Akkad and behind him lay the last of an interminable waiting time: long hot days and hot dry winds, nights like this one tormented by gusts and endless blowings from the furnace lands of the Hawkbled. He glanced over his shoulder toward the Shield Wall, a broken line in starlight. Beyond that wall in the Northern Sink lay the focus of his problems.

Once more he looked to the desert. As he stared into the hot darkness, day dawned, the sun rising out of dust scarves and placing a touch of lime into the storm's red streamers. He closed his eyes, willing himself to see how this day would appear from Arrakeen, and the city lay there in his consciousness, caught up like a scattering of boxes between the light and the new shadows. Desert . . . boxes . . . desert . . . boxes . . .

When he opened his eyes, the desert remained: a spreading curry expanse of wind-kicked sand. Oily shadows along the base of each dune reached out like rays of the night just past. They linked one time with the other. He thought of the night, squatting here with Stilgar restless beside him, the older man worried at the silence and the unexplained reasons for coming to this place. Stilgar must have many memories of passing this way with his beloved Muad'Dib. Even now Stilgar was moving, scanning all around, alert for dangers. Stilgar did not like the open in daylight. He was pure old Fremen in that.

Leto's mind was reluctant to leave the night and the clean exertions of a sand crossing. Once here in the rocks, the night had taken on its black stillness. He sympathized with Stilgar's daylight fears. Black was a single thing even when it contained boiling terrors. Light could be many things. Night held its fear smells and its things which came with slithering sounds. Dimensions separated in the night, everything amplified – thorns sharper, blades more cutting. But terrors of the day could be worse.

Stilgar cleared his throat.

Leto spoke without turning: 'I have a very serious problem, Stil.'

'So I surmised.' The voice beside Leto came low and wary. The child had sounded disturbingly of the father. It was a thing of forbidden magic which touched a cord of revulsion in Stilgar. Fremen knew the terrors of *possession*. Those found possessed were rightfully killed and their water cast upon the sand lest it contaminate the tribal cistern. The dead should remain dead. It was correct to find one's immortality in children, but children had no right to assume too exact a shape from their past.

'My problem is that my father left so many things undone,' Leto said. 'Especially the focus of our lives. The Empire cannot go on this way, Stil, without a proper focus for human life. I am speaking of life, you understand? Life, not death.'

'Once, when he was troubled by a vision, your father spoke in this vein to me,' Stilgar said.

Leto found himself tempted to pass off that questioning fear beside him with a light response, perhaps a suggestion that they break their fast. He realized that he was very hungry. They had eaten the previous noon and Leto had insisted on fasting through the night. But another hunger drew him now.

*The trouble with my life is the trouble with this place,* Leto thought. *No preliminary creation. I just go back and back and back until distances fade away. I cannot see the horizon; I cannot see Habbanya Ridge. I can't find the original place of testing.*

'There's really no substitute for prescience,' Leto said. 'Perhaps I should risk the spice . . .'

'And be destroyed as your father was?'

'A dilemma,' Leto said.

'Once your father confided in me that knowing the future too well was to be locked into that future to the exclusion of any freedom to change.'

'The paradox which is our problem,' Leto said. 'It's a subtle and powerful thing, prescience. The future becomes now. To be sighted in the land of the blind carries its own perils. If you try to interpret what you see for the blind, you tend to forget that the blind possess an inherent movement conditioned by their blindness. They are like a monstrous machine moving along its own path. They have their own momentum, their own fixations. I fear the blind, Stil. I fear them. They can so easily crush anything in their path.'

Stilgar stared at the desert. Lime dawn had become steel day. He said: 'Why have we come to this place?'

'Because I wanted you to see the place where I may die.'

Stilgar tensed. Then: 'So you *have* had a vision!'

'Perhaps it was only a dream.'

'Why do we come to such a dangerous place?' Stilgar glared down at his charge. 'We will return at once.'

'I won't die today, Stil.'

'No? What was this vision?'

'I saw three paths,' Leto said. His voice came out with the sleepy sound of remembrance. 'One of those futures requires me to kill our grandmother.'

Stilgar shot a sharp glance back toward Sietch Tabr, as though he feared the Lady Jessica could hear them across the sandy distance. 'Why?'

'To keep from losing the spice monopoly.'

'I don't understand.'

'Nor do I. But that is the thought of my dream when I use the knife.'

'Oh.' Stilgar understood the use of a knife. He drew a deep breath. 'What is the second path?'

'Ghani and I marry to seal the Atreides bloodline.'

'*Ghaaa!*' Stilgar expelled his breath in a violent expression of distaste.

'It was usual in ancient times for kings and queens to do this,' Leo said. 'Ghani and I have decided we will not breed.'

'I warn you to hold fast in that decision!' There was death in Stilgar's voice. By Fremen Law, incest was punishable by death on the hanging tripod. He cleared his throat, asked: 'And the third path?'

'I am called to reduce my father to human stature.'

'He was my friend, Muad'Dib,' Stilgar muttered.

'He was your god! I must undeify him.'

Stilgar turned his back on the desert, stared toward the oasis of his beloved Sietch Tabr. Such talk always disturbed him.

Leto sensed the sweaty smell of Stilgar's movement. It was such a temptation to avoid the purposeful things which had to be said here. They could talk half the day away, moving from the specific to the abstract as though drawn away from real decisions, from those immediate necessities which confronted them. And there was no doubt that House Corrino posed a real threat to real lives – his own and Ghani's. But everything he did now had to be weighed and tested against the secret necessities. Stilgar once had voted to have Farad'n assassinated, holding out for the subtle application of chaumurky: poison administered in a drink. Farad'n was known to be partial to certain sweet liquors. That could not be permitted.

'If I die here, Stil,' Leto said, 'you must beware of Alia. She is no longer your friend.'

'What is this talk of death and your aunt?' Now Stilgar was truly outraged. *Kill the Lady Jessica! Beware of Alia! Die in this place!*

'Small men change their faces at her command,' Leto said. 'A ruler need not be a prophet, Stil. Nor even godlike. A ruler need only be sensitive. I brought you here with me to clarify what our Imperium requires. It requires good government. That does not depend upon laws or precedent, but upon the personal qualities of whoever governs.'

'The Regency handles its Imperial duties quite well,' Stilgar said. 'When you come of age – '

'I *am* of age! I'm the oldest person here! You're a puling infant beside me. I can remember times more than fifty centuries past. Hah! I can even remember when we Fremen were on Thurgrod.'

'Why do you play with such fancies?' Stilgar demanded, his tone peremptory.

109

Leto nodded to himself. Why indeed? Why recount his memories of those other centuries? Today's Fremen were his immediate problem, most of them still only half-tamed savages, prone to laugh at unlucky innocence.

'The crysknife dissolves at the death of its owner,' Leto said. 'Muad'Dib has dissolved. Why are the Fremen still alive?'

It was one of those abrupt thought changes, which so confounded Stilgar. He found himself temporarily dumb. Such words contained meaning, but their intent eluded him.

'I am expected to be Emperor, but I must be the servant,' Leto said. He glanced across his shoulder at Stilgar. 'My grandfather for whom I was named added new words to his coat of arms when he came here to Dune: "Here I am; here I remain." '

'He had no choice,' Stilgar said.

'Very good, Stil. Nor have I any choice. I should be the Emperor by birth, by the fitness of my understanding, by all that has gone into me. I even know what the Imperium requires: good government.'

'Naïb has an ancient meaning,' Stilgar said. 'It is "servant of the Sietch." '

'I remember your training, Stil,' Leto said. 'For proper government, the tribe must have ways to choose men whose lives reflect the way a government should behave.'

From the depths of his Fremen soul, Stilgar said: 'You'll assume the Imperial Mantle if it's meet. First you must prove that you can behave in the fashion of a ruler!'

Unexpectedly, Leto laughed. Then: 'Do you doubt my sincerity, Stil?'

'Of course not.'

'My birthright?'

'You are who you are.'

'And if I do what is expected of me, that is the measure of my sincerity, eh?'

'It is the Fremen practice.'

'Then I cannot have inner feelings to guide my behavior?'

'I don't understand what –'

'If I always behave with propriety, no matter what it costs me to suppress my own desires, then that is the measure of me.'

'Such is the essence of self-control, youngster.'

'Youngster!' Leto shook his head. 'Ahhh, Stil, you provide me with the key to a rational ethic of government. I must be constant, every action rooted in the traditions of the past.'

'That is proper.'

'But my past goes deeper than yours!'

'What difference – '

'I have no first person singular, Stil. I am a multiple person with memories of traditions more ancient than you could imagine. That's my burden, Stil. I'm past-directed. I'm abrim with innate knowledge which resists newness and change. Yet Muad'Dib changed all this.' He gestured at the desert, his arm sweeping to encompass the Shield Wall behind him.

Stilgar turned to peer at the Shield Wall. A village had been built beneath the wall since Muad'Dib's time, houses to shelter a planetology crew helping spread plant life into the desert. Stilgar stared at the man-made intrusion into the landscape. Change? Yes. There was an alignment to the village, a trueness which offended him. He stood silently, ignoring the itching of grit particles under his stillsuit. That village was an offense against the thing this planet had been. Suddenly Stilgar wanted a circular howling of wind to leap over the dunes and obliterate that place. The sensation left him trembling.

Leto said: 'Have you noticed, Stil, that the new stillsuits are of sloppy manufacture? Our water loss is too high.'

Stilgar stopped himself on the point of asking: *Have I not said it?* Instead he said: 'Our people grow increasingly dependent upon the pills.'

Leto nodded. The pills shifted body temperature, reduced water loss. They were cheaper and easier than stillsuits. But they inflicted the user with other burdens, among them a tendency to slowed reaction time, occasional blurred vision.

'Is that why we came out here?' Stilgar asked. 'To discuss stillsuit manufacture?'

'Why not?' Leto asked. 'Since you will not face what I must talk about.'

'Why must I beware of your aunt?' Anger edged his voice.

'Because she plays upon the old Fremen desire to resist change, yet would bring more terrible change than you can imagine.'

'You make much out of little! She's a proper Fremen.'

'Ahhh, then the proper Fremen holds to the ways of the past and I have an ancient past. Stil, were I to give free reign to this inclination, I would demand a closed society, completely dependent upon the sacred ways of the past. I would control migration, explaining that this fosters new ideas, and new ideas are a threat to the entire structure of life. Each little planetary polis would go its own way, becoming what it would. Finally the Empire would shatter under the weight of its differences.'

Stilgar tried to swallow in a dry throat. These were words which Muad'Dib might have produced. They had his ring to them. They were paradox, frightening. But if one allowed any change . . . He shook his head.

'The past may show the right way to behave if you live in the past, Stil, but circumstances change.'

Stilgar could only agree that circumstances did change. How must one behave then? He looked beyond Leto, seeing the desert and not seeing it. Muad'Dib had walked there. The flat was a place of golden shadows as the sun climbed, purple shadows, gritty rivulets crested in dust vapors. The dust fog which usually hung over Habbanya Ridge was visible in the far distance now, and the desert between presented his eyes with dunes diminishing, one curve into another. Through the smoky shimmer of heat he saw the plants which crept out from the desert edge. Muad'Dib had caused life to sprout in that desolate place. Copper, gold, red flowers, yellow flowers, rust and russet, gray-green leaves, spikes and harsh shadows beneath bushes. The motion of the day's heat set shadows quivering, vibrating in the air.

Presently Stilgar said: 'I am only a leader of Fremen; you are the son of a Duke.'

'Not knowing what you said, you said it,' Leto said.

Stilgar scowled. Once, long ago, Muad'Dib had chided him thus.

'You remember it, don't you, Stil?' Leto asked. 'We were under Habbanya Ridge and the Sardaukar captain – remember him: Aramsham? He killed his friend to save himself. And you warned several times that day about preserving the lives of Sardaukar who'd seen our secret ways. Finally you said they would surely reveal what they'd seen; they must be killed. And my father said: "Not knowing what you said, you said it." And you were hurt. You told him you were only a *simple* leader of Fremen. Dukes must know more important things.'

Stilgar stared down at Leto. *We were under Habbanya Ridge! We!* This . . . this child, not even conceived on that day, knew what had taken place in exact detail, the kind of detail which could only be known to someone who had been there. It was only another proof that these Atreides children could not be judged by ordinary standards.

'Now you will listen to me,' Leto said. 'If I die or disappear in the desert, you are to flee from Sietch Tabr. I command it. You are to take Ghani and –'

'You are not yet my Duke! You're a . . . a child!'

112

'I'm an adult in a child's flesh,' Leto said. He pointed down to a narrow crack in the rocks below them. 'If I die here, it will be in that place. You will see the blood. You will know then. Take my sister and –'

'I'm doubling your guard,' Stilgar said. 'You're not coming out here again. We are leaving now and you –'

'Stil! You cannot hold me. Turn your mind once more to that time at Habbanya Ridge. Remember? The factory crawler was out there on the sand and a big Maker was coming. There was no way to save the crawler from the worm. And my father was annoyed that he couldn't save that crawler. But Gurney could think only of the men he'd lost in the sand. Remember what he said: "Your father would've been more concerned for the men he couldn't save." Stil, I charge you to save people. They're more important than things. And Ghani is the most precious of all because, without me, she is the only hope for the Atreides.'

'I will hear no more,' Stilgar said. He turned and began climbing down the rocks toward the oasis across the sand. He heard Leto following. Presently Leto passed him and, glancing back, said:

'Have you noticed, Stil, how beautiful the young women are this year?'

*The life of a single human, as the life of a family or an entire people, persists as memory. My people must come to see this as part of their maturing process. They are people as organism, and in this persistent memory they store more and more experiences in a subliminal reservoir. Humankind hopes to call upon this material if it is needed for a changing universe. But much that is stored can be lost in that chance play of accident which we call 'fate'. Much may not be integrated into evolutionary relationships, and thus may not be evaluated and keyed into activity by those ongoing environmental changes which inflict themselves upon flesh. The species can forget! This is the special value of the Kwisatz Haderach which the Bene Gesserits never suspected; the Kwisatz Haderach cannot forget.*

> – The Book of Leto
> After Harq al-Ada

Stilgar could not explain it, but he found Leto's casual observation profoundly disturbing. It ground through his awareness all the way back across the sand to Sietch Tabr, taking precedence over everything else Leto had said out there on The Attendant.

Indeed, the young women of Arrakis were very beautiful that year. And the young men, too. Their faces glowed serenely with water-richness. Their eyes looked outward and far. They exposed their features often without any pretense of stillsuit masks and the snaking lines of catchtubes. Frequently they did not even wear stillsuits in the open, preferring the new garments which, as they moved, offered flickering suggestions of the lithe young bodies beneath.

Such human beauty was set off against the new beauty of the landscape. By contrast with the old Arrakis, the eye could be spellbound by its collision with a tiny clump of green twigs growing among red-brown rocks. And the old sietch warrens of the cave-metropolis culture, complete with elaborate seals and moisture traps at every entrance, were giving way to open villages built often of mud bricks. Mud bricks!

*Why did I want the village destroyed?* Stilgar wondered, and he stumbled as he walked.

He knew himself to be of a dying breed. Old Fremen gasped in wonder at the prodigality of their planet – water wasted into the air for no more than its ability to mold building bricks. The water for a single one-family dwelling would keep an entire sietch alive for a year.

The new buildings even had transparent windows to let in the sun's heat and to dessicate the bodies within. Such windows opened outward.

New Fremen within their mud homes could look out upon their landscape. They no longer were enclosed and huddling in a sietch. Where the new vision moved, there also moved the imagination. Stilgar could feel this. The new vision joined Fremen to the rest of the Imperial universe, conditioned them to unbounded space. Once they'd been tied to water-poor Arrakis by their enslavement to its bitter necessities. They'd not shared that open-mindedness which conditioned inhabitants on most planets of the Imperium.

Stilgar could see the changes contrasting with his own doubts and fears. In the old days it had been a rare Fremen who even considered the possibility that he might leave Arrakis to begin a new life on one of the water-rich worlds. They'd not even been permitted the *dream* of escape.

He watched Leto's moving back as the youth walked ahead. Leto had spoken of prohibitions against movement off-planet. Well, that had always been a reality for most other-worlders, even where the dream was permitted as a safety valve. But planetary serfdom had reached its peak here on Arrakis. Fremen had turned inward, barricaded in their minds as they were barricaded in their cave warrens.

The very meaning of sietch – a place of sanctuary in times of trouble – had been perverted here into a monstrous confinement for an entire population.

Leto spoke the truth: Muad'Dib had changed all that.

Stilgar felt lost. He could feel his old beliefs crumbling. The new outward vision produced life which desired to move away from containment.

*'How beautiful the young women are this year.'*

The old ways (*My ways!* he admitted) had forced his people to ignore all history except that which turned inward onto their own travail. The old Fremen had read history out of their own terrible migrations, their flights from persecution into persecution. The old planetary government had followed the stated policy of the old Imperium. They had suppressed creativity and all sense of progress, of evolution. Prosperity had been dangerous to the old Imperium and its holders of power.

With an abrupt shock, Stilgar realized that these things were equally dangerous to the course which Alia was setting.

Again Stilgar stumbled and fell farther behind Leto.

In the old ways and old religions, there'd been no future, only an endless *now*. Before Muad'Dib, Stilgar saw, the Fremen had been conditioned to believe in failure, never in the possibility of accomplishment. Well . . . they'd believed Liet-Kynes, but he'd set a forty-generation timescale. That was no accomplishment; that was a dream which, he saw now, had also turned inward.

*Muad'Dib had changed that!*

During the Jihad, Fremen had learned much about the old Padishah Emperor, Shaddam IV. The eighty-first Padishah of House Corrino to occupy the Golden Lion Throne and reign over this Imperium of uncounted worlds had used Arrakis as a testing place for those policies which he'd hoped to implement in the rest of his empire. His planetary governors on Arrakis had cultivated a persistent pessimism to bolster their power base. They'd made sure that everyone on Arrakis, even the free-roaming Fremen, became familiar with numerous cases of injustice and insoluble problems; they had been taught to think of themselves as a helpless people for whom there was no succor.

*'How beautiful the young women are this year!'*

As he watched Leto's retreating back, Stilgar began to wonder how the youth had set these thoughts flowing – and just by uttering a seemingly simple statement. Because of that statement, Stilgar found himself viewing Alia and his own role on the Council in an entirely different way.

Alia was fond of saying that old ways gave ground slowly. Stilgar admitted to himself that he'd always found this statement vaguely reassuring. Change was dangerous. Invention must be suppressed. Individual willpower must be denied. What other function did the priesthood serve than to deny individual will?

Alia kept saying that opportunities for open competition had to be reduced to manageable limits. But that meant the recurrent threat of technology could only be used to confine populations – just as it had served its ancient masters. Any permitted technology had to be rooted in ritual. Otherwise . . . otherwise . . .

Again Stilgar stumbled. He was at the qanat now and saw Leto waiting beneath the apricot orchard which grew along the flowing water. Stilgar heard his feet moving through uncut grass.

*Uncut grass!*

*What can I believe?* Stilgar asked himself.

It was proper for a Fremen of his generation to believe that individuals needed a profound sense of their own limitations. Traditions were surely the most controlling element in a secure society. People had to know the boundaries of their time, of their society, of their territory. What was wrong with the sietch as a model for all thinking? A sense of enclosure should pervade every individual choice – should fence in the family, the community, and every step taken by a proper government.

Stilgar came to a stop and stared across the orchard at Leto. The youth stood there, regarding him with a smile.

*Does he know the turmoil in my head?* Stilgar wondered.

And the old Fremen Naib tried to fall back on the traditional catechism of his people. Each aspect of life required a single form, its inherent circularity based on secret inner knowledge of what will work and what will not work. The model for life, for the community, for every element of the larger society right up to and beyond the peaks of government – that model had to be the sietch and its counterpart in the sand: Shai-Hulud. The giant sandworm was surely a most formidable creature, but when threatened it hid in the impenetrable deeps.

*Change is dangerous!* Stilgar told himself. Sameness and stability were the proper goals of government.

But the young men and women were beautiful.

And they remembered the words of Muad'Dib as he deposed

116

Shaddam IV: 'It's not long life to the Emperor that I seek; it's long life to the Imperium.'

*Isn't that what I've been saying to myself?* Stilgar wondered.

He resumed walking, headed toward the sietch entrance slightly to Leto's right. The youth moved to intercept him.

Muad'Dib had said another thing, Stilgar reminded himself: *'Just as individuals are born, mature, breed, and die, so do societies and civilizations and governments.'*

Dangerous or not, there would be change. The beautiful young Fremen knew this. They could look outward and see it, prepare for it.

Stilgar was forced to stop. It was either that or walk right over Leto.

The youth peered up at him owlishly, said: 'You see, Stil? Tradition isn't the absolute guide you thought it was.'


> *A Fremen dies when he is too long from the desert; this we call 'the water sickness'.*
>
> – Stilgar, the Commentaries

'It is difficult for me, asking you to do this,' Alia said. 'But . . . I must insure that there's an empire for Paul's children to inherit. There's no other reason for the Regency.'

Alia turned from where she was seated at a mirror completing her morning toilet. She looked at her husband, measuring how he absorbed these words. Duncan Idaho deserved careful study in these moments; there was no doubt that he'd become something far more subtle and dangerous than the one-time sword-master of House Atreides. The outer appearance remained similar – the black goat hair over sharp dark features – but in the long years since his awakening from the ghola state he had undergone an inner metamorphosis.

She wondered now, as she had wondered many times, what the ghola rebirth-after-death might have hidden in the secret loneliness of him. Before the Tleilaxu had worked their subtle science on him, Duncan's reactions had borne clear labels for the Atreides – loyalty, fanatic adherence to the moral code of his mercenary forebears, swift to anger and swift to recover. He had been implacable in his resolve for revenge against House Harkonnen. And he had died saving Paul. But the Tleilaxu had brought his body from the Sardaukar and, in their regeneration vats, they had grown a zombie-katrundo: the flesh of Duncan Idaho, but none of his conscious memories. He'd been trained as a mentat and sent as a gift, a human computer for Paul, a fine tool equipped with a hypnotic compulsion to slay his owner. The flesh of Duncan Idaho had resisted that compulsion and, in the intolerable stress, his cellular past had come back to him.

Alia had decided long ago that it was dangerous to think of him as Duncan in the privacy of her thoughts. Better to think of him by his ghola name, Hayt. Far better. And it was essential that he get not the slightest glimpse of the old Baron Harkonnen sitting there in her mind.

Duncan saw Alia studying him, turned away. Love could not hide the changes in her, nor conceal from him the transparency of her motives. The many-faceted metal eyes which the Tleilaxu had given him were cruel in their ability to penetrate deception. They limned her now as a gloating, almost masculine figure, and he could not stand to see her thus.

'Why do you turn away?' Alia asked.

'I must think about this thing,' he said. 'The Lady Jessica is . . . an Atreides.'

'And your loyalty is to House Atreides, not to me,' Alia pouted.

'Don't put such fickle interpretations into me,' he said.

Alia pursed her lips. Had she moved too rapidly?

Duncan crossed to the chambered opening which looked down on a corner of the Temple plaza. He could see pilgrims beginning to gather there, the Arrakeen traders moving in to feed on the edges like a pack of predators upon a herd of beasts. He focused on a particular group of tradesmen, spice-fiber baskets over their arms. Fremen mercenaries a pace behind them. They moved with a stolid force through the gathering throng.

'They sell pieces of etched marble,' he said, pointing. 'Did you know that? They set the pieces out in the desert to be etched by stormsands. Sometimes they find interesting patterns in the stone. They call it a new art form, very popular: genuine storm-etched marble from Dune. I bought a piece of it last week – a golden tree with five tassels, lovely but very fragile.'

'Don't change the subject,' Alia said.

'I haven't changed the subject,' he said. 'It's beautiful, but it's not art. Humans create art by their own violence, by their own volition.' He put his right hand on the windowsill. 'The twins detest this city and I'm afraid I see their point.'

'I fail to see the association,' Alia said. 'The abduction of my mother is not a real abduction. She will be safe as your captive.'

'This city was built by the blind,' he said. 'Did you know that Leto and Stilgar went out from Sietch Tabr into the desert last week? They were gone the whole night.'

'It was reported to me,' she said. 'These baubles from the sand — would you have me prohibit their sale?'

'That'd be bad for business,' he said, turning. 'Do you know what Stilgar said when I asked why they went out on the sand that way? He said Leto wished to commune with the spirit of Muad'Dib.'

Alia felt the sudden coldness of panic, looked in the mirror a moment to recover. Leto would not venture from the sietch at night for such nonsense. Was it a conspiracy?

Idaho put a hand over his eyes to blot out the sight of her, said: 'Stilgar told me he went along with Leto because he still believes in Muad'Dib.'

'Of course he does!'

Idaho chuckled, a hollow sound. 'He said he still believes because Muad'Dib was always for the little people.'

'What did you say to that?' Alia asked, her voice betraying her fear.

Idaho dropped his hand from his eyes. 'I said, "That must make you one of the little people."'

'Duncan! That's a dangerous game. Bait *that* Fremen Naib and you could awaken a beast to destroy us all.'

'He still believes in Muad'Dib,' Idaho said. 'That's our protection.'

'What was his reply?'

'He said he knew his own mind.'

'I see.'

'No . . . I don't believe you do. Things that bite have longer teeth than Stilgar's.'

'I don't understand you today, Duncan. I ask you to do a very important thing, a thing vital to . . . What is all of this rambling?'

How petulant she sounded. He turned back to the chambered window. 'When I was trained as a mentat . . . It is very difficult, Alia, to learn how to work your own mind. You learn first that the mind must be allowed to work itself. That's very strange. You can work your own muscles, exercise them, strengthen them, but the mind acts of itself. Sometimes, when you have learned this about the mind, it shows you things you do not want to see.'

'And that's why you tried to insult Stilgar?'

'Stilgar doesn't know his own mind; he doesn't let it run free.'

'Except in the spice orgy.'

'Not even there. That's what makes him a Naib. To be a leader of men, he controls and limits his reactions. He does what is expected of him. Once you know this, you know Stilgar and you can measure the length of his teeth.'

'That's the Fremen way,' she said. 'Well, Duncan, will you do it, or won't you? She must be taken and it must be made to look like the work of House Corrino.'

He remained silent, weighing her tone and arguments in his mentat way. This abduction plan spoke of a coldness and a cruelty whose dimensions, thus revealed, shocked him. Risk her own mother's life for the reasons thus far produced? Alia was lying. Perhaps the whisperings about Alia and Javid were true. This thought produced an icy hardness in his stomach.

'You're the only one I can trust for this,' Alia said.

'I know that,' he said.

She took this as acceptance, smiled at herself in the mirror.

'You know,' Idaho said, 'the mentat learns to look at every human as a series of relationships.'

Alia did not respond. She sat, caught in a personal memory which drew a blank expression on her face. Idaho, glancing over his shoulder at her, saw the expression and shuddered. It was as though she communed with voices heard only by herself.

'Relationships,' he whispered.

And he thought: *One must cast off old agonies as a snake casts off its skin – only to grow a new set and accept all of their limitations. It was the same with governments – even the Regency. Old governments can be traced like discarded molts. I must carry out this scheme, but not in the way Alia commands.*

Presently Alia shook her shoulders, said: 'Leto should not be going out like that in these times. I will reprimand him.'

'Not even with Stilgar?'

'Not even with him.'

She arose from her mirror, crossed to where Idaho stood beside the window, put a hand on his arm.

He repressed a shiver, reduced this reaction to a mentat computation. Something in her revolted him.

Something in her.

He could not bring himself to look at her. He smelled the melange of her cosmetics, cleared his throat.

She said: 'I will be busy today examining Farad'n's gifts.'

'The clothing?'

'Yes. Nothing he does is what it seems. And we must remember that his Bashar, Tyekanik, is an adept of chaumurky, chaumas, and all the other subtleties of royal assassination.'

'The price of power,' he said, pulling away from her. 'But we're still mobile and Farad'n is not.'

She studied his chiseled profile. Sometimes the workings of his mind were diffiult to fathom. Was he thinking only that freedom of action gave life to a military power? Well, life on Arrakis had been too secure for too long. Senses once whetted by omnipresent dangers could degenerate when not used.

'Yes,' she said, 'we still have the Fremen.'

'Mobility,' he repeated. 'We cannot degenerate into infantry. That'd be foolish.'

His tone annoyed her, and she said: 'Farad'n will use any means to destroy us.'

'Ahhh, that's it,' he said. 'That's a form of initiative, a mobility which we didn't have in the old days. We had a code, the code of House Atreides. We always paid our way and let the enemy be the pillagers. That restriction no longer holds, of course. We're equally mobile, House Atreides and House Corrino.'

'We abduct my mother to save her from harm as much as for any other reason,' Alia said. 'We still live by the code!'

He looked down at her. She knew the dangers of inciting a mentat to compute. Didn't she realize what he had computed? Yet . . . he still loved her. He brushed a hand across his eyes. How youthful she looked. The Lady Jessica was correct: Alia gave the appearance of not having aged a day in their years together. She still possessed the soft features of her Bene Gesserit mother, but her eyes were Atreides – measuring, demanding, hawklike. And now something possessed of cruel calculation lurked behind those eyes.

Idaho had served House Atreides for too many years not to understand the family's strengths as well as their weaknesses. But this thing in Alia, this was new. The Atreides might play a devious game against enemies, but never against friends and allies, and not at all against Family. It was ground into the Atreides manner: support your own populace to the best of your ability; show them how much better they lived under the Atreides. Demonstrate your love for your friends by the candor of your behavior with them. What Alia asked now, though, was not Atreides. He felt this with all of his body's flesh and nerve structure. He was a unit, indivisible, feeling this alien attitude in Alia.

121

Abruptly his mentat sensorium clicked into full awareness and his mind leaped into the frozen trance where Time did not exist; only the computation existed. Alia would recognize what had happened to him, but that could not be helped. He gave himself up to the computation.

Computation: A *reflected* Lady Jessica lived out a pseudo-life in Alia's awareness. He saw this as he saw the reflected pre-ghola Duncan Idaho which remained a constant in his own awareness. Alia had this awareness by being one of the pre-born. He had it out of the Tleilaxu regeneration tanks. Yet Alia denied that reflection, risked her mother's life. Therefore Alia was not in contact with that pseudo-Jessica within. Therefore Alia was *completely* possessed by another pseudo-life to the exclusion of all others.

*Possessed!*

*Alien!*

*Abomination!*

Mentat fashion, he accepted this, turned to other facets of his problem. All of the Atreides were on this one planet. Would House Corrino risk attack from space? His mind flashed through the review of those conventions which had ended primitive forms of warfare:

One – All planets were vulnerable to attack from space; ergo: retaliation/revenge facilities were set up off-planet by every House Major. Farad'n would know that the Atreides had not omitted this elementary precaution.

Two – Force shields were a complete defense against projectiles and explosives of non-atomic type, the basic reason why hand-to-hand conflict had reentered human combat. But infantry had its limits. House Corrino might have brought their Sardaukar back to a pre-Arrakeen edge, but they still could be no match for the abandoned ferocity of Fremen.

Three – Planetary feudalism remained in constant danger from a large technical class, but the effects of the Butlerian Jihad continued as a damper on technological excesses. Ixians, Tleilaxu, and a few scattered outer planets were the only possible threat in this regard, and they were planet-vulnerable to the combined wrath of the rest of the Imperium. The Butlerian Jihad would not be undone. Mechanized warfare required a large technical class. The Atreides Imperium had channeled this force into other pursuits. No large technical class existed unwatched. And the Empire remained safely feudalist, naturally, since that was the best social form for spreading over widely dispersed wild frontiers – new planets.

Duncan felt his mentat awareness coruscate as it shot through memory data *of itself*, completely impervious to the passage of time. Arriving at the conviction that House Corrino would not risk an *illegal* atomic attack, he did this in flash-computation, the main decisional pathway, but he was perfectly aware of the elements which went into this conviction: The Imperium commanded as many nuclear and allied weapons as all the Great Houses combined. At least half the Great Houses would react without thinking if House Corrino broke the Convention. The Atreides off-planet retaliation system would be joined by overwhelming force, and no need to summon any of them. Fear would do the calling. Salusa Secundus and its allies would vanish in hot clouds. House Corrino would not risk such a holocaust. They were undoubtedly sincere in subscribing to the argument that nuclear weapons were a reserve held for one purpose: defense of humankind should a threatening 'other intelligence' ever be encountered.

The computational thoughts had clean edges, sharp relief. There were no blurred between-places. Alia chose abduction and terror because she had become alien, non-Atreides. House Corrino was a threat, but not in the ways which Alia argued in Council. Alia wanted the Lady Jessica removed because that searing Bene Gesserit intelligence had seen what only now had become clear to him.

Idaho shook himself out of the mentat trance, saw Alia standing in front of him, a coldly measuring expression on her face.

'Wouldn't you rather the Lady Jessica were killed?' he asked.

The alien-flash of her joy lay exposed before his eyes for a brief instant before being covered by false outrage. 'Duncan!'

Yes, this alien-Alia preferred matricide.

'You are afraid *of* your mother, not *for* her,' he said.

She spoke without a change in her measuring stare. 'Of course I am. She has reported about me to the Sisterhood.'

'What do you mean?'

'Don't you know the greatest temptation for a Bene Gesserit?' She moved closer to him, seductive, looked upward at him through her lashes. 'I thought only to keep myself strong and alert for the sake of the twins.'

'You speak of temptation,' he said, his voice mentat-flat.

'It's the thing which the Sisterhood hides most deeply, the thing they most fear. It's why they call me *Abomination*. They

123

know their inhibitions won't hold me back. Temptation – they always speak with heavy emphasis: *Great Temptation*. You see, we who employ the Bene Gesserit teachings can influence such things as the internal adjustment of enzyme balance within our bodies. It can prolong youth – far longer than with melange. Do you see the consequences should many Bene Gesserits do this? It would be noticed. I'm sure you compute the accuracy of what I'm saying. Melange is what makes us the target for so many plots. We control a substance which prolongs life. What if it became known that Bene Gesserits controlled an even more potent secret? You see! Not one Reverend Mother would be safe. Abduction and torture of Bene Gesserits would become a most common activity.'

'You've accomplished this enzyme balancing.' It was a statement, not a question.

'I've defied the Sisterhood! My mother's reports to the Sisterhood will make the Bene Gesserits unswerving allies of House Corrino.'

*How very plausible*, he thought.

He tested: 'But surely your own mother would not turn against you!'

'She was Bene Gesserit long before she was my mother. Duncan, she permitted her own son, my brother, to undergo the test of the *gom jabbar*! She arranged it! And she knew he might not survive it! Bene Gesserits have always been short on faith and long on pragmatism. She'll act against me if she believes it's in the best interests of the Sisterhood.'

He nodded. How convincing she was. It was a sad thought.

'We must hold the initiative,' she said. 'That's our sharpest weapon.'

'There's the problem of Gurney Halleck,' he said. 'Do I have to kill my old friend?'

'Gurney's off on some spy errand in the desert,' she said, knowing Idaho already was aware of this. 'He's safely out of the way.'

'Very odd,' he said, 'the Regent Governor òf Caladan running errands here on Arrakis.'

'Why not?' Alia demanded. 'He's her lover – in his dreams if not in fact.'

'Yes, of course.' And he wondered that she did not hear the insincerity in his voice.

'When will you abduct her?' Alia asked.

'It's better that you don't know.'

'Yes ... yes, I see. Where'll you take her?'

124

'Where she cannot be found. Depend upon it; she won't be left here to threaten you.'

The glee in Alia's eyes could not be mistaken. 'But where will . . .'

'If you do not know, then you can answer before a Truthsayer, if necessary, that you do not know where she is.'

'Ahhh, clever Duncan.'

*Now she believes I will kill the Lady Jessica,* he thought. And he said: 'Goodbye, beloved.'

She did not hear the finality in his voice, even kissed him lightly as he left.

And all the way down through the sietchlike maze of Temple corridors, Idaho brushed at his eyes. Tleilaxu eyes were not immune to tears.

> *You have loved Caladan*
> *And lamented its lost host —*
> *But pain discovers*
> *New lovers cannot erase*
> *Those forever ghost.*
>
> **– Refrain from The Habbanya Lament**

Stilgar quadrupled the sietch guard around the twins, but he knew it was useless. The lad was like his Atreides namesake, the grandfather Leto. Everyone who'd known the original Duke remarked on it. Leto had the measuring look about him, and caution, yes, but all of it had to be evaluated against that latent wildness, the susceptibility to dangerous decisions.

Ghanima was more like her mother. There was Chani's red hair, the set of Chani's eyes, and a calculating way about her when she adjusted to difficulties. She often said that she only did what she had to do, but where Leto led she would follow.

And Leto was going to lead them into danger.

Not once did Stilgar think of taking his problem to Alia. That ruled out Irulan, who ran to Alia with anything and everything. In coming to his decision, Stilgar realized he had accepted the possibility that Leto judged Alia correctly.

*She uses people in a casual and callous way,* he thought. *She even uses Duncan that way. It isn't so much that she'd turn on me and kill me. She'd* discard *me.*

Meanwhile the guard was strengthened and Stilgar stalked his sietch like a robed specter, prying everywhere. All the time, his mind seethed with the doubts Leto had planted there. If one could not depend upon tradition, then where was the rock upon which to anchor his life?

On the afternoon of the Convocation of Welcome for the Lady Jessica, Stilgar spied Ghanima standing with her grandmother at the entrance lip to the sietch's great assembly chamber. It was early and Alia had not yet arrived, but people already were thronging into the chamber, casting surreptitious glances at the child and adult as they passed.

Stilgar paused in a shadowed alcove out of the crowd flow and watched the pair of them, unable to hear their words above the murmuring throb of an assembling multitude. The people of many tribes would be here today to welcome back their old Reverend Mother. But she stared at Ghanima. Her eyes, the way they danced when she spoke! The movement fascinated him. Those deep blue, steady, demanding, measuring eyes. And that way of throwing her red-gold hair off her shoulder with a twist of the head: that was Chani. It was a ghostly resurrection, an uncanny resemblance.

Slowly Stilgar drew closer and took up his station in another alcove.

He could not associate Ghanima's observing manner with any other child of his experience – except her brother. Where was Leto? Stilgar glanced back up the crowded passage. His guards would have spread an alarm if anything were amiss. He shook his head. These twins assaulted his sanity. They were a constant abrasion against his peace of mind. He could almost hate them. Kin were not immune from one's hatred, but blood (and its precious water) carried demands for one's countenance which transcended most other concerns. These twins existed as his greatest responsibility.

Dust-filtered brown light came from the cavernous assembly chamber beyond Ghanima and Jessica. It touched the child's shoulders and the new white robe she wore, backlighting her hair as she turned to peer into the passage at the people thronging past.

*Why did Leto afflict me with these doubts?* he wondered. There was no doubt that it had been done deliberately. *Perhaps Leto wanted me to have a small share of his own mental experience.* Stilgar *knew* why the twins were different, but had always found his reasoning processes unable to accept what he knew. He had never experienced the womb as prison to an awak-

126

ened consciousness – a living awareness from the second month of gestation, so it was said.

Leto had once said that his memory was like 'an internal holograph, expanding in size and in detail from that original shocked awakening, but never changing shape or outline.

For the first time, as he watched Ghanima and the Lady Jessica, Stilgar began to understand what it must be like to live in such a scrambled web of memories, unable to retreat or find a sealed room of the mind. Faced with such a condition, one had to integrate madness, to select and reject from a multitude of offerings in a system where answers changed as fast as the questions.

There could be no fixed tradition. There could be no absolute answers to double-faced questions. What works? That which does not work. What does not work? That which works. He recognized this pattern. It was the old Fremen game of riddles. Question: 'It brings death and life.' Answer: 'The Coriolis wind.'

*Why did Leto want me to understand this?* Stilgar asked himself. From his cautious probings, Stilgar knew that the twins shared a common view of their difference: they thought of it as affliction. *The birth canal would be a draining place to such a one,* he thought. Ignorance reduces the shock of some experiences, but they would have no ignorance about birth. What would it be like to live a life where you knew all of the things that *could* go wrong? You would face a constant war with doubts. You would resent your difference from your fellows. It would be pleasant to inflict others with even a taste of that difference. 'Why me?' would be your first unanswered question.

*And what have I been asking myself?* Stilgar thought. A wry smile touched his lips. *Why me?*

Seeing the twins in this new way, he understood the dangerous chances they took with their uncompleted bodies. Ghanima had put it to him succinctly once after he'd berated her for climbing the precipitous west face to the rim above Sietch Tabr.

'Why should I fear death? I've been there before – many times.'

*How can I presume to teach such children?* Stilgar wondered. *How can anyone presume?*

Oddly, Jessica's thoughts were moving in a similar vein as she talked to her granddaughter. She'd been thinking how difficult it must be to carry mature minds in immature bodies. The body would have to learn what the mind already knew it could do – aligning responses and reflexes. The old Bene Gesserit *prana-*

*bindu* regimen would be available to them, but even there the mind would run where the flesh could not. Gurney had a supremely difficult task carrying out her orders.

'Stilgar is watching us from an alcove back there,' Ghanima said.

Jessica did not turn. But she found herself confounded by what she heard in Ghanima's voice. Ghanima loved the old Fremen as one would love a parent. Even while she spoke lightly of him and teased him, she loved him. The realization forced Jessica to see the old Naib in a new light, understanding in a gestalten revelation what the twins and Stilgar shared. This new Arrakis did not fit Stilgar well, Jessica realized. No more than this new universe fitted her grandchildren.

Unwanted and undemanded, a Bene Gesserit saying flowed through Jessica's mind: '*To suspect your own mortality is to know the beginning of terror; to learn irrefutably that you are mortal is to know the end of terror.*'

Yes, death would not be a hard yoke to wear, but life was a slow fire to Stilgar and the twins. Each found an ill-fitting world and longed for other ways where variations might be known without threat. They were children of Abraham, learning more from a hawk stooping over the desert than from any book yet written.

Leto had confounded Jessica only that morning as they'd stood beside the qanat which flowed below the sietch. He'd said: 'Water traps us, grandmother. We'd be better off living like dust because then the wind could carry us higher than the highest cliffs of the Shield Wall.'

Although she was familiar with such devious maturity from the mouths of these children, Jessica had been caught by this utterance, but had managed: 'Your father might've said that.'

And Leto, throwing a handful of sand into the air to watch it fall: 'Yes, he might've. But my father did not consider then how quickly water makes everything fall back to the ground from which it came.'

Now, standing beside Ghanima in the sietch, Jessica felt the shock of those words anew. She turned, glanced back at the still-flowing throng, let her gaze wander across Stilgar's shadowy shape in the alcove. Stilgar was no tame Fremen, trained only to carry twigs to the nest. He was still a hawk. When he thought of the color red, he did not think of flowers but of blood.

'You're so quiet, suddenly,' Ghanima said. 'Is something wrong?'

Jessica shook her head. 'It's something Leto said this morning, that's all.'

'When you went out to the plantings? What'd he say?'

Jessica thought of the curious look of adult wisdom which had come over Leto's face out there in the morning. It was the same look which came over Ghanima's face right now. 'He was recalling the time when Gurney came back from the smugglers to the Atreides banner,' Jessica said.

'Then you were talking about Stilgar,' Ghanima said.

Jessica did not question how this insight occurred. The twins appeared capable of reproducing each other's thought trains at will.

'Yes, we were,' Jessica said. 'Stilgar didn't like to hear Gurney calling . . . Paul his Duke, but Gurney's presence forced this upon all of the Fremen. Gurney kept saying "My Duke." '

'I see,' Ghanima said. 'And of course, Leto observed that *he* was not yet Stilgar's Duke.'

'That's right.'

'You know what he was doing to you, of course,' Ghanima said.

'I'm not sure I do,' Jessica admitted, and she found this admission particularly disturbing because it had not occurred to her that Leto was doing anything at all to her.

'He was trying to ignite your memories of our father,' Ghanima said. 'Leto's always hungry to know our father from the viewpoints of others who knew him.'

'But . . . doesn't Leto have . . .'

'Oh, he can listen to the *inner life*. Certainly. But that's not the same. You spoke about him, of course. Our father, I mean. You spoke of him as your son.'

'Yes.' Jessica clipped it off. She did not like the feeling that these twins could turn her on and off at will, open her memories for observation, touch any emotion which attracted their interest. Ghanima might be doing that right now!

'Leto said something to disturb you,' Ghanima said.

Jessica found herself shocked at the necessity to suppress anger. 'Yes . . . he did.'

'You don't like the fact that he knows our father as our mother knew him, and knows our mother as our father knew her,' Ghanima said. 'You don't like what that implies – what we may know about you.'

'I'd never really thought about it that way before,' Jessica said, finding her voice stiff.

'It's the knowledge of sensual things which usually disturbs,' Ghanima said. 'It's your conditioning. You find it extremely difficult to think of us as anything but children. But there's nothing our parents did together, in public or in private, that we would not know.'

For a brief instant Jessica found herself returning to the reaction which had come over her out there beside the qanat, but now she focused that reaction upon Ghanima.

'He probably spoke of your Duke's "rutting sensuality," ' Ghanima said. 'Sometimes Leto needs a bridle on his mouth!'

*Is there nothing these twins cannot profane?* Jessica wondered, moving from shock to outrage to revulsion. How dared they speak of *her* Leto's sensuality? Of course a man and woman who loved each other would share the pleasure of their bodies! It was a private and beautiful thing, not to be paraded in casual conversation between a child and an adult.

*Child and adult!*

Abruptly Jessica realized that neither Leto nor Ghanima had done this casually.

As Jessica remained silent, Ghanima said: 'We've shocked you. I apologize for both of us. Knowing Leto, I know he didn't consider apologizing. Sometimes when he's following a particular scent, he forgets how different we are . . . from you, for instance.'

Jessica thought: *And that is why you both do this, of course. You are teaching me!* And she wondered then: *Who else are you teaching? Stilgar? Duncan?*

'Leto tries to see things as you see them,' Ghanima said. 'Memories are not enough. When you try the hardest, just then, you most often fail.'

Jessica sighed.

Ghanima touched her grandmother's arm. 'Your son left many things unsaid which yet must be said, even to you. Forgive us, but he loved you. Don't you know that?'

Jessica turned away to hide the tears glistening in her eyes.

'He knew your fears,' Ghanima said. 'Just as he knew Stilgar's fears. Dear Stil. Our father was his "Doctor of Beasts" and Stil was no more than the green snail hidden in its shell.' She hummed the tune from which she'd taken these words. The music hurled the lyrics against Jessica's awareness without compromise:

> 'O Doctor of Beasts,
> To a green snail shell
> With its timid miracle
> Hidden, awaiting death,

You come as a deity!
Even snails know
That gods obliterate,
And cures bring pain,
That heaven is seen
Through a door of flame
O Doctor of Beasts,
I am the man-snail
Who sees your single eye
Peering into my shell!
Why, Muad'Dib? Why?

Ghanima said: 'Unfortunately, our father left many man-snails in our universe.'

*The assumption that humans exist within an essentially impermanent universe, taken as an operational precept, demands that the intellect becomes a totally aware balancing instrument. But the intellect cannot react thus without involving the entire organism. Such an organism may be recognized by its burning, driving behavior. And thus it is with a society treated as organism. But here we encounter an old inertia. Societies move to the goading of ancient, reactive impulses. They demand permanence. Any attempt to display the universe of impermanence arouses rejection patterns, fear, anger, and despair. Then how do we explain the acceptance of prescience? Simply: the giver of prescient visions, because he speaks of an absolute (permanent) realization, may be greeted with joy by humankind even while predicting the most dire events.*

– The Book of Leto
After Harq al-Ada

'It's like fighting in the dark,' Alia said.

She paced the Council Chamber in angry strides, moving from the tall silvery draperies which softened the morning sun at the eastern windows to the divans grouped beneath decorated wall panels at the room's opposite end. Her sandals crossed spice-fiber rugs, parquet wood, tiles of giant garnet and once more, rugs. At last she stood over Irulan and Idaho, who sat facing each other on divans of gray whale fur.

Idaho had resisted returning from Tabr, but she had sent peremptory orders. The abduction of Jessica was more important than ever now, but it had to wait. Idaho's mentat perceptions were required.

'These things are cut from the same pattern,' Alia said. 'They stink of a far-reaching plot.'

'Perhaps not,' Irulan ventured, but she glanced questioningly at Idaho.

Alia's face lapsed into an undisguised sneer. How could Irulan be that innocent? Unless . . . Alia bent a sharp and questioning stare onto the Princess. Irulan wore a simple black aba robe which matched the shadows in her spice-indigo eyes. Her blonde hair was tied in a tight coil at the nape of her neck, accenting a face thinned and toughened by years on Arrakis. She still retained the haughtiness she'd learned in the court of her father, Shaddam IV, and Alia often felt that this prideful attitude could mask the thoughts of a conspirator.

Idaho lounged in the black-and-green uniform of an Atreides House Guard, no insignia. It was an affectation which was secretly resented by many of Alia's actual guards, especially the amazons, who gloried in insignia of office. They did not like the plain presence of the ghola-swordmaster-mentat, the more so because he was the husband of their mistress.

'So the tribes want the Lady Jessica reinstated into the Regency Council,' Idaho said. 'How can that –'

'They make unanimous demand!' Alia said, pointing to an embossed sheet of spice-paper on the divan beside Irulan. 'Farad'n is one thing, but this . . . this has the stink of other alignments!'

'What does Stilgar think?' Irulan asked.

'His signature's on that paper!' Alia said.

'But if he . . .'

'How could he deny the mother of his god?' Alia sneered.

Idaho looked up at her, thinking: *That's awfully close to the edge with Irulan!* Again he wondered why Alia had brought him back here when she knew that he was needed at Sietch Tabr if the abduction plot were to be carried off. Was it possible she'd heard about the message sent to him by The Preacher? This thought filled his breast with turmoil. How could that mendicant mystic know the secret signal by which Paul Atreides had always summoned his swordmaster? Idaho longed to leave this pointless meeting and return to the search for an answer to that question.

'There's no doubt that The Preacher has been off-planet,' Alia said. 'The Guild wouldn't dare deceive us in such a thing. I will have him –'

'Careful!' Irulan said.

'Indeed, have a care,' Idaho said. 'Half the planet believe him to be –' He shrugged. ' – your brother.' And Idaho hoped he had carried this off with a properly casual attitude. How had the man known that signal?

'But if he's a courier, or a spy of the –'

'He's made contact with no one from CHOAM or House Corrino,' Irulan said. 'We can be sure of –'

'We can be sure of nothing!' Alia did not try to hide her scorn. She turned her back on Irulan, faced Idaho. He knew why he was here! Why didn't he perform as expected? He was in Council because Irulan was here. The history which had brought a Princess of House Corrino into the Atreides fold could never be forgotten. Allegiance, once changed, could change again. Duncan's mentat powers should be searching for flaws, for subtle deviations in Irulan's behavior.

Idaho stirred, glanced at Irulan. There were times when he resented the straight-line necessities imposed on mentat performance. He knew what Alia was thinking. Irulan would know it as well. But this Princess-wife to Paul Muad'Dib had overcome the decisions which had made her less than the royal concubine, Chani. There could be no doubt of Irulan's devotion to the royal twins. She had renounced family and Bene Gesserit in dedication to the Atreides.

'My mother is part of this plot!' Alia insisted. 'For what other reason would the Sisterhood send her back here at a time such as this?'

'Hysteria isn't going to help us,' Idaho said.

Alia whirled away from him, as he'd known she would. It helped him that he did not have to look at that once-beloved face which was now so twisted by alien possession.

'Well,' Irulan said, 'the Guild can't be completely trusted for –'

'The Guild!' Alia sneered.

'We can't rule out the enmity of the Guild or the Bene Gesserit,' Idaho said. 'But we must assign them special categories as essentially passive combatants. The Guild will live up to its basic rule: Never Govern. They're a parasitic growth, and they know it. They won't do anything to kill the organism which keeps them alive.'

'Their idea of which organism keeps them alive may be different from ours,' Irulan drawled. It was the closest she ever came to a sneer, that lazy tone of voice which said: 'You missed a point, mentat.'

Alia appeared puzzled. She had not expected Irulan to take this tack. It was not the kind of view which a conspirator would want examined.

133

'No doubt,' Idaho said. 'But the Guild won't come out overtly against House Atreides. The Sisterhood, on the other hand, might risk a certain kind of political break which – '

'If they do, it'll be through a front: someone or some group they can disavow,' Irulan said. 'The Bene Gesserit haven't existed all of these centuries without knowing the value of self-effacement. They prefer being behind the throne, not on it.'

*Self-effacement?* Alia wondered. Was that Irulan's choice?

'Precisely the point I make about the Guild,' Idaho said. He found the necessities of argument and explanation helpful. They kept his mind from other problems.

Alia strode back toward the sunlit windows. She knew Idaho's blind spot; every mentat had it. They had to make pronounce-ments. This brought about a tendency to depend upon absolutes, to see finite limits. They knew this about themselves. It was part of their training. Yet they continued to act beyond self-limiting parameters. *I should've left him at Sietch Tabr*, Alia thought. *It would've been better to just turn Irulan over to Javid for questioning.*

Within her skull, Alia heard a rumbling voice: 'Exactly!'

*Shut up! Shut up! Shut up!* she thought. A dangerous mistake beckoned her in these moments and she could not recognize its outlines. All she could sense was the danger. Idaho had to help her out of this predicament. He was a mentat. Mentats were necessary. The human-computer replaced the mechanical devices destroyed by the Butlerian Jihad. *Thou shalt not make a machine in the likeness of a human mind! But* Alia longed now for a compliant machine. They could not have suffered from Idaho's limitations. You could never distrust a machine.

Alia heard Irulan's drawling voice.

'A feint within a feint within a feint within a feint,' Irulan said. 'We all know the accepted pattern of attack upon power. I don't blame Alia for her suspicions. Of course she suspects every-one – even us. Ignore that for the moment, though. What remains as the prime arena of motives, the most fertile source of danger to the Regency?'

'CHOAM,' Idaho said, his voice mentat-flat.

Alia allowed herself a grim smile. The Combine Honnete Ober Advancer Mercantiles! But House Atreides dominated CHOAM with fifty-one percent of its shares. The Priesthood of Muad'Dib held another five percent, pragmatic acceptance by the Great Houses that Dune controlled the priceless melange. Not without reason was the spice often called 'the secret coinage'. Without melange, the Spacing Guild's heighliners could not move. Melange precipitated the 'navigation trance' by which a translight pathway could be 'seen' before it was traveled. Without melange and its amplification of the human immunogenic system, life expectancy for the very rich degenerated by a factor of at least four. Even the vast middle class of the Imperium ate diluted melange in small sprinklings with at least one meal a day.

But Alia had heard the mentat sincerity in Idaho's voice, a sound which she'd been awaiting with terrible expectancy.

CHOAM. The Combine Honnete was much more than House Atreides, much more than Dune, much more than the Priesthood or melange. It was inkvines, whale fur, shigawire, Ixian artifacts and entertainers, trade in people and places, the Hajj, those products which came from the borderline legality of Tleilaxu technology; it was addictive drugs and medical techniques; it was transportation (the Guild) and all of the supercomplex commerce of an empire which encompassed thousands of known planets plus some which fed secretly at the fringes, permitted there for services rendered. When Idaho said CHOAM, he spoke of a constant ferment, intrigue within intrigue, a play of powers where the shift of one duodecimal point in interest payments could change the ownership of an entire planet.

Alia returned to stand over the two seated on the divans. 'Something specific about CHOAM bothers you?' she asked.

'There's always the heavy speculative stockpiling of spice by certain Houses,' Irulan said.

Alia slapped her hands against her own thighs, then gestured at the embossed spice-paper beside Irulan. 'That *demanded* doesn't intrigue you, coming as it does –'

'All right!' Idaho barked. 'Out with it. What're you withholding? You know better than to deny the data and still expect me to function as –'

'There has been a recent very significant increase in trade for people with four specific specialties,' Alia said. And she wondered if this would be truly new information for his pair.

'Which specialties?' Irulan asked.

'Swordsmasters, twisted mentats from Tleilax, conditioned medics from the Suk school, and fincap accountants, most especially the latter. Why would questionable bookkeeping be in demand right now?' She directed the question at Idaho.

*Function as a mentat!* he thought. Well, that was better than dwelling on what Alia had become. He focused on her words, replaying them in his mind mentat fashion. *Swordmaster?* That

135

had been his own calling once. Swordmasters were, of course, more than personal fighters. They could repair force shields, plan military campaigns, design military support facilities, improvise weapons. *Twisted mentats?* The Tleilaxu persisted in this hoax, obviously. As a mentat himself, Idaho knew the fragile insecurity of Tleilaxu *twisting*. Great Houses which bought such mentats hoped to control them absolutely. Impossible! Even Piter de Vries, who'd served the Harkonnens in their assault on House Atreides, had maintained his own essential dignity, accepting death rather than surrender his inner core of selfdom at the end. *Suk doctors?* Their conditioning supposedly guaranteed them against disloyalty to their owner-patients. Suk doctors came very expensive. Increased purchase of Suks would involve substantial exchange of funds.

Idaho weighed these facts against an increase in fincap accountants.

'Prime computation,' he said, indicating a heavily weighted assurance that he spoke inductive fact. 'There's been a recent increase in wealth among Houses Minor. Some have to be moving quietly toward Great House status. Such wealth could only come from some specific shifts in political alignments.'

'We come at last to the Landsraad,' Alia said, voicing her own belief.

'The next Landsraad session is almost two standard years away,' Irulan reminded her.

'But political bargaining never ceases,' Alia said. 'And I'll warrant some among those tribal signatories – ' She gestured at the paper beside Irulan. ' – are among the Houses Minor who've shifted their alignments.'

'Perhaps,' Irulan said.

'The Landsraad,' Alia said. 'What better front for the Bene Gesserits? And what better agent for the Sisterhood than my own mother?' Alia planted herself directly in front of Idaho. 'Well, Duncan?'

*Why not function as a mentat?* Idaho asked himself. He saw the tenor of Alia's suspicions now. After all, Duncan Idaho had been personal house guard to the Lady Jessica for many years.

'Duncan?' Alia pressed.

'You should inquire closely after any advisory legislation which may be under preparation for the next session of the Landsraad,' Idaho said. 'They might take the legal position that a Regency can't veto certain kinds of legislation – specifically, adjustments of taxation and the policing of cartels. There are others, but . . .'

'Not a very good pragmatic bet on their part if they take that position,' Irulan said.

'I agree,' Alia said. 'The Sardaukar have no teeth and we still have our Fremen legions.'

'Careful, Alia,' Idaho said. 'Our enemies would like nothing better than to make us appear monstrous. No matter how many legions you command, power ultimately rides on popular suffrance in an empire as scattered as this one.'

'Popular suffrance?' Irulan asked.

'You mean Great House suffrance,' Alia said.

'And how many Great Houses will we face under this new alliance?' Idaho asked. 'Money is collecting in strange places!'

'The fringes?' Irulan asked.

Idaho shrugged. It was an unanswerable question. All of them suspected that one day the Tleilaxu or technological tinkerers on the Imperial fringes would nullify the Holtzmann Effect. On that day, shields would be useless. The whole precarious balance which maintained planetary feudatories would collapse.

Alia refused to consider that possibility. 'We'll ride with what we have,' she said. 'And what we have is a certain knowledge throughout the CHOAM directorate that *we* can destroy the spice if they force us to it. They won't risk that.'

'Back to CHOAM again,' Irulan said.

'Unless someone has managed to duplicate the sandtrout- sandworm cycle on another planet,' Idaho said. He looked speculatively at Irulan, excited by this question. 'Salusa Secundus?'

'My contacts there remain reliable,' Irulan said. 'Not Salusa.'

'Then my answer stands,' Alia said, staring at Idaho. 'We ride with what we have.'

*My move,* Idaho thought. He said: 'Why'd you drag me away from *important work*? You could've worked this out yourself.'

'Don't take that tone with me!' Alia snapped.

Idaho's eyes went wide. For an instant, he'd seen the alien on Alia's face, and it was a disconcerting sight. He turned his attention to Irulan, but she had not seen – or gave that appearance.

'I don't need an elementary education,' Alia said, her voice still edged with alien anger.

Idaho managed a rueful smile, but his breast ached.

'We never get far from wealth and all of its masks when we deal with power,' Irulan drawled. 'Paul was a social mutation and, as such, we have to remember that he shifted the old balance of wealth.'

'Such mutations are not irreversible,' Alia said, turning away from them as though she'd not exposed her terrible difference. 'Wherever there's wealth in this empire, they know this.'

'They also know,' Irulan said, 'that there are three people who could perpetuate that mutation: the twins and . . . She pointed at Alia.

*Are they insane, this pair?* Idaho wondered.

'They will try to assassinate me!' Alia rasped.

And Idaho sat in shocked silence; his mentat awareness whirling. Assassinate Alia? Why? They could discredit her too easily. They could cut her out of the Fremen pack and hunt her down at will. But the twins, now . . , He knew he was not in the proper mentat calm for such an assessment, but he had to try. He had to be as precise as possible. At the same time, he knew that precise thinking contained undigested absolutes. Nature was not precise. The universe was not precise when reduced to his scale; it was vague and fuzzy, full of unexpected movements and changes. Humankind as a whole had to be entered into this computation as a natural phenomenon. And the whole process of precise analysis represented a chopping off, a remove from the ongoing current of the universe. He had to get at that current, see it in motion.

'We were right to focus on CHOAM and the Landsraad,' Irulan drawled. 'And Duncan's suggestion offers a first line of inquiry for – '

'Money as a translation of energy can't be separated from the energy it expresses,' Alia said. 'We all know this. But we have to answer three specific questions: When? Using what weapons? Where?'

*The twins . . , the twins,* Idaho thought. *It's the twins who're in danger, not Alia.*

'You're not interested in who or how?' Irulan asked.

'If House Corrino or CHOAM or any other group employs human instruments on this planet,' Alia said 'we stand a better than sixty percent chance of finding them before they act. Knowing when they'll act and where gives us a bigger leverage on those odds. How? That's just asking *what weapons?*'

*Why can't they see it as I see it?* Idaho wondered.

'All right,' Irulan said. 'When?'

'When attention is focused on someone else,' Alia said.

'Attention was focused on your mother at the Convocation,' Irulan said. 'There was no attempt.'

'Wrong place,' Alia said.

*What is she doing?* Idaho wondered.

'Where, then?' Irulan asked.

'Right here in the Keep,' Alia said. 'It's the place where I'd feel most secure and least on my guard.'

'What weapons?' Irulan asked.

'Conventional – something a Fremen might have on his person: poisoned crysknife, maula pistol, a – '

'They've not tried a hunter-seeker in a long while,' Irulan said.

'Wouldn't work in a crowd,' Alia said. 'There'll have to be a crowd.'

'Biological weapon?' Irulan asked.

'An infectious agent?' Alia asked, not masking her incredulity. How could Irulan think an infectious agent would succeed against the immunological barriers which protected an Atreides?

'I was thinking more in the line of some animal,' Irulan said. 'A small pet, say, trained to bite a specific victim, inflicting a poison with its bite.'

'The House ferrets will prevent that,' Alia said.

'One of *them,* then?' Irulan asked.

'Couldn't be done. The House ferrets would reject an outsider, kill it. You know that.'

'I was just exploring possibilities in the hope that – '

'I'll alert my guards,' Alia said.

As Alia said *guards,* Idaho put a hand over his Tleilaxu eyes, trying to prevent the demanding involvement which swept over him. It was Rhajia, the movement of Infinity as expressed by Life, the latent cup of total immersion in mentat awareness which lay in wait for every mentat. It threw his awareness onto the universe like a net, falling, defining the shapes within it. He saw the twins crouching in darkness while giant claws raked the air about them.

'No,' he whispered.

'What?' Alia looked at him as though surprised to find him still there.

He took his hand from his eyes.

'The garments that House Corrino sent?' he asked 'Have they been sent on to the twins?'

'Of course,' Irulan said. 'They're perfectly safe.'

'No one's going to try for the twins at Sietch Tabr,' Alia said.

'Not with all of those Stilgar-trained guards around.'

Idaho stared at her. He had no particular datum to reinforce an argument based on mentat computations, but he knew. *He knew.* This thing he'd experienced came very close to the visionary power which Paul had known. Neither Irulan nor Alia would believe it, coming from him.

'I'd like to alert the port authorities against allowing the importation of any outside animals,' he said.

'You're not taking Irulan's suggestion seriously,' Alia protested.

'Why take any chances?' he asked.

'Tell that to the smugglers,' Alia said. 'I'll put my dependence on the House ferrets.'

Idaho shook his head. What could House ferrets do against claws the size of those envisioned? But Alia was right. Bribes in the right places, one acquiescent Guild navigator, and anyplace in the Empty Quarter became a landing port. The Guild would resist a front position in any attack on House Atreides, but if the price were high enough . . . Well, the Guild could only be thought of as something like a geological barrier which made attacks difficult, but not impossible. They could always protest that they were just 'a transportation agency'. How could they know to what use a particular cargo would be put?

Alia broke the silence with a purely Fremen gesture, a raised fist with thumb horizontal. She accompanied the gesture with a traditional expletive which meant, 'I give Typhoon Conflict.' She obviously saw herself as the only logical target for assassins, and the gesture protested a universe full of undigested threats. She was saying she would hurl the death wind at anyone who attacked her.

Idaho felt the hopelessness of any protest. He saw that she no longer suspected him. He was going back to Tabr and she expected a perfectly executed abduction of the Lady Jessica. He lifted himself from the divan in an adrenalin surge of anger, thinking: *If only Alia were the target! If only assassins could get to her!* For an instant, he rested his hand on his own knife, but it was not in him to do this. Far better, though, that she die a martyr than live to be discredited and hounded into a sandy grave.

'Yes,' Alia said, misinterpreting his expression as concern for her. 'You'd best hurry back to Tabr.' And she thought: *How foolish of me to suspect Duncan! He's mine, not Jessica's!* It had been the demand from the tribes that'd upset her, Alia thought.

She waved an airy good-bye to Idaho as he left.

Idaho left the Council Chamber feeling hopeless. Not only was Alia blind with her alien possession, but she became more insane with each crisis. She'd already passed her danger point and was doomed. But what could be done for the twins? Whom could he convince? Stilgar? And what could Stilgar do that he wasn't already doing?

*The Lady Jessica, then?*

Yes, he'd explore that possibility – but she, too, might be far gone in plotting with her Sisterhood. He carried few illusions about that Atreides concubine. She might do anything at the command of the Bene Gesserits – even turn against her own grandchildren.

> *Good government never depends upon laws, but upon the personal qualities of those who govern. The machinery of government is always subordinate to the will of those who administer that machinery. The most important element of government, therefore, is the method of choosing leaders.*
>
> – Law and Governance
> The Spacing Guild Manual

*Why does Alia wish me to share the morning audience?* Jessica wondered. *They've not voted me back into the Council.*

Jessica stood in the anteroom to the Keep's Great Hall. The anteroom itself would have been a great hall anywhere other than Arrakis. Following the Atreides lead, buildings in Arrakeen had become ever more gigantic as wealth and power concentrated, and this room epitomized her misgivings. She did not like this anteroom with its tiled floor depicting her son's victory over Shaddam IV.

She caught a reflection of her own face in the polished plasteel door which led into the Great Hall. Returning to Dune forced such comparisons upon her, and Jessica noted only the signs of aging in her own features: the oval face had developed tiny lines and the eyes were more brittle in their indigo reflection. She could remember when there had been white around the blue of her eyes. Only the careful ministrations of a professional dresser maintained the polished bronze of her hair. Her nose remained small, mouth generous, and her body was still slender, but even the Bene Gesserit-trained muscles had a tendency toward slowing with the passage of time. Some might not note this and say: 'You haven't changed a bit!' But the Sisterhood's training was a two-edged sword; small changes seldom escaped the notice of people thus trained.

And the lack of small changes in Alia had not escaped Jessica's notice.

Javid, the master of Alia's appointments, stood at the great door, being very official this morning. He was a robed genie with a cynical smile on his round face. Javid struck Jessica as a paradox: a well-fed Fremen. Noting her attention upon him, Javid smiled knowingly, shrugged. His attendance in Jessica's entourage had been short, as he'd known it would be. He hated Atreides, but he was Alia's man in more ways than one, if the rumors were to be believed.

Jessica saw the shrug, thought: *This is the age of the shrug. He knows I've heard all the stories about him and he doesn't care. Our civilization could well die of indifference within it before succumbing to external attack.*

The guards Gurney had assigned her before leaving for the smugglers and the desert hadn't liked her coming here without their attendance. But Jessica felt oddly safe. Let someone make a martyr of her in this place; Alia wouldn't survive it. Alia would know that.

When Jessica failed to respond to his shrug and smile, Javid coughed, a belching disturbance of his larynx which could only have been achieved with practice. It was like a secret language. It said: 'We understand the nonsense of all this pomp, My Lady. Isn't it wonderful what humans can be made to believe!'

*Wonderful!* Jessica agreed, but her face gave no indication of the thought.

The anteroom was quite full now, all of the morning's permitted supplicants having received their right of entrance from Javid's people. The outer doors had been closed. Supplicants and attendants kept a polite distance from Jessica, but observed that she wore the formal black aba of a Fremen Reverend Mother. This would raise many questions. No mark of Muad'Dib's priesthood could be seen on her person. Conversations hummed as the people divided their attention between Jessica and the small side door through which Alia would come to lead them into the Great Hall. It was obvious to Jessica that the old pattern which defined where the Regency's powers lay had been shaken.

*I did that just by coming here,* she thought. *But I came because Alia invited me.*

Reading the signs of disturbance, Jessica realized Alia was deliberately prolonging this moment, allowing the subtle currents to run their course here. Alia would be watching from a spy hole, of course. Few subtleties of Alia's behavior escaped Jessica, and she felt with each passing minute how right she'd been to accept the mission which the Sisterhood had pressed upon her.

'Matters cannot be allowed to continue in this way,' the leader of the Bene Gesserit delegation had argued. 'Surely the signs of decay have not escaped you – you of all people! We know why you left us, but we know also how you were trained. Nothing was stinted in your education. You are an adept of the Panoplia Prophetica and you must know when the souring of a powerful religion threatens us all.'

Jessica had pursed her lips in thought while staring out a window at the soft signs of spring at Castle Caladan. She did not like to direct her thinking in such a logical fashion. One of the first lessons of the Sisterhood had been to reserve an attitude of questioning distrust for anything which came in the guise of logic. But the members of the delegation had known that, too.

How moist the air had been that morning, Jessica thought, looking around Alia's anteroom. How fresh and moist. Here there was a sweaty dampness, to the air which evoked a sense of uneasiness in Jessica, and she thought: *I've reverted to Fremen ways.* The air was too moist in this sietch-above-ground. What was wrong with the Master of the Stills? Paul would never have permitted such laxness.

She noted that Javid, his shiny face alert and composed, appeared not to have noticed the fault of dampness in the anteroom's air. Bad training for one born on Arrakis.

The members of the Bene Gisserit delegation had wanted to know if she required proofs of their allegations. She'd given them an angry answer out of their own manuals: 'All proofs inevitably lead to propositions which have no proof! All things are known because we want to believe in them.'

'But we have submitted these questions to mentats,' the delegation's leader had protested.

Jessica had stared at the woman, astonished. 'I marvel that you have reached your present station and not yet learned the limits of mentats,' Jessica had said.

At which the delegation had relaxed. Apparently it had all been a test, and she had passed. They'd feared, of course, that she had lost all touch with those balancing abilities which were at the core of Bene Gesserit training.

Now Jessica became softly alert as Javid left his door station and approached her. He bowed. 'My Lady. It occurred to me that you might not've heard the latest exploit of The Preacher.'

'I get daily reports on everything which occurs here,' Jessica said. *Let him take that back to Alia!*

Javid smiled. 'Then you know he rails against your family. Only last night, he preached in the south suburb and no one dared touch him. You know why, of course.'

'Because they think he's my son come back to them,' Jessica said, her voice bored.

'This question has not yet been put to the mentat Idaho,' Javid said. 'Perhaps that should be done and the thing settled.'

Jessica thought: *Here's one who truly doesn't know a mentat's limits, although he dares put horns on one – in his dreams if not in fact.*

'Mentats share the fallibilities of those who use them,' she said. 'The human mind, as is the case with the mind of any animal, is a resonator. It responds to resonances in the environment. The mentat has learned to extend his awareness across many parallel loops of causality and to proceed along those loops for long chains of consequences.' *Let him chew on that!*

'This Preacher doesn't disturb you, then?' Javid asked, his voice abruptly formal and portentous.

'I find him a healthy sign,' she said. 'I don't want him bothered.'

Javid clearly had not expected that blunt a response. He tried to smile, failed. Then: 'The ruling Council of the church which deifies thy son will, of course, bow to your wishes if you insist. But certainly some explanation –'

'Perhaps you'd rather *I* explained how I fit into your schemes,' she said.

Javid stared at her narrowly. 'Madame, I see no logical reason why thou refusest to denounce this Preacher. He cannot be thy son. I make a reasonable request: denounce him.'

*This is a set piece,* Jessica thought. *Alia put him up to it.*

She said: 'No.'

'But he defiles the name of thy son! He preaches abominable things, cries out against thy holy daughter. He incites the populace against us. When asked, he said that even thou possessest the nature of evil and that thy –'

'Enough of this nonsense!' Jessica said. 'Tell Alia that I re-

144

fuse. I've heard nothing but tales of this Preacher since returning. He bores me.'

'Does it bore thee, Madame, to learn that in his latest defilement he has said that thou wilt not turn against him? And here, clearly, thou –'

'Evil as I am, I still won't denounce him,' she said,

'It is no joking matter, Madame!'

Jessica waved him away angrily. 'Begone!' She spoke with sufficient carrying power that others heard, forcing him to obey.

His eyes glared with rage, but he managed a stiff bow and returned to his position at the door.

This argument fitted neatly into the observations Jessica already had made. When he spoke of Alia, Javid's voice carried the husky undertones of a lover; no mistaking it. The rumors no doubt were true. Alia had allowed her life to degenerate in a terrible way. Observing this, Jessica began to harbor the suspicion that Alia was a willing participant in Abomination. Was it a perverse will to self-destruction? Because surely Alia was working to destroy herself and the power base which fed on her brother's teachings.

Faint stirrings of unease began to grow apparent in the anteroom. The aficionados of this place would know when Alia delayed too long, and by now they'd all heard about Jessica's peremptory dismissal of Alia's favorite.

Jessica sighed. She felt that her body had walked into this place with her soul creeping behind. Movements among the courtiers were so transparent! The seeking out of important people was a dance like the wind through a field of cereal stalks. The cultivated inhabitants of this place furrowed their brows and gave pragmatic rating numbers to the importance of each of their fellows. Obviously her rebuff of Javid had hurt him; few spoke to him now. But the others! Her trained eye could read the rating numbers in the satellites attending the powerful.

*They do not attend me because I am dangerous*, she thought. *I have the stink of someone Alia fears.*

Jessica glanced around the room, seeing eyes turn away. They were such seriously futile people that she found herself wanting to cry out against their ready-made justifications for pointless lives. Oh, if only The Preacher could see this room as it looked now!

A fragment of a nearby conversation caught her attention. A tall, slender Priest was addressing his coterie, no doubt supplicants here under his auspices. 'Often I must speak otherwise than I think,' he said, 'This is called diplomacy.'

The resultant laughter was too loud, too quickly silenced. People in the group saw that Jessica had overheard.

*My Duke would have transported such a one to the farthest available hellhole!* Jessica thought. *I've returned none too soon.*

She knew now that she'd lived on faraway Caladan in an insulated capsule which had allowed only the most blatant of Alia's excesses to intrude. *I contributed to my own dream-existence,* she thought. Caladan had been something like that insulation provided by a really first-class frigate riding securely in the hold of a Guild heighliner. Only the most violent maneuvers could be felt, and those as mere softened movements.

*How seductive it is to live in peace,* she thought.

The more she saw of Alia's court, the more sympathy Jessica felt for the words reported as coming from this blind Preacher. Yes, Paul might have said such words on seeing what had become of his realm. And Jessica wondered what Gurney had found out among the smugglers.

Her first reaction to Arrakeen had been the right one, Jessica realized. On that first ride into the city with Javid, her attention had been caught by armored screens around dwellings, the heavily guarded pathways and alleys, the patient watchers at every turn, the tall walls and indications of deep underground places revealed by thick foundations. Arrakeen had become an ungenerous place, a contained place, unreasonable and self-righteous in its harsh outlines.

Abruptly the anteroom's small side door opened. A vanguard of priestess amazons spewed into the room with Alia shielded behind them, haughty and moving with a confined awareness of real and terrible power. Alia's face was composed; no emotion betrayed itself as her gaze caught and held her mother's. But both knew the battle had been joined.

At Javid's command, the giant doors into the great Hall were opened, moving with a silent and inevitable sense of hidden energies.

Alia came to her mother's side as the guards enfolded them.

'Shall we go in now, mother?' Alia asked.

'It's high time,' Jessica said. And she thought, seeing the sense of gloating in Alia's eyes: *She thinks she can destroy me and remain unscathed! She's mad!*

And Jessica wondered if that might not have been what Idaho had wanted. He'd sent a message, but she'd been unable to

respond. Such an enigmatic message: *'Danger. Must see you.'*
It had been written in a variant of the old Chakobsa where the
particular word chosen to denote danger signified a plot.

*I'll see him immediately when I return to Tabr,* she thought.

> *This is the fallacy of power : ultimately it is effective only in
> an absolute, a limited universe. But the basic lesson of our relati-
> vistic universe is that things change. Any power must always meet
> a greater power. Paul Muad'Dib taught this lesson to the Sardau-
> kar on the Plains of Arrakeen. His descendants have yet to learn
> the lesson for themselves.*

> — The Preacher at Arrakeen

The first supplicant for the morning audience was a Kadeshian
troubadour, a pilgrim of the Hajj whose purse had been emptied
by Arrakeen mercenaries. He stood on the watergreen stone of
the chamber floor with no air of begging about him.

Jessica admired his boldness from where she sat with Alia
atop the seven-step platform. Identical thrones had been placed
here for mother and daughter, and Jessica made particular note
of the fact that Alia sat on the right, the *masculine* position.

As for the Kadeshian troubadour, it was obvious that Javid's
people had passed him for just this quality he now displayed,
his boldness. The troubadour was expected to provide some
entertainment for the courtiers of the Great Hall; it was the
payment he'd make in lieu of the money he no longer possessed.

From the report of the Priest-Advocate who now pled the
troubadour's case, the Kadeshian had retained only the clothing
on his back and the baliset slung over one shoulder on a leather
cord.

'He says he was fed a dark drink,' the Advocate said, barely
hiding the smile which sought to twist his lips. 'If it please your
Holiness, the drink left him helpless but awake while his purse
was cut.'

Jessica studied the troubadour while the Advocate droned
on and on with a false subservience, his voice full of mucky
morals. The Kadeshian was tall, easily two meters. He had a
roving eye which showed intelligent alertness and humor. His
golden hair was worn to the shoulders in the style of his planet,
and there was a sense of virile strength in the broad chest and

147

neatly tapering body which a gray Hajj robe could not conceal. His name was given as Tagir Mohandis and he was descended from merchant engineers, proud of his ancestry and himself.

Alia finally cut off the pleading with a hand wave, spoke without turning: 'The Lady Jessica will render first judgment in honor of her return to us.'

'Thank you, daughter,' Jessica said, stating the order of ascendancy to all who heard. *Daughter!* So this Tagir Mohandis was part of their plan. Or was he an innocent dupe? This judgment was designed to open attack on herself, Jessica realized. It was obvious in Alia's attitude.

'Do you play the instrument well?' Jessica asked, indicating the nine-string baliset on the troubadour's shoulder.

'As well as the great Gurney Halleck himself!' Tagir Mohandis spoke loudly for all in the hall to hear, and his words evoked an interested stir among the courtiers.

'You seek the gift of transport money,' Jessica said. 'Where would that money take you?'

'To Salusa Secundus and Farad'n's court,' Mohandis said. 'I've heard he seeks troubadours and minstrels, that he supports the arts and builds a great renaissance of cultivated life around him.'

Jessica refrained from glancing at Alia. They'd known, of course, what Mohandis would ask. She found herself enjoying this byplay. Did they think her unable to meet this thrust?

'Will you play for your passage?' Jessica asked. 'My terms are Fremen terms. If I enjoy your music, I may keep you here to smooth away my cares; if your music offends me. I may send you to toil in the desert for your passage money. If I deem your playing just right for Farad'n, who is said to be an enemy of the Atreides, then I will send you to him with my blessing. Will you play on these terms, Tagir Mohandis?'

He threw his head back in a great roaring laugh. His blond hair danced as he unslung the baliset and tuned it deftly to indicate acceptance of her challenge.

The crowd in the chamber started to press closer, but were held back by courtiers and guards.

Presently Mohandis strummed a note, holding the bass hum of the side strings with a fine attention to their compelling vibration. Then, lifting his voice in a mellow tenor, he sang, obviously improvising, but his touch so deft that Jessica was enthralled before she focused on his lyrics:

148

'You say you long for Caladan seas,
Where once you ruled, Atreides,
Without surcease –
But exiles dwell in stranger-lands!

You say 'twere bitter, men so rude,
To sell your dreams of Shai-Hulud,
For tasteless food –
And exiles, dwell in stranger-lands.

You make Arrakis grow infirm,
Silence the passage of the worm
And end your term –
As exiles, dwell in stranger-lands.

Alia! They name you Coan-Teen,
That spirit who is never seen
Until –'

'*Enough!*' Alia screamed. She pushed herself half out of her throne. 'I'll have you –'

'Alia!' Jessica spoke just loud enough, voice pitched just right to avoid confrontation while gaining full attention. It was a masterful use of Voice and all who heard it recognized the trained powers in this demonstration. Alia sank back into her seat and Jessica noted that she showed not the slightest discomfiture.

*This, too, was anticipated*, Jessica thought. *How very interesting.*

'The judgment on this first one's mine,' Jessica reminded her.

'Very well.' Alia's words were barely audible.

'I find this one a fitting gift for Farad'n,' Jessica said. 'He has a tongue which cuts like a crysknife. Such bloodletting as that tongue can administer would be healthy for our own court, but I'd rather he ministered to House Corrino.'

A light rippling of laughter spread through the hall.

Alia permitted herself a snorting exhalation. 'Do you know what he called me?'

'He didn't call you anything, daughter. He but reported that which he or anyone else could hear in the streets. There they call you Coan-Teen . . .'

'The female death-spirit who walks without feet,' Alia snarled.

'If you put away those who report accurately, you'll keep only those who know what you want to hear,' Jessica said, her voice sweet. 'I can think of nothing more poisonous than to rot in the stink of your own reflections.'

Audible gasps came from those immediately below the thrones.

Jessica focused on Mohandis, who remained silent, standing completely uncowed. He awaited whatever judgment was passed upon him as though it did not matter. Mohandis was exactly

149

the kind of man her Duke would have chosen to have by his side in troubled times: one who acted with confidence of his own judgment, but accepted whatever befell, even death, without berating his fate. Then why had he chosen this course?

'Why did you sing those particular words?' Jessica asked him.

He lifted his head to speak clearly. 'I'd heard that the Atreides were honorable and open-minded. I'd a thought to test it and perhaps to stay here in your service, thereby having the time to seek out those who robbed me and deal with them in my own fashion.'

'He dares test *us*!' Alia muttered.

'Why not?' Jessica asked.

She smiled down at the troubadour to signal goodwill. He had come into this hall only because it offered him opportunity for another adventure, another passage through his universe. Jessica found herself tempted to bind him to her own entourage, but Alia's reaction boded evil for brave Mohandis. There were also signs which said this was the course expected of the Lady Jessica – take a brave and handsome troubadour into her service as she'd taken brave Gurney Halleck. Best Mohandis were sent on his way, though it rankled to lose such a fine specimen to Farad'n.

'He shall go to Farad'n,' Jessica said. 'See that he gets his passage money. Let his tongue draw the blood of House Corrino and see how he survives it.'

'Alia glowered at the floor, then produced a belated smile. 'The wisdom of the Lady Jessica prevails,' she said, waving Mohandis away.

*That did not go the way she wanted*, Jessica thought, but there were indicators in Alia's manner that a more potent test remained.

Another suplicant was being brought forward.

Jessica, noting her daughter's reaction, felt the gnawing of doubts. The lesson learned from the twins was needed here. Let Alia be *Abomination*, still she was one of the pre-born. She could know her mother as she knew herself. It did not compute that Alia would misjudge her mother's reactions in the matter of the troubadour. *Why did Alia stage that confrontation? To distract me?*

There was no more time to reflect. The second supplicant had taken place below the twin thrones, his Advocate at his side.

The suplicant was a Fremen this time, an old man with the

sand marks of the desert-born on his face. He was not tall, but had a wiry body and the long *dishdasha* usually worn over a stillsuit gave him a stately appearance. The robe was in keeping with his narrow face and beaked nose, the glaring eyes of blue-on-blue. He wore no stillsuit and seemed uncomfortable without it. The gigantic space of the Audience Hall must seem to him like the dangerous open air which robbed his flesh of its price-less moisture. Under the hood, which had been thrown partly back, he wore the knotted *keffiya* headdress of a Naib.

'I am Ghadhean al-Fali,' he said, placing one foot on the steps to the thrones to signify his status above that of the mob. 'I was one of Muad'Dib's death commandos and I am here con-cerning a matter of the desert.'

Alia stiffened only slightly, a small betrayal. Al-Fali's name had been on that demand to place Jessica on the Council.

*A matter of the desert!* Jessica thought.

Ghadhean al-Fali had spoken before his Advocate could open the pleading. With that formal Fremen phrase he had placed them on notice that he brought them something of concern to all of Dune – and that he spoke with the authority of a Fedaykin who had offered his life beside that of Paul Muad'Dib. Jessica doubted that this was what Ghadhean al-Fali had told Javid or the Advocate General in seeking audience here. Her guess was confirmed as an official of the Priesthood rushed forward from the rear of the chamber waving the black cloth of intercession.

'My Ladies!' the official called out. 'Do not listen to this man! He comes under false –'

Jessica, watching the Priest run toward them, caught a move-ment out of the corner of her eyes, saw Alia's hand signaling in the old Atreides battle language: '*Now!*' Jessica could not deter-mine where the signal was directed, but acted instinctively with a lurch to the left, taking throne and all. She rolled away from the the crashing throne as she fell, came to her feet as she heard the sharp *spat* of a maula pistol . . . and again. But she was mov-ing with the first sound, felt something tug at her right sleeve. She drove into the throng of supplicants and courtiers gathered below the dais. Alia, she noted, had not moved.

Surrounded by people, Jessica stopped.

Ghadhean al-Fali, she saw, had dodged to the other side of the dais, but the Advocate remained in his original position.

It had all happened with the rapidity of an ambush, but every-one in the Hall knew where trained reflexes should have taken anyone caught by surprise. Alia and the Advocate stood frozen in their exposure.

A disturbance toward the middle of the room caught Jessica's attention and she forced a way through the throng, saw four supplicants holding the Priest official. His black cloth of intercession lay near his feet, a maula pistol exposed in its folds.

Al-Fali thrust his way past Jessica, looked from the pistol to the Priest. The Fremen let out a cry of rage, came up from his belt with an *achag* blow, the fingers of his left hand rigid. They caught the Priest in the throat and he collapsed, strangling. Without a backward glance at the man he had killed, the old Naib turned an angry face toward the dais.

'Dalal-il 'an-nubuwwa!' al-Fali called, placing both palms against his forehead, then lowering them. 'The Qadis as-Salaf will not let me be silenced! If I do not slay those who interfere, others will slay them!'

*He thinks he was the target,* Jessica realized. She looked down at her sleeve, put a finger in the neat hole left by the maula pellet. Poisoned, no doubt.

The supplicants had dropped the Priest. He lay writhing on the floor, dying with his larynx crushed. Jessica motioned to a pair of shocked courtiers standing at her left, said: 'I want that man saved for questioning. If he dies, you die!' As they hesitated, peering toward the dais, she used Voice on them: 'Move!'

The pair moved.

Jessica thrust herself to al-Fali's side, nudged him: 'You are a fool, Naib! They were after me, not you.'

Several people around them heard her. In the immediate shocked silence, al-Fali glanced at the dais with its one toppled throne and Alia still seated on the other. The look of realization which came over his face could've been read by a novice.

'Fedaykin,' Jessica said, reminding him of his old service to her family, 'we who have been scorched know how to stand back to back.'

'Trust me, My Lady,' he said, taking her meaning immediately.

A gasp behind Jessica brought her whirling, and she felt al-Fali move to stand with his back to her. A woman in the gaudy garb of a city Fremen was straightening from beside the Priest on the floor. The two courtiers were nowhere to be seen. The woman did not even glance at Jessica, but lifted her voice in the ancient keening of her people – the call for those who serviced the deathstills, the call for them to come and gather a body's water into the tribal cistern. It was a curiously incongruous noise coming from one dressed as this woman was. Jessica felt the persistence of the old ways even as she saw the falseness in this city woman. The creature in the gaudy dress obviously had killed the Priest to make sure he was silenced.

*Why did she bother?* Jessica wondered. *She had only to wait for the man to die of asphyxiation.* The act was a desperate one, a sign of deep fear.

Alia sat forward on the edge of her throne her eyes aglitter with watchfulness. A slender woman wearing the braid knots of Alia's own guards strode past Jessica, bent over the Priest, straightened, and looked back at the dais. 'He is dead.'

'Have him removed,' Alia called. She motioned to guards below the dais. 'Straighten the Lady Jessica's chair.'

*So you'll try to brazen it out!* Jessica thought. Did Alia think anyone had been fooled? Al-Fali had spoken of the Qadis as-Salaf, calling on the holy fathers of Fremen mythology as his protectors. But no supernatural agency had brought a maula pistol into this room where no weapons were permitted. A conspiracy involving Javid's people was the only answer, and Alia's unconcern about her own person told everyone she was a part of that conspiracy.

The old Naib spoke over his shoulder to Jessica: 'Accept my apologies, My Lady. We of the desert come to you as our last desperate hope, and now we see that you still have need of us.'

'Matricide does not sit well on my daughter,' Jessica said.

'The tribes will hear of this,' al-Fali promised.

'If you have such desperate need of me,' Jessica asked, 'why did you not approach me at the Convocation in Sietch Tabr?'

'Stilgar would not permit it.'

*Ahhh,* Jessica thought, *the rule of the Naibs! In Tabr, Stilgar's word was law.*

The toppled throne had been straightened. Alia motioned for her mother to return, said: 'All of you please note the death of that traitor-Priest. Those who threaten me die.' She glanced at al-Fali. 'My thanks to you, Naib.'

'Thanks for a mistake,' al-Fali muttered. He looked at Jessica. 'You were right. My rage removed one who should've been questioned.'

Jessica whispered: 'Mark those two courtiers and the woman in the colorful dress, Fedaykin. I want them taken and questioned.'

'It will be done,' he said.

153

'If we get out of here alive,' Jessica said, 'Come, let us go back and play our parts.'

'As you say, My Lady.'

Together, they returned to the dais, Jessica mounting the steps and resuming her position beside Alia, al-Fali remaining in the supplicant's position below.

'Now,' Alia said.

'One moment, daughter,' Jessica said. She held up her sleeve, exposed the hole with a finger through it. 'The attack was aimed at me. The pellet almost found me even as I was dodging. You will all note that the maula pistol is no longer down there.' She pointed. 'Who has it?'

There was no response.

'Perhaps it could be traced,' Jessica said.

'What nonsense!' Alia said. '*I* was the –'

Jessica half turned toward her daughter, motioned with her left hand. 'Someone down there has that pistol. Don't you have a fear that –'

'One of my guards has it!' Alia said.

'Then that guard will bring the weapon to me,' Jessica said.

'She's already taken it away.'

'How convenient,' Jessica said.

'What are you saying?' Alia demanded.

Jessica allowed herself a grim smile. 'I am saying that two of your people were charged with saving that *traitor-Priest*. I warned them that they would die if he died. They will die.'

'I forbid it!'

Jessica merely shrugged.

'We have a brave Fedaykin here,' Alia said, motioning toward al-Fali. 'This argument can wait.'

'It can wait forever,' Jessica said, speaking in Chakobsa, her words double-barbed to tell Alia that no argument would stop the death command.

'We shall see!' Alia said. She turned to al-Fali. 'Why are you here, Ghadhean al-Fali?'

'To see the mother of Muad'Dib,' the Naib said. 'What is left of the Fedaykin, that band of brothers who served her son, pooled their poor resources to buy my way in here past the avaricious guardians who shield the Atreides from the realities of Arrakis.'

Alia said: 'Anything the Fedaykin require, they have only –'

'He came to see me,' Jessica interrupted. 'What is your desperate need, Fedaykin?'

154

Alia said: 'I speak for the Atreides here! What is –'

'Be silent, you murderous Abomination!' Jessica snapped. 'You tried to have me killed, *daughter*! I say it for all here to know. You can't have everyone in this hall killed to silence them – as that Priest was silenced. Yes, the Naib's blow would've killed the man, but he could've been saved. He could've been questioned! You have no concern that he was silenced. Spray your protests upon us as you will, your guilt is written in your actions!'

Alia sat in frozen silence, face pale. And Jessica, watching the play of emotions across her daughter's face, saw a terrifyingly familiar movement of Alia's hands, an unconscious response which once had identified a deadly enemy of the Atreides. Alia's fingers moved in a tapping rhythm – little finger twice, index finger three times, ring finger twice, little finger once, ring finger twice . . . and back through the tapping in the same order.

*The old Baron!*

The focus of Jessica's eyes caught Alia's attention and she glanced down at her hand, held it still, looked back at her mother to see the terrible recognition. A gloating smile locked Alia's mouth.

'So you have your revenge upon us,' Jessica whispered.

'Have you gone mad, mother?' Alia asked.

'I wish I had,' Jessica said. And she thought: *She knows I will confirm this to the Sisterhood. She knows. She may even suspect I'll tell the Fremen and force her into a Trial of Possession. She cannot let me leave here alive.*

'Our brave Fedaykin waits while we argue,' Alia said.

Jessica forced her attention back to the old Naib. She brought her responses under control, said: 'You came to see me, Ghadhean.'

'Yes, My Lady. We of the desert see terrible things happening. The Little Makers came out of the sand as was foretold in the oldest prophecies. Shai-Halud no longer can be found except in the deeps of the Empty Quarter. We have abandoned our friend, the desert!'

Jessica glanced at Alia, who merely motioned for Jessica to continue. Jessica looked out over the throng in the Chamber, saw the shocked alertness on every face. The import of the fight between mother and daughter had not been lost on this throng, and they must wonder why the audience continued. She returned her attention to al-Fali.

'Ghadhean, what is this talk of Little Makers and the scarcity of sandworms?'

'Mother of Moisture,' he said, using her old Fremen title, 'we were warned of this in the Kitab al-Ibar. We beseech thee. Let it not be forgotten that on the day Muad'Dib died, Arrakis turned by itself! We cannot abandon the desert.'

'Hah!' Alia sneered. 'The superstitious riffraff of the Inner Desert fear the ecological transformation. They –'

'I hear you, Ghadhean,' Jessica said. 'If the worms go, the spice goes. If the spice goes, what coin do we have to buy our way?'

Sounds of surprise: gasps and startled whispers could be heard spreading across the Great Hall. The Chamber echoed to the sound.

Alia shrugged. 'Superstitious nonsense!'

Al-Fali lifted his right hand to point at Alia. 'I speak to the Mother of Moisture, not to the Coan-Teen!'

Alia's hands gripped the arms of her throne, but she remained seated.

Al-Fali looked at Jessica. 'Once it was the land where nothing grew. Now there are plants. They spread like lice upon a wound. There have been clouds and rain along the belt of Dune! Rain, My Lady! Oh, precious mother of Muad'Dib, as sleep is death's brother, so is rain on the Belt of Dune. It is the death of us all.'

'We do only what Liet-Kynes and Muad'Dib himself designed for us to do,' Alia protested. 'What is all of this superstitious gabble? We revere the words of Liet-Kynes, who told us: "I wish to see this entire planet caught up in a net of green plants." So it will be.'

'And what of the worms and the spice?' Jessica asked.

'There'll always be *some* desert,' Alia said. 'The worms will survive.'

*She's lying,* Jessica thought. *Why does she lie?*

'Help us, Mother of Moisture,' al-Fali pleaded.

With an abrupt sensation of double vision, Jessica felt her awareness lurch, propelled by the old Naib's words. It was the unmistakable *adab,* the demanding memory which came upon one of itself. It came without qualifications and held her senses immobile while the lesson of the past was impressed upon her awareness. She was caught up in it completely, a fish in the net. Yet she felt the demand of it as a *human-most* moment, each small part a reminder of creation. Every element of the lesson-memory was real but insubstantial in its constant change, and she knew this was the closest she might ever come to experiencing the prescient dietgrasp which had inflicted itself upon her son.

*Alia lied because she was possessed by one who would destroy the Atreides. She was, in herself, the first destruction. Then al-Fali spoke the truth: the sandworms are doomed unless the course of the ecological transformation is modified.*

In the pressure of revelation, Jessica saw the people of the audience reduced to slow motion, their roles identified for her. She could pick the ones charged with seeing that she did not leave here alive! And the path through them lay there in her awareness as though outlined in bright light – confusion among them, one of them feinted to stumble into another, whole groups tangled. She saw, also, that she might leave this Great Hall only to fall into other hands. Alia did not care if she created a martyr. No – the *thing which possessed her* did not care.

Now, in this frozen time, Jessica chose a way to save the old Naib and send him as messenger. The way through the audience remained indelibly clear. How simple it was! They were buffoons with barricaded eyes, their shoulders held in positions of immovable defense. Each position upon the great floor could be seen as an atrophic collision from which dead flesh might slough away to reveal skeletons. Their bodies, their clothes, and their faces described individual hells – the insucked breast of concealed terrors, the glittering hook of a jewel become substitute armor; the mouths were judgments full of frightened absolutes, cathedral prisms of eyebrows showing lofty and religious sentiments which their loins denied.

Jessica sensed dissolution in the shaping forces loosed upon Arrakis. Al-Fali's voice had been like a distrans in her soul, awakening a beast from the deepest part of her.

In an eyeblink Jessica moved from the *adab* into the universe of movement, but it was a different universe from the one which had commanded her attenion only a second before.

Alia was starting to speak, but Jessica said: 'Silence!' Then: 'There are those who fear that I have returned without reservation to the Sisterhood. But since that day in the desert when the Fremen gave the gift of life to me and to my son, I have been Fremen!' And she lapsed into the old tongue which only those in this room who could profit by it would understand: 'Onsar akhaka zeliman aw maslumen!' *Support your brother in his time of need, whether he be just or unjust!*

Her words had the desired effect, a subtle shifting of positions within the Chamber.

But Jessica raged on: 'The Ghadhean al-Fali, an honest Fremen, comes here to tell me what others should have revealed to me. Let no one deny this! The ecological transformation has become a tempest out of control!'

Wordless confirmations could be seen throughout the room.

'And my daughter delights in this!' Jessica said. 'Mektub al-mellah! You carve wounds upon my flesh and write there in salt! Why did the Atreides find a home here? Because the *Mohalata* was natural to us. To the Atreides, government was always a protective partnership: *Mohalata*, as the Fremen have always known it. Now look at her!' Jessica pointed at Alia. 'She laughs alone at night in contemplation of her own evil! Spice production will fall to nothing, or at best a fraction of its former level! And when word of *that* gets out –'

'We'll have a corner on the most priceless product in the universe!' Alia shouted.

'We'll have a corner on hell!' Jessica raged.

And Alia lapsed into the most ancient Chakobsa, the Atreides private language with its difficult glottal stops and clicks: 'Now, you know, *mother*! Did you think a granddaughter of Baron Harkonnen would not appreciate all of the lifetimes you crushed into my awareness before I was even born? When I raged against what you'd done to me, I had only to ask myself what the Baron would've done. And he answered! Understand me, Atreides bitch! He answered *me*!'

Jessica heard the venom and the confirmation of her guess. *Abomination!* Alia had been overwhelmed within, possessed by that *cahueit* of evil, the Baron Vladimir Harkonnen. The Baron himself spoke from her mouth now, uncaring of what was revealed. He wanted her to see his revenge, wanted her to know that he could not be cast out.

*I'm supposed to remain here helpless in my knowledge*, Jessica thought. With the thought, she launched herself onto the path the *adab* had revealed, shouting: 'Fedaykin, follow me!'

It turned out there were six Fedaykin in the room, and five of them won through behind her.

Leto leaned out the covert exit from the sietch, saw the bight of the cliff towering above his limited view. Late afternoon sunlight cast long shadows in the cliff's vertical striations. A skeleton butterfly flew in and out of the shadows, its webbed wings a transparent lacery against the light. How delicate that butterfly was to exist here, he thought.

Directly ahead of him lay the apricot orchard, with children working there to gather the fallen fruit. Beyond the orchard was the qanat. He and Ghanima had given the slip to their guards by losing themselves in a sudden crush of incoming workers. It had been a relatively simple matter to worm their way down an air passage to its connection with the steps to the covert exit. Now they had only to mingle themselves with the children, work their way to the qanat and drop into the tunnel. There they could move beside the predator fish which kept sandtrout from encysting the tribe's irrigation water. No Fremen would yet think of a human risking accidental immersion in water.

He stepped out of the protective passages. The cliff stretched away on both sides of him, turned horizontal just by the act of his own movement.

Ghanima moved closely behind him. Both carried small fruit baskets woven of spice-fiber, but each basket carried a sealed package: Fremkit, maula pistol, crysknife . . . and the new robes sent by Farad'n.

Ghanima followed her brother into the orchard, mingled with the working children. Stillsuit masks concealed every face. They were just two more workers here, but she felt the action drawing her life away from protective boundaries and known ways. What a simple step it was, that step from one danger into another!

In their baskets those new garments sent by Farad'n conveyed a purpose well understood by both of them. Ghanima had accented this knowledge by sewing their personal motto, '*We Share*', in Chakobsa above the hawk crest at each breast.

159

It would be twilight soon and, beyond the qanat which marked off sietch cultivation, there would come a special quality of evening which few places in the universe could match. It would be that softly lighted desert world with its persistent solitude, its saturated sense that each creature in it was alone in a new universe.

'We've been seen,' Ghanima whispered, bending to work beside her brother.

'Guards?'

'No – others.'

'Good.'

'We must move swiftly,' she said.

Leto acknowledged this by moving away from the cliff through the orchard. He thought with his father's thoughts: *Everything remains mobile in the desert or perishes.* Far out on the sand he could see The Attendant's outcropping, reminder of the need for mobility. The rocks lay static and rigid in their watchful enigma, fading yearly before the onslaught of wind-driven sand. One day The Attendant would be sand.

As they neared the qanat they heard music from a high entrance of the sietch. It was an old-style Fremen group – two-holed flutes, tambourines, tympani made on spice-plastic drums with skins stretched taut across one end. No one asked what animal on this planet provided that much skin.

*Stilgar will remember what I told him about that cleft in The Attendant,* Leto thought. *He'll come in the dark when it's too late – and then he'll know.*

Presently they were at the qanat. They slipped into an open tube, climbed down the inspection ladder to the service ledge. It was dusky, damp, and cold in the qanat and they could hear the predator fish splashing. Any sandtrout trying to steal this water would find its water-softened inner surface attacked by the fish. Humans must be wary of them, too.

'Careful,' Leto said, moving down the slippery ledge. He fastened his memory to times and places his flesh had never known. Ghanima followed.

At the end of the qanat they stripped to their stillsuits and put on the new robes. They left the old Fremen robes behind as they climbed out another inspection tube, wormed their way over a dune and down the far side. There they sat shielded from the sietch, strapped on maula pistols and crysknives, slipped the Fremkit packs onto their shoulders. They no longer could hear the music.

Leto arose, struck out through the valley between the dunes.

Ghanima fell into step behind him, moving with practiced unrhythmical quiet over the open sand.

Below the crest of each dune they bent low and crept across into the hidden lee, there to pause and peer backward seeking pursuit. No hunters had emerged upon the desert by the time they reached the first rocks.

In the shadows of the rocks they worked their way around The Attendant, climbed to a ledge looking out upon the desert. Colors blinked far out on the *bled*. The darkening air held the fragility of fine crystal. The landscape which met their gaze was beyond pity, nowhere did it pause – no hesitations in it at all. The gaze stayed upon no single place in its scanning movements across that immensity.

*It is the horizon of eternity,* Leto thought.

Ghanima crouched beside her brother, thinking: *The attack will come soon.* She listened for the slightest sound, her whole body transformed into a single sense of taut probing.

Leto sat equally alert. He knew now the culmination of all the training which had gone into the lives he shared so intimately. In this wilderness one developed a firm dependence upon the senses, *all* of the senses. Life became a hoard of stored perceptions, each one linked only to momentary survival.

Presently Ghanima climbed up the rocks and peered through a notch at the way they had come. The safety of the sietch seemed a lifetime away, a bulk of dumb cliffs rising out of brown-purple distance, dust-blurred edges at the rim where the last of the sunlight cast its silver streaks. Still no pursuit could be seen in the intervening distance. She returned to Leto's side.

'It'll be a predatory animal,' Leto said. 'That's my tertiary computation.'

'I think you stopped computing too soon,' Ghanima said. 'It'll be more than one animal. House Corrino has learned not to put all of its hopes into a single bag.'

Leto nodded agreement.

His mind felt suddenly heavy with the multitude of lives which his *difference* provided him: all of those lives, his even before birth. He was saturated with living and wanted to flee from his own consciousness. The inner world was a heavy beast which could devour him.

Restlessly he arose, climbed to the notch Ghanima had used, peered at the cliffs of the sietch. Back there, beneath the cliff, he could see how the qanat drew a line between life and death.

161

On the oasis edge he could see camel sage, onion grass, gobi feather grass, wild alfalfa. In the last of the light he could make out the black movements of birds pick-hopping in the alfalfa. The distant grain tassels were ruffled by a wind which drew shadows that moved right up to the orchard. The motion caught at his awareness, and he saw that the shadows hid within their fluid form a larger change, and that larger change gave ransom to the turning rainbows of a silver-dusted sky.

*What will happen out here?* he asked himself.

And he knew it would either be death or the play of death, himself the object. Ghanima would be the one to return, believing the reality of a death she had seen or reporting sincerely from a deep hypnotic compulsion that her brother was, indeed, slain.

The unknowns of this place haunted him. He thought how easy it would be to succumb to the demand for prescience, to risk launching his awareness into an unchanging, absolute future. The small vision of his dream was bad enough, though. He knew he dared not risk the larger vision.

Presently, he returned to Ghanima's side:

'No pursuit yet,' he said.

'The beasts they send for us will be large,' Ghanima said. 'We may have time to see them coming.'

'Not if they come in the night.'

'It'll be dark very soon,' she said.

'Yes. It's time we went down into *our* place.' He indicated the rocks to their left and below them where wind-sand had eaten a tiny cleft in the basalt. It was large enough to admit them, but small enough to keep out large creatures. Leto felt himself reluctant to go there, but knew it must be done. That was the place he'd pointed out to Stilgar.

'They may really kill us,' he said.

'This is the chance we have to take,' she said. 'We owe it to our father.'

'I'm not arguing.'

And he thought: *This is the correct path; we do the thing.* But he knew how dangerous it was to be right in this universe. Their survival now demanded vigor and fitness and an understanding of the limitations in every moment. Fremen ways were their best armor, and the Bene Gesserit knowledge was a force held in reserve. They were both thinking now as Atreides-trained battle veterans with no other defenses than a Fremen toughness which was not even hinted at by their childish bodies and their formal attire.

162

Leto fingered the hilt of the poison-tipped crysknife at his waist. Unconsciously Ghanima duplicated the gesture.

'Shall we go down now?' Ghanima asked. As she spoke she saw the movement far below them, small movement made less threatening by distance. Her stillness alerted Leto before she could utter a warning.

'Tigers,' he said.

'Laza tigers,' she corrected him.

'They see us,' he said.

'We'd better hurry,' she said. 'A maula would never stop those creatures. They will've been well trained for this.'

'They'll have a human director somewhere around,' he said, leading the way at a fast lope down the rocks to the left.

Ghanima agreed, but kept it to herself, saving her strength. There'd be a human around somewhere. Those tigers couldn't be allowed to run free until the proper moment.

The tigers moved fast in the last of the light, leaping from rock to rock. They were eye-minded creatures and soon it would be night, the time of the ear-minded. The bell-call of a nightbird came from The Attendant's rocks to emphasize the change. Creatures of the darkness already were hustling in the shadows of the etched crevasses.

Still the tigers remained visible to the running twins. The animals flowed with power, a rippling sense of golden sureness in every movement.

Leto felt that he had stumbled into this place to free himself from his soul. He ran with the sure knowledge that he and Ghanima could reach their narrow notch in time, but his gaze kept returning with fascination to the oncoming beasts.

*One stumble and we're lost*, he thought.

That thought reduced the sureness of his knowledge, and he ran faster.

*You Bene Gesserit call your activity of the Panoplia Prophetica a 'Science of Religion'. Very well. I, a seeker after another kind of scientist, find this an appropriate definition. You do, indeed, build your own myths, but so do all societies. You I must warn, however. You are behaving as so many other misguided scientists have behaved. Your actions reveal that you wish to take something out of [away from] life. It is time you were reminded of that which you so often profess: One cannot have a single thing without its opposite.*

– The Preacher at Arrakeen:
A Message to the Sisterhood

In the hour before dawn, Jessica sat immobile on a worn rug of spice-cloth. Around her were the bare rocks of an old and poor sietch, one of the original settlements. It lay below the rim of Red Chasm, sheltered from the westerlies of the desert. Al-Fali and his brothers had brought her here; now they awaited word from Stilgar. The Fedaykin had moved cautiously in the matter of communication, however. Stilgar was not to know their location.

The Fedaykin already knew they were under a *procès-verbal*, an official report of crimes against the Imperium. Alia was taking the tack that her mother had been suborned by enemies of the realm, although the Sisterhood had not yet been named. The high-handed, tyrannical nature of Alia's power was out in the open, however, and her belief that because she controlled the Priesthood she controlled the Fremen was about to be tested.

Jessica's message to Stilgar had been direct and simple: '*My daughter is possessed and must be put to the trial.*'

Fears destroyed values, though, and it already was known that some Fremen would prefer not to believe this accusation. Their attempts to use the accusation as a passport had brought on two battles during the night, but the ornithopters al-Fali's people had stolen had brought the fugitives to this precarious safety: Red Chasm Sietch. Word was going out to the Fedaykin from here, but fewer than two hundred of them remained on Arrakis. The others held posts throughout the Empire.

Reflecting upon these facts, Jessica wondered if she had come to the place of her death. Some of the Fedaykin believed it, but the death commandos accepted this easily enough. Al-Fali had merely grinned at her when some of his young men voiced their fears.

'When God hath ordained a creature to die in a particular place, He causeth that creature's wants to direct him to that place,' the old Naib had said.

The patched curtains at her doorway rustled; al-Fali entered. The old man's narrow, windburned face appeared drawn, his eyes feverish. Obviously he had not rested.

'Someone comes,' he said.

'From Stilgar?'

'Perhaps.' He lowered his eyes, glanced leftward in the manner of the old Fremen who brought bad news.

'What is it?' Jessica demanded.

'We have word from Tabr that your grandchildren are not here.' He spoke without looking at her.

'Alia . . .'

'She has ordered that the twins be given over to her custody, but Sietch Tabr reports that the children are not there. That is all we know.'

'Stilgar's sent them into the desert,' Jessica said.

'Possibly, but it is known that he was searching for them all through the night. Perhaps it was a trick on his part . . .'

'That's not Stilgar's way,' she said, and thought: *Unless the twins put him up to it.* But that didn't feel right either. She wondered at herself: no sensations of panic to suppress, and her fears for the twins were tempered by what Ghanima had revealed. She peered up at al-Fali, found him studying her with pity in his eyes. She said: 'They've gone into the desert by themselves.'

'Alone? Those two children!'

She did not bother to explain that 'those two children' probably knew more about desert survival than most living Fremen. Her thoughts were fixed, instead, on Leto's odd behavior when he'd insisted that she allow herself to be abducted. She'd put the memory aside, but this moment demanded it. He'd said she would know the moment to obey him.

'The messenger should be in the sietch by now,' al-Fali said. 'I will bring him to you.' He let himself out through the patched curtain.

Jessica stared at the curtain. It was red cloth of spice-fiber, but the patches were blue. The story was that this sietch had refused to profit from Muad'Dib's religion, earning the enmity of Alia's Priesthood. The people here reportedly had put their capital into a scheme to raise dogs as large as ponies, dogs bred for intelligence as guardians of children. The dogs had all died. Some said it was poison and the Priests were blamed.

She shook her head to drive out these reflections, recognizing them for what they were: *ghafla*; the gadfly distraction.

Where had those children gone? To Jacurutu? They had a plan. *They tried to enlighten me to the extent they thought I'd accept*, she remembered. And when they'd reached the limits as they saw them, Leto had commanded her to obey.

*He'd* commanded *her!*

Leto had recognized what Alia was doing; that much was obvious. Both twins had spoken of their aunt's 'affliction', even when defending her. Alia was gambling on the *rightness* of her position in the Regency. Demanding custody of the twins confirmed that. Jessica found a harsh laugh shaking her own breast. The Reverend Mother Gaius Helen Mohiam had been fond of explaining this particular error to her student, Jessica. *'If you focus your awareness only upon your own rightness, then you invite the forces of opposition to overwhelm you. This is a common error. Even I, your teacher, have made it.'*

'And even I, your student, have made it,' Jessica whispered to herself.

She heard fabrics whispering in the passage beyond the curtain. Two young Fremen entered, part of the entourage they'd picked up during the night. The two were obviously awed at being in the presence of Muad'Dib's mother. Jessica had read them completely: they were non-thinkers, attaching themselves to any fancied power for the identity which this gave them. Without a reflection from her they were empty. Thus, they were dangerous.

'We were sent ahead by al-Fali to prepare you,' one of the young Fremen said.

Jessica felt an abrupt clenching tightness in her breast, but her voice remained calm. 'Prepare me for what?'

'Stilgar has sent Duncan Idaho as his messenger.'

Jessica pulled her aba hood up over her hair, an unconscious gesture. *Duncan?* But he was Alia's tool.

The Fremen who'd spoken took a half step forward. 'Idaho says he has come to take you to safety, but al-Fali does not see how this can be.'

'It seems passing strange, indeed,' Jessica said. 'But there are stranger things in our universe. Bring him.'

They glanced at each other but obeyed, leaving together with such a rush that they tore another rent in the worn curtain.

Presently Idaho stepped through the curtain, followed by the two Fremen and al-Fali bringing up the rear, hand on his crys-knife. Idaho appeared composed. He wore the dress casuals of an

Atreides House Guard, a uniform which had changed little in more than fourteen centuries. Arrakis had replaced the old gold-handled plasteel blade with a crysknife, but that was minor.

'I'm told you wish to help me,' Jessica said.

'As odd as that may seem,' he said.

'But didn't Alia send you to abduct me?' she asked.

A slight raising of his black eyebrows was the only mark of surprise. The many-faceted Tleilaxu eyes continued to stare at her with glittering intensity. 'Those were her orders,' he said.

Al-Fali's knuckles went white on his crysknife, but he did not draw.

'I've spent much of this night reviewing the mistakes I made with my daughter,' she said.

'There were many,' Idaho agreed, 'and I shared in most of them.'

She saw now that his jaw muscles were trembling.

'It was easy to listen to the arguments which led us astray,' Jessica said. 'I wanted to leave this place . . . You . . . you wanted a girl you saw as a younger version of me.'

He accepted this silently.

'Where are my grandchildren?' she demanded, voice going harsh.

He blinked. Then: 'Stilgar believes they have gone into the desert – hiding. Perhaps they saw this crisis coming.'

Jessica glanced at al-Fali, who nodded his recognition that she had anticipated this.

'What is Alia doing?' Jessica asked.

'She risks civil war,' he said.

'Do you believe it'll come to that?'

Idaho shrugged. 'Probably not. These are softer times. There are more people willing to listen to pleasant arguments.'

'I agree,' she said. 'Well and good, what of my grandchildren?'

'Stilgar will find them – if . . .'

'Yes, I see.' It was really up to Gurney Halleck then. She turned to look at the rock wall on her left. 'Alia grasps the power firmly now.' She looked back at Idaho. 'You understand? One uses power by grasping it lightly. To grasp too strongly is to be taken over by power, and thus to become its victim.'

'As my Duke always told me,' Idaho said.

Somehow Jessica knew he meant the older Leto, not Paul. She asked: 'Where am I to be taken in this . . . abduction?'

Idaho peered down at her as though trying to see into the shadows created by the hood.

167

Al-Fali stepped forward: 'My Lady, you are not seriously thinking . . .'

'Is it not my right to decide my own fate?' Jessica asked.

'But this . . . ' Al-Fali's head nodded toward Idaho.

'This was my loyal guardian before Alia was born,' Jessica said. 'Before he died saving my son's life and mine. We Atreides always honor certain obligations.'

'Then you will go with me?' Idaho asked.

'Where would you take her?' al-Fali asked.

'Best that you don't know,' Jessica said.

Al-Fali scowled but remained silent. His face betrayed indecision, an understanding of the wisdom in her words but an unresolved doubt of Idaho's trustworthiness.

'What of the Fedaykin who helped me?' Jessica asked.

'They have Stilgar's countenance if they can get to Tabr,' Idaho said. Jessica faced al-Fali: 'I command you to go there, my friend. Stilgar can use Fedaykin in the search for my grandchildren.'

The old Naib lowered his gaze. 'As Muad'Dib's mother commands.'

*He's still obeying Paul*, she thought.

'We should be out of here quickly,' Idaho said. 'The search is certain to include this place, and that early.'

Jessica rocked forward and arose with that fluid grace which never quite left the Bene Gesserit, even when they felt the pangs of age. And she felt old now after her night of flight. Even as she moved, her mind remained on that peculiar interview with her grandson. What was he really doing? She shook her head, covered the motion by adjusting her hood. It was too easy to fall into the trap of underestimating Leto. Life with ordinary children conditioned one to a false view of the inheritance which the twins enjoyed.

Her attention was caught by Idaho's pose. He stood in the relaxed preparedness for violence, one foot ahead of the other, a stance which she herself had taught him. She shot a quick look at the two young Fremen, at al-Fali. Doubts still assailed the old Fremen Naib and the two young men felt this.

'I trust this man with my life,' she said, addressing herself to al-Fali. 'And it is not the first time.'

'My Lady,' al-Fali protested. 'It's just . . . ' He glared at Idaho. 'He's the husband of the Coan-Teen!'

'And he was trained by my Duke and by me,' she said.

'But he's a *ghola*!' The words were torn from al-Fali.

'My son's ghola,' she reminded him.

It was too much for a former Fedaykin who'd once pledged himself to support Muad'Dib to the death. He sighed, stepped aside, and motioned the two young men to open the curtains.

Jessica stepped through, Idaho behind her. She turned, spoke to al-Fali in the doorway. 'You are to go to Stilgar. He's to be trusted.'

'Yes . . . ' But she still heard doubts in the old man's voice.

Idaho touched her arm. 'We should go at once. Is there anything you wish to take?'

'Only my common sense,' she said.

'Why? Do you fear you're making a mistake?'

She glanced up at him. 'You were always the best 'thopter pilot in our service, Duncan.'

This did not amuse him. He stepped ahead of her, moving swiftly, retracing the way he'd come. Al-Fali fell into step beside Jessica. 'How did you know he came by 'thopter?'

'He wears no stillsuit,' Jessica said.

Al-Fali appeared abashed by this obvious perception. He would not be silenced, though. 'Our messenger brought him here directly from Stilgar's. They could've been seen.'

'Were you seen, Duncan?' Jessica asked Idaho's back.

'You know better than that,' he said. 'We flew lower than the dune tops.'

They turned into a side passage which led downward in spiral steps, debouching finally into an open chamber well lighted by glowglobes high in the brown rock. A single ornithopter sat facing the far wall, crouched there like an insect waiting to spring. The wall would be false rock, then – a door opening onto the desert. As poor as this sietch was, it still maintained the instruments of secrecy and mobility.

Idaho opened the ornithopter's door for her, helped her into the right-hand seat. As she moved past him, she saw perspiration on his forehead where a lock of the black goat-hair lay tumbled. Unbidden, Jessica found herself recalling that head spouting blood in a noisy cavern. The steely marbles of the Tleilaxu eyes brought her out of that recollection. Nothing was as it seemed anymore. She busied herself fastening her seatbelt.

'It's been a long time since you've flown me, Duncan,' she said.

'Long and far time,' he said. He was already checking the controls.

Al-Fali and the two younger Fremen waited beside the controls to the false rock, prepared to open it.

'Do you think I harbor doubts about you?' Jessica asked, speaking softly to Idaho.

Idaho kept his attention on an engine instrument, ignited the impellers and watched a needle move. A smile touched his mouth, a quick and harsh gesture in his sharp features, gone as quickly as it had come.

'I am still Atreides,' Jessica said. 'Alia is not.'

'Have no fear,' he grated. 'I still serve the Atreides.'

'Alia is no longer Atreides,' Jessica repeated.

'You needn't remind me!' he snarled. 'Now shut up and let me fly this thing.'

The desperation in his voice was quite unexpected, out of keeping with the Idaho she'd known. Putting down a renewed sense of fear, Jessica asked: 'Where are we going, Duncan? You can tell me now.'

But he nodded to al-Fali and the false rock opened outward into bright silvery sunlight. The ornithopter leaped outward and up, its wings throbbing with the effort, the jets roaring, and they mounted into an empty sky. Idaho set a southwesterly course toward Sihaya Ridge which could be seen as a dark line upon the sand.

Presently he said: 'Do not think harshly of me, My Lady.'

'I haven't thought harshly of you since that night you came into our Arrakeen Great Hall roaring drunk on spice-beer,' she said. But his words renewed her doubts, and she fell into the relaxed preparedness of complete *prana-bindu* defense.

'I remember that night well,' he said. 'I was very young and .., inexperienced.'

'But the best swordmaster in my Duke's retinue.'

'Not quite, My Lady. Gurney could best me six times out of ten.' He glanced at her. 'Where is Gurney?'

'Doing my bidding.'

He shook his head.

'Do you know where we're going?' she asked.

'Yes, My Lady.'

'Then tell me.'

'Very well. I promised that I would create a believable plot against House Atreides. Only one way, really, to do that.' He pressed a button on the control wheel and cocoon restraints whipped from Jessica's seat, enfolded her in unbreakable softness, leaving only her head exposed. 'I'm taking you to Salusa Secundus,' he said. 'To Farad'n.'

In a rare, uncontrolled spasm, Jessica surged against the restraints, felt them tighten, easing only when she relaxed, but not before she felt the deadly shigawire concealed in the protective sheathing.

'The shigawire release has been disconnected,' he said, not looking at her. 'Oh, yes, and don't try Voice on me. I've come a long way since the days when you could move me that way.' He looked at her. 'The Tleilaxu armored me against such wiles.'

'You're obeying Alia,' Jessica said, 'and she –'

'Not Alia,' he said. 'We do The Preacher's bidding. He wants you to teach Farad'n as once you taught . . . Paul.'

Jessica remained in frozen silence, remembering Leto's words, that she would find an interesting student. Presently she said: 'This Preacher – is he my son?'

Idaho's voice seemed to come from a great distance: 'I wish I knew.'

*The universe is just there; that's the only way a Fedaykin can view it and remain the master of his senses. The universe neither threatens nor promises. It holds things beyond our sway : the fall of a meteor, the eruption of a spiceblow, growing old and dying. These are the realities of this universe and they must be faced regardless of how you feel about them. You cannot fend off such realities with words. They will come at you in their own wordless way and then, then you will understand what is meant by 'life and death'. Understanding this, you will be filled with joy.*

        – Muad'Dib to his Fedaykin

'And those are the things we have set in motion,' Wensicia said. 'These things were done for *you*.'

Farad'n remained motionless, seated across from his mother in her morning room. The sun's golden light came from behind him, casting his shadow on the white-carpeted floor. Light reflected from the wall behind his mother drew a nimbus around her hair. She wore her usual white robe trimmed in gold – reminders of royal days. Her heart-shaped face appeared composed, but he knew she was watching his every reaction. His stomach felt empty, although he'd just come from breakfast.

'You don't approve?' Wensicia asked.

'What is there to disapprove?' he asked.

'Well . . . that we kept this from you until now?'

'Oh, that.' He studied his mother, tried to reflect upon his complex position in this matter. He could only think on a thing he had noticed recently, that Tyekanik no longer called her 'My Princess'. What did he call her? Queen Mother?

*Why do I feel a sense of loss?* he wondered. *What am I losing?* The answer was obvious: he was losing his carefree days, time for those pursuits of the mind which so attracted him. If this plot unfolded by his mother came off, those things would be gone forever. New responsibilities would demand his attention. He found that he resented this deeply. How dared they take such liberties with his time? And without even consulting him!

'Out with it,' his mother said. 'Something's wrong.'

'What if this plan fails?' he asked, saying the first thing that came into his mind.

'How can it fail?'

'I don't know . . . Any plan can fail. How're you using Idaho in all of this?'

'Idaho? What's this interest in . . . Oh, yes – that mystic fellow Tyek brought here without consulting me. That was wrong of him. The mystic spoke of Idaho, didn't he?'

It was a clumsy lie on her part, and Farad'n found himself staring at his mother in wonderment. She'd known about The Preacher all along!

'It's just that I've never seen a ghola,' he said.

She accepted this, said: 'We're saving Idaho for something important.'

Farad'n chewed silently at his upper lip.

Wensicia found herself reminded of his dead father. Dalak had been like that at times, very inward and complex, difficult to read. Dalak, she reminded herself, had been related to Count Hasimar Fenring, and there'd been something of the dandy and the fanatic in both of them. Would Farad'n follow in that path? She began to regret having Tyek lead the lad into the Arrakeen religion. Who knew where that might take him?

'What does Tyek call you now?' Farad'n asked.

'What's that?' She was startled by this shift.

'I've noticed that he doesn't call you "My Princess" anymore.'

*How observant he is*, she thought, wondering why this filled her with disquiet. *Does he think I've taken Tyek as a lover? Nonsense, it wouldn't matter one way or the other. Then why this question?*

172

'He calls me "My Lady",' she said.

'Why?'

'Because that's the custom in all of the Great Houses.'

*Including the Atreides*, he thought.

'It's less suggestive if overheard,' she explained. 'Some will think we've given up our legitimate aspirations.'

'Who would be that stupid?' he asked.

She pursed her lips, decided to let it pass. A small thing, but great campaigns were made up of many small things.

'The Lady Jessica shouldn't have left Caladan,' he said.

She shook her head sharply. What was this? His mind was darting around like a crazy thing! She said: 'What do you mean?'

'She shouldn't have gone back to Arrakis,' he said. 'That's bad strategy. Makes one wonder. Would've been better to have her grandchildren visit her on Caladan.'

*He's right*, she thought, dismayed that this had never occurred to her. Tyek would have to explore this immediately. Again she shook her head. *No!* What was Farad'n doing? He must know that the Priesthood would never risk both twins in space.

She said this.

'Is it the Priesthood or the Lady Alia?' he asked, noting that her thoughts had gone where he had wanted. He found exhilaration in this new importance, the mind-games available in political plotting. It had been a long time since his mother's mind had interested him. She was too easily maneuvered.

'You think Alia wants power for herself?' Wensicia asked.

He looked away from her. Of course Alia wanted the power for herself! All of the reports from that accursed planet agreed on this. His thoughts took off on a new course.

'I've been reading about their Planetologist,' he said. 'There has to be a clue to the sandworms and the haploids in there somewhere, if only . . .'

'Leave that to others now!' she said, beginning to lose patience with him. 'Is this all you have to say about the things we've done for you?'

'You didn't do them for me,' he said.

'Wha-a-at?'

'You did it for House Corrino,' he said, 'and you're House Corrino right now. I've not been invested.'

'You have responsibilities!' she said. 'What about all of the people who depend upon you?'

As if her words put the burden upon him, he felt the weight

of all those hopes and dreams which followed House Corrino.

'Yes,' he said, 'I understand about them, but I find some of the things done in my *name* distasteful.'

'Dis . . . How can you say such a thing? We do what any Great House would do in promoting its own fortunes!'

'Do you? I think you've been a bit gross. No! Don't interrupt me. If I'm to be an Emperor, then you'd better learn how to listen to me. Do you think I cannot read between the lines? How were those tigers trained?'

She remained speechless at this cutting demonstration of his perceptive abilities.

'I see,' he said, 'Well, I'll keep Tyek because I know you led him into this. He's a good officer under most circumstances, but he'll fight for his own principles only in a friendly arena.'

'His . . . *principles*?'

'The difference between a good officer and a poor one is strength of character and about five heartbeats,' he said. 'He has to stick by his principles wherever they're challenged.'

'The tigers were necessary,' she said.

'I'll believe that if they succeed,' he said. 'But I will not condone what had to be done in training them. Don't protest. It's obvious. They were *conditioned*. You said it yourself.'

'What're you going to do?' she asked.

'I'm going to wait and see,' he said. 'Perhaps I'll become Emperor.'

She put a hand to her breast, sighed. For a few moments there he'd terrified her. She'd almost believed he would denounce her. Principles! But he was committed now; she could see that.

Farad'n got up, went to the door and rang for his mother's attendants. He looked back: 'We are through, aren't we?'

'Yes.' She raised a hand as he started to leave. 'Where're you going?'

'To the library. I've become fascinated lately by Corrino history.' He left her then, sensing how he carried his new commitment with him.

*Damn her!*

But he knew he was committed. And he recognized that there was a deep emotional difference between history as recorded on shigawire and read at leisure, a deep difference between that kind of history and the history which one lived. This new living history which he felt gathering around him possessed a sense of plunging into an irreversible future. Farad'n could feel himself

174

driven now by the desires of all those whose fortunes rode with him. He found it strange that he could not pin down his own desires in this.

> *It is said of Muad'Dib that once when he saw a weed trying to grow between two rocks, he moved one of the rocks. Later, when the weed was seen to be flourishing, he covered it with the remaining rock. 'That was its fate,' he explained.*
>
> — The Commentaries

'Now!' Ghanima shouted.

Leto, two steps ahead of her in reaching the narrow cut in the rocks, did not hesitate. He dove into the slit, crawled forward until darkness enfolded him. He heard Ghanima drop behind him, a sudden stillness, and her voice, not hurrying or fearful:

'I'm stuck.'

He stood up, knowing this would bring his head within reach of questing claws, reversed himself in the narrow passage, crept back until he felt Ghanima's outstretched hand.

'It's my robe,' she said. 'It's caught.'

He heard rocks falling directly below them, pulled on her hand but felt only a small gain.

There was panting below them, a growl.

Leto tensed himself, wedging his hips against the rock, heaved on Ghanima's arm. Cloth ripped and he felt her jerk toward him. She hissed and he knew she felt pain, but he pulled once more, harder. She came farther into the hole, then all the way, dropping beside him. They were too close to the end of the cut, though. He turned, dropped to all fours, scrambled deeper. Ghanima pulled herself along behind him. There was a panting intensity to her movements which told him she'd been hurt. He came to the end of the opening, rolled over and peered upward out of the narrow gap of their sanctuary. The opening was about two meters above him, filled with stars. Something large obscured the stars.

A rumbling growl filled the air around the twins. It was deep, menacing, an ancient sound: hunter speaking to its prey.

'How badly are you hurt?' Leto asked, keeping his voice even.

She matched him, tone for tone: 'One of them clawed me. Breached my stillsuit along the left leg. I'm bleeding.'

'How bad?'

175

'Vein. I can stop it.

'Use pressure,' he said. 'Don't move. I'll take care of our friends.'

'Careful,' she said. 'They're bigger than I expected.'

Leto unsheathed his crysknife, reached up with it. He knew the tiger would be questing downward, claws raking the narrow passage where its body could not go.

Slowly, slowly, he extended the knife. Abruptly something struck the top of the blade. He felt the blow all along his arm, almost lost his grip on the knife. Blood gushed along his hand, spattered his face, and there came an immediate scream which deafened him. The stars became visible. Sómething threshed and flung itself down the rocks toward the sand in a violent cater-wauling.

Once more, the stars were obscured and he heard the hunter's growl. The second tiger had moved into place, unmindful of its companion's fate.

'They're persistent,' Leto said.

'You got one for sure,' Ghanima said. 'Listen!'

The screams and thrashing convulsions below them were growing fainter. The second tiger remained, though, a curtain against the stars.

Leto sheathed his blade, touched Ghanima's arm. 'Give me your knife. I want a fresh tip to make sure of this one.'

'Do you think they'll have a third one in reserve?' She asked.

'Not likely. Laza tigers hunt in pairs.'

'Just as we do,' she said.

'As we do,' he agreed. He felt the handle of her crysknife slip into his palm, gripped it tightly. Once more he began that careful upward questing. The blade encountered only empty air, even when he reached into a level dangerous to his body. He withdrew, pondering this.

'Can't you find it?'

'It's not behaving the way the other one did.'

'It's still there. Smell it?'

He swallowed in a dry throat. A fetid breath, moist with the musky smell of the cat, assaulted his nostrils. The stars were still blocked from view. Nothing could be heard of the first cat; the crysknife poison had completed its work.

'I think I'm going to have to stand up,' he said.

'No!'

'It has to be teased into reach of the knife.'

'Yes, but we agreed that if one of us could avoid being wounded . . .'

'And you're wounded, so you're the one going back,' he said.

'But if you're badly injured, I won't be able to leave you,' she said.

'Do you have a better idea?'

'Give me back my knife.'

'But your leg!'

'I can stand on the good one.'

'That thing could take your head off with one sweep. Maybe the maula . . .'

'If there's anything out there to hear, they'll know we came prepared for –'

'I don't like your taking this risk!' he said.

'Whoever's out there mustn't learn we have maulas – not yet.' She touched his arm. 'I'll be careful, keep my head down.'

As he remained silent, she said: 'You know I'm the one who has to do this. Give me back my knife.'

Reluctantly he quested with his free hand, found her hand and returned the knife. It was the logical thing to do, but logic warred with every emotion in him.

He felt Ghanima pull away, heard the sandy rasping of her robe against the rock. She gasped, and he knew she must be standing. *Be very careful!* he thought. And he almost pulled her back to insist they use a maula pistol. But that could warn anyone out there that they had such weapons. Worse, it could drive the tiger out of reach, and they'd be trapped in here with a wounded tiger waiting for them in some unknown place out on those rocks.

Ghanima took a deep breath, braced her back against one wall of the cleft. *I must be quick*, she thought. She reached upward with the knife point. Her left leg throbbed where the claws had raked it. She felt the crusting of blood against her skin there and the warmth of a new flow. *Very quick!* She sank her senses into the calm preparation for crisis which the Bene Gesserit Way provided, put pain and all other distractions out of her awareness. The cat must reach down! Slowly she passed the blade along the opening. Where was the damned animal? Once more she raked the air. Nothing. The tiger would have to be lured into attack.

Carefully she probed with her sense of smell. Warm breath came from her left. She poised herself, drew in a deep breath, screamed: 'Taqwa!' It was the old Fremen battlecry, its meaning found in the most ancient legends: '*The price of freedom!*' With

177

the cry she tipped the blade and stabbed along the cleft's dark opening. Claws found her elbow before the knife touched flesh, and she had time only to tip her wrist toward the pain before agony raked her arm from elbow to wrist. Through the pain, she felt the poison tip sink into the tiger. The blade was wrenched from her numb fingers. But again the narrow gap of the cleft lay open to the stars and the wailing voice of a dying cat filled the night. They followed it by its death throes, a thrashing passage down the rocks. Presently the death-silence came.

'It got my arm,' Ghanima said, trying to bind a loose fold of her robe around the wound.

'Badly?'

'I think so. I can't feel my hand.'

'Let me get a light and –'

'Not until we get under cover!'

'I'll hurry.'

She heard him twisting to reach his Fremkit, felt the dark slickness of a nightshield as it was slipped over her head, tucked in behind him. He didn't bother to make it moisture tight.

'My knife's on this side,' she said. 'I can feel the handle with my knee.'

'Leave it for now.'

He ignited a single small globe. The brilliance of it made her blink. Leto put the globe on the sandy floor at one side, gasped as he saw her arm. One claw had opened a long, gaping wound which twisted from the elbow along the back of her arm almost to the wrist. The wound described the way she had rotated her arm to present the knife tip to the tiger's paw.

Ghanima glanced once at the wound, closed her eyes and began reciting the litany against fear.

Leto found himself sharing her need, but put aside the clamor of his own emotions while he set about binding up the wound. It had to be done carefully to stop the flow of blood while retaining the appearance of a clumsy job which Ghanima might have done by herself. He made her tie off the knot with her free hand, holding one end of the bandage in her teeth.

'Now let's look at the leg,' he said.

She twisted around to present the other wound. It was not as bad: two shallow claw cuts along the calf. They had bled freely into the stillsuit, however. He cleaned it up as best he could, bound the wound beneath the stillsuit. He sealed the suit over the bandage.

178

'I got sand in it,' he said. 'Have it treated as soon as you get back.'

'Sand in our wounds,' she said. 'That's an old story for Fremen.'

He managed a smile, sat back.

Ghanima took a deep breath. 'We've pulled it off.'

'Not yet.'

She swallowed, fighting to recover from the aftermath of shock. Her face appeared pale in the light of the glowglobe. And she thought: *Yes, we must move fast now. Whoever controlled those tigers could be out there right now.*

Leto, staring at his sister, felt a sudden wrenching sense of loss. It was a deep pain which shot through his breast. He and Ghanima must separate now. For all of those years since birth they had been as one person. But their plan demanded now that they undergo a metamorphosis, going their separate ways into uniqueness where the sharing of daily experiences would never again unite them as they once had been united.

He retreated into the necessarily mundane. 'Here's my Fremkit. I took the bandages from it. Someone may look.'

'Yes.' She exchanged kits with him.

'Someone out there has a transmitter for those cats,' he said. 'Most likely he'll be waiting near the qanat to make certain of us.'

She touched her maula pistol where it sat atop the Fremkit, picked it up and thrust it into the sash beneath her robe. 'My robe's torn.'

'Yes.'

'Searchers may get here soon,' he said. 'They may have a traitor among them. Best you slip back alone. Get Harah to hide you.'

'I'll . . . I'll start the search for the traitor as soon as I get back,' she said. She peered into her brother's face, sharing his painful knowledge that from this point on they would accumulate a store of differences. Never again would they be as one, sharing knowledge which no one else could understand.

'I'll go to Jacurutu,' he said.

'Fondak,' she said.

He nodded his agreement. Jacurutu/Fondak – they had to be the same place. It was the only way the legendary place could have been hidden. Smugglers had done it, of course. How easy for them to convert one label into another, acting under the cover of the unspoken convention by which they were allowed to exist. The ruling family of a planet must always have a back

179

door for escape in extremis. And a small share in smuggling profits kept the channels open. In Fondak/Jacurutu, the smugglers had taken over a completely operative sietch untroubled by a resident population. And they had hidden Jacurutu right out in the open, secure in the tabu which kept Fremen from it.

'No Fremen will think to search for me in such a place,' he said. 'They'll inquire among the smugglers, of course, but . . .'

'We'll do as agreed,' she said. 'It's just . . .'

'I know.' Hearing his own voice, Leto realized they were drawing out these last moments of sameness. A wry grin touched his mouth, adding years to his appearance. Ghanima realized she was seeing him through a veil of time, looking at an older Leto. Tears burned her eyes.

'You needn't give water to the dead just yet,' he said, brushing a finger against the dampness on her cheeks. 'I'll go out far enough that no one will hear, and I'll call a worm.' He indicated the collapsed Maker hooks strapped to the outside of his Fremkit. 'I'll be at Jacurutu before dawn two days from now.'

'Ride swiftly, my old friend,' she whispered.

'I'll come back to you, my only friend,' he said. 'Remember to be careful at the qanat.'

'Choose a good worm,' she said, giving him the Fremen words of parting. Her left hand extinguished the glowglobe, and the nightseal rustled as she pulled it aside, folded it and tucked it into her kit. She felt him go, hearing only the softest of sounds quickly fading into silence as he crept down the rocks into the desert.

Ghanima steeled herself then for what she had to do. Leto must be dead to her. She had to make herself believe it. There could be no Jacurutu in her mind, no brother out there seeking a place lost in Fremen mythology. From this point onward she could not think of Leto as alive. She must condition herself to react out of a total belief that her brother was dead, killed here by Laza tigers. Not many humans could fool a Truthsayer, but she knew that she could do it . . . might have to do it. The multi-lives she and Leta shared had taught them the way: a hypnotic process old in Sheba's time, although she might be the only human alive who could recall Sheba as a reality. The deep compulsions had been designed with care and, for a long time after Leto had gone, Ghanima reworked her self-awareness, building the lonely sister, the surviving twin, until it was a believable totality. As she did this, she found the inner world becoming silent, blanked away from intrusion into her consciousness. It was a side effect she had not expected.

*If only Leto could have lived to learn this,* she thought, and she did not find the thought a paradox. Standing, she peered down at the desert where the tiger had taken Leto. There was a sound growing in the sand out there, a familiar sound to Fremen: the passage of a worm. Rare as they had become in these parts, a worm still came. Perhaps the first cat's death throes . . . Yes, Leto had killed one cat before the other one got him. It was oddly symbolic that a worm should come. So deep was her compulsion that she saw three dark spots far down on the sand: the two tigers and Leto. Then the worm came and there was only sand with its surface broken into new waves by the passage of Shai-Hulud. It had not been a very large worm . . . but large enough. And her compulsion did not permit her to see a small figure riding on the ringed back.

Fighting her grief, Ghanima sealed her Fremkit, crept cautiously from her hiding place. Hand on her maula pistol, she scanned the area. No sign of a human with a transmitter. She worked her way up the rocks and across to the far side, creeping through moonshadows, waiting and waiting to be sure no assassin lurked in her path.

Across the open space she could see torches at Tabr, the wavering activity of a search. A dark patch moved across the sand toward The Attendant. She chose her path to run far to the north of the approaching party, went down to the sand and moved into the dune shadows. Careful to make her steps fall in a broken rhythm which would not attract a worm, she set out into the lonely distance which separated Tabr from the place where Leto had died. She would have to be careful at the qanat, she knew. Nothing must prevent her from telling how her brother had perished saving her from the tigers.

*Governments, if they endure, always tend increasingly toward aristocratic forms. No government in history has been known to evade this pattern. And as the aristocracy develops, government tends more and more to act exclusively in the interests of the ruling class – whether that class be hereditary royalty, oligarchs of financial empires, or entrenched bureaucracy.*

> – Politics as Repeat Phenomenon:
> Bene Gesserit Training Manual

'Why does he make us this offer?' Farad'n asked. 'That's most essential.'

He and the Bashar Tyekanik stood in the lounge of Farad'n's private quarters. Wensicia sat at one side on a low blue divan, almost as audience rather than participant. She knew her position and resented it, but Farad'n had undergone a terrifying change since that morning when she'd revealed their plots to kill him.

It was late afternoon at Corrino Castle and the low light accented the quiet comfort of his lounge – a room lined with actual books reproduced in plastino, with shelves revealing a horde of player spools, data blocks, shigawire reels, mnemonic amplifiers. There were signs all around that this room was much used – worn places on the books, bright metal on the amplifiers, frayed corners on the data blocks. There was only the one divan, but many chairs – all of them sensiform floaters designed for unobtrusive comfort.

Farad'n stood with his back to a window. He wore a plain Sardaukar uniform in gray and black with only the golden lion-claw symbols on the wings of his collar as decoration. He had chosen to receive the Bashar and his mother in this room, hoping to create an atmosphere of more relaxed communication than could be achieved in a more formal setting. But Tyekanik's constant 'My Lord this' and 'My Lady that' kept them at a distance.

'My Lord, I don't think he'd make this offer were he unable to deliver,' Tyekanik said.

'Of course not!' Wensicia intruded.

Farad'n merely glanced at his mother to silence her, asked: 'We've put no pressure on Idaho, made no attempt to seek delivery on The Preacher's promise?'

'None,' Tyekanik said.

'Then why does Duncan Idaho, noted all of his life for his

fanatic loyalty to the Atreides, offer now to deliver the Lady Jessica into our hands?'

'These rumors of trouble on Arrakis . . .' Wensicia ventured.

'Unconfirmed,' Farad'n said. 'It is possible that The Preacher has precipitated this?'

'Possible,' Tyekanik said, 'but I fail to see a motive.'

'He speaks of seeking asylum for her,' Farad'n said. 'That might follow if those rumors . . .'

'Precisely,' his mother said.

'Or it could be a ruse of some sort,' Tyekanik said.

'We can make several assumptions and explore them,' Farad'n said. 'What if Idaho has fallen into disfavor with his Lady Alia?'

'That might explain matters,' Wensicia said, 'but he –'

'No word yet from the smugglers?' Farad'n interrupted. 'Why can't we –'

'Transmission is always slow in this season,' Tyekanik said, 'and the needs of security . . .'

'Yes, of course, but still . . .' Farad'n shook his head. 'I don't like our assumption.'

'Don't be too quick to abandon it,' Wensicia said. 'All of those stories about Alia and that Priest, whatever his name is . . .'

'Javid,' Farad'n said. 'But the man's obviously –'

'He's been a very valuable source of information for us,' Wensicia said.

'I was about to say that he's obviously a double agent,' Farad'n said. 'How could he indict himself in this? He's not to be trusted. There are too many signs . . .'

'I fail to see them,' she said.

He was suddenly angry with her defenses. 'Take my word for it, mother! The signs are there; I'll explain later.'

'I'm afraid I must agree,' Tyekanik said.

Wensicia lapsed into hurt silence. How dared they push her out of Council like this? As though she were some lightheaded fancy woman with no –

'We mustn't forget that Idaho was once a ghola,' Farad'n said. 'The Tleilaxu . . .' He glanced sidelong at Tyekanik.

'That avenue will be explored,' Tyekanik said. He found himself admiring the way Farad'n's mind worked: alert, questing, sharp. Yes, the Tleilaxu, in restoring life to Idaho, might have planted a powerful barb in him for their own use.

'But I fail to apprehend a Tleilaxu motive,' Farad'n said.

'An investment in our fortunes,' Tyekanik said. 'A small insurance for future favors?'

'Large investment, I'd call it,' Farad'n said.

'Dangerous,' Wensicia said.

Farad'n had to agree with her. The Lady Jessica's capabilities were notorious in the Empire. After all, she'd been the one who'd trained Muad'Dib.

'If it became known that we hold her,' Farad'n said.

'Yes, that'd be a two-edged sword,' Tyekanik said. 'But it need not be known.'

'Let us assume,' Farad'n said, 'that we accept this offer. What's her value? Can we exchange her for something of greater importance?'

'Not openly,' Wensicia said.

'Of course not!' He peered expectantly at Tyekanik.

'That remains to be seen,' Tyekanik said.

Farad'n nodded. 'Yes. I think if we accept, we should consider the Lady Jessica as money banked for indeterminate use. After all, wealth doesn't necessarily have to be spent on any particular thing. It's just ... potentially useful.'

'She'd be a very dangerous captive,' Tyekanik said.

'There is that to consider, indeed,' Farad'n said. 'I'm told that her Bene Gesserit Ways permit her to manipulate a person just by the subtle employment of her voice.'

'Or her body,' Wensicia said. 'Irulan once divulged to me some of the things she'd learned. She was showing off at the time, and I saw no demonstrations. Still the evidence is pretty conclusive that Bene Gesserits have their ways of achieving their ends.'

'Were you suggesting,' Farad'n asked, 'that she might seduce me?'

Wensicia merely shrugged.

'I'd say she's a little old for that, wouldn't you?' Farad'n asked.

'With a Bene Gesserit, nothing's certain,' Tyekanik said.

Farad'n experienced a shiver of excitement tinged with fear. Playing this game to restore House Corrino's high seat of power both attracted and repelled him. How attractive it remained, the urge to retire from this game into his preferred pursuits -- historical research and learning the manifest duties for ruling here on Salusa Secundus. The restoration of his Sardaukar forces was a task in itself ... and for that job, Tyek was still a good tool. One planet was, after all, an enormous responsibility. But the Empire was an even greater responsibility, far more attractive as an instrument of power. And the more he read about Muad-'Dib/Paul Atreides, the more fascinated Farad'n became with the uses of power. As titular head of House Corrino, heir of Shaddam IV, what a great achievement it would be to restore his line to the Lion Throne. He wanted that! He wanted it. Farad'n had found that, by repeating this enticing litany to himself several times, he could overcome momentary doubts.

Tyekanik was speaking: ' . . . and of course, the Bene Gesserit teach that peace encourages aggression, thus igniting war. The paradox of – '

'How did we get on this subject?' Farad'n asked, bringing his attention back from the arena of speculation.

'Why,' Wensicia said sweetly, having noted the wool-gathering expression on her son's face, 'I merely asked if Tyek was familiar with the driving philosophy behind the Sisterhood.'

'Philosophy should be approached with irreverence,' Farad'n said, turning to face Tyekanik. 'In regard to Idaho's offer, I think we should inquire further. When we think we know something, that's precisely the moment when we should look deeper into the thing.'

'It will be done,' Tyekanik said. He liked this cautious streak in Farad'n, but hoped it did not extend to those military decisions which required speed and precision.

With seeming irrelevancy, Farad'n asked: 'Do you know what I find most interesting about the history of Arrakis? It was the custom in primitive times for Fremen to kill on sight anyone not clad in a stillsuit with its easily visible and characteristic hood.'

'What is your fascination with the stillsuit?' Tykanik asked.

'So you've noticed, eh?'

'How could we not notice?' Wensicia asked.

Farad'n sent an irritated glance at his mother. Why did she interrupt like that? He returned his attention to Tyekanik.

'The stillsuit is the key to that planet's character, Tyek. It's the hallmark of Dune. People tend to focus on the physical characteristics: the stillsuit conserves body moisture, recycles it, and makes it possible to exist on such a planet. You know, the Fremen custom was to have one stillsuit for each member of a family, *except* for food gatherers. They had spares. But please note, both of you – ' He moved to include his mother in this.
' – how garments which appear to be stillsuits, but really aren't, have become high fashion throughout the Empire. It's such a dominant characteristic for humans to copy the conqueror!'

'Do you really find such infromation valuable?' Tyekanik asked, his tone puzzled.

'Tyek, Tyek – without such information, one cannot govern. I said the stillsuit was the key to their character and it is! It's a conservative thing. The mistakes they make will be conservative mistakes.'

Tyekanik glanced at Wensicia, who was staring at her son with a worried frown. This characteristic of Farad'n's both attracted and worried the Bashar. It was so unlike Shaddam. Now, there had been an essential Sardaukar: a military killer with few inhibitions. But Shaddam had fallen to the Atreides under that damnable Paul. Indeed, what he read of Paul Atreides revealed just such characteristics as Farad'n now displayed. It was possible that Farad'n might hesitate less than the Atreides over brutal necessities, but that was his Sardaukar training.

'Many have governed without using this kind of information,' Tyekanik said.

Farad'n merely stared at him for a moment. Then: 'Governed and failed.'

Tyekanik's mouth drew into a stiff line at this obvious allusion to Shaddam's failure. That had been a Sardaukar failure, too, and no Sardaukar could recall it easily.

Having made his point, Farad'n said: 'You see, Tyek, the influence of a planet upon the mass unconscious of its inhabitants has never been fully appreciated. To defeat the Atreides, we must understand not only Caladan but Arrakis: one planet soft and the other a training ground for hard decisions. That was a unique event, that marriage of Atreides and Fremen. We must know how it worked or we won't be able to match it, let alone defeat it.'

'What does this have to do with Idaho's offer?' Wensicia demanded.

Farad'n glanced pityingly down at his mother. 'We begin their defeat by the kinds of stress we introduce into their society. That's a very powerful tool: stress. And the lack of it is important, too. Did you not mark how the Atreides helped things grow soft and easy here?'

Tyekanik allowed himself a curt nod of agreement. That was a good point. The Sardaukar could not be permitted to grow too soft. This offer from Idaho still bothered him, though. He said: 'Perhaps it'd be best to reject the offer.'

'Not yet,' Wensicia said. 'We've a spectrum of choices open to us. Our task is to identify as much of the spectrum as we can. My son is right: we need more information.'

Farad'n stared at her, measuring her intent as well as the

186

surface meaning of her words. 'But will we know when we've passed the point of no alternate choice?' he asked.

A sour chuckle came from Tyekanik. 'If you ask me, we're long past the point of no return.'

Farad'n tipped his head back to laugh aloud. 'But we still have alternate choices, Tyek! When we come to the end of our rope, that's an important place to recognize!'

*In this age when the means of human transport include devices which can span the deeps of space in transtime, and other devices which can carry men swiftly over virtually impassable planetary surfaces, it seems odd to think of attempting long journeys afoot. Yet this remains a primary means of travel on Arrakis, a fact attributed partly to preference and partly to the brutal treatment which this planet reserves for anything mechanical. In the strictures of Arrakis, human flesh remains the most durable and reliable resource for the Hajj. Perhaps it is the implicit awareness of this fact which makes Arrakis the ultimate mirror of the soul.*

*– Handbook of the Hajj*

Slowly, cautiously, Ghanima made her way back to Tabr, holding herself to the deepest shadows of the dunes, crouching in stillness as the search party passed to the south of her. Terrible awareness gripped her: the worm which had taken the tigers and Leto's body, the dangers ahead. He was gone; her twin was gone. She put aside all tears and nurtured her rage. In this, she was pure Fremen. And she knew this, reveling in it.

She understood what was said about Fremen. They were not supposed to have a conscience, having lost it in a burning for revenge against those who had driven them from planet to planet in the long wandering. That was foolishness, of course. Only the rawest primitive had no conscience. Fremen possessed a highly evolved conscience which centered on their own welfare as a people. It was only to outsiders that they seemed brutish – just as outsiders appeared brutish to Fremen. Every Fremen knew very well that he could do a brutal thing and feel no guilt. Fremen did not feel guilt for the same things that aroused such feelings in others. Their rituals provided a freedom from guilts which might otherwise have destroyed them. They knew in their deepest awareness that any transgression could be ascribed, at least in part, to well recognized extenuating circumstances: 'the failure of authority', or 'a *natural* bad tendency' shared by all

187

humans, or to 'bad luck', which any sentient creature should be able to identify as a collision between mortal flesh and the outer chaos of the universe.

In this context Ghanima felt herself to be the pure Fremen, a carefully prepared extension of tribal brutality. She needed only a target – and that, obviously, was House Corrino. She longed to see Farad'n's blood spilled on the ground at her feet.

No enemy awaited her at the qanat. Even the search parties had gone elsewhere. She crossed the water on an earth bridge, crept through tall grass toward the covert exit of the sietch. Abruptly light flared ahead of her and Ghanima threw herself flat on the ground. She peered out through stalks of giant alfalfa. A woman had entered the covert passage from the outside, and someone had remembered to prepare that passage in the way any sietch entrance should be prepared. In troubled times, one greeted anyone entering the sietch with bright light, temporarily blinding the newcomer and giving guards time to decide. But such a greeting was never meant to be broadcast out over the desert. The light visible here meant the outer seals had been left aside.

Ghanima felt a tug of bitterness at this betrayal of sietch security: this flowing light. The ways of the lace-shirt Fremen were to be found everywhere!

The light continued to throw its fan over the ground at the cliff base. A young girl ran out of the orchard's darkness into the light, something fearful about her movements. Ghanima could see the bright circle of a glowglobe within the passage, a halo of insects around it. The light illuminated two dark shadows in the passage: a man and the girl. They were holding hands as they stared into each other's eyes.

Ghanima sensed something wrong about the man and woman there. They were not just two lovers stealing a moment from the search. The light was suspended above and beyond them in the passage. The two talked against a glowing arch, throwing their shadows into the outer night where anyone could be a watcher of their movements. Now and again the man would free a hand. The hand would come gesturing into the light, a sharp and furtive movement which, once completed, returned to the shadows.

Lonely sounds of night creatures filled the darkness around Ghanima, but she screened out such distractions.

What was it about those two?

The man's motions were so static, so careful.

He turned. Reflection from the woman's robe illuminated him, exposing a raw red face with a large blotchy nose. Ghanima drew in a deep, silent breath of recognition. *Palimbasha!* He was a grandson of a Naib whose sons had fallen in Atreides service. The face – and another thing revealed by the open swinging of his robe as he turned – drew for Ghanima a complete picture. He wore a belt beneath the robe, and attached to the belt was a box which glistened with keys and dials. It was an instrument of the Tleilaxu or the Ixians for certain. And it had to be the transmitter which had released the tigers. Palimbasha. This meant another Naibate family had gone over to House Corrino.

Who was the woman, then? No matter. She was someone being used by Palimbasha.

Unhidden, a Bene Gesserit thought came into Ghanima's mind: *Each planet has its own period, and each life likewise.*

She recalled Palimbasha well, watching him there with that woman, seeing the transmitter, the furtive movements. Palimbasha taught in the sietch school. Mathematics. The man was a mathematical boor. He had attempted to explain Muad'Dib through mathematics until censured by the Priesthood. He was a mind-slaver and his enslaving process could be understood with extreme simplicity: he transferred technical knowledge without a transfer of values.

*I should've suspected him earlier,* she thought. *The signs were all there.*

Then, with an acid tightening of her stomach: *He killed my brother!*

She forced herself to calmness. Palimbasha would kill her, too, if she tried to pass him there in the covert passage. Now she understood the reason for this un-Fremen display of light, this betrayal of the hidden entrance. They were watching by that light to see if either of their victims had escaped. It must be a terrible time of waiting for them, not knowing. And now that Ghanima had seen the transmitter, she could explain certain of the hand motions, Palimbasha was depressing one of the transmitter's keys frequently, an angry gesture.

The presence of this pair said much to Ghanima. Likely every way into the sietch carried a similar watcher in its depths.

She scratched her nose where dust tickled it. Her wounded leg still throbbed and the knife arm ached when it didn't burn. The fingers remained numb. Should it come to a knife, she would have to use the blade in her left hand.

Ghanima thought of using the maula pistol, but its characteristic sound would be sure to attract unwanted attention. Some other way would have to be found.

Palimbasha turned away from the entrance once more. He was a dark object against the light. The woman turned her attention to the outer night while she talked. There was a trained alertness about the woman, a sense that she knew how to look into the shadows, using the edges of her eyes. She was more than just a useful tool, then. She was part of the deeper conspiracy.

Ghanima recalled now that Palimbasha aspired to be a Kaymakam, a political governor under the Regency. He would be part of a larger plan, that was clear. There would be many others with him. Even here in Tabr. Ghanima examined the edges of the problem thus exposed, probed into it. If she could take one of these guardians alive, many others would be forfeit.

The *whiffle* of a small animal drinking at the qanat behind her caught Ghanima's awareness. Natural sounds and natural things. Her memory searched through a strange silent barrier in her mind, found a priestess of Jowf captured in Assyria by Sennacherib. The memories of that priestess told Ghanima what would have to be done here. Palimbasha and his woman there were mere children, wayward and dangerous. They knew nothing of Jowf, knew not even the name of the planet where Sennacherib and the priestess had faded into dust. The thing which was about to happen to the pair of conspirators, if it were explained to them, could only be explained in terms of beginning here.

And ending here.

Rolling onto her side, Ghanima freed her Fremkit, slipped the sandsnorkel from its bindings. She uncapped the sandsnorkel, removed the long filter within it. Now she had an open tube. She selected a needle from the repair pack, unsheathed her crysknife, and inserted the needle into the poison hollow at the knife's tip, that place where once a sandworm's nerve had fitted. Her injured arm made the work difficult. She moved carefully and slowly, handling the poisoned needle with caution while she took a wad of spice-fiber from its chamber in the kit. The needle's shank fitted tightly into the fiber wad, forming a missile which went tightly into the tube of the sandsnorkel.

Holding the weapon flat, Ghanima wormed her way closer to the light, moving slowly to cause minimal disturbance in the alfalfa. As she moved, she studied the insects around the light. Yes, there were piume flies in that fluttering mob. They were notorious biters of human flesh. The poisoned dart might go

190

unnoticed, swatted aside as a biting fly. A decision remained: Which one of those two to take – the man or the woman!

*Muriz.* The name came unbidden into Ghanima's mind. That was the woman's name. It recalled things said about her. She was one of those who fluttered around Palimbasha as the insects fluttered around the light. She was easily swayed, a weak one.

Very well. Palimbasha had chosen the wrong companion for this night.

Ghanima put the tube to her mouth and, with the memory of the priestess of Jowf clearly in her awareness, she sighted carefully, expelled her breath in one strong surge.

Palimbasha batted at his cheek, drew away a hand with a speck of blood on it. The needle was nowhere to be seen, flicked away by the motion of his own hand.

The woman said something soothing and Palimbasha laughed. As he laughed, his legs began to give away beneath him. He sagged against the woman, who tried to support him. She was still staggering with the dead weight when Ghanima came up beside her and pressed the point of an unsheathed crysknife against her waist.

In a conversational tone, Ghanima said: 'Make no sudden moves, Muriz. My knife is poisoned. You may let go of Palimbasha now. He is dead.'

*In all major socializing forces you will find an underlying movement to gain and maintain power through the use of words. From witch doctor to priest to bureaucrat it is all the same. A governed populace must be conditioned to accept power-words as actual things, to confuse the symbolized system with the tangible universe. In the maintenance of such a power structure, certain symbols are kept out of the reach of common understanding – symbols such as those'dealing with economic manipulation of those which define the local interpretation of sanity. Symbol-secrecy of this form leads to the development of fragmented sub-languages, each being a signal that its users are accumulating some form of power. With this insight into a power process, our Imperial Security Force must be ever alert to the formation of sub-languages.*

– Lecture to the Arrakeen War College
by The Princess Irulan

'It is perhaps unnecessary to tell you,' Farad'n said, 'but to avoid any errors I'll announce that a mute has been stationed with orders to kill you both should I show signs of succumbing to witchery.'

He did not expect to see any effect from these words. Both the Lady Jessica and Idaho gratified expectations.

Farad'n had chosen with care the setting for this first examination of the pair. Shaddam's old State Audience Chamber. What it lacked in grandeur it made up for with exotic appointments. Outside it was a winter afternoon, but the windowless chamber's lighting simulated a timeless summer day bathed in golden light from artfully scattered glowglobes of the purest Ixian crystal.

The news from Arrakis filled Farad'n with quiet elation. Leto, the male twin, was dead, killed by an assassin-tiger. Ghanima, the surviving sister, was in the custody of her aunt and reputedly was a hostage. The full report did much to explain the presence of Idaho and the Lady Jessica. Sanctuary was what they wanted. Corrino spies reported an uneasy truce on Arrakis. Alia had agreed to submit herself to a test called 'the Trial of Possession', the purpose of which had not been fully explained. However, no date had been set for this trial and two Corrino spies believed it might never take place. This much was certain, though: there had been fighting between desert Fremen and the Imperial Military Fremen, an abortive civil war which had brought government to a temporary standstill. Stilgar's holdings were now neutral ground, designated after an exchange of hostages. Ghanima evidently had been considered one of these hostages, although the working of this remained unclear.

Jessica and Idaho had been brought to the audience securely bound in suspensor chairs. Both were held down by deadly thin strands of shigawire which would cut flesh at the slightest struggle. Two Sardaukar troopers had brought them, checked the bindings, and had gone away silently.

The warning had, indeed, been unnecessary. Jessica had seen the armed mute standing against a wall at her right, an old but efficient projectile weapon in his hand. She allowed her gaze to roam over the room's exotic inlays. The broad leaves of the rare iron bush had been set with eye pearls and interlaced to form the center of the domed ceiling. The floor beneath her was alternate blocks of diamond wood and kabuzu shell arranged within rectangular borders of passaquet bones. These had been set on end, laser-cut and polished. Selected hard materials decorated the walls in stress-woven patterns which outlined the four positions of the Lion symbol claimed by descendants of the late Shaddam IV. The lions were executed in wild gold.

Farad'n had chosen to receive the captives while standing. He wore uniform shorts and a light golden jacket of elf-silk open at the throat. His only decoration was the princely starburst of his royal family worn at the left breast. He was attended by the Bashar Tyekanik wearing Sardaukar dress tans and heavy boots, an ornate lasegun carried in a front holster at the belt buckle. Tyekanik, whose heavy visage was known to Jessica from Bene Gesserit reports, stood three paces to the left and slightly behind Farad'n. A single throne of dark wood sat on the floor near the wall directly behind the two.

'Now,' Farad'n said, addressing Jessica, 'do you have anything to say?'

'I would inquire why we are bound thus?' Jessica said, indicating the shigawire.

'We have only just now received reports from Arrakis to explain your presence here,' Farad'n said. 'Perhaps I'll have you released presently.' He smiled. 'If you – ' He broke off as his mother entered by the State doors behind the captives.

Wensicia hurried past Jessica and Idaho without a glance, presented a small message cube to Farad'n, actuated it. He studied the glowing face, glancing occasionally at Jessica's back to the cube. The glowing face went dark and he returned the cube to his mother, indicated that she should show it to Tyekanik. While she was doing this, he scowled at Jessica.

Presently Wensicia stationed herself at Farad'n's right hand, the darkened cube in her hand, partly concealed in a fold of her white gown.

Jessica glanced to her right at Idaho, but he refused to meet her gaze.

'The Bene Gesserit are displeased with me,' Farad'n said. 'They believe I was responsible for the death of your grandson.'

Jessica held her face emotionless, thinking: *So Ghanima's story is to be trusted, unless* . . . She didn't like the suspected unknowns.

Idaho closed his eyes, opened them to glance at Jessica. She continued to stare at Farad'n. Idaho had told her about his Rhajia vision, but she'd seemed unworried. He didn't know how to catalogue her lack of emotion. She obviously knew something, though, that she wasn't revealing.

'This is the situation,' Farad'n said, and he proceeded to explain everything he'd learned about events on Arrakis, leaving out nothing. He concluded: 'Your granddaughter survives, but

193

she's reportedly in the custody of the Lady Alia. This should gratify you.'

'Did you kill my grandson?' Jessica asked.

Farad'n answered truthfully: 'I did not. I recently learned of a plot, but it was not of my making.'

Jessica looked at Wensicia, saw the gloating expression on that heart-shaped face, thought: *Her doing! The lioness schemes for her cub.* This was a game the lioness might live to regret.

Returning her attention to Farad'n, Jessica said: 'But the Sisterhood believes you killed him.'

Farad'n turned to his mother. 'Show her the message.'

As Wensicia hesitated, he spoke with an edge of anger which Jessica noted for future use. 'I said show it to her!'

Face pale, Wensicia presented the message face of the cube to Jessica, activated it. Words flowed across the face, responding to Jessica's eye movements: *'Bene Gesserit Council on Wallach IX files formal protest against House Corrino in assassination of Leto Atreides II. Arguments and showing of evidence are assigned to Landsraad Internal Security Commission. Neutral ground will be chosen and names of judge will be submitted for approval by all parties. Your immediate response required. Sabit Rekush for the Landsraad.'*

Wensicia returned to her son's side.

'How do you intend to respond?' Jessica asked.

Wensicia said: 'Since my son has not yet been formally invested as head of House Corrino, I will – Where are you going?' This last was addressed to Farad'n who, as she spoke, turned and headed for a side door near the watchful mute.

Farad'n paused, half turned. 'I'm going back to my books and the other pursuits which hold much more interest for me.'

'How dare you?' Wensicia demanded. A dark flush spread from her neck up across her cheeks.

'I'll dare quite a few things in my own name,' Farad'n said. 'You have made decisions in my name, decisions which I find extremely distasteful. Either I will make the decisions in my own name from this point on or you can find yourself another heir for House Corrino.'

Jessica passed her gaze swiftly across the participants in this confrontation, seeing the real anger in Farad'n. The Bashar Aide stood stiffly at attention, trying to make it appear that he had heard nothing. Wensicia hesitated on the brink of screaming rage. Farad'n appeared perfectly willing to accept any outcome from his throw of the dice. Jessica rather admired his poise, seeing many things in his confrontation which could be of value to her. It seemed that the decision to send assassin-tigers against her grandchildren had been made without Farad'n's knowledge. There could be little doubt of his truthfulness in saying he'd learned of the plot after its inception. There was no mistaking the real anger in his eyes as he stood there, ready to accept any decision.

Wensicia took a deep, trembling breath. Then: 'Very well. The formal investiture will take place tomorrow. You may act in advance of it now.' She looked at Tyekanik, who refused to meet her gaze.

*There'll be a screaming fight once mother and son get out of here,* Jessica thought. *But I do believe he has won.* She allowed her thoughts to return then to the message from the Landsraad. The Sisterhood had judged their messengers with a finesse which did credit to Bene Gesserit planning. Hidden in the formal notice of protest was a message for Jessica's eyes. The fact of the message said the Sisterhood's spies knew Jessica's situation and they'd gauged Farad'n with a superb nicety to guess he'd show it to his captive.

'I'd like an answer to my question,' Jessica said, addressing herself to Farad'n as he returned to face her.

'I shall tell the Landsraad that I had nothing to do with this assassination,' Farad'n said. 'I will add that I share the Sisterhood's distaste for the manner of it, although I cannot be completely displeased at the outcome. My apologies for any grief this may have caused you. Fortune passes everywhere.'

*Fortune passes everywhere!* Jessica thought. That'd been a favorite saying of her Duke, and there'd been something in Farad'n's manner which said he knew this. She forced herself to ignore the possibility that they'd really killed Leto. She had to assume that Ghanima's fears for Leto had motivated a complete revelation of the twins' plan. The smugglers would put Gurney in position to meet Leto then and the Sisterhood's devices would be carried out. Leto had to be tested. He had to be. Without the testing he was doomed as Alia was doomed. And Ghanima . . . Well, that could be faced later. There was no way to send the pre-born before a Reverend Mother Gaius Helen Mohiam.

Jessica allowed herself a deep sigh. 'Sooner or later,' she said, 'it'll occur to someone that you and my granddaughter could unite our two Houses and heal old wounds.'

'This has already been mentioned to me as a possibility,'

Farad'n said, glancing briefly at his mother. 'My response was that I'd prefer to await the outcome of recent events on Arrakis. There's no need for a hasty decision.'

'There's always the possibility that you've already played into my daughter's hands,' Jessica said.

Farad'n stiffened. 'Explain!'

'Matters on Arrakis are not as they may seem to you,' Jessica said. 'Alia plays her own game, Abomination's game. My grand-daughter is in danger unless Alia can contrive a way to use her.'

'You expect me to believe that you and your daughter oppose each other, that Atreides fights Atreides?'

Jessica looked at Wensicia, back to Farad'n. 'Corrino fights Corrino.'

A wry smile moved Farad'n's lips. 'Well taken. How would I have played into your daughter's hands?'

'By becoming implicated in my grandson's death, by abducting me.'

'Abduct . . .'

'Don't trust this witch,' Wensicia cautioned.

'I'll choose whom to trust, mother,' Farad'n said. 'Forgive me, Lady Jessica, but I don't understand this matter of abduction. I'd understand that you and your faithful retainer – '

'Who is Alia's husband,' Jessica said.

Farad'n turned a measuring stare at Idaho, looked to the Bashar. 'What think you, Tyek?'

The Bashar apparently was having thoughts similar to those Jessica professed. He said: 'I like her reasoning. Caution!'

'He's a ghola-mentat,' Farad'n said. 'We could test him to the death and not find a certain answer.'

'But it's a safe working assumption that we may've been tricked,' Tyekanik said.

Jessica knew the moment had come to make her move. Now if Idaho's grief only kept him locked in the part he'd chosen. She disliked using him this way, but there were larger considerations.

'To begin with,' Jessica said, 'I might announce publicly that I came here of my own free choice.'

'Interesting,' Farad'n said.

'You'd have to trust me and grant me the complete freedom of Salusa Secundus,' Jessica said. 'There could be no appearance that I spoke out of compulsion.'

'No!' Wensicia protested.

Farad'n ignored her. 'What reason would you give?'

'That I'm the Sisterhood's plenipotentiary sent here to take over your education.'

'But the Sisterhood accuses –'

'That'd require a decisive action from you,' Jessica said.

'Don't trust her!' Wensicia said.

With extreme politeness, Farad'n glanced at her, said: 'If you interrupt me once more, I'll have Tyek remove you. He heard you consent to the formal investiture. That binds him to *me* now.'

'She's a witch, I tell you!' Wensicia looked to the mute against the side wall.

Farad'n hesitated. Then: 'Tyek, what think you? Have I been witched?'

'Not in my judgment. She –'

'You've both been witched!'

'Mother.' His tone was flat and final.

Wensicia clenched her fists, tried to speak, whirled, and fled the room.

Addressing himself once more to Jessica, Farad'n asked: 'Would the Bene Gesserit consent to this?'

'They would.'

Farad'n absorbed the implications of this, smiled tightly. 'What does the Sisterhood want in all of this?'

'Your marriage to my granddaughter.'

Idaho shot a questioning look at Jessica, made as though to speak, but remained silent.

Jessica said: 'You were going to say something, Duncan?'

'I was going to say that the Bene Gesserit want what they've always wanted: a universe which won't interfere with them.'

'An obvious assumption,' Farad'n said, 'but I hardly see why you intrude with it.'

Idaho's eyebrows managed the shrug which the shigawire would not permit his body. Disconcertingly, he smiled.

Farad'n saw the smile, whirled to confront Idaho. 'I amuse you?'

'This whole situation amuses me. Someone in your family has compromised the Spacing Guild by using them to carry instruments of assassination to Arrakis, instruments whose intent could not be concealed. You've offended the Bene Gesserit by killing a male they wanted for their breeding pro–'

'You call me a liar, ghola?'

'No. I believe you didn't know about the plot. But I thought the situation needed bringing into focus.'

'Don't forget that he's a mentat,' Jessica cautioned.

'My very thought,' Farad'n said. Once more he faced Jessica. 'Let us say that I free you and you make your announcement. That still leaves the matter of your grandson's death. The mentat is correct.'

'Was it your mother?' Jessica asked.

'My Lord!' Tyekanik warned.

'It's all right, Tyek.' Farad'n waved a hand easily. 'And if I say it was my mother?'

Risking everything in the test of this internal break among the Corrino, Jessica said: 'You must denounce her and banish her.'

'My Lord,' Tyekanik said, 'there could be trickery within trickery here.'

Idaho said: 'And the Lady Jessica and I are the ones who've been tricked.'

Farad'n's jaw hardened.

And Jessica thought: *Don't interfere, Duncan! Not now!* But Idaho's words had sent her own Bene Gesserit abilities at logic into motion. He shocked her. She began to wonder if there were the possibility that she was being used in ways she didn't understand. Ghanima and Leto . . . The pre-born could draw upon countless inner experiences, a storehouse of advice far more extensive than the living Bene Gesserit depended upon. And there was that other question: Had her own Sisterhood been completely candid with her? They still might not trust her. After all, she'd betrayed them once . . . to her Duke.

Farad'n looked at Idaho with a puzzled frown. 'Mentat, I need to know what this Preacher is to you.'

'He arranged the passage here. I . . . We did not exchange ten words. Others acted for him. He could be . . . He could be Paul Atreides, but I don't have enough data for certainty. All I know for certain is that it was time for me to leave and he had the means.'

'You speak of being tricked,' Farad'n reminded him.

'Alia expects you to kill us quietly and conceal the evidence of it,' Idaho said. 'Having rid her of the Lady Jessica, I'm no longer useful. And the Lady Jessica, having served her Sisterhood's purposes, is no longer useful to them. Alia will be calling the Bene Gesserit to account, but they will win.'

Jessica closed her eyes in concentration. He was right! She could hear the mentat firmness in his voice, that deep sincerity of pronouncement. The pattern fell into place without a chink.

She took two deep breaths and triggered the mnemonic trance, rolled the data through her mind, came out of the trance and opened her eyes. It was done while Farad'n moved from in front of her to a position within half a step of Idaho – a space of no more than three steps.

'Say no more, Duncan,' Jessica said, and she thought mournfully of how Leto had warned her against Bene Gesserit conditioning.

Idaho, about to speak, closed his mouth.

'I command here,' Farad'n said. 'Continue, mentat.'

Idaho remained silent.

Farad'n half turned to study Jessica.

She stared at a point on the far wall, reviewing what Idaho and the trance had built. The Bene Gesserit hadn't abandoned the Atreides line, of course. But they wanted control of a Kwisatz Haderach and they'd invested too much in the long breeding program. They wanted the open clash between Atreides and Corrino, a situation where they could step in as arbiters. And Duncan was right. They'd emerge with control of both Ghanima and Farad'n. It was the only compromise possible. The wonder was that Alia hadn't seen it. Jessica swallowed past a tightness in her throat. Alia . . . Abomination! Ghanima was right to pity her. But who was left to pity Ghanima?

'The Sisterhood has promised to put you on the throne with Ghanima as your mate,' Jessica said.

Farad'n took a backward step. Did the witch read minds?

'They worked secretly and not through your mother,' Jessica said. 'They told you I was not privy to their plan.'

Jessica read revelation in Farad'n's face. How open he was. But it was true, the whole structure. Idaho had demonstrated masterful abilities as a mentat in seeing through to the fabric on the limited data available to him.

'So they played a double game and told you,' Farad'n said.

'They told me nothing of this,' Jessica said. 'Duncan was correct: they tricked me.' She nodded to herself. It had been a classic delaying action in the Sisterhood's traditional pattern – a reasonable story, easily accepted because it squared with what one might believe of their motives. But they wanted Jessica out of the way – a flawed sister who'd failed them once.

Tyekanik moved to Farad'n's side. 'My Lord, these two are too dangerous to –'

'Wait a bit, Tyek,' Farad'n said. 'There are wheels within

199

wheels here.' He faced Jessica. 'We've had reasons to believe
that Alia might offer herself as my bride.'

Idaho gave an involuntary start, controlled himself. Blood
began dripping from his left wrist where the shigawire had cut.

Jessica allowed herself a small, eye-widening response. She
who'd known the original Leto as lover, father of her children,
confidant and friend, saw his trait of cold reasoning filtered now
through the twistings of an Abomination.

'Will you accept?' Idaho asked.

'It is being considered.'

'Duncan, I told you to be silent,' Jessica said. She addressed
Farad'n. 'Her price was two inconsequential deaths – the two of
us.'

'We suspected treachery,' Farad'n said. 'Wasn't it your son
who said "treachery breeds treachery"?'

'The Sisterhood is out to control both Atreides and Corrino,'
Jessica said. 'Isn't that obvious?'

'We're toying now with the idea of accepting your offer, Lady
Jessica, but Duncan Idaho should be sent back to his loving wife.'

*Pain is a function of nerves,* Idaho reminded himself. *Pain
comes as light comes to the eyes. Effort comes from the muscles,
not from nerves.* It was an old mentat drill and he completed it in
the space of one breath, flexed his right wrist and severed an
artery against the shigawire.

Tyekanik leaped to the chair, hit its trip lock to release the
bindings, shouted for medical aid. It was revealing that assistants
came swarming at once through doors hidden in wall panels.

*There was always a bit of foolishness in Duncan,* Jessica
thought.

Farad'n studied Jessica a moment while the medics ministered
to Idaho. 'I didn't say I was going to accept his Alia.'

'That's not why he cut his wrist,' Jessica said.

'Oh? I thought he was simply removing himself.'

'You're not that stupid,' Jessica said. 'Stop pretending with
me.'

He smiled. 'I'm well aware that Alia would destroy me. Not
even the Bene Gesserit would expect me to accept her.'

Jessica bent a weighted stare upon Farad'n. What was this
young scion of House Corrino? He didn't play the fool well.
Again, she recalled Leto's words that she'd encounter an interesting student. And The Preacher wanted this as well, Idaho said.
She wished she'd met this Preacher.

'Will you banish Wensicia?' Jessica asked.

'It seems a reasonable bargain,' Farad'n said.

Jessica glanced at Idaho. The medics had finished with him. Less dangerous restraints held him in the floater chair.

'Mentats should beware of absolutes,' she said.

'I'm tired,' Idaho said. 'You've no idea how tired I am.'

'When it's overexploited, even loyalty wears out finally,' Farad'n said.

Again Jessica shot that measuring stare at him.

Farad'n, seeing this, thought: *In time she'll know me for certain and that could be valuable. A renegade Bene Gesserit of my own! It's the one thing her son had that I don't have. Let her get only a glimpse of me now. She can see the rest later.*

'A fair exchange,' Farad'n said. 'I accept your offer on your terms.' He signaled the mute against the wall with a complex flickering of fingers. The mute nodded. Farad'n bent to the chair's control, released Jessica.

Tyekanik asked: 'My Lord, are you sure?'

'Isn't it what we discussed?' Farad'n asked.

'Yes, but . . .'

Farad'n chuckled, addressed Jessica. 'Tyek suspects my sources. But one learns from books and reels only that certain things can be done. Actual learning requires that you do those things.'

Jessica mused on this as she lifted herself from the chair. Her mind returned to Farad'n's hand signals. He had an Atreides-style battle language! It spoke of careful analysis. Someone here was consciously copying the Atreides.

'Of course,' Jessica said, 'you'll want me to teach you as the Bene Gesserit are taught.'

Farad'n beamed at her. 'The one offer I cannot resist,' he said.

> *The password was given to me by a man who died in the dungeons of Arrakeen. You see, that is where I got this ring in the shape of a tortoise. It was in the suk outside the city where I was hidden by the rebels. The password? Oh, that has been changed many times since then. It was 'Persistence'. And the countersign was 'Tortoise'. It got me out of there alive. That's why I bought this ring : a reminder.*
>
> – Tagir Mohandis: Conversations with a Friend

Leto was far out on the sand when he heard the worm behind him, coming to his thumper there and the dusting of spice he'd spread around the dead tigers. There was a good omen for this beginning of their plan: worms were scarce enough in these parts most times. The worm was not essential, but it helped. There would be no need for Ghanima to explain a missing body.

By this time he knew that Ghanima had worked herself into the belief that he was dead. Only a tiny, isolated capsule of awareness would remain to her, a walled-off memory which could be recalled by words uttered in the ancient language shared only by the two of them in all of this universe. *Secher Nbiw.* If she heard those words: *Golden Path* ... only then would she remember him. Until then, he was dead.

Now Leto felt truly alone.

He moved with the random walk which made only those sounds natural to the desert. Nothing in his passage would tell that worm back there that human flesh moved here. It was a way of walking so deeply conditioned in him that he didn't need to think about it. The feet moved of themselves, no measurable rhythm to their pacing. Any sound his feet made could be ascribed to the wind, to gravity. No human passed here.

When the worm had done its work behind him, Leto crouched behind a dune's slipface and peered back toward The Attendant. Yes, he was far enough. He planted a thumper and summoned his transportation. The worm came swiftly, giving him barely enough time to position himself before it engulfed the thumper. As it passed, he went up its side on the Maker hooks, opened the sensitive leading edge of a ring, and turned the mindless beast southeastward. It was a small worm, but strong. He could sense the strength in its twisting as it hissed across the dunes. There was a following breeze and he felt the heat of their passage, the friction which the worm converted to the beginnings of spice within itself.

As the worm moved, his mind moved. Stilgar had taken him up for his first worm journey. Leto had only to let his memory flow and he could hear Stilgar's voice: calm and precise, full of politeness from another age. Not for Stilgar the threatening staggers of a Fremen drunk on spice-liquor. Not for Stilgar the loud voice and bluster of these times. No – Stilgar had his duties. He was an instructor of royalty: 'In the olden times, the birds were named for their songs. Each wind had its name. A six-klick wind was called a Pastaza, a twenty-klick wind was Cueshma, and a hundred-klick wind was Heinali – Heinali, the man-pusher. Then there was the wind of the demon on the open desert: Hulasikali Wala, the wind that eats flesh.'

And Leto, who'd already known these things, had nodded his gratitude at the wisdom of such instruction.

But Stilgar's voice could be filled with many valuable things.

'There were in olden times certain tribes which were known to be water hunters. They were called Iduali, which meant "water insects", because those people wouldn't hesitate to steal the water of another Fremen. If they caught you alone in the desert they would not even leave you the water of your flesh. There was this place where they lived: Sietch Jacurutu. That's where the other tribes banded and wiped out the Iduali. That was a long time ago, before Keynes even – in my great-great-grandfather's days. And from that day to this, no Fremen has gone to Jacurutu. It is tabu.'

Thus had Leto been reminded of knowledge which lay in his memory. It had been an important lesson about the working of memory. A memory was not enough, even for one whose past was as multiform as his, unless its use was known and its value revealed to judgment. Jacurutu would have water, a windtrap, all of the attributes of a Fremen sietch, plus the value without compare that no Fremen would venture there. Many of the young would not even know such a place as Jacurutu had ever existed. Oh, they would know about Fondak, of course, but that was a smuggler place.

It was a perfect place for the dead to hide – among the smugglers and the dead of another age.

*Thank you, Stilgar.*

The worm tired before dawn. Leto slid off its side and watched it dig itself into the dunes, moving slowly in the familiar pattern of the creatures. It would go deep and sulk.

*I must wait out the day,* he thought.

He stood atop a dune and scanned all around: emptiness, emptiness, emptiness. Only the wavering track of the vanished worm broke the pattern.

The slow cry of a nightbird challenged the first green line of light along the eastern horizon. Leto dug himself into the sand's concealment, inflated a stilltent around his body and sent the tip of a sandsnorkel questioning for air.

For a long time before sleep came, he lay in the enforced darkness thinking about the decision he and Ghanima had made. It had not been an easy decision, especially for Ghanima. He had not told her all of his vision, nor all of the reasoning derived from it. It was a vision, not a dream, in his thinking now. But the peculiarity of this thing was that he saw it as a vision of a vision. If any argument existed to convince him that his father still lived, it lay in that vision-vision.

*The life of the prophet locks us into his vision,* Leto thought. *And a prophet could only break out of the vision by creating his death at variance with that vision.* That was how it appeared in Leto's doubled vision, and he pondered this as it related to the choice he had made. *Poor Baptist John,* he thought. *If he'd only the courage to die some other way . . . But perhaps his choice had been the bravest one. How do I know what alternatives faced him? I know what alternatives faced my father, though.*

Leto sighed. To turn his back on his father was like betraying a god. But the Atreides Empire needed shaking up. It had fallen into the worst of Paul's vision. How casually it obliterated men. It was done without a second thought. The mainspring of a religious insanity had been wound tight and left ticking.

*And we're locked in my father's vision.*

A way out of that insanity lay along the Golden Path, Leto knew. His father had seen it. But humanity might come out of that Golden Path and look back down it at Muad'Dib's time, seeing that as a better age. Humankind had to experience the alternative to Muad'Dib, though, or never understand its own myths.

*Security . . . peace . . . prosperity . . .*

Given the choice, there was little doubt what most citizens of this Empire would select.

*Though they hate me,* he thought. *Though Ghani hate me.*

His right hand itched, and he thought of the terrible glove in his vision-vision. *It will be,* he thought. *Yes, it will be.*

*Arrakis, give me strength,* he prayed. His planet remained strong and alive beneath him and around him. Its sand pressed close against the stilltent. Dune was a giant counting its massed riches. It was a beguiling entity, both beautiful and grossly ugly. The only coin its merchants really knew was the bloodpulse of their own power, no matter how that power had been amassed. They possessed this planet the way a man might possess a captive mistress, or the way the Bene Gesserits possessed their Sisters.

No wonder Stilgar hated the merchant-priests.

*Thank you, Stilgar.*

Leto recalled the beauties of the old sietch ways, the life lived before the coming of the Imperium's technocracy, and his mind flowed as he knew Stilgar's dreams flowed. Before the glow-globes and lasers, before the ornithopters and spice-crawlers there'd been another kind of life: brown-skinned mothers with babies on their hips, lamps which burned spice-oil amidst a heavy fragrance of cinnamon, Naibs who persuaded their people while knowing none could be compelled. It had been a darkswarming of life in rocky burrows . . .

*A terrible glove will restore the balance,* Leto thought. Presently, he slept.

> *I saw his blood and a piece of his robe which had been ripped by sharp claws. His sister reports vividly of the tigers, the sureness of their attack. We have questioned one of the plotters, and others are dead or in custody. Everything points to a Corrino plot. A Truthsayer has attested to this testimony.*
>
> > – Stilgar's Report
> > to the Landsraad Commission

Farad'n studied Duncan Idaho through the spy circuit, seeking a clue to that strange man's behavior. It was shortly after noon and Idaho waited outside the quarters assigned to the Lady Jessica, seeking audience with her. Would she see him? She'd know they were spied upon, of course. But would she see him?

Around Farad'n lay the room where Tyekanik had guided the training of the Laza tigers – an illegal room, really, filled as it was with forbidden instruments from the hands of the Tleilaxu and Ixians. By the movement of switches at his right hand, Farad'n could look at Idaho from six different angles, or shift to the interior of the Lady Jessica's suite where the spying facilities were equally sophisticated.

Idaho's eyes bothered Farad'n. Those pitted metal orbs which the Tleilaxu had given their ghola in the regrowth tanks marked their possessor as profoundly different from other humans. Farad'n touched his own eyelids, feeling the hard surfaces of the permanent contact lenses which concealed the total blue of his spice addiction. Idaho's eyes must record a different universe. How could it be otherwise. It almost tempted Farad'n to seek out the Tleilaxu surgeons and answer that question himself.

*Why did Idaho try to kill himself?*

*Was that really what he'd tried? He must've known we wouldn't permit it.*

*Idaho remained a dangerous question mark.*

Tyekanik wanted to keep him on Salusa or kill him. Perhaps that would be best.

Farad'n shifted to the frontal view. Idaho sat on a hard bench outside the door to the Lady Jessica's suite. It was a windowless foyer with light wood walls decorated by lance pennants. Idaho had been on that bench more than an hour and appeared ready to wait there forever. Farad'n bent close to the screen. The loyal swordmaster of the Atreides, instructor of Paul Muad'Dib, had been treated kindly by his years on Arrakis. He'd arrived with a youthful spring in his step. A steady spice diet must have helped him, of course. And that marvelous metabolic balance which the Tleilaxu tanks always imparted. Did Idaho really remember his past before the tanks? No other whom the Tleilaxu had revived could claim this. What an enigma this Idaho was!

The reports of his death were in the library. The Sardaukar who'd slain him reported his prowess: nineteen of their number dispatched by Idaho before he'd fallen. Nineteen Sardaukar! His flesh had been well worth sending to the regrowth tanks. But the Tleilaxu had made a mentat out of him. What a strange creature lived in that regrown flesh. How did it feel to be a human computer in addition to all of his other talents?

*Why did he try to kill himself?*

Farad'n knew his own talents and held few illusions about them. He was a historian-archaeologist and judge of men. Necessity had forced him to become an expert on those who would serve him – necessity and a careful study of the Atreides. He saw it as the price always demanded of aristocracy. To rule required accurate and incisive judgments about those who wielded your power. More than one ruler had fallen through mistakes and excesses of his underlings.

Careful study of the Atreides revealed a superb talent in choosing servants. They'd known how to maintain loyalty, how to keep a fine edge on the ardor of their warriors.

Idaho was not acting in character.

*Why?*

Farad'n squinted his eyes, trying to see past the skin of this man. There was a sense of duration about Idaho, a feeling that he could not be worn down. He gave the impression of being self-contained, an organized and firmly integrated whole. The Tleilaxu tanks had set something more than human into motion. Farad'n sensed this. There was a self-renewing movement about the man, as though he acted in accordance with immutable laws, beginnnig anew at every ending. He moved in a fixed orbit with an endurance about him like that of a planet around a star. He would respond to pressure without breaking – merely shifting his orbit slightly but not really changing anything basic.

*Why did he cut his wrist?*

Whatever his motive, he had done it for the Atreides, for his ruling House. The Atreides were the star of his orbit.

*Somehow he believes that my holding the Lady Jessica here strengthens the Atreides.*

And Farad'n reminded himself: *A mentat thinks this.*

It gave the thought an added depth. Mentats made mistakes, but not often.

Having come to this conclusion. Farad'n almost summoned his aides to have them send the Lady Jessica away with Idaho. He poised himself on the point of acting, withdrew.

Both of those people – the ghola-mentat and the Bene Gesserit witch – remained counters of unknown denomination in this game of power. Idaho must be sent back because that would certainly stir up troubles on Arrakis. Jessica must be kept here, drained of her strange knowledge to benefit House Corrino.

Farad'n knew it was a subtle and deadly game he played. But he had prepared himself for this possibility over the years, ever since he'd realized that he was more intelligent, more sensitive than those around him. It had been a frightening discovery for a child, and he knew the library had been his refuge as well as his teacher.

Doubts ate at him now, though, and he wondered if he was quite up to this game. He'd alienated his mother, lost her counsel, but her decisions had always been dangerous to him. Tigers! Their training had been an atrocity and their use had been stupidity. How easy they were to trace! She should be thankful to suffer nothing more than banishment. The Lady Jessica's advice had fitted his needs with a lovely precision there. She must be made to divulge the way of that Atreides thinking.

His doubts began to fade away. He thought of his Sardaukar once more growing tough and resilient through the rigorous training and the denial of luxury which he commanded. His Sardaukar legions remained small, but once more they were a man-to-man match for the Fremen. That served little purpose as long as the limits imposed by the Treaty of Arrakeen governed the relative size of the forces. Fremen could overwhelm him by their numbers – unless they were tied up and weakened by civil war.

It was too soon for a battle of Sardaukar against Fremen. He needed time. He needed new allies from among the discontented Houses Major and the newly powerful from the Houses Minor.

He needed access to CHOAM financing. He needed the time for his Sardaukar to grow stronger and the Fremen to grow weaker.

Again Farad'n looked at the screen which revealed the patient ghola. Why did Idaho want to see the Lady Jessica at this time? He would know they were spied upon, that every word, every gesture would be recorded and analyzed.

*Why?*

Farad'n glanced away from the screen to the ledge beside his control console. In the pale electronic light he could make out the spools which contained the latest reports from Arrakis. His spies were thorough; he had to give them credit. There was much to give him hope and pleasure in those reports. He closed his eyes, and the high points of those reports passed through his mind in the oddly editorial form to which he'd reduced the spools for his own uses:

*As the planet is made fertile, Fremen are freed of land pressures and their new communities lose the traditional sietch-stronghold character. From infancy, in the old sietch culture, the Fremen was taught by the rota: 'Like the knowledge of your own being, the sietch forms a firm base from which you move out into the world and into the universe.'*

*The traditional Fremen says: 'Look to the Massif,' meaning that the master science is the Law. But the new social structure is loosening those old legal restrictions; discipline grows lax. The new Fremen leaders know only their Low Catechism of ancestry plus the history which is camouflaged in the myth structure of their songs. People of the new communities are more volatile, more open; they quarrel more often and are less responsive to authority. The old sietch folk are more disciplined, more inclined to group actions and they tend to work harder; they are more careful of their resources. The old folk still believe that the orderly society is the fulfillment of the individual. The young grow away from this belief. Those remnants of the older culture which remain look at the young and say: 'The death wind has etched away their past.'*

Farad'n liked the pointedness of his own summary. The new diversity on Arrakis could only bring violence. He had the essential concepts firmly etched into the spools:

*The religion of Muad'Dib is based firmly in the old Fremen sietch cultural tradition while the new culture moves farther and farther from those disciplines.*

Not for the first time, Farad'n asked himself why Tyekanik had embraced that religion. Tyekanik behaved oddly in his new morality. He seemed utterly sincere, but carried along as though against his will. Tyekanik was like one who had stepped into the whirlwind to test it and had been caught up by forces beyond his control. Tyekanik's conversion annoyed Farad'n by its character-less completeness. It was a reversion to very old Sardaukar ways. He warned that the young Fremen might yet revert in a similar way, that the inborn, ingrained traditions would prevail.

Once more Farad'n thought about those report spools. They told of a disquieting thing: the persistence of a cultural remnant from the most ancient Fremen times – 'The Water of Concep-tion'. The amniotic fluid of the newborn was saved at birth, distilled into the first water fed to that child. The traditional form required a godmother to serve the water, saying: 'Here is the water of thy conception.' Even the young Fremen still followed this tradition with their own new-born.

*The water of thy conception.*

Farad'n found himself revolted by the idea of drinking water distilled from the amniotic fluid which had borne him. And he thought about the surviving twin, Ghanima, her mother dead when she'd taken that strange water. Had she reflected later upon that odd link with her past? Probably not. She'd been raised Fremen. What was natural and acceptable to Fremen had been natural and acceptable to her.

Momentarily Farad'n regretted the death of Leto II. It would have been interesting to discuss this point with him. Perhaps an opportunity would come to discuss it with Ghanima.

*Why did Idaho cut his wrists?*

The question persisted every time he glanced at the spy screen. Again doubts assailed Farad'n. He longed for the ability to sink into the mysterious spice trance as Paul Muad'Dib had done, there to seek out the future and *know* the answers to his questions. No matter how much spice he ingested, though, his ordinary awareness persisted in its singular flow of *now*, reflecting a universe of uncertainties.

The spy screen showed a servant opening the Lady Jessica's door. The woman beckoned Idaho, who arose from the bench and went through the door. The servant would file a complete report later, but Farad'n, his curiosity once more fully aroused, touched another switch on his console, watched as Idaho entered the sitting room of the Lady Jessica's quarters.

How calm and contained the mentat appeared. And how fathomless were his ghola eyes.

*Above all else, the mentat must be a generalist, not a specialist. It is wise to have decisions of great moment monitored by generalists. Experts and specialists lead you quickly into chaos. They are a source of useless nit-picking, the ferocious quibble over a comma. The mentat-generalist, on the other hand, should bring to decision-making a healthy common sense. He must not cut himself off from the broad sweep of what is happening in his universe. He must remain capable of saying : 'There's no real mystery about this at the moment. This is what we want now. It may prove wrong later, but we'll correct that when we come to it.' The mentat-generalist must understand that anything which we can identify as our universe is merely part of larger phenomena. But the expert looks backward; he looks into the narrow standards of his own specialty. The generalist looks outward; he looks for living principles, knowing full well that such principles change, that they develop. It is to the characteristics of change itself that the mentat-generalist must look. There can be no permanent catalogue of such change, no handbook or manual. You must look at it with as few preconceptions as possible, asking yourself : 'Now what is this thing doing?'*

— The Mentat Handbook

It was the day of the Kwisatz Haderach, the first Holy Day of those who followed Muad'Dib. It recognized the deified Paul Atreides as that person who was everywhere simultaneously, the male Bene Gesserit who mingled both male and female ancestry in an inseparable power to become the One-with-All. The faithful called this day *Ayil*, the Sacrifice, to commemorate the death which made his presence 'real in all places'.

The Preacher chose the early morning of this day to appear once more in the plaza of Alia's temple, defying the order for his arrest which everyone knew had been issued. The delicate truce prevailed between Alia's Priesthood and those desert tribes which had rebelled, but the presence of this truce could be felt as a tangible thing which moved everyone in Arrakeen with uneasiness. The Preacher did not dispel that mood.

It was the twenty-eighth day of official mourning for Muad-'Dib's son, six days following the memorial rite at Old Pass which had been delayed by the rebellion. Even the fighting had not stopped the Hajj, though. The Preacher knew the plaza would be heavily thronged on this day. Most pilgrims tried to time their stay on Arrakis to cross *Ayil*, 'to feel then the Holy Presence of the Kwisatz Haderach on His day.'

The Preacher entered the plaza at first light, finding the place already thronging with the faithful. He kept a hand lightly on the shoulder of his young guide, sensing the cynical pride in the lad's walk. Now, when the Preacher approached, people noticed every nuance of his behavior. Such attention was not entirely distasteful to the young guide. The Preacher merely accepted it as a necessity.

Taking his stance on the third of the Temple's steps, The Preacher waited for the hush to come. When silence had spread like a wave through the throng and the hurrying footsteps of others come to listen could be heard at the plaza's limits, he cleared his throat. It was still morning-cold around him and light had not yet come down into the plaza from the building tops. He felt the gray hush of the great square as he began to speak.

'I have come to give homage and to preach in the memory of Leto Atreides II,' he said, calling out in that strong voice so reminiscent of a wormsman from the desert. 'I do it in compassion for all who suffer. I say to you what the dead Leto has learned, that tomorrow has not yet happened and may never happen. This moment here is the only observable time and place for us in our universe. I tell you to savor this moment and understand what it teaches. I tell you to learn that a government's growth and its death are apparent in the growth and death of its citizens.'

A disturbed murmur passed through the plaza. Did he mock the death of Leto II? They wondered if Priest Guards would rush out now and arrest The Preacher.

Alia knew there would be no such interruption of The Preacher. It was her order that he be left unmolested on this day. She had disguised herself in a good stillsuit with a moisture mask to conceal her nose and mouth, and a common hooded robe to hide her hair. She stood in the second row beneath the Preacher, watching him carefully. Was this Paul? The years might have changed him thus. And he had always been superb with Voice, a fact which made it difficult to identify him by his speech. Still, this Preacher made his voice do what he wanted. Paul could not have done it better. She felt that she had to know his identity before she could act against him. How his words dazzled her!

She sensed no irony in The Preacher's statement. He was using the seductive attraction of definite sentences uttered with a driving sincerity. People might stumble only momentarily at his meanings, realizing that he had meant them to stumble, teaching

211

them in this fashion. Indeed, he picked up the crowd's response, saying: 'Irony often masks the inability to think beyond one's assumptions. I am not being ironic. Ghanima has said to you that the blood of her brother cannot be washed off. I concur.

'It will be said that Leto has gone where his father went, has done what his father did. Muad'Dib's Church says he chose in behalf of his own humanity a course which might appear absurd and foolhardy, but which history will validate. That history is being rewritten even now.

'I say to you that there is another lesson to be learned from these lives and their endings.'

Alia, alert to every nuance, asked herself why The Preacher said *endings* instead of *deaths*. Was he saying that one or both were now truly dead? How could that be? A Truthsayer had confirmed Ghanima's story. What was this Preacher doing, then? Was he making a statement of myth or reality?

'Note this other lesson well!' The Preacher thundered, lifting his arms. 'If you would possess your humanity, let go of the universe!'

He lowered his arms, pointed his empty sockets directly at Alia. He seemed to be speaking intimately to her, an action so obvious that several around her turned to peer inquiringly in her direction. Alia shivered at the power in him. This could be Paul. It could!

'But I realize that humans cannot bear very much reality,' he said. 'Most lives are a flight from selfhood. Most prefer the truths of the stable. You stick your heads into the stanchions and munch contentedly until you die. Others use you for their purposes. Not once do you live outside the stable to lift your head and be your own creature. Muad'Dib came to tell you about that. Without understanding his message, you cannot revere him!'

Someone in the throng, possibly a Priest in disguise, could stand no more. His hoarse male voice was lifted in a shout: 'You don't live the life of Muad'Dib! How dare you to tell others how they must revere him!'

'Because he's dead!' The Preacher bellowed.

Alia turned to see who had challenged The Preacher. The man remained hidden from her, but his voice came over the intervening heads in another shout: 'If you believe him truly dead, then you are alone from this time forward!'

Surely it was a Priest, Alia thought. But she failed to recognize the voice.

'I come only to ask a simple question,' The Preacher said. 'Is

Muad'Dib's death to be followed by the moral suicide of all men? Is that the inevitable aftermath of a Messiah?'

'Then you admit him Messiah!' the voice from the crowd shouted.

'Why not, since I'm the prophet of his times?' The Preacher asked.

There was such calm assurance in his tone and manner that even his challenger fell silent. The crowd responded with a disturbed murmur, a low animal sound.

'Yes,' The Preacher repeated, 'I am the prophet of these times.'

Alia, concentrating on him, detected the subtle inflections of Voice. He'd certainly controlled the crowd. Was he Bene Gesserit trained? Was this another ploy of the Missionaria Protectiva? Not Paul at all, but just another part of the endless power game?

'I articulate the myth and the dream!' The Preacher shouted. 'I am the physician who delivers the child and announces that the child is born. Yet I come to you at a time of death. Does that not disturb you? It should shake your souls!'

Even as she felt anger at his words, Alia understood the pointed way of his speech. With others, she found herself edging closer up the steps, crowding toward this tall man in desert garb. His young guide caught her attention: how bright-eyed and saucy the lad appeared! Would Muad'Dib employ such a cynical youth?

'I mean to disturb you!' The Preacher shouted. 'It is my intention! I come here to combat the fraud and illusion of your conventional, institutionalized religion. As with all such religions, your institution moves toward cowardice, it moves toward mediocrity, inertia, and self-satisfaction.'

Angry murmurs began to arise in the center of the throng.

Alia felt the tensions and gloatingly wondered if there might not be a riot. Could The Preacher handle these tensions? If not, he could die right here!

'That Priest who challenged me!' The Preacher called, pointing into the crowd.

*He knows!* Alia thought. A thrill ran through her, almost sexual in its undertones. This Preacher played a dangerous game, but he played it consummately.

'You, Priest in your mufti,' The Preacher called, 'you are a chaplain to the self-satisfied. I come not to challenge Muad'Dib but to challenge you! Is your religion real when it costs you nothing and carries no risk? Is your religion real when you fatten upon it? Is your religion real when you commit atrocities in its

213

name? Whence comes your downward degeneration from the original revelation? Answer me, Priest!'

But the challenger remained silent. And Alia noted that the crowd once more was listening with avid submission to The Preacher's every word. By attacking the Priesthood, he had their sympathy! And if her spies were correct, most of the pilgrims and Fremen on Arrakis believed this man was Muad'Dib.

'The son of Muad'Dib risked!' The Preacher shouted, and Alia heard tears in his voice. 'Muad'Dib risked! They paid their price! And what did Muad'Dib achieve? A religion which is doing away with him!'

*How different those words if they come from Paul himself,* Alia thought. *I must find out!* She moved closer up the steps and others moved with her. She pressed through the throng until she could almost reach out and touch this mysterious prophet. She smelled the desert on him, a mixture of spice and flint. Both The Preacher and his young guide were dusty, as though they'd recently come from the *bled.* She could see where The Preacher's hands were deeply veined along the skin protruding from the wrist seals of his stillsuit. She could see that one finger of his left hand had worn a ring; the indentation remained. Paul had worn a ring on that finger: the Atreides Hawk which now reposed in Sietch Tabr. Leto would have worn it had he lived . . . or had she permitted him to ascend the throne.

Again The Preacher aimed his empty sockets at Alia, spoke intimately, but with a voice which carried across the throng.

'Muad'Dib showed you two things: a certain future and an uncertain future. With full awareness, he confronted the ultimate uncertainty of the larger universe. He stepped off *blindly* from his position on this world. He showed us that men must do this always, choosing the uncertain instead of the certain.' His voice, Alia noted, took on a pleading tone at the end of this statement.

Alia glanced around, slipped a hand onto the hilt of her crysknife. *If I killed him right now, what would they do?* Again, she felt a thrill rush through her. *If I killed him and revealed myself, denouncing The Preacher as imposter and heretic!*

But what if they proved it was Paul?

Someone pushed Alia even closer to him. She felt herself enthralled by his presence even as she fought to still her anger. Was this Paul? Gods below! What could she do?

'Why has another Leto been taken from us?' The Preacher demanded. There was real pain in his voice. 'Answer me if you can! Ahhhh, their message is clear: abandon certainty.' He repeated it in a rolling stentorian shout: 'Abandon certainty! That's life's deepest command. That's what life's all about. We're a probe into the unknown, into the uncertain. Why can't you hear Muad'Dib? If certainty is knowing absolutely an absolute future, then that's only death disguised! Such a future becomes *now*! He showed you this!'

With a terrifying directness The Preacher reached out, grabbed Alia's arm. It was done without any groping or hesitation. She tried to pull away, but he held her in a painful grip, speaking directly into her face as those around them edged back in confusion.

'What did Paul Atreides tell you, woman?' he demanded.

*How does he know I'm a woman?* she asked herself. She wanted to sink into her inner lives, ask their protection, but the world within remained frighteningly silent, mesmerized by this figure from their past.

'He told you that completion equals death!' The Preacher shouted. 'Absolute prediction is completion . . . is death!'

She tried to pry his fingers away. She wanted to grab her knife and slash him away from her, but dared not. She had never felt this daunted in all of her life.

The Preacher lifted his chin to speak over her to the crowd, shouted: 'I give you Muad'Dib's words! He said, "I'm going to rub your faces in things you try to avoid. I don't find it strange that all you want to believe is only that which comforts you. How else do humans invent the traps which betray us into mediocrity? How else do we define cowardice?" That's what Muad'Dib told you!'

Abruptly he released Alia's arm, thrust her into the crowd. She would have fallen but for the press of people supporting her.

'To exist is to stand out, away from the background,' The Preacher said. 'You aren't thinking or really existing unless you're willing to risk even your own sanity in the judgment of your existence.'

Stepping down, The Preacher once more took Alia's arm – no faltering or hesitation. He was gentler this time, though. Leaning close, he pitched his voice for her ears alone, said: 'Stop trying to pull me once more into the background, sister.'

Then, hand on his young guide's shoulder, he stepped into the throng. Way was made for the strange pair. Hands reached out to touch The Preacher, but people reached with an awesome tenderness, fearful of what they might find beneath that dusty Fremen robe.

Alia stood alone in her shock as the throng moved out behind The Preacher.

Certainty filled her. It was Paul. No doubt remained. It was her brother. She felt what the crowd felt. She had stood in the sacred presence and now her universe tumbled all about her. She wanted to run after him, pleading for him to save her from herself, but she could not move. While others pressed to follow The Preacher and his guide, she stood intoxicated with an absolute despair, a distress so deep that she could only tremble with it, unable to command her own muscles.

*What will I do? What will I do?* she asked herself.

Now she did not even have Duncan to lean upon, nor her mother. The inner lives remained silent. There was Ghanima, held securely under guard within the Keep, but Alia could not bring herself to take this distress to the surviving twin.

*Everyone has turned against me. What can I do?*

> *The one-eyed view of our universe says you must not look far afield for problems. Such problems may never arrive. Instead, tend to the wolf within your fences. The packs ranging outside may not even exist.*
>
> – The Azhar Book: Shamra I:4

Jessica awaited Idaho at the window of her sitting room. It was a comfortable room with soft divans and old-fashioned chairs. There wasn't a suspensor in any of her rooms, and the glowglobes were crystal from another age. Her window overlooked a courtyard garden one story down.

She heard the servant open the door, then the sound of Idaho's footsteps on the wood floor, then on the carpet. She listened without turning, kept her gaze upon the dappled light of the courtyard's green floor. The silent, fearful warfare of her emotions must be suppressed now. She took the deep breaths of her *prana-bindu* training, felt the outflow of enforced calmness.

The high sun threw its searchlight along a dustbeam into the courtyard, highlighting the silver wheel of a spider-web stretched in the branches of a linden tree which reached almost to her window. It was cool within her quarters, but outside the sealed window there was air which trembled with petrified heat. Castle Corrino sat in a stagnant place which belied the greens in her courtyard.

She heard Idaho stop directly behind her.

Without turning, she said: 'The gift of words is the gift of deception and illusion, Duncan. Why do you wish words with me?'

'It may be that only one of us will survive,' he said.

'And you wish me to make a good report of your efforts?' She turned, saw how calmly he stood there, watching her with those gray metal eyes which held no center of focus. How blank they were!

'Duncan, is it possible that you're jealous of your place in history?'

She spoke accusingly and remembered as she spoke that other time when she'd confronted this man. He'd been drunk then, set to spy upon her, and was torn by conflicting obligations. But that had been a pre-ghola Duncan. This was not the same man at all. This one was not divided in his actions, not torn.

He proved her summation by smiling. 'History holds its own court and delivers its own judgments,' he said. 'I doubt that I'll be concerned when my judgment's handed down.'

'Why are you here?' she asked.

'For the same reason you're here, My Lady.'

No outward sign betrayed the shocking power of those simple words, but she reflected at a furious pace: *Does he really know why I'm here?* How could he? Only Ghanima knew. Then had he enough data for a mentat computation? That was possible. And what if he said something to give her away? Would he do that if he shared her reason for being here? He must know their every movement, every word was being spied upon by Farad'n or his servants.

'House Atreides has come to a bitter crossroads,' she said. 'Family turned against itself. You were among my Duke's most loyal men, Duncan. When the Baron Harkonnen –'

'Let us not speak of Harkonnens,' he said. 'That was another age and your Duke is dead.' And he wondered: *Can't she guess that Paul revealed the Harkonnen blood in the Atreides?* What a risk that had been for Paul, but it had bound Duncan Idaho even more firmly to him. The trust in the revelation had been a coin almost too great to imagine. Paul had known what the Baron's people had done to Idaho.

'House Atreides is not dead,' Jessica said.

'What is House Atreides?' he asked. 'Are you House Atreides? Is it Alia? Ghanima? Is it the people who serve this House? I look at those people and they bear the stamp of a travail beyond

217

words! How can they be Atreides? Your son said it rightly: "Travail and persecution are the lot of all who follow me." I would break myself away from that, My Lady.'

'Have you really gone over to Farad'n?'

'Isn't that what you've done, My Lady? Didn't you come here to convince Farad'n that a marriage to Ghanima would solve all of our problems?'

*Does he really think that?* she wondered. *Or is he talking for the watchful spies?*

'House Atreides has always been essentially an idea,' she said. 'You know that, Duncan. We bought loyalty with loyalty.'

'Service to the people,' Idaho sneered. 'Ahhh, many's the time I've heard your Duke say it. He must lie uneasy in his grave, My Lady.'

'Do you really think us fallen that low?'

'My lady, did you not know that there are Fremen rebels – they call themselves "Maquis of the Inner Desert" – who curse House Atreides and even Muad'Dib?'

'I heard Farad'n's report,' she said, wondering where he was leading this conversation and to what point.

'More than that, My Lady. More than Farad'n's report. I've heard their curse myself. Here's the way of it: "Burning be on you, Atreides! You shall have no souls, nor spirits, nor bodies, nor shades nor magic nor bones, nor hair nor utterances nor words. You shall have no grave, nor house nor hole nor tomb. You shall have no garden, nor tree nor bush. You shall have no water, nor bread nor light nor fire. You shall have no children, nor family nor heirs nor tribe. You shall have no head, nor arms nor legs nor gait nor seed. You shall have no seats on any planet. Your souls shall not be permitted to come up from the depths, and they shall never be among those permitted to live upon the earth. On no day shall you behold Shai-Hulud, but you shall be bound and fettered in the nethermost abomination and your souls shall never enter into the glorious light for ever and ever." That's the way of the curse, My Lady. Can you imagine such hatred from Fremen? They consign all Atreides to the left hand of the damned, to the Woman-Sun which is full of burning.'

Jessica allowed herself a shudder. Idaho undoubtedly had delivered those words with the same voice in which he'd heard the original curse. Why did he expose this to House Corrino? She could picture an outraged Fremen, terrible in his anger, standing before his tribe to vent that ancient curse. Why did Idaho want Farad'n to hear it?

'You make a strong argument for the marriage of Ghanima and Farad'n,' she said.

'You always did have a single-minded approach to problems,' he said. 'Ghanima's Fremen. She can marry only one who pays no *fai*, no tax for protection. House Corrino gave up its entire CHOAM holdings to your son and his heirs. Farad'n exists on Atreides suffrance. And remember when your Duke planted the Hawk flag on Arrakis, remember what he said: "Here I am; here I remain!" His bones are still there. And Farad'n would have to live on Arrakis, his Sardaukar with him.'

Idaho shook his head at the very thought of such an alliance.

'There's an old saying that one peels a problem like an onion,' she said, her voice cold. *How dare he patronize me? Unless he's performing for Farad'n's watchful eyes . . .*

'Somehow, I can't see Fremen and Sardaukar sharing a planet,' Idaho said. 'That's a layer which doesn't come off the onion.'

She didn't like the thoughts which Idaho's words might arouse in Farad'n and his advisors, spoke sharply: 'House Atreides is still the law in this Empire!' And she thought: *Does Idaho want Farad'n to believe he can regain the throne without the Atreides?*

'Oh, yes,' Idaho said. 'I almost forgot. Atreides Law! As translated, of course, by the Priests of the Golden Elixir. I have but to close my eyes and I hear your Duke telling me that real estate is always gained and held by violence or the threat of it. Fortune passes everywhere, as Gurney used to sing it. The end justifies the means? Or do I have my proverbs mixed up? Well, it doesn't matter whether the mailed fist is brandished openly by Fremen legions or Sardaukar, or whether it's hidden in the Atreides Law – the fist is still there. And the onion layer won't come off, My Lady. You know, I wonder which fist Farad'n will demand?'

*What is he doing?* Jessica wondered. House Corrino would soak up this argument and gloat over it!

'So you think the Priests wouldn't let Ghanima marry Farad'n?' Jessica ventured, probing to see where Idaho's words might be leading.

'Let her? Gods below! The Priests will let Alia do whatever she decrees. She could marry Farad'n herself!'

*Is that where he's fishing?* Jessica wondered.

'No, My Lady,' Idaho said. 'That's not the issue. This Empire's people cannot distinguish between Atreides government and the government of Beast Rabban. Men die every day in Arrakeen's dungeons. I left because I could not give my sword arm another hour to the Atreides! Don't you understand what

219

I'm saying, why I came here to you as the nearest Atreides representative? The Atreides Empire has betrayed your Duke and your son. I loved your daughter, but she went one way and I went another. If it comes down to it, I'll advise Farad'n to accept Ghanima's hand – or Alia's – only on his own terms!'

*Ahhh, he sets the stage for a formal withdrawal with honor from Atreides service,* she thought. But these other matters of which he spoke, could he possibly know how well they did her work for her? She scowled at him. 'You know spies are listening to every word, don't you?'

'Spies?' He chuckled. 'They listen as I would listen in their place. Don't you know how my loyalties move in a different way? Many's the night I've spent alone in the desert, and the Fremen are right about that place. In the desert, especially at night, you encounter the dangers of hard thinking.'

'Is that where you heard Fremen curse us?'

'Yes. Among the al-Ourouba. At The Preacher's bidding I joined them, My Lady. We call ourselves the Zarr Sadus, those who refuse to submit to the Priests. I am here to make formal announcement to an Atreides that I've removed myself to enemy territory.'

Jessica studied him, looking for betrayals of minutiae, but Idaho gave no indication that he spoke falsely or with hidden plans. Was it really possible that he'd gone over to Farad'n? She was reminded of her Sisterhood's maxim: *In human affairs, nothing remains enduring; all human affairs revolve in a helix, moving around and out.* If Idaho had really left the Atreides fold, that would explain his present behavior. He was moving around and out. She had to consider this as a possibility.

*But why had he emphasized that he did The Preacher's bidding?*

Jessica's mind raced and, having considered alternatives, she realized she might have to kill Idaho. The plan upon which she had staked her hopes remained so delicate that nothing could be allowed to interfere with it. Nothing. And Idaho's words hinted that he knew her plan. She gauged their relative positions in the room, moving and turning to place herself in position for a lethal blow.

'I've always considered the normalizing effect of the *faufreluches* to be a pillar of our strength,' she said. Let him wonder why she shifted their conversation to the system of class distinction. 'The Landsraad Council of the Great Houses, the regional Sysselraads, all deserve our –'

'You do not distract me,' he said.

And Idaho wondered at how transparent her actions had become. Was it that she had grown lax in concealment, or had he finally breached the walls of her Bene Gesserit training? The latter, he decided, but some of it was in herself – a changing as she aged. It saddened him to see this just the way it saddened him to see the small ways the new Fremen differed from the old. The passing of the desert was the passing of something precious to humans and he could not describe this thing, no more than he could describe what had happened to the Lady Jessica.

Jessica stared at Idaho in open astonishment, not trying to conceal her reaction. Could he read her that easily?

'You will not slay me,' he said. He used the Fremen words of warning: 'Don't throw your blood upon my knife.' And he thought: *I've become very much the Fremen.* It gave him a wry sense of continuity to realize how deeply he had accepted the ways of the planet which had harbored his second life.

'I think you'd better leave,' she said.

'Not until you accept my withdrawal from Atreides service.'

'Accepted!' She bit it off. And only after she'd uttered the word did she realize how much pure reflex had gone into this exchange. She needed time to think and reconsider. How had Idaho known what she would do? She did not believe him capable of leaping Time in the spice way.

Idaho backed away from her until he felt the door behind him. He bowed. 'Once more I call you My Lady, and then never again. My advice to Farad'n will be to send you back to Wallach, quietly and quickly, at the earliest practical moment. You are too dangerous a toy to keep around. Although I don't believe he thinks of you as a toy. You are working for the Sisterhood, not for the Atreides. I wonder now if you ever worked for the Atreides. You witches move too deeply and darkly for mere mortals ever to trust.'

'A ghola considers himself a mere mortal,' she jibed.

'Compared to you,' he said.

'Leave!' she ordered.

'Such is my intention.' He slipped out the door, passing the curious stare of the servant who'd obviously been listening.

*It's done,* he thought. *And they can read it in only one way.*

*Only in the realm of mathematics can you understand Muad'Dib's precise view of the future. Thus : first, we postulate any number of point-dimensions in space. (This is the classic n-fold extended aggregate, an aggregate of n dimensions.) With this framework, Time as commonly understood becomes an aggregate of one-dimensional properties. Applying this to the Muad'Dib phenomenon, we find that we either are confronted by new properties of Time or (by reduction through the infinity calculus) we are dealing with separate systems which contains n body properties. For Muad'Dib, we assume the latter. As demonstrated by the reduction, the point-dimensions of the n-fold can only have separate existence within different frameworks of Time. Separate dimensions of Time are thus demonstrated to coexist. This being the inescapable case, Muad'Dib's predictions required that he perceive the n-fold not as extended aggregate but as an operation within a single framework. In effect, he froze his universe into that one framework which was his view of Time.*

*— Palimbasha:*
**Lectures at Sietch Tabr**

Leto lay at the crest of a dune, peering across open sand at a sinuous rock outcropping. The rock lay like an immense worm atop the sand, flat and threatening in the morning sunlight. Nothing stirred there. No bird circled overhead; no animal scampered among the rocks. He could see the slots of a windtrap almost at the center of the 'worm's' back. There'd be water here. The rock-worm held the familiar appearance of a sietch shelter, except for the absence of living things. He lay quietly, blending with sand, watching.

One of Gurney Halleck's tunes kept flowing through his mind, monotonously persistent:

> *Beneath the hill where the fox runs lightly.*
> *A dappled sun shines brightly*
> *Where my one love's still.*
>
> *Beneath the hill in the fennel brake*
> *I spy my love who cannot wake.*
> *He hides in a grave*
> *Beneath the hill.*

Where was the entrance to that place? Leto wondered.

He felt the certainty that this must be Jacurutu/Fondak, but there was something wrong here beyond the lack of animal movement. Something flickered at the edges of conscious perception, warning him.

What hid beneath the hill?

Lack of animals was bothersome. It aroused his Fremen sense of caution: *The absence says more than the presence when it comes to desert survival.* But there was a windtrap. There would be water and humans to use it. This was the tabu place which hid behind Fondak's name, its other identity lost even to the memories of most Fremen. And no birds or animals could be seen there.

No humans – yet here the Golden Path began.

His father had once said: 'There's unknown all around at every moment. That's where you seek knowledge.'

Leto glanced out to his right along the dune crests. There'd been a mother storm recently. Lake Azrak, the gypsum plain, had been exposed from beneath its sandy cover. Fremen superstition said that whoever saw the Biyan, the White Lands, was granted a two-edged wish, a wish which might destroy you. Leto saw only a gypsum plain which told him that open water had existed once here on Arrakis.

As it would exist once more.

He peered upward, swinging his gaze all around in the search for movement. The sky was porous after the storm. Light passing through it generated a sensation of milky presence, of a silver sun lost somewhere above the dust veil which persisted in the high altitudes.

Once more Leto brought his attention back to the sinuous rock. He slipped the binoculars from his Fremkit, focused their motile lenses and peered at the naked grayness, this outcropping where once the men of Jacurutu had lived. Amplification revealed a thorn bush, the one called Queen of Night. The bush nestled in shadows at a cleft which might be an entrance into the old sietch. He scanned the length of the outcropping. The silver sun turned reds into gray, casting a diffuse flatness over the long expanse of rock.

He rolled over, turning his back on Jacurutu, scanned the circle of his surroundings through the binoculars. Nothing in that wilderness preserved the marks of human passage. The wind already had obliterated his tracks, leaving only a vague roundness where he had dropped from his worm in the night.

Again he looked at Jacurutu. Except for the windtrap, there was no sign that men had ever passed this way. And without that sinuous length of rock, there was nothing here to subtract from the bleached sand, a wilderness from horizon to horizon,

Leto felt suddenly that he was in this place because he had refused to be confined in the system which his ancestors bequeathed him. He thought of how people looked at him, that universal mistake in every glance except Ghanima's.

*Except for that ragged mob of other memories, this child was never a child.*

*I must accept responsibility for the decision we made*, he thought.

Once more he scanned the length of rock. By all the descriptions this had to be Fondak, and no other place could be Jacurutu. He felt a strange resonant relationship with the tabu of this place. In the Bene Gesserit Way, he opened his mind to Jacurutu, seeking to know nothing about it. *Knowing* was a barrier which prevented learning. For a few moments he allowed himself merely to resonate, making no demands, asking no questions.

The problem lay within the lack of animal life, but it was a particular thing which alerted him. He perceived it then: there were no scavenger birds – no eagles, no vultures, no hawks. Even when other life hid, these remained. Every watering place in this desert held its chain of life. At the end of the chain were the omnipresent scavengers. Nothing had come to investigate his presence. How well he knew the 'watchdogs of the sietch', that line of crouched birds on the cliff's edge at Tabr, primitive undertakers waiting for flesh. As the Fremen said: 'Our competitors.' But they said it with no sense of jealousy because questing birds often told when strangers approached.

*What if this Fondak has been abandoned even by the smugglers?*

Leto paused to drink from one of his catchtubes.

*What if there's truly no water here?*

He reviewed his position. He'd run two worms into the sand getting here, riding them with his flail through the night, leaving them half dead. This was the Inner Desert where the smugglers' haven was to be found. If life existed here, if it *could* exist, it would have to be in the presence of water.

*What if there's no water? What if this isn't Fondak/Jacurutu?*

Once more he aimed his binoculars at the windtrap. Its outer edges were sand-etched, in need of maintenance, but enough of it remained. There should be water.

*But what if there isn't?*

An abandoned sietch might lose its water to the air, to any

224

number of catastrophes. Why were there no scavenger birds? Killed for their water? By whom? How could all of them be eliminated? Poison?

*Poisoned water.*

The legend of Jacurutu contained no story of the cistern poisoned, but it might have been. If the original flocks were slain, would they not have been renewed by this time? The Iduali were wiped out generations ago and the stories never mentioned poison. Again he examined the rock with his binoculars. How could an entire sietch have been wiped out? Certainly some must have escaped. All of the inhabitants of a sietch were seldom at home. Parties roamed the desert, trekked to the towns.

With a sigh of resignation Leto put away his binoculars. He slipped down the hidden face of the dune, took extra care to dig in his stilltent and conceal all sign of his intrusion as he prepared to spend the hot hours. The sluggish currents of fatigue stole along his limbs as he sealed himself in the darkness. Within the tent's sweaty confines he spent much of the day drowsing, imagining mistakes he could have made. His dreams were defensive, but there could be no self-defense in this trial he and Ghanima had chosen. Failure would scald their souls. He ate spice-biscuits and slept, awakened to eat once more, to drink and return to sleep. It had been a long journey to this place, a severe test for the muscles of a child.

Toward evening he awoke refreshed, listened for signs of life. He crept out of his sandy shroud. There was dust high in the sky blowing one way, but he could feel sand stinging his cheek from another direction — sure sign there would be a weather change. He sensed a storm coming.

Cautiously he crept to the crest of his dune, peered once more at those enigmatic rocks. The intervening air was yellow. The signs spoke of a Coriolis storm approaching, the wind that carried death in its belly. There'd be a great winding sheet of wind-driven sand that might stretch across four degrees of latitude. The desolate emptiness of the gypsum pan was a yellow surface now, reflecting the dust clouds. The false peace of evening enfolded him. Then the day collapsed and it was night, the quick night of the Inner Desert. The rocks were transformed into angular peaks frosted by the light of First Moon. He felt sandthorns stinging his skin. A peal of dry thunder sounded like an echo from distant drums and, in the space between moonlight and darkness he saw sudden movement: bats. He could hear the stirring of their wings, their tiny squeaks.

*Bats.*

By design or accident, this place conveyed a sense of abandoned desolation. It was where the half-legendary smuggler stronghold should be: Fondak. But what if it were not Fondak? What if the tabu still ruled and this were only the shell of ghostly Jacurutu?

Leto crouched in the lee of his dune and waited for the night to settle into its own rhythms. Patience and caution – caution and patience. For a time he amused himself by reviewing Chaucer's route from London to Canterbury, listing the places from Southwark: two miles to the watering-place of St Thomas, five miles to Deptford, six miles to Greenwich, thirty miles to Rochester, forty miles to Sittingbourne, fifty-five miles to Boughton under Blean, fifty-eight miles to Harbledown, and sixty miles to Canterbury. It gave him a sense of timeless buoyancy to know that few in his universe would recall Chaucer or know any London except the village on Gansireed. St Thomas was preserved in the Orange Catholic Bible and the Azhar Book, but Canterbury was gone from the memories of men, as was the planet which had known it. There lay the burden of his memories, of all those lives which threatened to engulf him. He had made that trip to Canterbury once.

His present trip was longer, though, and more dangerous.

Presently he crept over the dune's crest and made his way toward the moonlit rocks. He blended with shadows, slid across the crests, made no sounds that might signal his presence.

The dust had gone as it often did just before a storm, and the night was brilliant. The day had revealed no movement, but he heard small creatures rustling in the darkness as he neared the rocks.

In a valley between two dunes he came upon a family of jerboa which scampered away at his approach. He eased over the next crest, his emotions beset by salty anxieties. That cleft he had seen – did it lead up to an entrance? And there were other concerns: the old-time sietch had always been guarded by traps – poisoned barbs in pits, poisoned spines on plants. He felt himself caught up in the Fremen agrapha: *The ear-minded night.* And he listened for the slightest sound.

The gray rocks towered above him now, made giant by his nearness. As he listened, he heard birds invisible in that cliff, the soft calling of winged prey. They were the sounds of daybirds, but abroad by night. What had turned their world around? Human predation?

Abruptly Leto froze against the sand. There was fire on the

cliff, a ballet of glittering and mysterious gems against the night's black gauze, the sort of signal a sietch might send to wanderers across the *bled*. Who were these occupants of this place? He crept forward into the deepest shadows at the cliff's base, felt along the rock with a hand, sliding his body behind the hand as he sought the fissure he'd seen by daylight. He located it on his eighth step, slipped the sandsnorkel from his kit and probed the darkness. As he moved, something tight and binding dropped over his shoulders and arms, immobilizing him.

*Trapvine!*

He resisted the urge to struggle; that only made the vine pull tighter. He dropped the snorkel, flexed the fingers of his right hand, trying for the knife at his waist. He felt like a bare innocent for not throwing something into that fissure from a distance, testing the darkness for its dangers. His mind had been too occupied by the fire on the cliff.

Each movement tightened the trapvine, but his fingers at last touched the knife hilt. Stealthily, he closed his hand around the hilt, began to slip it free.

Flaring light enveloped him, arresting all movement.

'Ahhh, a fine catch in our net.' It was a heavy masculine voice from behind Leto, something vaguely familiar in the tone. Leto tried to turn his head, aware of the vine's dangerous propensity to crush a body which moved too freely.

A hand took his knife before he could see his captor. The hand moved expertly over his body, extracting the small devices he and Ghanima carried as a matter of survival. Nothing escaped the searcher, not even the shigawire garrote concealed in his hair.

Leto still had not seen the man.

Fingers did something with the trapvine and he found he could breathe easier, but the man said: 'Do not struggle, Leto Atreides. I have your water in my cup.'

By supreme effort Leto remained calm, said: 'You know my name?'

'Of course! When one baits a trap, it's for a purpose. One aims for a specific quarry, not so?'

Leto remained silent, but his thoughts whirled.

'You feel betrayed!' the heavy voice said. Hands turned him around, gently but with an obvious show of strength. An adult male was telling the child what the odds were.

Leto stared up into the glare from twin floater flares, saw the black outline of a stillsuit-masked face, the hood. As his eyes

227

adjusted he made out a dark strip of skin, the utterly shadowed eyes of melange addiction.

'You wonder why we went to all this trouble,' the man said. His voice issued from the shielded lower part of his face with a curious muffled quality, as though he tried to conceal an accent.

'I long ago ceased to wonder at the numbers of people who want the Atreides twins dead,' Leto said. 'Their reasons are obvious.'

As he spoke, Leto's mind flung itself against the unknown as against a cage, questing wildly for answers. A baited trap? But who had known except Ghanima? Impossible! Ghanima wouldn't betray her own brother. Then did someone know him well enough to predict his actions? Who? His grandmother? How could she?

'You could not be permitted to go on as you were,' the man said. 'Very bad. Before ascending the throne, you need to be educated.' The whiteless eyes stared down at him. 'You wonder how one could presume to educate such a person as yourself? You, with the knowledge of a multitude held there in your memories? That's just it, you see! You think yourself educated, but all you are is a repository of dead lives. You don't yet have a life of your own. You're just a walking surfeit of others, all with one goal – to seek death. Not good in a ruler, being a death seeker. You'd strew your surroundings with corpses. Your father, for example, never understood the –'

'You dare speak of him that way?'

'Many's the time I've dared it. He was only Paul Atreides, after all. Well, boy, welcome to your school.'

The man brought a hand from beneath his robe, touched Leto's cheek. Leto felt the jolt of a slapshot and found himself winding downward into a darkness where a green flag waved. It was the green banner of the Atreides with its day and night symbols, its Dune staff which concealed a water tube. He heard the water gurgling as unconsciousness enfolded him. Or was it someone chuckling?

*We can still remember the golden days before Heisenberg, who showed humans the walls enclosing our predestined arguments. The lives within me find this amusing. Knowledge, you see, has no uses without purpose, but purpose is what builds enclosing walls.*

– Leto Atreides II
His Voice

Alia found herself speaking harshly to the guards she confronted in the Temple foyer. There were nine of them in the dusty green uniforms of the suburban patrol, and they were still panting and sweating with their exertions. The light of late afternoon came in the door behind them. The area had been cleared of pilgrims.

'So my orders mean nothing to you?' she demanded.

And she wondered at her own anger, not trying to contain it but letting it run. Her body trembled with unleashed tensions. Idaho gone . . . the Lady Jessica . . . no reports . . . only rumors that they were on Salusa. Why hadn't Idaho sent a message? What had he done? Had he learned finally about Javid?

Alia wore the yellow of Arrakeen mourning, the color of the burning sun from Fremen history. In a few minutes she would be leading the second and final funeral procession to Old Gap, there to complete the stone marker for her lost nephew. The work would be completed in the night, fitting homage to one who'd been destined to lead Fremen.

The priestly guards appeared defiant in the face of her anger, not shamed at all. They stood in front of her, outlined by the waning light. The odor of their perspiration was easily detected through the light and inefficient stillsuits of city dwellers. Their leader, a tall blond Kaza with the bourka symbols of the Cadelam family, flung his stillsuit mask aside to speak more clearly. His voice was full of the prideful intonations to be expected from a scion of the family which once had ruled at Sietch Abbir.

'Certainly we tried to capture him!'

The man was obviously outraged at her attack. 'He speaks blasphemy! We know your orders, but we heard him with our own ears!'

'And you failed to catch him,' Alia said, her voice low and accusing.

One of the other guards, a short young woman, tried to defend them. 'The crowds were thick there! I swear people interfered with us!'

'We'll keep after him,' the Cadelam said. 'We'll not always fail.'

Alia scowled. 'Why won't you understand and obey me?'

'My Lady, we —'

'What will you do, scion of the *Cade Lamb*, if you capture him and find him to be, in truth, my brother?'

He obviously did not hear her special emphasis on his name, although he could not be a priestly guard without some education and the wit to go with it. Did he want to sacrifice himself?

The guardsman swallowed, then: 'We must kill him ourselves, for he breeds disorder.'

The others stood aghast at this, but still defiant. They knew what they had heard.

'He calls upon the tribes to band against you,' the Cadelam said.

Alia knew how to handle him now. She spoke in a quiet, matter-of-fact tone: 'I see. Then if you must sacrifice yourself this way, taking him openly for all to see who you are and what you do, then I guess you must.'

'Sacrifice my . . . ' He broke off, glanced at his companions. As Kaza of this group, their appointed leader, he had the right to speak for them, but he showed signs that he wished he'd remained silent. The other guards stirred uncomfortably. In the heat of the chase they'd defied Alia. One could only reflect now upon such defiance of the 'Womb of Heaven'. With obvious discomfort the guards opened a small space between themselves and their Kaza.

'For the good of the Church, our official reaction would have to be severe,' Alia said. 'You understand that, don't you?'

'But he —'

'I've heard him myself,' she said. 'But this is a special case.'

'He cannot be Muad'Dib, My Lady!'

*How little you know!* she thought. She said: 'We cannot risk taking him in the open, harming him where others could see it. If another opportunity presents itself, of course.'

'He's always surrounded by crowds these days!'

'Then I fear you must be patient. Of course, if you insist on defying me . . . ' She left the consequences hanging in the air, unspoken, but well understood. The Cadelam was ambitious, a shining career before him.

'We didn't mean defiance, My Lady.' The man had himself

under control now. 'We acted hastily; I can see that. Forgive us, but he –'

'Nothing has happened; nothing to forgive,' she said, using the common Fremen formula. It was one of the many ways a tribe kept peace in its ranks, and this Cadelam was still Old Fremen enough to remember that. His family carried a long tradition of leadership. Guilt was the Naib's whip, to be used sparingly. Fremen served best when free of guilt or resentment.

He showed his realization of her judgment by bowing his head, saying: 'For the good of the tribe; I understand.'

'Go refresh yourselves,' she said. 'The procession begins in a few minutes.'

'Yes, My Lady.' They bustled away, every movement revealing their relief at this escape.

Within Alia's head a bass voice rumbled: 'Ahhhhh, you handled that most adroitly. One or two of them still believe you desire The Preacher dead. They'll find a way.'

'Shut up!' she hissed. 'Shut up! I should never have listened to you! Look what you've done . . .'

'Set you on the road to immortality,' the bass voice said.

She felt it echoing in her skull like a distant ache, thought: *Where can I hide? There's no place to go!*

'Ghanima's knife is sharp,' the Baron said. 'Remember that.'

Alia blinked. Yes, that was something to remember. Ghanima's knife was sharp. That knife might yet cut them out of their present predicament.

> *If you believe certain words, you believe their hidden arguments. When you believe something is right or wrong, true or false, you believe the assumptions in the words which express the arguments. Such assumptions are often full of holes, but remain most precious to the convinced.*
>
> – The Open–Ended Proof
> from The Panoplia Prophetica

Leto's mind floated in a stew of fierce odors. He recognized the heavy cinnamon of melange, the confined sweat of working bodies, the acridity of an uncapped deathstill, dust of many sorts with flint dominant. The odors formed a trail through dreamsand, created shapes of fog in a dead land. He knew these odors should tell him something, but part of him could not yet listen,

Thoughts like wraiths floated through his mind: *In this time I have no finished features; I am all of my ancestors. The sun setting into the sand is the sun setting into my soul. Once this multitude within me was great, but that's ended. I'm Fremen and I'll have a Fremen ending. The Golden Path is ended before it began. It's nothing but a windblown trail. We Fremen knew all the tricks to conceal ourselves: we left no feces, no water, no tracks ... Now, look at my trail vanish.*

A masculine voice spoke close to his ear: 'I could kill you, Atreides. I could kill you, Atreides.' It was repeated over and over until it lost meaning, became a wordless thing carried within Leto's dreaming, a litany of sorts: 'I could kill you, Atreides.'

Leto cleared his throat and felt the reality of this simple act shake his senses. His dry throat managed: 'Who ...'

The voice beside him said: 'I'm an educated Fremen and I've killed my man. You took away our gods, Atreides. What do we care about your stinking Muad'Dib? Your god's dead!'

Was that a real Ouraba voice or another part of his dream? Leto opened his eyes, found himself unfettered on a hard couch. He looked upward at rock, dim glowglobes, an unmasked face staring down at him so close he could smell the breath with its familiar odors of a sietch diet. The face was Fremen; no mistaking the dark skin, those sharp features and water-wasted flesh. This was no fat city dweller. Here was a desert Fremen.

'I am Namri, father of Javid,' the Fremen said. 'Do you know me now, Atreides?'

'I know Javid,' Leto husked.

'Yes, your family knows my son well. I am proud of him. You Atreides may know him even better soon.'

'What ...'

'I am one of your schoolmasters, Atreides. I have only one function: I am the one who could kill you. I'd do it gladly. In this school, to graduate is to live; to fail is to be given into my hands.'

Leto heard implacable sincerity in that voice. It chilled him. This was a human gom jabbar, a high-handed enemy to test his right of entrance into the human concourse. Leto sensed his grandmother's hand in this and, behind her, the faceless masses of the Bene Gesserit. He writhed at this thought.

'Your education begins with me,' Namri said. 'That is just. It is fitting. Because it could end with me. Listen to me carefully now. My every word carries your life in it. Everything about me holds your death within it.'

Leto shot his glance around the room: rock walls, barren — only this couch, the dim glowglobes, and a dark passage behind Namri.

'You will not get past me,' Namri said. And Leto believed him.

'Why're you doing this?' Leto asked.

'That's already been explained. Think what plans are in your head! You are here and you cannot put a future into your present condition. The two don't go together: now and future. But if you really know your past, if you look backward and see where you've been, perhaps there'll be reason once more. If not, there will be your death.'

Leto noted that Namri's tone was not unkind, but it was firm and no denying the death in it.

Namri rocked back on his heels, stared at the rock ceiling. 'In olden times Fremen faced east at dawn. *Eos*, you know? That's dawn in one of the old tongues.'

Bitter pride in his voice, Leto said: 'I speak that tongue.'

'You have not listened to me, then,' Namri said, and there was a knife edge in his voice. 'Night was the time of chaos. Day was the time of order. That's how it was in the time of that tongue you say you speak: darkness–disorder, light–order. We Fremen changed that. *Eos* was the light we distrusted. We preferred the light of a moon, or the stars. Light was too much order and that can be fatal. You see what you *Eos*-Atreides have done? Man is a creature of only that light which protects him. The sun was our enemy on Dune.' Namri brought his gaze down to Leto's level. 'What light do you prefer, Atreides?'

By Namri's poised attitude, Leto sensed that this question carried deep weight. Would the man kill him if he failed to answer correctly? He might. Leto saw Namri's hand resting quietly next to the polished hilt of a crysknife. A ring in the form of a magic tortoise glittered on the Fremen's knife hand.

Leto eased himself up onto his elbows, sent his mind questing into Fremen beliefs. They trusted the Law and loved to hear its lessons expounded in analogy, these old Fremen. The light of the moon?

'I prefer . . . the light of *Lisanu L'haqq*,' Leto said, watching Namri for subtle revelations. The man seemed disappointed, but his hand moved away from his knife. 'It is the light of truth, the light of the perfect man in which the influence of al-Mutakallim can clearly be seen,' Leto continued. 'What other light would a human prefer?'

'You speak as one who recites, not one who believes,' Namri said.

And Leto thought: *I did recite*. But he began to sense the drift of Namri's thoughts, how his words were filtered through early training in the ancient riddle game. Thousands of these riddles went into Fremen training, and Leto had but to bend his attention upon this custom to find examples flooding his mind. *'Challenge: Silence? Answer: The friend of the hunted.'*

Namri nodded to himself as though he shared this thought, said: 'There is a cave which is the cave of life for Fremen. It is an actual cave which the desert has hidden. Shai-Hulud, the great-grandfather of all Fremen, sealed up that cave. My Uncle Ziamad told me about it and he never lied to me. There is such a cave.'

Leto heard the challenging silence when Namri finished speaking. *Cave of life?* 'My Uncle Stilgar also told me of that cave,' Leto said. 'It was sealed to keep cowards from hiding there.'

The reflection of a glowglobe glittered in Namri's shadowed eyes. He asked: 'Would you Atreides open that cave? You seek to control life through a ministry: your Central Ministry for Information, Auqaf and Hajj. The Maulana in charge is called Kausar. He has come a long way from his family's beginnings at the salt mines of Niazi. Tell me, Atreides, what is wrong with your ministry?'

Leto sat up, aware now that he was fully into the riddle game with Namri and that the forfeit was death. The man gave every indication that he'd use that crysknife at the first wrong answer.

Namri, recognizing this awareness in Leto, said: 'Believe me, Atreides. I am the clod-crusher. I am the Iron Hammer.'

Now Leto understood. Namri saw himself as Mirzabah, the Iron Hammer with which the dead are beaten who cannot reply satisfactorily to the questions they must answer before entry into paradise.

*What was wrong with the central ministry which Alia and her priests had created?*

Leto thought of why he'd come into the desert, and a small hope returned to him that the Golden Path might yet appear in his universe. What this Namri implied by his question was no more than the motive which had driven Muad'Dib's own son into the desert.

'God's it is to show the way,' Leto said.

Namri's chin jerked down and he stared sharply at Leto. 'Can it be true that you believe this?' he demanded.

'It's why I am here,' Leto said.

'To find the way?'

'To find it for myself.' Leto put his feet over the edge of the cot. The rock floor was uncarpeted, cold. 'The Priests created their ministry to hide the way.'

'You speak like a true rebel,' Namri said, and he rubbed the tortoise ring on his finger. 'We shall see. Listen carefully once more. You know the high Shield Wall at Jalalud-Din? That Wall bears my family's marks carved there in the first days. Javid, my son, has seen those marks. Abedi Jalal, my nephew, has seen them. Mujahid Shafqat of the Other Ones, he too has seen our marks. In the season of the storms near Sukkar, I came down with my friend Yakup Abad near that place. The winds were blistering hot like the whirl-winds from which we learned our dances. We did not take time to see the marks because a storm blocked the way. But when the storm passed we saw the vision of Thatta upon the blown sand. The face of Shakir Ali was there for a moment, looking down upon his city of tombs. The vision was gone in the instant, but we all saw it. Tell me, Atreides, where can I find that city of tombs?'

*The whirlwinds from which we learned our dances,* Leto thought. *The vision of Thatta and Shakir Ali.* These were the words of a Zensunni Wanderer, those who considered themselves to be the only true men of the desert.

*And Fremen were forbidden to have tombs.*

'The city of tombs is at the end of the path which all men follow,' Leto said. And he dredged up the Zensunni beatifics. 'It is in a garden one thousand paces square. There is a fine entry corridor two hundred and thirty-three paces long and one hundred paces wide all paved with marble from ancient Jaipur. Therein dwells at-Razzaq, he who provides food for all who ask. And on the Day of Reckoning, all who stand up and seek the city of tombs shall not find it. For it is written: That which you know in one world, you shall not find in another.'

'Again you recite without belief,' Namri sneered. 'But I'll accept it for now because I think you know why you're here.' A cold smile touched his lips. 'I give you a *provisional* future, Atreides.'

Leto studied the man warily. Was this another question in disguise?

'Good!' Namri said. 'Your awareness has been prepared. I've sunk home the barbs. One more thing, then. Have you heard that they wear imitation stillsuits in the cities of far Kadrish?'

As Namri waited, Leto quested in his mind for a hidden meaning. *Imitation stillsuits? They were worn on many planets.* He said: 'The foppish habits of Kadrish are an old story often repeated. The wise animal blends into its surroundings.'

Namri nodded slowly. Then: 'The one who trapped you and brought you here will see you presently. Do not try to leave this place. It would be your death.' Arising as he spoke, Namri went out into the dark passage.

For a long time after he had gone, Leto stared into the passage. He could hear sounds out there, the quiet voices of men on guard duty. Namri's story of the mirage-vision stayed with Leto. It brought up the long desert crossing to this place. It no longer mattered whether this were Jacurutu/Fondak. Namri was not a smuggler. He was something much more potent. And the game Namri played smelled of the Lady Jessica; it stank of the Bene Gesserit. Leto sensed an enclosing peril in this realization. But that dark passage where Namri had gone was the only exit from this room. And outside lay a strange sietch – beyond that, the desert. The harsh severity of that desert, its ordered chaos with mirages and endless dunes, came over Leto as part of the trap in which he was caught. He could recross that sand, but where would flight take him? The thought was like stagnant water. It would not quench his thirst.

*Because of the one-pointed Time awareness in which the conventional mind remains immersed, humans tend to think of everything in a sequential, word-oriented framework. This mental trap produces very short-term concepts of effectiveness and consequences, a condition of constant, unplanned response to crises.*

– Liet-Kynes
The Arrakis Workbook

*Words and movements simultaneous,* Jessica reminded herself and she bent her thoughts to those necessary mental preparations for the coming encounter.

The hour was shortly after breakfast, the golden sun of Salusa Secundus just beginning to touch the far wall of the enclosed garden which she could see from her window. She had dressed herself carefully: the black hooded cloak of a Reverend Mother, but it carried the Atreides crest in gold worked into an embroidered ring around the hem and again at the cuff of each sleeve.

Jessica arranged the drape of her garment carefully as she turned her back on the window, holding her left arm across her waist to present the Hawk motif of the crest.

Farad'n noted the Atreides symbols, commenting on them as he entered, but he betrayed no anger or surprise. She detected subtle humor in his voice and wondered at it. She saw that he had clad himself in the gray leotard which she had suggested. He sat on the low green divan to which she directed him, relaxing with his right arm along the back.

*Why do I trust her?* he wondered. *This is a Bene Gesserit witch!*

Jessica, reading the thought in the contrast between his relaxed body and the expression on his face, smiled and said: 'You trust me because you know our bargain is a good one and you want what I can teach you.'

She saw the pinch of a scowl touch his brow, waved her left hand to calm him. 'No, I don't read minds. I read the face, the body, the mannerisms, tone of voice, set of arms. Anyone can do this once they learn the Bene Gesserit Way.'

'And you will teach me?'

'I'm sure you've studied the reports about us,' she said. 'Is there anywhere a report that we fail to deliver on a direct promise?'

'No reports, but . . .'

'We survive in part by the complete confidence which people can have in our truthfulness. That has not changed.'

'I find this reasonable,' he said. 'I'm anxious to begin.'

'I'm surprised you've never asked the Bene Gesserit for a teacher,' she said. 'They would've leaped at the opportunity to put you in their debt.'

'My mother would never listen to me when I urged her to do this,' he said. 'But now . . . ' He shrugged, an eloquent comment on Wensicia's banishment. 'Shall we start?'

'It would've been better to begin this when you were much younger,' Jessica said. 'It'll be harder for you now, and it'll take much longer. You'll have to begin by learning patience, extreme patience. I pray you'll not find it too high a price.'

'Not for the reward you offer.'

She heard the sincerity, the pressure of expectations, and the touch of awe in his voice. These formed a place to begin. She said: 'The art of patience, then – starting with some elementary *prana-bindu* exercises for the legs and arms, for your breathing. We'll leave the hands and fingers for later. Are you ready?'

She seated herself on a stool facing him.

Farad'n nodded, holding an expectant expression on his face to conceal the sudden onset of fear. Tyekanik had warned him that there must be a trick in the Lady Jessica's offer, something brewed by the Sisterhood. 'You cannot believe that she has abandoned them again or that they have abandoned her.' Farad'n had stopped the argument with an angry outburst for which he'd been immediately sorry. His emotional reaction had made him agree more quickly with Tyekanik's precautions. Farad'n glanced at the corners of the room, the subtle gleam of *jems* in the coving. All that glittered was not *jems*: everything in this room would be recorded and good minds would review every nuance, every word, every movement.

Jessica smiled, noting the direction of his gaze, but not revealing that she knew where his attention had wandered. She said: 'To learn patience in the Bene Gesserit Way, you must begin by recognizing the essential, raw instability of our universe. We call nature – meaning this totality in all of its manifestations – the Ultimate Non-Absolute. To free your vision and permit you to recognize this conditional nature's changing ways, you will hold your two hands at arm's length in front of you. Stare at your extended hands, first the palms and then the backs. Examine the fingers, front and back. Do it.'

Farad'n complied, but he felt foolish. These were his own hands. He knew them.

'Imagine your hands aging,' Jessica said. 'They must grow very old in your eyes. Very, very old. Notice how dry the skin . . .'

'My hands don't change,' he said. He already could feel the muscles of his upper arms trembling.

'Continue to stare at your hands. Make them old, as old as you can imagine. It may take time. But when you see them age, reverse the process. Make your hands young again – as young as you can make them. Strive to take them from infancy to great age at will, back and forth, back and forth.'

'They don't change!' he protested. His shoulders ached.

'If you demand it of your senses, your hands will change,' she said. 'Concentrate upon visualizing the flow of time which you desire: infancy to age, age to infancy. It may take you hours, days, months. But it can be achieved. Reversing that change-flow will teach you to see every system as something spinning in relative stability . . . only relative.'

'I thought I was learning patience.' She heard anger in his voice, and edge of frustration.

'And relative stability,' she said. 'This is the perspective which you create with your own belief, and beliefs can be manipulated by imagination. You've learned only a limited way of looking at the universe. Now you must make the universe your own creation. This will permit you to harness any relative stability to your own uses, to whatever uses you are capable of imagining.'

'How long did you say it takes?'

'Patience,' she reminded him.

A spontaneous grin touched his lips. His eyes wavered toward her.

'Look at your hands!' she snapped.

The grin vanished. His gaze jerked back to a fixated concentration upon his extended hands.

'What do I do when my arms get tired?' he asked.

'Stop talking and concentrate,' she said. 'If you become too tired, stop. Return to it after a few minutes of relaxation and exercise. You must persist in this until you succeed. At your present stage, this is more important than you could possibly realize. Learn this lesson or the others will not come.'

Farad'n inhaled a deep breath, chewed his lips, stared at his hands. He turned them slowly: front, back, front, back . . . His shoulders trembled with fatigue. Front, back . . . Nothing changed.

Jessica arose, crossed to the only door.

He spoke without removing his attention from his hands. 'Where are you going?'

'You'll work better on this if you're alone. I'll return in about an hour. Patience.'

'I know!'

She studied him a moment. How intent he looked. He reminded her with a heart-tugging abruptness of her own lost son. She permitted herself a sigh: 'When I return I'll give you the exercise lessons to relieve your muscles. Give it time. You'll be astonished at what you can make your body and your senses do.'

She let herself out.

The omnipresent guards took up station three paces behind her as she strode down the hall. Their awe and fear were obvious. They were Sardaukar, thrice-warned of her prowess, raised on the stories of their defeat by the Fremen of Arrakis. This witch was a Fremen Reverend Mother, a Bene Gesserit and an Atreides.

Jessica, glancing back, saw their stern faces as a milepost in her design. She turned away as she came to the stairs, went down them and through a short passage into the garden below her windows.

*Now if only Duncan and Gurney can do their parts,* she thought as she felt the gravel of a pathway beneath her feet, saw the golden light filtered by greenery.

> *You will learn the integrated communication methods as you complete the next step in your mentat education. This is a gestalten function which will overlay data paths in your awareness, resolving complexities and masses of input from the mentat index-catalogue techniques which you already have mastered. Your initial problem will be the breaking tensions arising from the divergent assembly of minutiae/data on specialized subjects. Be warned. Without mentat overlay integration, you can be immersed in the Babel Problem, which is the label we give to the omnipresent dangers of achieving wrong combinations from accurate information.*
>
> — The Mentat Handbook

The sound of fabrics rubbing together sent sparks of awareness through Leto. He was surprised that he had tuned his sensitivity to the point where he automatically identified the fabrics from their sound: the combination came from a Fremen robe rubbing against the coarse hangings of a door curtain. He turned toward the sound. It came from the passage where Namri had gone minutes before. As Leto turned, he saw his captor enter. It was the same man who had taken him prisoner: the same dark strip of skin above the stillsuit mask, the identical searing eyes. The man lifted a hand to his mask, slipped the catchtube from his nostrils, lowered the mask and, in the same motion, flipped his hood back. Even before he focused on the scar of the inkvine whip along the man's jaw, Leto recognized him. The recognition was a totality in his awareness with the search for confirming details coming afterward. No mistake about it, this rolling lump of humanity, this warrior-troubadour, was Gurney Halleck!

Leto clenched his hands into fists, overcome momentarily by the shock of recognition. No Atreides retainer had ever been more loyal. None better at shield fighting. He'd been Paul's trusted confidant and teacher.

He was the Lady Jessica's servant.

These recognitions and more surged through Leto's mind. Gurney was his captor. Gurney and Namri were in this conspiracy together. And Jessica's hand was in it with them.

'I understand you've met our Namri,' Halleck said. 'Pray believe him, young sir. He has one function and one function only. He's the one capable of killing you should the need arise.'

Leto responded automatically with his father's tones: 'So you've joined my enemies, Gurney! I never thought the – '

'Try none of your devil tricks on me, lad,' Halleck said. 'I'm proof against them all. I follow your grandmother's orders. Your education has been planned to the last detail. It was she who approved my selection of Namri. What comes next, painful as it may seem, is at her command.'

'And what does she command?'

Halleck lifted a hand from the folds of his robe, exposed a Fremen injector, primitive but efficient. Its transparent tube was charged with blue fluid.

Leto squirmed backward on the cot, was stopped by the rock wall. As he moved, Namri entered, stood beside Halleck with hand on cryaknife. Together they blocked the only exit.

'I see you've recognized the spice essence,' Halleck said. 'You're to take the *worm trip*, lad. You must go through it. Otherwise, what your father dared and you dare not would hang over you for the rest of your days.'

Leto shook his head wordlessly. This was the thing he and Ghanima knew could overwhelm them. Gurney was an ignorant fool! How could Jessica . . . Leto felt the father-presence in his memories. It surged into his mind, trying to strip away his defenses. Leto wanted to shriek outrage, could not move his lips. But this was the wordless thing which his pre-born awareness most feared. This was prescient trance, the reading of immutable future with all of its fixity and its terrors. Surely Jessica could not have ordered such an ordeal for her own grandson. But her presence loomed in his mind, filling him with acceptance arguments. Even the litany of fear was pressed upon him with a repetitive droning: '*I must not fear. Fear is the mind-killer. Fear is the little death that brings total obliteration. I will face my fear. I will permit it to pass over me and through me. And when it has gone past . . .*'

With an oath already ancient when Chaldea was young, Leto tried to move, tried to leap at the two men standing over him, but his muscles refused to obey. As though he already existed in the trance, Leto saw Halleck's hand move, the injector approach.

The light of a glowglobe sparkled within the blue fluid. The injector touched Leto's left arm. Pain lanced through him, shot upward to the muscles of his neck, into his head.

Abruptly Leto saw a young woman sitting outside a crude hut in dawnlight. She sat right there in front of him roasting coffee beans to a rose brown, adding cardamom and melange. The voice of a rebeck echoed from somewhere behind him. The music echoed and echoed until it entered his head, still echoing. It suffused his body and he felt himself to be large, very large, not a child at all. And his skin was not his own. He knew that sensation! His skin was not his own. Warmth spread through his body. As abruptly as his first vision, he found himself standing in darkness. It was night. Stars like a rain of embers fell in gusts from a brilliant cosmos.

Part of him knew there was no escaping, but still he tried to fight it until the father-presence intruded. 'I will protect you in the trance. The others within will not take you.'

Wind tumbled Leto, rolled him, hissing, pouring dust and sand over him, cutting his arms, his face, abrading his clothes, whipping the loose-torn ends of now useless fabric. But he felt no pain and he saw the cuts heal as rapidly as they appeared. Still he rolled with the wind. And his skin was not his own.

*It will happen!* he thought

But the thought was distant and came as though it were not his own, not really his own; no more than his skin.

The vision absorbed him. It evolved into a stereologic memory which separated past and present, future and present, future and past. Each separation mingled into a trinocular focus which he sensed as the multidimensional relief map of his own future existence.

He thought: *Time is a measure of space, just as a range-finder is a measure of space, but measuring locks us into the place we measure.*

He sensed the trance deepening. It came as an amplification of internal consciousness which his self-identity soaked up and through which he felt himself changing. It was living Time and he could arrest an instant of it. Memory fragments, future and past, deluged him. But they existed as montage-in-motion. Their relationships underwent a constant dance. His memory was a lens, an illuminating searchlight which picked out fragments, isolating them, but forever failing to stop the ceaseless motion and modification which surged into his view.

That which he and Ghanima had planned came through the

searchlight, dominating everything, but now it terrified him. Vision reality ached in him. The uncritical inevitability made his ego cringe.

*And his skin was not his own!* Past and present tumbled through him, surging across the barriers of his terror. He could not separate them. One moment he felt himself setting forth on Butlerian Jihad, eager to destroy any machine which simulated human awareness. That had to be the past – over and done with. Yet his senses hurtled through the experience, absorbing the most minute details. He heard a minister- companion speaking from a pulpit: *'We must negate the machines-that-think. Humans must set their own guidelines. This is not something machines can do. Reasoning depends upon programming, not on hardware, and we are the ultimate program!'*

He heard the voice clearly, knew his surroundings – a vast wooden hall with dark windows. Light came from sputtering flames. And his minister-companion said: *'Our Jihad is a "dump program". We dump the things which destroy us as humans!'*

And it was in Leto's mind that the speaker had been a servant of computers, one who knew them and serviced them. But the scene vanished and Ghanima stood in front of him, saying: *'Gurney knows. He told me. They're Duncan's words and Duncan was speaking as a mentat. "In doing good, avoid notoriety; in doing evil, avoid self-awareness."'*

That had to be future – far future. But he felt the reality. It was as intense as any past from his multitude of lives. And he whispered. 'Isn't that true, father?'

But the father-presence within spoke warningly: *'Don't invite disaster! You're learning stroboscopic awareness now. Without it you could overrun yourself, lose your place-mark in Time.'*

And the bas-relief imagery persisted. Intrusions hammered at him. Past-present-now. There was no true separation. He knew he had to flow with this thing, but the flowing terrified him. How could he return to any recognizable place? Yet he felt himself being forced to cease every effort of resistance. He could not grasp his new universe in motionless, labeled bits. No bit would stand still. Things could not be forever ordered and formulated. He had to find the rhythm of change and see between the changes to the changing itself. Without knowing where it began he found himself moving within a gigantic *moment bienheureux*, able to see the past in the future, present in past, the *now* in both past and future. It was the accumulation of centuries experienced between one heartbeat and the next.

Leto's awareness floated free, no objective psyche to compensate for consciousness, no barriers, Namri's 'provisional future' remained lightly in his memory, but it shared awareness with many futures. And in this shattering awareness, all of his past, every inner life became his own. With the help of the greatest within him, he dominated. They were *his*.

He thought: *When you study an object from a distance, only its principle may be seen.* He had achieved the distance and he could see his own life now: the multi-past and its memories were his burden, his joy, and his necessity. But the *worm trip* had added another dimension and his father no longer stood guard within him because the need no longer existed. Leto saw through the distances clearly – past and present. And the past presented him with an ultimate ancestor – one who was called Harum and without whom the distant future would not be. These clear distances provided new principles, new dimensions of sharing. Whichever life he now chose, he'd live it out in an autonomous sphere of mass experience, a trail of lives so convoluted that no single lifetime could count the generations of it. Aroused, this mass experience held the power to subdue his selfdom. It could make itself felt upon an individual, a nation, a society or an entire civilization. That of course, was why Gurney had been taught to fear him; why Namri's knife waited. They could not be allowed to see his power within him. No one could ever see it in its fullness – not even Ghanima.

Presently Leto sat up, saw that only Namri remained, watching.

In an old voice, Leto said: 'There's no single set of limits for all men. Universal prescience is an empty myth. Only the most powerful local currents of Time may be foretold. But in an infinite universe, *local* can be so gigantic that your mind shrinks from it.'

Namri shook his head, not understanding.

'Where's Gurney?' Leto asked.

'He left lest he have to watch me slay you.'

'Will you slay me, Namri?' It was almost a plea to have the man do it.

Namri took his hand from his knife. 'Since you ask me to do it, I will not. If you were indifferent, though . . .'

'The malady of indifference is what destroys many things,' Leto said. He nodded to himself. 'Yes . . . even civilizations die of it. It's as though that were the price demanded for achieving new levels of complexity or consciousness.' He looked up at

Namri. 'So they told you to look for indifference in me?' And he saw Namri was more than a killer – Namri was devious.

'As a sign of unbridled power,' Namri said, but it was a lie.

'Indifferent power, yes.' Leto sat up, sighed deeply. 'There was no moral grandeur to my father's life, Namri; only a local trap which he built for himself.'

> *O Paul, thou Muad'Dib,*
> *Mahdi of all men,*
> *Thy breath exhaled*
> *Sent forth the hurican.*
>
> **– Songs of Muad'Dib**

'Never!' Ghanima said. 'I'd kill him on our wedding night.' She spoke with a barbed stubbornness which thus far had resisted all blandishments. Alia and her advisors had been at it half the night, keeping the royal quarters in a state of unrest, sending out for new advisors, for food and drink. The entire Temple and its adjoining Keep seethed with the frustrations of unmade decisions.

Ghanima sat composedly on a green floater chair in her own quarters, a large room with rough tan walls to simulate sietch rock. The ceiling, however, was imbar crystal which flickered with blue light, and the floor was black tile. The furnishings were sparse: a small writing table, five floater chairs and a narrow cot set into an alcove, Fremen fashion. Ghanima wore a robe of yellow mourning.

'You are not a free person who can settle every aspect of her own life,' Alia said for perhaps the hundredth time. *The little fool must come to realize this sooner or later! She must approve the betrothal to Farad'n. She must! Let her kill him later, but the betrothal requires open acknowledgment by the Fremen affianced.*

'He killed my brother,' Ghanima said, holding to the single note which sustained her. 'Everyone knows this. Fremen would spit at the mention of my name were I to consent to this betrothal.'

*And that is one of the reasons why you must consent,* Alia thought. She said: 'His mother did it. He has banished her for it. What more do you want of him?'

'His blood,' Ghanima said. 'He's a Corrino.'

245

'He has denounced his own mother,' Alia protested. 'And why should you worry about the Fremen rabble? They'll accept whatever we tell them to accept. Ghani, the peace of the Empire demands that –'

'I will not consent,' Ghanima said. 'You cannot announce the betrothal without me.'

Irulan, entering the room as Ghanima spoke, glanced inquiringly at Alia and the two female advisors who stood dejectedly beside her. Irulan saw Alia throw up her arms in disgust and drop into a chair facing Ghanima.

'You speak to her, Irulan,' Alia said.

Irulan pulled a floater into place, sat down beside Alia.

'You're a Corrino, Irulan,' Ghanima said. 'Don't press your luck with me.' Ghanima got up, crossed to her cot and sat on it cross-legged, glaring back at the women. Irulan, she saw, had dressed in a black aba to match Alia's, the hood thrown back to reveal her golden hair. It was mourning hair under the yellow glow of the floating globes which illuminated the room.

Irulan glanced at Alia, stood up and crossed to stand facing Ghanima. 'Ghani, I'd kill him myself if that were the way to solve matters. And Farad'n's my own blood, as you so kindly emphasized. But you have duties far higher than your commitment to Fremen...'

'That doesn't sound any better coming from you than it does from my precious aunt,' Ghanima said. 'The blood of a brother cannot be washed off. That's more than some little Fremen aphorism.'

Irulan pressed her lips together. Then: 'Farad'n holds your grandmother captive. He holds Duncan and if we don't –'

'I'm not satisfied with your stories of how all this happened,' Ghanima said, peering past Irulan at Alia. 'Once Duncan died rather than let enemies take my father. Perhaps this new ghola-flesh is no longer the same as –'

'Duncan was charged with protecting your grandmother's life!' Alia said, whirling in her chair. 'I'm confident he chose the only way to do that.' And she thought: *Duncan! Duncan! You weren't supposed to do it this way.*

Ghanima, reading the overtones of contrivance in Alia's voice, stared across at her aunt. 'You're lying, O Womb of Heaven. I've heard about your fight with my grandmother. What is it you fear to tell us about her and your precious Duncan?'

'You've heard it all,' Alia said, but she felt a stab of fear at this bald accusation and what it implied. Fatigue had made her

246

careless, she realized. She arose, said. 'Everything I know, you know.' Turning to Irulan: 'You work on her. She must be made to –'

Ghanima interrupted with a coarse Fremen expletive which came shockingly from the immature lips. Into the quick silence she said: 'You think me a mere child, that you have years in which to work on me, that eventually I'll accept. Think again, O Heavenly Regent. You know better than anyone the years I have within me. I'll listen to them, not to you.'

Alia barely suppressed an angry retort, stared hard at Ghanima. *Abomination?* Who was this child? A new fear of Ghanima began to rise in Alia. Had she accepted her own compromise with the lives which came to her pre-born? Alia said: 'There's time yet for you to see reason.'

'There may be time yet for me to see Farad'n's blood spurt around my knife,' Ghanima said. 'Depend on it. If I'm ever left alone with him, one of us will surely die.'

'You think you loved your brother more than I?' Irulan demanded. 'You play a fool's game! I was mother to him as I was to you. I was –'

'You never knew him,' Ghanima said. 'All of you, except at times my *beloved aunt,* persist in thinking us children. You're the fools! Alia knows! Look at her run away from . . .'

'I run from nothing,' Alia said, but she turned her back on Irulan and Ghanima, and stared at the two amazons who were pretending not to hear this argument. They'd obviously given up on Ghanima. Perhaps they sympathized with her. Angrily, Alia sent them from the room. Relief was obvious on their faces as they obeyed.

'You run,' Ghanima persisted.

'I've chosen a way of life which suits me,' Alia said, turning back to stare at Ghanima sitting cross-legged on the cot. Was it possible she'd made that terrible inner compromise? Alia tried to see the signs of it in Ghanima, but was unable to read a single betrayal. Alia wondered then: *Has she seen it in me? But how could she?*

'You feared to be the window for a multitude,' Ghanima accused. 'But we're the preborn and we know. You'll be their window, conscious or unconscious. You cannot deny them.' And she thought: *Yes, I know you – Abomination. And perhaps I'll go as you have gone, but for now I can only pity you and despise you.*

Silence hung between Ghanima and Alia, an almost palpabable

247

thing which alerted the Bene Gesserit training in Irulan. She glanced from one to the other, then: 'Why're you so quiet suddenly?'

'I've just had a thought which requires considerable reflection,' Alia said.

'Reflect at your leisure, dear aunt,' Ghanima sneered.

Alia, putting down fatigue-inflamed anger, said: 'Enough for now! Leave her to think. Perhaps she'll come to her senses.'

Irulan arose, said: 'It's almost dawn anyway. Ghani, before we go would you care to hear the latest message from Farad'n? He . . .'

'I would not,' Ghanima said. 'And hereafter, cease calling me by that ridiculous diminutive. Ghani! It merely supports the mistaken assumption that I'm a child you can . . .'

'Why'd you and Alia grow so suddenly quiet?' Irulan asked, reverting to her previous question, but casting it now in a delicate mode of Voice.

Ghanima threw her head back in laughter. 'Irulan! You'd try Voice on me?'

'What?' Irulan was taken aback.

'You'd teach your grandmother to suck eggs,' Ghanima said. 'I'd what?'

'The fact that I remember the expression and you've never even heard it before should give you pause,' Ghanima said. 'It was an old expression of scorn when you Bene Gesserit were young. But if that doesn't chasten you, ask yourself what your royal parents could've been thinking of when they named you Irulan? Or is it Ruinal?'

In spite of her training, Irulan flushed. 'You're trying to goad me, Ghanima.'

'And you tried to use Voice on me. On me! I remember the first human efforts in that direction. I remember *then*, Ruinous Irulan. Now, get out of here, all of you.'

But Alia was intrigued now, caught by an inner suggestion which sloughed her fatigue aside. She said: 'Perhaps I've a suggestion which could change your mind, Ghani.'

'Still Ghani!' A brittle laugh escaped Ghanima, then: 'Reflect but a moment: If I desire to kill Farad'n, I need but fall in with your plans. I presume you've thought of that. Beware of *Ghani* in a tractable mood. You see, I'm being utterly candid with you.'

'That's what I hoped,' Alia said. 'If you . . .'

'The blood of a brother cannot be washed away.' Ghanima said. 'I'll not go before my Frèmen loved ones a traitor to that.

248

*Never to forgive, never to forget.* Isn't that our catechism? I warn you here, and I'll say it publicly: you cannot betroth me to Farad'n. Who, knowing me would believe it? Farad'n himself could not believe it, Fremen, hearing of such a betrothal, would laugh into their sleeves and say; "See! She lures him into a trap". If you . . .'

'I understand that,' Alia said, moving to Irulan's side. Irulan, she noted, was standing in shocked silence, aware already of where this conversation was headed.

'And so I would be luring him into a trap,' Ghanima said. 'If that's what you want, I'll agree, but he may not fall. If you wish this false betrothal as the empty coin with which to buy back my grandmother and your precious Duncan, so be it. But it's on your head. Buy them back. Farad'n, though, is mine. Him I'll kill.'

Irulan whirled to face Alia before she could speak. 'Alia! If we go back on our word . . . ' She let it hang there a moment while Alia smilingly reflected on the potential wrath among the Great Houses in Faufrelaches Assembled, the destructive consequences to believe in Atreides honor, the loss of religious trust, all of the great and small building blocks which would tumble.

'It'd rule against us,' Irulan protested. 'All belief in Paul's prophethood would be destroyed. It . . . the Empire . . . '

'Who could dare question our right to decide what is wrong and what is right?' Alia asked, voice mild. 'We meditate between good and evil. I need but proclaim . . .'

'You can't do this!' Irulan protested. 'Paul's memory . . .'

'Is just another tool of Church and State,' Ghanima said. 'Don't speak foolishness, Irulan.' Ghanima touched the crysknife at her waist, looked up at Alia. 'I've misjudged my clever aunt. Regret of all that's Holy in Muad'Dib's Empire. I have indeed, misjudged you. Lure Farad'n into our parlor if you will.'

'This is recklessness,' Irulan pleaded.

'You agree to this betrothal, Ghanima?' Alia asked, ignoring Irulan.

'On my terms,' Ghanima said, hand still on her crysknife.

'I wash my hands of this,' Irulan said, actually wringing her hands. 'I was willing to argue for a true betrothal to heal – '

'We'll give you a wound much more difficult to heal, Alia and I,' Ghanima said. 'Bring him quickly, if he'll come. And perhaps he will. Would he suspect a child of my tender years? Let us plan the formal ceremony of betrothal to require his presence.

249

Let there be an opportunity for me to be alone with him ▪ ▪ ▪ just a minute or two ▪ ▪ .'

Irulan shuddered at this evidence that Ghanima was, after all, Fremen entire, child no different from adult in this terrible bloodiness. After all, Fremen children were accustomed to slay the wounded on the battlefield, releasing women from this chore that they might collect the bodies and haul them away to the deathstills. And Ghanima, speaking with the voice of a Fremen child, piled horror upon horror by the studied maturity of her words, by the ancient sense of vendetta which hung like an aura around her.

'Done,' Alia said, and she fought to keep voice and face from betraying her glee. 'We'll prepare the formal charter of betrothal. We'll have the signatures witnessed by the proper assemblage from the Great Houses. Farad'n cannot possibly doubt –'

'He'll doubt, but he'll come,' Ghanima said. 'And he'll have guards. But will they think to guard him from me?'

'For the love of all that Paul tried to do,' Irulan protested, 'let us at least make Farad'n's death appear an accident, or the result of malice by outside –'

'I'll take joy in displaying my bloody knife to my brethren,' Ghanima said.

'Alia, I beg you,' Irulan said. 'Abandon this rash insanity. Declare *kanly* against Farad'n, anything to –'

'We don't require formal declaration of vendetta against him,' Ghanima said. 'The whole Empire knows how we must feel.' She pointed to the sleeve of her robe. 'We wear the yellow of mourning. When I exchange it for the black of a Fremen betrothed, will that fool anyone?'

'Pray that it fools Farad'n,' Alia said, 'and the delegates of the Great Houses we invite to witness the –'

'Every one of those delegates will turn against you,' Irulan said. 'You know that!'

'Excellent point,' Ghanima said. 'Choose those delegates with care, Alia. They must be ones we won't mind eliminating later.'

Irulan threw up her arms in despair, turned and fled.

'Have her put under close surveillance lest she try to warn her nephew,' Ghanima said.

'Don't try to teach me how to conduct a plot,' Alia said. She turned and followed Irulan, but at a slower pace. The guards outside and the waiting aides were sucked up in her wake like sand particles drawn into the vortex of a rising worm.

Ghanima shook her head sadly from side to side as the door closed, thought: *It's as poor Leto and I thought. Gods below! I wish it'd been me the tiger killed instead of him.*

*Many forces sought control of the Atreides twins and, when the death of Leto was announced, this movement of plot and counterplot was amplified. Note the relative motivations: the Sisterhood feared Alia, an adult Abomination, but still wanted those genetic characteristics carried by the Atreides. The Church hierarchy of Auqaf and Hajj saw only the power implicit in control of Muad'Dib's heir. CHOAM wanted a doorway to the wealth of Dune. Farad'n and his Sardaukar sought a return to glory for House Corrino. The Spacing Guild feared the equation Arrakis= melange; without the spice they could not navigate. Jessica wished to repair what her disobedience to the Bene Gesserit had created. Few thought to ask the twins what their plans might be, until it was too late.*

- The Book of Kreos

Shortly after the evening meal, Leto saw a man walking past the arched doorway to his chamber, and his mind went with the man. The passage had been left open and Leto had seen some activity out there – spice hampers being wheeled past, three women with the obvious off-world sophistication of dress which marked them as smugglers. This man who took Leto's mind walking might have been no different except that he moved like Stilgar, a much younger Stilgar.

It was a peculiar walk his mind took. Time filled Leto's awareness like a stellar globe. He could see infinite timespaces, but he had to press into his own future before knowing in which moment his flesh lay. His multifaceted memory-lives surged and receded, but they were his now. They were like waves on a beach, but if they rose too high, he could command them and they would retreat, leaving the royal Harum behind.

Now and again he would listen to those memory-lives. One would rise like a prompter, poking its head up out of the stage and calling cues for his behavior. His father came during the mind-walk and said: 'You are a child seeking to be a man. When you are a man, you will seek in vain for the child you were.'

All the while, he felt his body being plagued by the fleas and lice of an old sietch poorly maintained. None of the attendants who brought his heavily spice-laced food appeared bothered by the creatures. Did these people have immunity from such

251

things, or was it only that they had lived with them so long they could ignore discomfort?

Who were these people assembled around Gurney? How had they come to this place? Was this Jacurutu? His multi-memories produced answers he did not like. They were ugly people and Gurney was the ugliest. Perfection floated here, though, dormant and awaiting beneath an ugly surface.

Part of him knew he remained spice-bound, held in bondage by the heavy dosages of melange in every meal. His child's body wanted to rebel while his persona raved with the immediate presence of memories carried over from thousands of eons.

His mind returned from its walk, and he wondered if his body had really stayed behind. Spice confused the senses. He felt the pressures of self-limitations piling up against him like the long barachan dunes of the *bled* slowly building themselves a ramp against a desert cliff. One day a few trickles of sand would flow over the cliff, then more and more and more . . . and only the sand would remain exposed to the sky.

But the cliff would still be there underneath.

*I'm still within the trance,* he thought

He knew he would come soon to a branching of life and death. His captors kept sending him back into the spice thralldom, unsatisfied with his responses at every return. Always, treacherous Namri waited there with his knife. Leto knew countless pasts and futures, but he had yet to learn what would satisfy Namri . . . or Gurney Halleck. They wanted something outside of the visions. The life and death branching lured Leto. His life, he knew, would have to possess some inner meaning which carried it above the vision circumstances. Thinking of this demand, he felt that his inner awareness was his true being and his outer existence was the trance. This terrified him. He did not want to go back to the sietch with its fleas, its Namri, its Gurney Halleck.

*I'm a coward,* he thought

But a coward, even a coward, might die bravely with nothing but a gesture. Where was that gesture which could make him whole once more? How could he awaken from trance and vision into the universe which Gurney demanded? Without that turning, without an awakening from aimless visions, he knew he could die in a prison of his own choosing. In this he had at last come to cooperate with his captors. Somewhere he had to find wisdom, an inner balance which would reflect upon the universe and return to him an image of calm strength. Only then might he seek his Golden Path and survive the skin which was not his own.

Someone was playing the baliset out there in the sietch. Leto felt that his body probably heard the music in the present. He sensed the cot beneath his back. He could hear music. It was Gurney at the baliset. No other fingers could quite compare with his mastery of that most difficult instrument. He played an old Fremen song, one called a *hadith* because of its internal narrative and the voice which invoked those patterns required for survival on Arrakis. The song told the story of human occupations within a sietch.

Leto felt the music move him through a marvelous ancient cavern. He saw women trampling spice residue for fuel, curding the spice for fermentation, forming spice-fabrics. Melange was everywhere in the sietch.

Those moments came when Leto could not distinguish between the music and the people of the cavern vision. The whine and slap of a power loom was the whine and slap of the baliset. But his inner eyes beheld fabrics of human hair, the long fur of mutated rats, threads of desert cotton, and strips curled from the skin of birds. He saw a sietch school. The ecolanguage of Dune raged through his mind on its wings of music. He saw the sun-powered kitchen, the long chamber where stillsuits were made and maintained. He saw weather forecasters reading the sticks they'd brought in from the sand.

Somewhere during this journey, someone brought him food and spooned it into his mouth, holding his head up with a strong arm. He knew this as a real-time sensation, but the marvelous play of motion continued within him.

As though it came in the next instant after the spice-laden food, he saw the hurtling of a sandstorm. Moving images within the sand breath became the golden reflections of a moth's eyes, and his own life was reduced to the viscous trail of a crawling insect.

Words from the Panoplia Prophetica raved through him: 'It is said that there is nothing firm, nothing balanced, nothing durable in all the universe – that nothing remains in its state, that each day, some time each hour, brings change.'

*The old Missionaria Protectiva knew what they were doing,* he thought. *They knew about Terrible Purposes. They knew how to manipulate people and religions. Even my father didn't escape them, not in the end.*

There lay the clue he'd been seeking. Leto studied it. He felt

253

strength flowing back into his flesh. His entire multifaceted being turned over and looked out upon the universe. He sat up and found himself alone in the gloomy cell with only the light from the outer passage where the man had walked past and taken his mind an eon ago.

'Good fortune to us all!' he called in the traditional Fremen way.

Gurney Halleck appeared in the arched doorway, his head a black silhouette against the light from the outer passage.

'Bring light,' Leto said.

'You wish to be tested further?'

Leto laughed. 'No. It's my turn to test you.'

'We shall see.' Halleck turned away, returning in a moment with a bright blue glowglobe in the crook of his left elbow. He released it in the cell, allowing it to drift above their heads.

'Where's Namri?' Leto asked.

'Just outside where I can call him.'

'Ahh, Old Father Eternity always waits patiently,' Leto said. He felt curiously released, poised on the edge of discovery.

'You call Namri by the name reserved for Shai-Hulud?' Halleck asked.

'His knife's a worm's tooth,' Leto said. 'Thus, he's Old Father Eternity.'

Halleck smiled grimly, but remained silent.

'You still wait to pass judgment on me,' Leto said. 'And there's no way to exchange information, I'll admit, without making judgments. You can't ask the universe to be exact, though.'

A rustling sound behind Halleck alerted Leto to Namri's approach. He stopped half a pace to Halleck's left.

'Ahhh, the left hand of the damned,' Leto said.

'It's not wise to joke about the Infinite and the Absolute,' Namri growled. He glanced sideways at Halleck.

'Are you God, Namri, that you invoke absolutes?' Leto asked. But he kept his attention on Halleck. Judgment would come from there.

Both men merely stared at him without answering.

'Every judgment teeters on the brink of error,' Leto explained. 'To claim absolute knowledge is to become monstrous. Knowledge is an unending adventure at the edge of uncertainty.'

'What word game is this you play?' Halleck demanded.

'Let him speak,' Namri said.

'It's the game Namri initiated with me,' Leto said, and saw the old Fremen's head nod agreement. He'd certainly recognized the riddle game. 'Our senses always have at least two levels,' Leto said.

'Trivia and message,' Namri said.

'Excellent!' Leto said. 'You gave me trivia; I give you message. I see, I hear, I detect odors, I touch; I feel changes in temperature, taste. I sense the passage of time. I may take emotive samples. Ahhhhh! I am happy. You see, Gurney? Namri? There's no mystery about a human life. It's not a problem to be solved, but a reality to be experienced.'

'You try our patience, lad,' Namri said. 'Is this the place where you wish to die?'

But Halleck put out a restraining hand.

'First, I am not a lad,' Leto said. He made the first sign at his right ear. 'You'll not slay me; I've placed a water burden upon you.'

Namri drew his crysknife half out of its sheath. 'I owe you nothing!'

'But God created Arrakis to train the faithful,' Leto said. 'I've not only showed you my faith, I've made you conscious of your own existence. Life requires dispute. You've been made to *know* – by me! – that your reality differs from all others; thus, you know you're alive.'

'Irreverence is a dangerous game to play with me,' Namri said. He held his crysknife half drawn.

'Irreverence is a most necessary ingredient of religion,' Leto said. 'Not to speak of its importance in philosophy. Irreverence is the only way left to us for testing our universe.'

'So you think you understand the universe?' Halleck asked, and he opened a space between himself and Namri.

'Ye-esss,' Namri said, and there was death in his voice.

'The universe can be understood only by the wind,' Leto said. 'There's no mighty seat of reason which dwells within the brain. Creation is discovery. God discovered us in the Void because we moved against a background which He already knew. The wall was blank. Then there was movement.'

'You play hide and seek with death,' Halleck warned.

'But you are both my friends,' Leto said. He faced Namri. 'When you offer a candidate as Friend of your Sietch, do you not slay a hawk and an eagle as the offering? And is this not the response: "God send each man at his end, such hawks, such eagles, and such friends"?'

Namri's hand slid from his knife. The blade slipped back into its sheath. He stared wide-eyed at Leto. Each sietch kept its friendship ritual secret, yet here was a selected part of the rite.

Halleck, though, asked: 'Is this place your end?'

'I know what you need to hear from me, Gurney,' Leto said, watching the play of hope and suspicion across the ugly face. Leto touched his own breast. 'This child was never a child. My father lives within me, but he is not me. You loved him, and he was a gallant human whose affairs beat upon high shores. His intent was to close down the cycle of wars, but he reckoned without the movement of infinity as expressed by life. That's Rhajia! Namri knows. Its movement can be seen by any mortal. Beware paths which narrow future possibilities. Such paths divert you from infinity into lethal traps.'

'What is it I need to hear from you?' Halleck asked.

'He's just word playing,' Namri said, but his voice carried deep hesitation, doubts.

'I ally myself with Namri against my father,' Leto said. 'And my father within allies himself with us against what was made of him.'

'Why?' Halleck demanded.

'Because it's the *amor fati* which I bring to humankind, the act of ultimate self-examination. In this universe, I choose to ally myself against any force which brings humiliation upon humankind. Gurney! Gurney! You were not born and raised in the desert. Your flesh doesn't know the truth of which I speak. But Namri knows. In the open land, one direction is as good as another.'

'I still have not heard what I must hear,' Halleck snarled.

'He speaks for war and against peace,' Namri said.

'No,' Leto said. 'Nor did my father speak against war. But look what was made of him. Peace has only one meaning in this Imperium. It's the maintenance of a single way of life. You are commanded to be contented. Life must be uniform on all planets as it is in the Imperial Government. The major object of priestly study is to find the correct forms of human behavior. For this they go to the words of Muad'Dib! Tell me, Namri, are you content?'

'No.' The words came out flat, spontaneous rejection.

'Then do you blaspheme?'

'Of course not!'

'But you aren't contented. You see, Gurney? Namri proves it to us. Every question, every problem doesn't have a single correct answer. One must permit diversity. A monolith is unstable. Then why do you demand a single correct statement from me? Is that to be the measure of your monstrous judgment?'

'Will you force me to have you slain?' Halleck asked, and there was agony in his voice.

'No, I'll have pity upon you,' Leto said. 'Send word to my grandmother that I'll cooperate. The Sisterhood may come to regret my cooperation, but an Atreides gives his word.'

'A Truthsayer should test that,' Namri said. 'These Atreides . . .'

'He'll have his chance to say before his grandmother what must be said,' Halleck said. He nodded with his head toward the passage.

Namri paused before leaving, glanced at Leto. 'I pray we do the right thing in leaving him alive.'

'Go, friends,' Leto said. 'Go and reflect.'

As the two men departed, Leto threw himself onto his back, feeling the cold cot against his spine. Movement sent his head spinning over the edge of his spice-burdened consciousness. In that instant he saw the entire planet – every village, every town, every city, the desert places and the planted places. All of the shapes which smashed against his vision bore intimate relationships to a mixture of elements within themselves and without. He saw the structures of Imperial society reflected in physical structures of its planets and their communities. Like a gigantic unfolding within him, he saw this revelation for what it must be: a window into the society's invisible parts. Seeing this, Leto realized that every system had such a window. Even the system of himself and his universe. He began peering into windows, a cosmic voyeur.

This was what his grandmother and the Sisterhood sought! He knew it. His awareness flowed on a new, higher level. He felt the past carried in his cells, in his memories, in the archetypes which haunted his assumptions, in the myths which hemmed him, in his languages and their prehistoric detritus. It was all of the shapes out of his human and nonhuman past, all of the lives which he now commanded, all integrated in him at last. And he felt himself as a thing caught up in the ebb and flow of nucleotides. Against the backdrop of infinity he was a protozoan creature in which birth and death were virtually simultaneous, but he was both infinite and protozoan, a creature of molecular memories.

*We humans are a form of colony organism!* he thought.

They wanted his cooperation. Promising cooperation had won him another reprieve from Namri's knife. By summoning to co-

257

operation, they sought to recognize a healer.

And he thought: *But I'll not bring them social order in the way they expect it!*

A grimace contorted Leto's mouth. He knew he'd not be as unconsciously malevolent as was his father – despotism at one terminal and slavery at the other – but this universe might pray for those 'good old days'.

His father-within spoke to him then, cautiously probing, unable to demand attention but pleading for audience.

And Leto answered: 'No. We will give them complexities to occupy their mind. There are many modes of flight from danger. How will they know I'm dangerous unless they experience me for thousands of years? Yes, father-within, we'll give them question marks.'

---

> *There is no guilt or innocence in you. All of that is past. Guilt belabors the dead and I am not the Iron Hammer. You multitude of the dead are merely people who have done certain things, and the memory of those things illuminates my path.*
>
> > – Leto II to His Memory-Lives
> > After Harq al-Ada

'It moves of itself!' Farad'n said, and his voice was barely a whisper.

He stood above the Lady Jessica's bed, a brace of guards close behind him. The Lady Jessica had propped herself up in the bed. She was clad in a parasilk gown of shimmering white with a matching band around her copper hair. Farad'n had come bursting in upon her moments before. He wore the gray leotard and his face was sweaty with excitement and the exertions of his dash through the palace corridors.

'What time is it?' Jessica asked.

'Time?' Farad'n appeared puzzled.

One of the guards spoke up: 'It is the third hour past midnight, My Lady.' The guard glanced fearfully at Farad'n. The young prince had come dashing through the night-lighted corridors, picking up startled guards in his wake.

'But it moves,' Farad'n said. He held out his left hand, then his right. 'I saw my own hands shrink into chubby fists, and I remembered! They were my hands when I was an infant. I

258

remembered being an infant, but it was . . . a clearer memory. I was reorganizing my old memories!'

'Very good,' Jessica said. His excitement was infectious. 'And what happened when your hands became old?'

'My . . . mind was . . . sluggish,' he said. 'I felt an ache in my back. Right here.' He touched a place over his left kidney.

'You've learned a most important lesson,' Jessica said. 'Do you know what that lesson is?'

He dropped his hands to his sides, stared at her. Then: 'My mind controls my reality.' His eyes glittered, and he repeated it, louder this time: 'My mind controls my reality!'

'That is the beginning of *prana-bindu* balance,' Jessica said. 'It is only the beginning, though.'

'What do I do next?' he asked.

'My Lady,' the guard who had answered her question ventured now to interrupt. 'The hour,' he said.

*Aren't their spy posts manned at this hour?* Jessica wondered. She said: 'Begone. We have work to do.'

'But My Lady,' the guard said, and he looked fearfully from Farad'n to Jessica and back.

'You think I'm going to seduce him?' Jessica asked.

The man stiffened.

Farad'n laughed, a joyous outburst. He waved a hand in dismissal. 'You heard her. Begone.'

The guards looked at each other, but they obeyed.

Farad'n sat on the edge of her bed. 'What next?' He shook his head. 'I wanted to believe you, yet I did not believe. Then . . . it was as though my mind melted. I was tired. My mind gave up its fighting against you. It happened. Just like that!' He snapped his fingers.

'It was not me that your mind fought against,' Jessica said. '

'Of course not,' he admitted. 'I was fighting against myself, all the nonsense I've learned. What next now?'

Jessica smiled. 'I confess I didn't expect you to succeed this rapidly. It's been only eight days and . . . ?'

'I was patient,' he said, grinning.

'And you've begun to learn patience, too,' she said.

'Begun?'

'You've just crept over the lip of this learning,' she said. 'Now you're truly an infant. Before . . . you were only a potential, not even born.'

The corners of his mouth drew down.

'Don't be so gloomy,' she said. 'You've done it. That's im-

259

portant. How many can say they were born anew?'

'What comes next?' he insisted.

'You will practice this thing you've learned,' she said. 'I want you able to do this at will, easily. Later you'll fill a new place in your awareness which this has opened. It will be filled by the ability to test any reality against your own demands.'

'Is that all I do now . . . practice the –'

'No. Now you can begin the muscle training. Tell me, can you move the little toe on your left foot without moving any other muscle of your body?'

'My . . . ' She saw a distant expression come over his face as he tried to move the toe. He looked down at his foot presently, staring at it. Sweat broke out on his forehead. A deep breath escaped him. 'I can't do it.'

'Yes you can,' she said. 'You will learn to do it. You will learn every muscle in your body. You will know these muscles the way you know your hands.'

He swallowed hard at the magnitude of this prospect. Then: 'What are you doing to me? What is your plan for me?'

'I intend to turn you loose upon the universe,' she said. 'You will become whatever it is you most deeply desire.'

He mulled this for a moment. 'Whatever I desire?'

'Yes.'

'That's impossible!'

'Unless you learn to control your desires the way you control your reality,' she said. And she thought: *There! Let his analysts examine that. They'll advise cautious approval, but Farad'n will move a step closer to realization of what I'm really doing.*

He proved her surmise by saying: 'It's one thing to tell a person he'll realize his heart's desire. It's another thing to actually deliver that realization.'

'You've come farther than I thought,' Jessica said. 'Very good. I promise you: if you complete this program of learning, you'll be your own man. Whatever you do, it'll be because that's what you want to do.'

*And let a Truthsayer try to pry that apart*, she thought.

He stood up, but the expression he bent upon her was warm, a sense of camaraderie in it. 'You know, I believe you. Damned if I know why, but I do. And I won't say a word about the other things I'm thinking.'

Jessica watched his retreating back as he let himself out of her bedchamber. She turned off the glowglobes, lay back. This Farad'n was a deep one. He'd as much as told her that he was

260

beginning to see her design, but he was joining her conspiracy of his own volition.

*Wait until he begins to learn his own emotions,* she thought. With that, she composed herself for the return to sleep. The morrow, she knew, would be plagued by casual encounters with palace personnel asking seemingly innocuous questions.

> Humankind periodically goes through a speedup of its affairs, thereby experiencing the race between the renewable vitality of the living and the beckoning vitiation of decadence. In this periodic race, any pause becomes luxury. Only then can one reflect that all is permitted; all is possible.
>
> -- **The Apocrypha of Muad'Dib**

*The touch of sand is important,* Leto told himself.

He could feel the grit beneath him where he sat beneath a brilliant sky. They had force-fed him another heavy dosage of melange, and Leto's mind turned upon itself like a whirlpool. An unanswered question lay deep within the funnel of the whirlpool: *Why do they insist that I say it?* Gurney was stubborn; no doubt of that. And he'd had his orders from his Lady Jessica.

They'd brought him out of the sietch into the daylight for this 'lesson'. He had the strange sensation that he'd let his body take the short trip from the sietch while his inner being mediated a battle between the Duke Leto I and the old Baron Harkonnen. They'd fought within him, through him, because he would not let them communicate directly. The fight had taught him what had happened to Alia. Poor Alia.

*I was right to fear the spice trip,* he thought.

A welling bitterness toward the Lady Jessica filled him. Her damned gom jabbar! Fight it and win, or die in the attempt. She couldn't put a poisoned needle against his neck, but she could send him into the valley of peril which had claimed her own daughter.

Snuffling sounds intruded upon his awareness. They wavered, growing louder, then softer, louder . . . softer. There was no way for him to determine whether they had current reality or came from the spice.

Leto's body sagged over his folded arms. He felt hot sand through his buttocks. There was a rug directly in front of him, but he sat on open sand. A shadow lay across the rug: Namri.

Leto stared into the muddy pattern of the rug, feeling bubbles ripple there. His awareness drifted on its own current through a landscape which stretched out to a horizon of shock-headed greenery.

His skull thrummed with drums. He felt heat, fever. The fever was a pressure of burning which filled his senses, crowding out awareness of flesh until he could only feel the moving shadows of his peril. Namri and the knife. Pressure . . . pressure . . . Leto lay at last suspended between sky and sand, his mind lost to all but the fever. Now he waited for something to happen, sensing that any occurrence would be a first-and-only thing.

Hot-hot pounding sunshine crashed brilliantly around him, without tranquillity, without remedy. *Where is my Golden Path?* Everywhere bugs crawled. Everywhere. *My skin is not my own.* He sent messages along his nerves, waited out the dragging other-person responses.

*Up head*, he told his nerves.

A head which might have been his own crept upward, looked out at patches of blankness in the bright light.

Someone whispered: 'He's deep into it now.'

No answer.

Burn fire sun building heat on heat.

Slowly, outbending, the current of his awareness took him drifting through a last screen of green blankness and there, across low folding dunes, distant no more than a kilometer beyond the stretched out chalk line of a cliff, *there* lay the green burgeoning future, upflung, flowing into endless green, greenswelling, green-green moving outward endlessly.

In all of that green there was not one great worm.

Riches of wild growth, but nowhere Shai-Hulud.

Leto sensed that he had ventured across old boundaries into a new land which only the imagination had witnessed, and that he looked now directly through the very next veil which a yawning humankind called *Unknown.*

It was bloodthirsty reality.

He felt the red fruit of his life swaying on a limb, fluid slipping away from him, and the fluid was the spice essence flowing through his veins.

Without Shai-Hulud, no more spice.

He had seen a future without the great gray worm-serpent of Dune. He knew this, yet could not tear himself from the trance to rail against such a passage.

Abruptly his awareness plunged back – back, back, away from

such a deadly future. His thoughts went into his bowels, becoming primitive, moved only by intense emotions. He found himself unable to focus on any particular aspect of his vision or his surroundings, but there was a voice within him. It spoke an ancient language and he understood it perfectly. The voice was musical and lilting, but its words bludgeoned him.

'It is not the present which influences the future, thou fool, but the future which forms the present. You have it all backward. Since the future is set, an unfolding of events which will assure that future is fixed and inevitable.'

The words transfixed him. He felt terror rooted in the heavy matter of his body. By this he knew his body still existed, but the reckless nature and enormous power of his vision left him feeling contaminated, defenseless, unable to signal a muscle and gain its obedience. He knew he was submitting more and more to the onslaught of those collective lives whose memories once had made him believe he was real. Fear filled him. He thought that he might be losing the inner command, falling at last into Abomination.

Leto felt his body twisting in terror.

He had come to depend upon his victory and the newly won benevolent cooperation of those memories. They had turned against him, all of them – even royal Harum whom he'd trusted. He lay shimmering on a surface which had no roots, unable to give any expression to his own life. He tried to concentrate upon a mental picture of himself, was confronted by overlapping frames, each a different age: infant into doddering ancient. He recalled his father's early training: *Let the hands grow young, then old.* But his whole body was immersed now in this lost reality and the entire image progression melted into other faces, the features of those who had given him their memories.

A diamond thunderbolt shattered him.

Leto felt pieces of his awareness drifting apart, yet he retained a sense of himself somewhere between being and nonbeing. Hope quickening, he felt his body breathing. In . . . Out. He took in a deep breath: *yin.* He let it out: *yang.*

Somewhere just beyond his grasp lay a place of supreme independence, a victory over all of the confusions inherent in his multitude of lives – no false sense of command, but a true victory. He knew his previous mistake now: he had sought power in the reality of his trance, choosing that rather than face the fears which he and Ghanima had fed in each other.

*Fear defeated Alia!*

But the seeking after power spread another trap, diverting him into fantasy. He saw the illusion. The entire illusion process rotated half a turn and now he knew a center from which he could watch without purpose the flight of his visions, of his inner lives.

Elation flooded him. It made him want to laugh, but he denied himself this luxury, knowing it would bar the doors of memory.

*Ahhhh, my memories,* he thought. *I have seen your illusion. You no longer invent the next moment for me. You merely show me how to create new moments, I'll not lock myself on the old tracks.*

This thought passed through his awareness as though wiping a surface clean and in its wake he felt his entire body, an *einfalle* which reported in most minute detail on every cell, every nerve. He entered a state of intense quiet. In this quiet, he heard voices, knowing they came from a great distance, but he heard them clearly as though they echoed in a chasm.

One of the voices was Halleck's. 'Perhaps we gave him too much of it.'

Namri answered. 'We gave him exactly what she told us to give him.'

'Perhaps we should go back out there and have another look at him.' Halleck.

'Sabiha is good at such things; she'll call us if anything starts to go wrong.' Namri.

'I don't like this business of Sabiha.' Halleck.

'She's a necessary ingredient.' Namri.

Leto felt bright light outside himself and darkness within, but the darkness was secretive, protective, and warm. The light began to blaze up and he felt that it came from the darkness within, swirling outward like a brilliant cloud. His body became transparent, drawing him upward, yet he retained that *einfalle* contact with every cell and nerve. The multitude of inner lives fell into alignment, nothing tangled or mixed. They became very quiet in duplication of his own inner silence, each memory-life discrete, an entity incorporeal and undivided.

Leto spoke to them then: 'I am your spirit. I am the only life you can realize. I am the house of your spirit in the land which is nowhere, the land which is your only remaining home. Without me, the intelligible universe reverts to chaos. Creative and abysmal are inextricably linked in me; only I can mediate between them. Without me, mankind will sink into the mire and vanity of *knowing.* Through me, you and they will find the only way out of chaos: *understanding by living.*'

With this he let go of himself and became himself, his own person compassing the entirety of his past. It was not victory, not defeat, but a new thing to be shared with any inner life he chose. Leto savored this newness, letting it possess every cell, every nerve, giving up what the *einfalle* had presented to him and recovering the totality in the same instant.

After a time, he awoke in white darkness. With a flash of awareness he knew where his flesh was: seated on sand about a kilometer from the cliff wall which marked the northern boundary of the sietch. He knew that sietch now: Jacurutu for certain . . . and Fondak. But it was far different from the myths and legends and the rumors which the smugglers allowed.

A young woman sat on a rug directly in front of him, a bright glowglobe anchored to her left sleeve and drifting just above her head. When Leto looked away from the glowglobe, there were stars. He knew this young woman; she was the one from his vision earlier, the roaster of coffee. She was Namri's niece, as ready with a knife as Namri was. There was the knife in her lap. She wore a simple green robe over a gray stillsuit. *Sabiha,* that was her name. And Namri had his own plans for her.

Sabiha saw the awakening in his eyes, said: 'It's almost dawn. You've spent the whole night here.'

'And most of a day,' he said. 'You make good coffee.'

This statement puzzled her, but she ignored it with a single-mindedness which spoke of harsh training and explicit instructions for her present behavior.

'It's the hour of assassins,' Leto said. 'But your knife is no longer needed.' He glanced at the crysknife in her lap.

'Namri will be the judge of that,' she said.

*Not Halleck, then.* She only confirmed his inner knowledge.

'Shai-Hulud is a great garbage collector and eraser of unwanted evidence,' Leto said. 'I've used him thus myself.'

She rested her hand lightly on the knife handle.

'How much is revealed by where we sit and how we sit,' he said. 'You sit upon the rug and I upon the sand.'

Her hands closed over the knife handle.

Leto yawned, a gaping and stretching which made his jaw ache. 'I've had a vision which included you,' he said.

Her shoulders relaxed slightly.

'We've been very one-sided about Arrakis,' he said. 'Barbaric of us. There's a certain momentum in what we've been doing, but now we must undo some of our work. The scales must be brought into better balance.'

A puzzled frown touched Sabiha's face.

'My vision,' he said. 'Unless we restore the dance of life here on Dune, the dragon on the floor of the desert will be no more.'

Because he'd used the Old Fremen name for the great worm, she was a moment understanding him. Then: 'The worms?'

'We're in a dark passage,' he said. 'Without spice, the Empire falls apart. The Guild will not move. Planets will slowly lose their clear memories of each other. They'll turn inward upon themselves. Space will become a boundary when the Guild navigators lose their mastery. We'll cling to our dunetops and be ignorant of that which is above us and below us.'

'You speak very strangely,' she said. 'How have you seen *me* in your vision?'

*Trust Fremen superstition!* he thought. He said: 'I've become pasigraphic. I'm a living glyph to write out the changes which must come to pass. If I do not write them, you'll encounter such heartache as no human should experience.'

'What words are these?' she asked, but her hand remained lightly on the knife.

Leto turned his head toward the cliffs of Jacurutu, seeing the beginning glow which would be Second Moon making its pre-dawn passage behind the rocks. The death-scream of a desert hare shocked its way through him. He saw Sabiha shudder. There came the beating of wings – a predator bird, night creature here. He saw the ember glow of many eyes as they swept past above him, headed for crannies in the cliff.

'I must follow the dictates of my new heart,' Leto said. 'You look upon me as a mere child, Sabiha, but if –'

'They warned me about you,' Sabiha said, and now her shoulders were stiff with readiness.

He heard the fear in her voice, said: 'Don't fear me, Sabiha. You've lived eight more years than this flesh of mine. For that, I honor you. But I have untold thousands more years of other lives, far more than you have known. Don't look upon me as a child. I have bridged the many futures and, in one, saw us entwined in love. You and I, Sabiha.'

'What are . . . This can't . . .' She broke off in confusion.

'The idea could grow on you,' he said. 'Now help me back to the sietch, for I've been in far places and am weak with the weariness of my travels. Namri must hear where I have been.'

He saw the indecision in her, said: 'Am I not the Guest of

the Cavern? Namri must learn what I have learned. We have many things to do lest our universe degenerate.'

'I don't believe that . . . about the worms,' she said.

'Nor about us entwined in love?'

She shook her head. But he could see the thoughts drifting through her mind like windblown feathers. His words both attracted and repelled her. To be consort of power, that certainly carried high allure. Yet there were her uncle's orders. But one day this son of Muad'Dib might rule here on Dune and in the farthest reaches of their universe. She encountered then an extremely Fremen, cavern-hiding aversion to such a future. The consort of Leto would be seen by everyone, would be an object of gossip and speculation. She could have wealth, though, and . . .

'I am the son of Muad'Dib, able to see the future,' he said.

Slowly she replaced her knife in its sheath, lifted herself easily from the rug, crossed to his side and helped him to his feet. Leto found himself amused by her actions then: she folded the rug neatly and draped it across her right shoulder. He saw her measuring the difference in their sizes, reflecting upon his words: *Entwined in love?*

*Size is another thing that changes,* he thought.

She put a hand on his arm then to help him and control him. He stumbled and she spoke sharply: 'We're too far from the sietch for *that*!' Meaning the unwanted sound which might attract a worm.

Leto felt that his body had become a dry shell like that abandoned by an insect. He knew this shell: it was one with the society which had been built upon the melange trade and its Religion of the Golden Elixir. It was emptied by its excesses. Muad'Dib's high aims had fallen into wizardry which was enforced by the military arm of Auqaf. Muad'Dib's religion had another name now; it was Shein-san-Shao, an Ixian label which designated the intensity and insanity of those who thought they could bring the universe to paradise at the point of a cryskin fe. But that too would change as Ix had changed. For they were merely the ninth planet of their sun, and had even forgotten the language which had given them their name.

'The Jihad was a kind of mass insanity,' he muttered.

'What?' Sabiha had been concentrating on the problem of making him walk without rhythm, hiding their presence out here on open sand. She was a moment focusing on his words, then interpreted them as another product of his obvious fatigue. She felt the weakness of him, the way he'd been drained by the trance.

267

It seemed pointless and cruel to her. If he were to be killed as Namri said, then it should be done quickly without all of this by-play. Leto had spoken of a marvelous revelation, though. Perhaps that was what Namri sought. Certainly that must be the motive behind the behavior of this child's own grandmother. Why else would Our Lady of Dune give her sanction to these perilous acts against a child?

*Child?*

Again she reflected upon his words. They were at the cliff base now and she stopped her charge, letting him relax a moment here where it was safer. Looking down at him in the dim starlight, she asked: 'How could there be no more worms?'

'Only I can change that,' he said. 'Have no fear. I can change anything.'

'But it's –'

'Some questions have no answers,' he said. 'I've seen that future, but the contradictions would only confuse you. This is a changing universe and we are the strangest change of all. We resonate to many influences. Our futures need constant updating. Now, there's a barrier which we must remove. This requires that we do brutal things, that we go against our most basic, our dearest wishes . . . But it must be done.'

'What must be done?'

'Have you ever killed a friend?' he asked and, turning, led the way into the gap which sloped upward to the sietch's hidden entrance. He moved as quickly as his trance-fatigue would permit, but she was right behind him, clutching his robe and pulling him to a stop.

'What's this of killing a friend?'

'He'll die anyway,' Leto said. 'I don't have to do it, but I could prevent it. If I don't prevent it, is that not killing him?'

'Who is this . . . who will die?'

'The alternative keeps me silent,' he said. 'I might have to give my sister to a monster.'

Again he turned away from her, and this time when she pulled at his robe he resisted, refusing to answer her questions. *Best she not know until the time comes,* he thought.

*Natural selection has been described as an environment selec-
tively screening for those who will have progeny. Where humans
are concerned, though, this is an extremely limiting viewpoint.
Reproduction by sex tends toward experiment and innovation. It
raises many questions, including the ancient one about whether
environment is a selective agent after the variation occurs, or
whether environment plays a pre-selective role in determining the
variations which it screens. Dune did not really answer those
questions; it merely raised new questions which Leto and the
Sisterhood may attempt to answer over the next five hundred
generations.*

> – The Dune Catastrophe
> After Harq al-Ada

The bare brown rocks of the Shield Wall loomed in the distance,
visible to Ghanima as the embodiment of that apparition which
threatened her future. She stood at the edge of the roof garden
atop the Keep, the setting sun at her back. The sun held a deep
orange glow from intervening dust clouds, a color as rich as the
rim of a worm's mouth. She sighed, thinking: *Alia . . . Alia . . . Is
your fate to be my fate?*

The inner lives had grown increasingly clamorous of late.
There was something about female conditioning in a Fremen
society – perhaps it was a real sexual difference, but whatever –
the female was more susceptible to that inner tide. Her grandmother had warned about it as they'd schemed, drawing on the
accumulated wisdom of the Bene Gesserit but awakening that
wisdom's threats within Ghanima.

'Abomination,' the Lady Jessica had said, 'our term for the
pre-born, has a long history of bitter experiences behind it. The
way of it seems to be that the inner lives divide. They split into
the benign and the malignant. The benign remain tractable, useful. The malignant appear to unite in one powerful psyche, trying
to take over the living flesh and its consciousness. The process
is known to take considerable time, but its signs are well known.'

'Why did you abandon Alia?' Ghanima asked.

'I fled in terror of what I'd created,' Jessica said, her voice low.
'I gave up. And my burden now is that . . . perhaps I gave up too
soon.'

'What do you mean?'

'I cannot explain yet, but . . . maybe . . . no! I'll not give you
false hopes. *Ghafla*, the abominable distraction, has a long history

in human mythology. It was called many things, but chiefly it was called *possession*. That's what it seems to be. You lose your way in the malignancy and it takes possession of you.'

'Leto . . . feared the spice,' Ghanima said, finding that she could talk about him quietly. The terrible price demanded of them!

'And wisely,' Jessica had said. She would say no more.

But Ghanima had risked an exploration of her inner memories, peering past an odd blurred veil and futilely expanding on the Bene Gesserit fears. To explain what had befallen Alia did not ease it one bit. The Bene Gesserit accumulation of experience had pointed to a possible way out of the trap, though, and when Ghanima ventured the inner sharing, she first called upon the Mohalata, a partnership of the benign which might protect her.

She recalled that sharing as she stood in the sunset glow at the edge of the Keep's roof garden. Immediately she felt the memory-presence of her mother. Chani stood there, an apparition between Ghanima and the distant cliffs.

'Enter here and you will eat the fruit of the Zaqquum, the food of hell!' Chani said. 'Bar this door, my daughter; it is your only safety.'

The inner clamor lifted itself around the vision and Ghanima fled, sinking her consciousness into the Sisterhood's Credo, reacting out of desperation more than trust. Quickly she recited the Credo, moving her lips, letting her voice rise to a whisper:

'*Religion is the emulation of the adult by the child. Religion is the encystment of past beliefs: mythology, which is guesswork, the hidden assumptions of trust in the universe, those pronouncements which men have made in search of personal power, all of it mingled with shreds of enlightenment. And always the ultimate unspoken commandment is "Thou shalt not question!" But we question. We break that commandment as a matter of course. The work to which we have set ourselves is the liberating of the imagination, the harnessing of imagination to humankind's deepest sense of creativity.*'

Slowly a sense of order returned to Ghanima's thoughts. She felt her body trembling, though, and knew how fragile was this peace she had attained – and that blurring veil remained in her mind.

'Leb Kamai,' she whispered, 'Heart of my enemy, you shall not be my heart.'

And she called up a memory of Farad'n's features, the saturnine young face with its heavy brows and firm mouth.

*Hate will make me strong,* she thought. *In hate, I can resist Alia's fate.*

But the trembling fragility of her position remained, and all she could think about was how much Farad'n resembled his uncle, the late ShaddamIV.

'Here you are!'

It was Irulan coming up from Ghanima's right, striding along the parapet with movements reminiscent of a man. Turning, Ghanima thought: *And she's Shaddam's daughter.*

'Why will you persist in sneaking out alone?' Irulan demanded, stopping in front of Ghanima and towering over her with a scowling face.

Ghanima refrained from saying that she was not alone, that guards had seen her emerge onto the roof. Irulan's anger went to the fact they were in the open here and that a distant weapon might find them.

'You're not wearing a stillsuit,' Ghanima said. 'Did you know that in the old days someone caught outside the sietch without a stillsuit was automatically killed. To waste water was to endanger the tribe.'

'Water! Water!' Irulan snapped. 'I want to know why you endanger yourself this way. Come back inside. You make trouble for all of us.'

'What danger is there now?' Ghanima asked. 'Stilgar has purged the traitors. Alia's guards are everywhere.'

Irulan peered upward at the darkening sky. Stars were already visible against a gray-blue backdrop. She returned her attention to Ghanima. 'I won't argue. I was sent to tell you we have word from Farad'n. He accepts, but for some reason he wishes to delay the ceremony.'

'How long?'

'We don't know yet. It's being negotiated. But Duncan is being sent home.'

'And my grandmother?'

'She chooses to stay on Salusa for the time being.'

'Who can blame her?' Ghanima asked.

'That silly fight with Alia!'

'Don't try to gull me, Irulan! That was no silly fight. I've heard the stories.'

'The Sisterhood's fears —'

'Are real,' Ghanima said. 'Well, you've delivered your message. Will you use this opportunity to have another try at dissuading me?'

271

'I've given up.'

'You should know better than to try lying to me,' Ghanima said.

'Very well! I'll keep trying to dissuade you. This course is madness.' And Irulan wondered why she let Ghanima become so irritating. A Bene Gesserit didn't need to be irritated at anything. She said: 'I'm concerned by the extreme danger to you. You know that. Ghani, Ghani . . . you're Paul's daughter. How can you – '

'Because I'm his daughter,' Ghanima said. 'We Atreides go back to Agamemnon and we know what's in our blood. Never forget that, childless wife of my father. We Atreides have a bloody history and we're not through with the blood.'

Distracted, Irulan asked: 'Who's Agamemnon?'

'How sparse your vaunted Bene Gesserit education proves itself,' Ghanima said. 'I keep forgetting that you foreshorten history. But my memories go back to , . . ' She broke off; best not to arouse those shades from their fragile sleep.

'Whatever you remember,' Irulan said, 'you must know how dangerous this course is to – '

'I'll kill him,' Ghanima said. 'He owes me a life.'

'And I'll prevent it if I can.'

'We already know this. You won't get the opportunity. Alia is sending you south to one of the new towns until after it's done.'

Irulan shook her head in dismay. 'Ghani, I took my oath that I'd guard you against any danger. I'll do it with my own life if necessary. If you think I'm going to languish in some brick-walled djedida while you . . . '

'There's always the Huanui,' Ghanima said, speaking softly. 'We have the deathstill as an alternative. I'm sure you couldn't interfere from there.'

Irulan paled, put a hand to her mouth, forgetting for a moment all of her training. It was a measure of how much care she had invested in Ghanima, this almost complete abandonment of everything except animal fear. She spoke out of that shattering emotion, allowing it to tremble on her lips. 'Ghani, I don't fear for myself. I'd throw myself into the worm's mouth for you. Yes, I'm what you call me, the childless wife of your father, but you're the child I never had. I beg you . . . ' Tears glistened at the corners of her eyes.

Ghanima fought down a tightness in her throat; said: 'There is another difference between us. You were never Fremen. I'm nothing else. This is a chasm which divides us. Alia knows. Whatever else she may be, she knows this.'

'You can't tell what Alia knows,' Irulan said, speaking bitterly. 'If I didn't know her for Atreides, I'd swear she has set herself to destroy her own Family.'

*And how do you know she's still Atreides?* Ghanima thought, wondering at this blindness in Irulan. This was a Bene Gesserit, and who knew better than they the history of Abomination? She would not let herself even think about it, let alone believe it. Alia must have worked some witchery on this poor woman.

Ghanima said: 'I owe you a water debt. For that, I'll guard your life. But your cousin's forfeit. Say no more of that.'

Irulan stilled the trembling of her lips, wiped her eyes. 'I did love your father,' she whispered. 'I didn't even know it until he was dead.'

'Perhaps he isn't dead,' Ghanima said. 'The Preacher . . .'

'Ghani! Sometimes I don't understand you. Would Paul attack his own family?'

Ghanima shrugged, looked out at the darkening sky. 'He might find amusement in such a –'

'How can you speak so lightly of this –'

'To keep away the dark depths,' Ghanima said. 'I don't taunt you. The gods know I don't. But I'm not just my father's daughter. I'm every person who's contributed seed to the Atreides. You won't think of Abomination, but I can't think of anything else. I'm the pre-born. I know what's within me.'

'That foolish old superstition about –'

'Don't!' Ghanima reached a hand toward Irulan's mouth. 'I'm every Bene Gesserit of their damnable breeding program up to and including my grandmother. And I'm very much more.' She tore at her left palm, drawing blood with a fingernail. 'This is a young body, but its experiences . . . Oh, *gods,* Irulan! My experiences! No!' She put out her hand once more as Irulan moved closer. 'I know all of those futures which my father explored. I've the wisdom of so many lifetimes, and all the ignorance, too . . . all the frailties. If you'd help me, Irulan, first learn who I am.'

Instinctively Irulan bent and gathered Ghanima into her arms, holding her close, cheek against cheek.

*Don't let me have to kill this woman,* Ghanima thought. *Don't let that happen.*

As this thought swept through her, the whole desert passed into night.

*One small bird has called thee*
*From a beak streaked crimson.*
*It cried once over Sietch Tabr*
*And thou went forth unto Funeral Plain.*

**— Lament for Leto II**

Leto awoke to the tinkle of water rings in a woman's hair. He looked to the open doorway of his cell and saw Sabiha sitting there. In the half-immersed awareness of the spice he saw her outlined by all that his vision revealed about her. She was two years past the age when most Fremen women were wed or at least betrothed. Therefore her family was saving her for something . . . or someone. She was nubile . . . obviously. His vision-shrouded eyes saw her as a creature out of humankind's Terranic past: dark hair and pale skin, deep sockets which gave her blue-in-blue eyes a greenish cast. She possessed a small nose and a wide mouth above a sharp chin. And she was a living signal to him that the Bene Gesserit plan was known — or suspected — here in Jacurutu. So they hoped to revive Pharaonic Imperialism through him, did they? Then what was their design to force him into marrying his sister? Surely Sabiha could not prevent that.

His captors knew the plan, though. And how had they learned it? They'd not shared its vision. They'd not gone with him where life became a moving membrane in other dimensions. The reflexive and circular subjectivity of the visions which revealed Sabiha were his and his alone.

Again the water rings tinkled in Sabiha's hair and the sound stirred up his visions. He knew where he had been and what he had learned. Nothing could erase that. He was not riding a great Maker palanquin now, the tinkle of water rings among the passengers a rhythm for their passage songs. No . . . He was here in the cell of Jacurutu, embarked on that most dangerous of all journeys: away from the back to the *Ahl as-sunna wal-jamas*, from the real world of the senses and back to that world.

What was she doing there with the water rings tinkling in her hair? Oh, yes. She was mixing more of the brew which they thought held him captive: food laced with spice essence to keep him half in and half out of the real universe until either he died or his grandmother's plan succeeded. And every time he thought he'd won, they sent him back. The Lady Jessica was right, of

274

course – that old witch! But what a thing to do. The total recall of all those lives within him was of no use at all until he could organize the data and remember it at will. Those lives had been the raw stuff of anarchy. One or all of them could have overwhelmed him. The spice and its peculiar setting here in Jacurutu had been a desperate gamble.

*Now Gurney waits for the sign and I refuse to give it to him. How long will his patience last?*

He stared out at Sabiha. She'd thrown her hood back and revealed the tribal tattoos at her temples. Leto did not recognize the tattoos, at first, then remembered where he was. Yes, Jacurutu still lived.

Leto did not know whether to be thankful toward his grandmother or hate her. She wanted him to have conscious-level instincts. But instincts were only racial memories of how to handle crises. His direct memories of those other lives told him far more than that. He had it all organized now, and could see the peril of revealing himself to Gurney. No way of keeping the revelation from Namri. And Namri was another problem.

Sabiha entered the cell with a bowl in her hands. He admired the way the light from outside made rainbow circles at the edges of her hair. Gently she raised his head and began feeding him from the bowl. It was only then he realized how weak he was. He allowed her to feed him while his mind went roving, recalling the session with Gurney and Namri. They believed him! Namri more than Gurney, but even Gurney could not deny what his senses had already reported to him about the planet.

Sabiha wiped his mouth with a hem of her robe.

*Ahhh, Sabiha,* he thought recalling that other vision which filled his heart with pain. *Many nights have I dreamed beside the open water, hearing the winds pass overhead. Many nights my flesh lay beside the snake's den and I dreamed of Sabiha in the summer heat. I saw her storing spice-bread baked on red-hot sheets of plasteel. I saw the clear water in the qanat, gentle and shining, but a stormwind ran through my heart. She sips coffee and eats. Her teeth shine in the shadows. I see her braiding my water rings into her hair. The amber fragrance of her bosom strikes through to my innermost senses. She torments me and oppresses me by her very existence.*

The pressure of his multi-memories exploded the time-frozen englobement which he had tried to resist. He felt twining bodies, the sounds of sex, rhythms laced in every sensory impression: lips, breathing, moist breaths, tongues. Somewhere in his vision there were helix shapes, coal-colored, and he felt the beat of those shapes as they turned within him. A voice pleaded in his skull: 'Please, please, please, please . . .' There was an adult beefswelling in his loins and he felt his mouth open, holding, clinging to the girder-shape of ecstasy. Then a sigh, a lingering groundswelling sweetness, a collapse.

Oh, how sweet to let that come into existence!

'Sabiha,' he whispered. 'Oh, my Sabiha.'

When her charge had clearly gone deeply into the trance after his food, Sabiha took the bowl and left, pausing at the doorway to speak to Namri. 'He called my name again.'

'Go back and stay with him,' Namri said. 'I must find Halleck and discuss this with him.'

Sabiha deposited the bowl beside the doorway and returned to the cell. She sat on the edge of the cot, staring at Leto's shadowed face.

Presently he opened his eyes and put a hand out, touching her cheek. He began to talk to her then, telling her about the vision in which she had lived.

She covered his hand with her own as he spoke. How sweet he was . . . how very swee— She sank onto the cot, cushioned by his hand, unconscious before he pulled the hand away. Leto sat up, feeling the depths of his weakness. The spice and its visions had drained him. He searched through his cells for every spare spark of energy, climbed from the cot without disturbing Sabiha. He had to go, but he knew he'd not get far. Slowly he sealed his stillsuit, drew the robe around him, slipped through the passage to the outer shaft. There were a few people about, busy at their own affairs. They knew him, but he was not their responsibility. Namri and Halleck would know what he was doing; Sabiha could not be far away.

He found the kind of side passage he needed and walked boldly down it.

Behind him Sabiha slept peacefully until Halleck roused her.

She sat up, rubbed her eyes, saw the empty cot, saw her uncle standing behind Halleck, the anger on their faces.

Namri answered the expression on her face: 'Yes, he's gone.'

'How could you let him escape?' Halleck raged. 'How is this possible?'

'He was seen going toward the lower exit,' Namri said, his voice oddly calm.

Sabiha cowered in front of them, remembering.

'How?' Halleck demanded.

'I don't know. I don't know.'

'It's night and he's weak,' Namri said. 'He won't get far.'

Halleck whirled on him. 'You want the boy to die!'

'It wouldn't displease me.'

Again Halleck confronted Sabiha. 'Tell me what happened.'

'He touched my cheek. He kept talking about his vision . . . us together.' She looked down at the empty cot. 'He made me sleep. He put some magic on me.'

Halleck glanced at Namri. 'Could he be hiding inside somewhere?'

'Nowhere inside. He'd be found, seen. He was headed for the exit. He's out there.'

'Magic,' Sabiha muttered.

'No magic,' Namri said. 'He hypnotized her. Almost did it to me, you remember? Said I was his friend.'

'He's very weak,' Halleck said.

'Only in his body,' Namri said. 'He won't go far, though. I disabled the heel pumps of his stillsuit. He'll die with no water if we don't find him.'

Halleck almost turned and struck Namri, but held himself in rigid control. Jessica had warned him that Namri might have to kill the lad. Gods below! What a pass they'd come to, Atreides against Atreides. He said: 'Is it possible he just wandered away in the spice trance?'

'What difference does it make?' Namri asked. 'If he escapes us he must die.'

'We'll start searching at first light,' Halleck said. 'Did he take a Fremkit?'

'There're always a few beside the doorseal,' Namri said. 'He'd've been a fool not to take one. Somehow he has never struck me as a fool.'

'Then send a message to our friends,' Halleck said. 'Tell them what's happened.'

'No messages this night,' Namri said. 'There's a storm coming. The tribes have been tracking it for three days now. It'll be here by midnight. Already communication's blanked out. The satellites signed off this sector two hours ago.'

A deep sigh shook Halleck. The boy would die out there for sure if the sandblast storm caught him. It would eat the flesh from his bones and sliver the bones to fragments. The contrived false death would become real. He slapped a fist into an open palm. The storm could trap them in the sietch. They couldn't

277

even mount a search. And storm static had already isolated the sietch.

'Distrans,' he said, thinking they might imprint a message onto a bat's voice and dispatch it with the alarm.

Namri shook his head. 'Bats won't fly in a storm. Come on, man. They're more sensitive than we are. They'll cower in the cliffs until it's past. Best to wait for the satellites to pick us up again. Then we can try to find his remains.'

'Not if he took to Fremkit and hid in the sand,' Sabiha said.

Cursing under his breath, Halleck whirled away from them, strode out into the sietch.

*Peace demands solutions, but we never reach living solutions; we only work toward them. A fixed solution is, by definition, a dead solution. The trouble with peace is that it tends to punish mistakes instead of rewarding brilliance.*

    – The Words of My Father:
    an account of Muad'Dib
    reconstructed by Harq al-Ada

'She's training him? She's training Farad'n?'

Alia glared at Duncan Idaho with a deliberate mix of anger and incredulity. The Guild heighliner had swung into orbit around Arrakis at noon local. An hour later the lighter had put Idaho down at Arrakeen, unannounced, but all casual and open. Within minutes a 'thopter had deposited him atop the Keep. Warned of his impending arrival, Alia had greeted him there, coldly formal before her guards, but now they stood in her quarters beneath the north rim. He had just delivered his report, truthfully, precisely, emphasizing each datum in mentat fashion.

'She has taken leave of her senses,' Alia said.

He treated the statement as a mentat problem. 'All the indicators are that she remains well balanced, sane. I should say her sanity index was –'

'Stop that!' Alia snapped. 'What can she be thinking of?'

Idaho, who knew that his own emotional balance depended now upon retreat into mentat coldness, said: 'I compute she is thinking of her granddaughter's betrothal.' His features remained carefully bland, a mask for the raging grief which threatened to engulf him. There was no Alia here. Alia was dead. For a time he'd maintained a myth-Alia before his senses, someone he'd manufactured out of his own needs, but a mentat could carry on such self-deception for only a limited time. This creature in human guise was possessed; a demonpsyche drove her. His steely eyes with their myriad facets available at will reproduced upon his vision centers a multiplicity of myth-Alias. But when he combined them into a single image, no Alia remained. Her features moved to other demands. She was a shell within which outrages had been committed.

'Where's Ghanima?' he asked.

She waved the question aside. 'I've sent her with Irulan to stay in Stilgar's keeping.'

*Neutral territory,* he thought. *There's been another negotiation with rebellious tribes. She's losing ground and doesn't know it . . . or does she? Is there another reason? Has Stilgar gone over to her?*

'The betrothal,' Alia mused. 'What are conditions in the Corrino House?'

'Salusa swarms with *outrine* relatives, all working upon Farad'n, hoping for a share in his return to power.'

And she's training him in the Bene Gesserit . . . '

'Is it not fitting for Ghanima's husband?'

Alia smiled to herself, thinking of Ghanima's adamant rage. Let Farad'n be trained. Jessica was training a corpse. It would all work out.

'I must consider this at length,' she said. 'You're very quiet, Duncan.'

'I await your questions.'

'I see. You know, I was very angry with you. Taking her to Farad'n!'

'You commanded me to make it real.'

'I was forced to put out the report that you'd both been taken captive,' she said.

'I obeyed your orders.'

'You're so literal at times, Duncan. You almost frighten me. But if you hadn't, well . . . '

'The Lady Jessica's out of harm's way,' he said. 'And for Ghanima's sake we should be grateful that –'

'Exceedingly grateful,' she agreed. And she thought: *He's no longer trustworthy. He has that damnable Atreides loyalty. I must make an excuse to send him away . . . and have him eliminated. An accident, of course.*

She touched his cheek.

Idaho forced himself to respond to the caress, taking her hand and kissing it.

'Duncan, Duncan, how sad it is,' she said. 'But I cannot keep you here with me. Too much is happening and I've so few I can completely trust.'

He released her hand, waited.

'I was *forced* to send Ghanima to Tabr,' she said. 'Things are in deep unrest here. Raiders from the Broken Lands breached the qanats at Kagga Basin and spilled all of their waters into the sands. Arrakeen was on short rations. The Basin's alive with sandtrout yet, reaping the water harvest. They're being dealt with, of course, but we're spread very thin.'

He'd already noted how few amazons of Alia's guard were to be seen in the Keep. And he thought: *The Maquis of the Inner Desert will keep on probing her defenses. Doesn't she know that?*

'Tabr is still neutral territory,' she said. 'Negotiations are continuing there right now. Javid's there with a delegation from the Priesthood. But I'd like you at Tabr to watch them, especially Irulan.'

'She *is* Corrino,' he agreed.

But he saw in her eyes that she was rejecting him. How transparent this Alia-creature had become!

She waved a hand. 'Go now, Duncan, before I soften and keep you here beside me. I've missed you so . . .'

'And I've missed you,' he said, allowing all of his grief to flow into his voice.

She stared at him, startled by the sadness. Then: 'For my sake, Duncan.' And she thought: *Too bad, Duncan.* She said: 'Zia will take you to Tabr. We need the 'thopter back here.'

*Her pet amazon*, he thought. *I must be careful of that one.*

'I understand,' he said, once more taking her hand and kissing it. He stared at the dear flesh which once had been his Alia's. He could not bring himself to look at her face as he left. Someone else stared back at him from her eyes.

As he mounted to the Keep's roofpad, Idaho probed a growing sense of unanswered questions. The meeting with Alia had been extremely trying for the mentat part of him which kept reading data signs. He waited beside the 'thopter with one of the Keep's amazons, stared grimly southward. Imagination took his gaze beyond the Shield Wall to Sietch Tabr. *Why does Zia take me to Tabr? Returning a 'thopter is a menial task. What is the delay? Is Zia getting special instructions?*

Idaho glanced at the watchful guard, mounted to the pilot's

position in the 'thopter. He leaned out, said: 'Tell Alia I'll send the 'thopter back immediately with one of Stilgar's men.'

Before the guard could protest he closed the door and started the 'thopter. He could see her standing there indecisively. Who could question Alia's consort? He had the 'thopter airborne before she could make up her mind what to do.

Now, alone in the 'thopter, he allowed his grief to spend itself in great wracking sobs. Alia was gone. They had parted forever. Tears flowed from his Tleilaxu eyes and he whispered: 'Let all the waters of Dune flow into the sand. They will not match my tears.'

This was a non-mentat excess, though, and he recognized it as such, forcing himself to sober assessment of present necessities. The 'thopter demanded his attention. The reactions of flying brought him some relief, and he had himself once more in hand.

*Ghanima with Stilgar again. And Irulan.*

Why had Zia been designated to accompany him? He made it a mentat problem and the answer chilled him. *I was to have a fatal accident.*

> *This rocky shrine to the skull of a ruler grants no prayers. It has become the grave of lamentations. Only the wind hears the voice of this place. The cries of night creatures and the passing wonder of two moons, all say his day has ended. No more suppliants come. The visitors have gone from the feast. How bare the pathway down this mountain.*
>
> — Lines at the Shrine of an Atreides Duke Anon.

The thing had the deceptive appearance of simplicity to Leto: avoiding the vision, do that which has not been seen. He knew the trap in his thought, how the casual threads of a locked future twisted themselves together until they held you fast, but he had a new grip on those threads. Nowhere had he seen himself running from Jacurutu. The thread to Sabiha must be cut first.

He crouched now in the last daylight at the eastern edge of the rock which protected Jacurutu. His Fremkit had produced energy tablets and food. He waited now for strength. To the west lay Lake Azrak, the gypsum plain where once there'd been open water in the days before the worm. Unseen to the east lay the Bene Sherk, a scattering of new settlements encroaching upon the open *bled.* To the south lay the Tanzerouft, the Land of

Terror: thirty-eight hundred kilometers of wasteland broken only by patches of grass-locked dunes and windtraps to water them – the work of the ecological transformation remaking the landscape of Arrakis. They were serviced by airborne teams and no one stayed for long.

*I will go south*, he told himself. *Gurney will expect me to do that.* This was not the moment to do the completely unexpected.

It would be dark soon and he could leave this temporary hiding place. He stared at the southern skyline. There was a whistling of dun sky along that horizon, rolling there like smoke, a burning line of undulant dust – a storm. He watched the high center of the storm rising up out of the Great Flat like a questing worm. For a full minute he watched the center, saw that it did not move to the right or the left. The old Fremen saying leaped into his mind: *When the center does not move, you are in its path.*

That storm changed matters.

For a moment he stared back westward the direction of Tabr, feeling the deceptive gray-tan peace of the desert evening, seeing the white gypsum pan edged by wind-rounded pebbles, the desolate emptiness with its unreal surface of glaring white reflecting dust clouds. Nowhere in any vision had he seen himself surviving the gray serpent of a mother storm or buried too deeply in sand to survive. There was only that vision of rolling in wind . . . but that might come later.

And a storm was out there, winding across many degrees of latitude, whipping its world into submission. It could be risked. There were old stories, always heard from a friend of a friend, that one could lock an exhausted worm on the surface by propping a Maker hook beneath one of its wide rings and, having immobilized it, ride out a storm in the leeward shadow. There was a line between audacity and abandoned recklessness which tempted him. That storm would not come before midnight at the earliest. There was time. How many threads could be cut here? All, including the final one?

*Gurney will expect me to go south, but not into a storm.*

He stared down to the south, seeking a pathway, saw the fluent ebony brushstroke of a deep gorge curving through Jacurutu's rock. He saw sand curls in the bowels of the gorge, chimera sand. It uttered its haughty runnels onto the plain as though it were water. The gritty taste of thirst whispered in his mouth as he shouldered his Fremkit and let himself down onto the path which led into the canyon. It was still light enough that he might be seen, but he knew he was gambling with time.

As he reached the canyon's lip, the quick night of the central desert fell upon him. He was left with the parched glissando of moonglow to light his way toward the Tanzerouft. He felt his heartbeat quicken with all of the fears which his wealth of memories provided. He sensed that he might be going down into Huanui-naa, as Fremen fears labeled the greatest storms: the Earth's Deathstill. But whatever came, it would be visionless. Every step left farther behind him the spice-induced *dhyana*, that spreading awareness of his intuitive-creative nature with its unfolding to the motionless chain of causality. For every hundred steps he took now, there must be at least one step aside, beyond words and into communion with his newly grasped internal reality.

*One way or another, father, I'm coming to you.*

There were birds invisible in the rocks around him, making themselves known by small sounds. Fremen-wise, he listened for their echoes to guide his way where he could not see. Often as he passed crannies he marked the baleful green of eyes, creatures crouched in hiding because they knew a storm approached.

He emerged from the gorge onto the desert. Living sand moved and breathed beneath him, telling of deep actions and latent fumaroles. He looked back and up to the moon-touched lava caps on Jacurutu's buttes. The whole structure was metamorphic, mostly pressure-formed. Arrakis still had something to say in its own future. He planted his thumper to call a worm and, when it began beating against the sand, took his position to watch and listen. Unconsciously his right hand went to the Atreides hawk ring concealed in a knotted fold of his *dishdasha*. Gurney had found it, but had left it. What had he thought, seeing Paul's ring?

*Father, expect me soon.*

The worm came from the south. It angled in to avoid the rocks, not as large a worm as he'd hoped, but that could not be remedied. He gauged its passage, planted his hooks, and went up the scaled side with a quick scrambling as it swept over the thumper in a swishing dust spray. The worm turned easily under the pressure of his hooks. The wind of its passage began to whip his robe. He bent his gaze on the southern stars, dim through dust, and pointed the worm that way.

*Right into the storm.*

As First Moon rose, Leto gauged the storm height and put off his estimate of its arrival. Not before daylight. It was spreading out, gathering more energy for a great leap. There'd be plenty of work for the ecological transformation teams. It was as though the planet fought them with a conscious fury out here, the fury increasing as the transformation took in more land.

All night he pressed the worm southward, sensing the reserves of its energy in the movements transmitted through his feet. Occasionally he let the beast fall off to the west which it was forever trying to do, moved by the invisible boundaries of its territory or by a deep-seated awareness of the coming storm. Worms buried themselves to escape the sandblast winds, but this one would not sink beneath the desert while Maker hooks held any of its rings open.

At midnight the worm was showing many signs of exhaustion. He moved back along its great ridges and worked the flail, allowing it to slow down but continuing to drive it southward.

The storm arrived just after daybreak. First there was the beady stretched-out immobility of the desert dawn pressing dunes one into another. Next, the advancing dust caused him to seal his face flaps. In the thickening dust the desert became a dun picture without lines. Then sand needles began cutting his cheeks, stinging his lids. He felt the coarse grit on his tongue and knew the moment of decision had come. Should he risk the old stories by immobilizing the almost exhausted worm? He took only a heartbeat to discard this choice, worked his way back to the worm's tail, slacked off his hooks. Barely moving now, the worm began to burrow. But the excesses of the creature's heat-transfer system still churned up a cyclone oven behind him in the quickening storm. Fremen children learned the danger of this position near the worm's tail with their earliest stories. Worms were oxygen factories; fire burned wildly in their passage, fed by the lavish exhalations from the chemical adaptations to friction within them.

Sand began to whip around his feet. Leto loosed his hooks and leaped wide to avoid the furnace at the tail. Everything depended now on getting beneath the sand where the worm had loosened it.

Grasping the static compaction tool in his left hand, he burrowed into a dune's slipface, knowing the worm was too tired to turn back and swallow him in its great white-orange mouth. As he burrowed with his left hand, his right hand worked the still-tent from his Fremkit and he readied it for inflation. It was all done in less than a minute: he had the tent into a hard-walled sand pocket on the lee face of a dune. He inflated the tent and crawled into it. Before sealing the sphincter, he reached out with the compaction tool, reversed its action. The slipface came sliding down over the tent. Only a few sand grains entered as he sealed the opening.

Now he had to work even more quickly. No sandsnorkel would reach up there to keep him supplied with breathing air. This was a great storm, the kind few survived. It would cover this place with tons of sand. Only the tender bubble of the stilltent with its compacted outer shell would protect him.

Leto stretched flat on his back, folded his hands over his breast and sent himself into a dormancy trance where his lungs would move only once an hour. In this he committed himself to the unknown. The storm would pass and, if it did not expose his fragile pocket, he might emerge . . . or he might enter the *Madinat as-salam*, the Abode of Peace. Whatever happened, he knew he had to break the threads, one by one, leaving him at last only the Golden Path. It was that, or he could not return to the caliphate of his father's heirs. No more would he live the lie of that *Desposyni*, that terrible caliphate, chanting to the demiurge of his father. No more would he keep silent when a priest mouthed offensive nonsense: *'His crysknife will dissolve demons!'*

With this commitment, Leto's awareness slipped into the web of timeless *dao*.

*There exist obvious higher-order influences in any planetary system. This is often demonstrated by introducing terraform life onto newly discovered planets. In all such cases, the life in similar zones develops striking similarities of adaptive form. This form signifies much more than shape; it connotes a survival organization and a relationship of such organizations. The human quest for this interdependent order and our niche within it represents a profound necessity. The quest can, however, be perverted into a conservative grip on sameness. This has always proved deadly for the entire system.*

— The Dune Catastrophe
After Harq al-Ada

'My son didn't really see *the future*; he saw the process of creation and its relationship to the myths in which men sleep,' Jessica said, She spoke swiftly but without appearing to rush the matter. She knew the hidden observers would find a way to interrupt as soon as they recognized what she was doing.

Farad'n sat on the floor outlined in a shaft of afternoon sunlight which slanted through the window behind him. Jessica could just see the top of a tree in the courtyard garden when she glanced across from her position standing against the far wall. It was a new Farad'n she saw: more slender, more sinewy. The months of training had worked their inevitable magic on him. His eyes glittered when he stared at her.

'He saw the shapes which existing forces would create unless they were diverted,' Jessica said. 'Rather than turn against his fellow men, he turned against himself. He refused to accept only that which comforted him because that was moral cowardice.'

Farad'n had learned to listen silently testing, probing, holding his questions until he had shaped them into a cutting edge. She had been talking about the Bene Gesserit view of molecular memory expressed as ritual and had, quite naturally, diverged to the Sisterhood's way of analyzing Paul Muad'Dib. Farad'n saw a shadow play in her words and actions, however, a projection of unconscious forms at variance with the surface intent of her statements.

'Of all our observations, this is the most crucial,' she'd said. 'Life is a mask through which the universe expresses itself. We assume that all of humankind and its supportive life forms represent a *natural* community and that the fate of all life is at stake in the fate of the individual. Thus, when it comes to that ultimate self-examination, the *amor fati*, we stop playing god and revert to teaching. In the crunch, we select individuals and we set them as free as we're able.'

He saw now where she had to be going and knowing its effect upon those who watched through the spy eyes, refrained from casting an apprehensive glance at the door. Only a trained eye could have detected his momentary imbalance, but Jessica saw it and smiled. A smile, after all, could mean anything.

'This is a sort of graduation ceremony,' she said. 'I'm very pleased with you, Farad'n. Will you stand, please.'

He obeyed, blocking off her view of the treetop through the window behind him.

Jessica held her arms stiffly at her side, said: 'I am charged to say this to you. "I stand in the sacred human presence. As I do now, so should you stand someday. I pray to your presence that this be so. The future remains uncertain and so it should, for it is the canvas upon which we paint our desires. Thus always the human condition faces a beautifully empty canvas. We possess only this moment in which to dedicate ourselves continuously to the sacred presence which we share and create." '

As Jessica finished speaking, Tyekanik came through the door on her left, moving with a false casualness which the scowl on his face belied. 'My Lord,' he said. But it already was too late. Jessica's words and all of the preparation which had gone before had done their work. Farad'n no longer was Corrino. He was now Bene Gesserit.

> *What you of the CHOAM directorate seem unable to understand is that you seldom find real loyalties in commerce. When did you last hear of a clerk giving his life for the company? Perhaps your deficiency rests in the false assumption that you can order men to think and cooperate. This has been a failure of everything from religions to general staffs throughout history. General staffs have a long record of destroying their own nations. As to religions, I recommend a rereading of Thomas Aquinas. As to you of CHOAM, what nonsense you believe! Men must want to do things out of their own innermost drives. People, not commercial organizations or chains of command, are what make great civilizations work. Every civilization depends upon the quality of the individuals it produces. If you over-organize humans, over-legalize them, suppress their urge to greatness – they cannot work and their civilization collapses.*

> – A letter to CHOAM
> Attributed to The Preacher

Leto came out of the trance with a softness of transition which did not define one condition as separate from another. One level of awareness simply moved into the other.

He knew where he was. A restoration of energy surged through him, but he sensed another message from the stale deadliness of the oxygen-depleted air within the stilltent. If he refused to move, he knew he would remain caught in the timeless web, the eternal *now* where all events coexisted. This prospect enticed him. He saw Time as a convention shaped by the collective mind of all sentience. Time and Space were categories imposed on the universe by his Mind. He had but to break free of the multiplicity where prescient visions lured him. Bold selection could change provisional futures.

What boldness did this moment require?

The trance state lured him. Leto felt that he had come from the *alam al-mythal* into the universe of reality only to find them identical. He wanted to maintain the Rihani magic of this revelation, but survival demanded decisions of him. His relentless taste for life sent its signals along his nerves.

Abruptly he reached out his right hand to where he had left the sand-compaction tool. He gripped it, rolled onto his stomach, and breached the tent's sphincter. A pool of sand drifted across his hand. Working in darkness, goaded by the stale air, he worked swiftly, tunneling upward at a steep angle. Six times his body lengths he went before he broke out into darkness and clean air. He slipped out onto the moonlit windface of a long curving dune, found himself about a third of the way from the dune's top.

It was Second Moon above him. It moved swiftly across him, departing beyond the dune, and the stars were laid out above him like bright rocks beside a path. Leto searched for the constellation of The Wanderer, found it, and let his gaze follow the outstretched arm to the brilliant glittering of Foum al-Hout, the polar star of the south.

*There's your damned universe for you!* he thought. Seen close up it was a hustling place like the sand all around him, a place of change, of uniqueness piled upon uniqueness. Seen from a distance, only the patterns lay revealed and those patterns tempted one to belief in absolutes.

*In absolutes, we may lose our way.* This made him think of the familiar warning from a Fremen ditty: *'Who loses his way in the Tanzerouft loses his life.'* The patterns could guide and they could trap. One had to remember that patterns change.

He took a deep breath, stirred himself into action. Sliding back down his passage, he collapsed the tent, brought it out and re-packed the Fremkit.

A wine glow began to develop along the eastern horizon. He shouldered the pack, climbed to the dunecrest and stood there in the chill predawn air until the rising sun felt warm on his right cheek. He stained his eyepits then to reduce reflection, knowing that he must woo this desert now rather than fight her. When he had put the stain back into the pack he sipped from one of his catchtubes, drew in a sputtering of drops and then air.

Dropping to the sand, he began going over his stillsuit, coming at last to the heel pumps. They had been cut cleverly with a needle knife. He slipped out of the suit and repaired it, but the damage had been done. At least half of his body's water was gone. Were it not for the stilltent's catch . . . He mused on this as he donned the suit, thinking how odd it was that he'd not anticipated this. Here was an obvious danger of visionless future.

Leto squatted on the dunetop then, pressed himself against the loneliness of this place. He let his gaze wander, fishing in the sand for a whistling vent, any irregularity of the dunes which might indicate spice or worm activity. But the storm had stamped its uniformity upon the land. Presently he removed a thumper from the kit, armed it, and sent it rotating to call Shai-Hulud from his depths. He then moved off to wait.

The worm was a long time coming. He heard it before he saw it, and turned eastward where the earthshaking susurration made the air tremble, waited for the first glimpse of orange from the mouth rising out of the sand. The worm lifted itself from the depths in a gigantic hissing of dust which obscured its flanks. The curving gray wall swept past Leto and he planted his hooks, went up the side in easy steps. He turned the worm southward in a great curving track as he climbed.

Under his goading hooks, the worm picked up speed. Wind whipped his robe against him. He felt himself to be goaded as the worm was goaded, an intense current of creation in his loins. Each planet has its own period and each life likewise, he reminded himself.

The worm was a type Fremen called a 'growler'. It frequently dug in its foreplates while the tail was driving. This produced rumbling sounds and caused part of its body to rise clear of the sand in a moving hump. It was a fast worm, though, and when they picked up a following wind the furnace exhalation of his tail sent a hot breeze across him. It was filled with acrid odors carried on the freshet of oxygen.

As the worm sped southward, Leto allowed his mind to run free. He tried to think of this passage as a new ceremony for his life, one which kept him from considering the price he'd have to pay for his Golden Path. Like the Fremen of old, he knew he'd have to adopt many new ceremonies to keep his personality from dividing into its memory parts, to keep the ravening hunters of his soul forever at bay. Contradictory images, never to be unified, must now be encysted in a living tension, a polarizing force which drove him from within.

*Always newness,* he thought. *I must always find the new threads out of my vision.*

In the early afternoon his attention was caught by a protuberance ahead and slightly to the right of his course. Slowly the protuberance became a narrow butte, an upthrust rock precisely where he'd expected it.

*Now Namri . . . Now Sabiha, let us see how your brethren take to my presence,* he thought. This was a most delicate thread ahead of him, dangerous more for its lures than its open threats.

The butte was a long time changing dimensions. And it appeared for a while that it approached him instead of him approaching it.

The worm, tiring now, kept veering left. Leto slid down the immense slope to set his hooks anew and keep the giant on a straight course. A soft sharpness of melange came to his nostrils, the signal of a rich vein. They passed the leprous blotches of violet sand where a spiceblow had erupted and he held the worm firmly until they were well past the vein. The breeze, redolent with the gingery odor of cinnamon, pursued them for a time until Leto rolled the worm onto its new course, headed directly toward the rising butte.

Abruptly colors blinked far out on the southern *bled*: the unwary rainbow flashing of a man-made artifact in that immensity. He brought up his binoculars, focused the oil lenses, and saw in the distance the outbanking wings of a spice-scout glittering in the sunlight. Beneath it a big harvester was shedding its wings like a chrysalis before lumbering off. When Leto lowered the binoculars the harvester dwindled to a speck, and he felt himself overcome by the *hadhdhab*, the immense omnipresence of the desert. It told him how those spice-hunters would see him, a dark object between desert and sky, which was the Fremen symbol for *man*. They'd see him, of course, and they'd be cautious. They'd wait. Fremen were always suspicious of one another in the desert until they recognized the newcomer or saw for certain that he posed no threat. Even within the fine patina of Imperial civilization and its sophisticated rules they remained half-tamed savages, aware always that a crysknife dissolved at the death of its owner.

*That's what can save us*, Leto thought. *That wildness.*

In the distance the spice-scout banked right, then left, a signal to the ground. He imagined the occupants scanning the desert behind him for sign that he might be more than a single rider on a single worm.

Leto rolled the worm to the left, held it until it had reversed its course, dropped down the flank, and leaped clear. The worm, released from his goading, sulked on the surface for a few breaths, then sank its front third and lay there recuperating, a sure sign that it had been ridden too long.

He turned away from the worm; it would stay there now. The scout was circling its crawler, still giving wing signals. They were smuggler-paid renegades for certain, wary of electronic communications. The hunters would be on spice out there. That was the message of the crawler's presence.

The scout circled once more, dipped its wings, came out of the circle and headed directly toward him. He recognized it for a type of light 'thopter his grandfather had introduced on Arrakis. The craft circled once above him, went out along the dune where he stood, and banked to land against the breeze. It came down within ten meters of him, stirring up a scattering of dust. The door on his side cracked enough to emit a single figure in a heavy Fremen robe with a spear symbol at the right breast.

The Fremen approached slowly, giving each of them time to study the other. The man was tall with the total indigo of spice-eyes. The stillsuit mask concealed the lower half of his face and the hood had been drawn down to protect his brows. The movement of the robe revealed a hand beneath it holding a maula pistol.

The man stopped two paces from Leto, looked down at him with a puzzled crinkling around the eyes.

'Good fortune to us all,' Leto said.

The man peered all around, scanning the emptiness, then returned his attention to Leto. 'What do you here, child?' he demanded. His voice was muffled by the stillsuit mask. 'Are you trying to be the cork in a wormhole?'

Again Leto used traditional Fremen formula: 'The desert is my home.'

'Wenn?' the man demanded. *Which way do you go?*

'I travel south from Jacurutu.'

An abrupt laugh erupted from the man. 'Well, Batigh! You are the strangest thing I've ever seen in the Tanzerouft.'

'I'm not your Little Melon,' Leto said, responding to *Batigh*. That was a label with dire overtones. The Little Melon on the desert's edge offered its water to any finder.

'We'll not drink you, Batigh,' the man said. 'I am Muriz. I am the arifa of this taif.' He indicated with a head motion the distant spice-crawler.

Leto noted how the man called himself the Judge of his group and referred to the others as *taif*, a band or company. They were not *ichwan*, not a band of brothers. Paid renegades for sure. Here lay the thread he required.

When Leto remained silent, Muriz asked: 'Do you have a name?'

'Batigh will do.'

A chuckle shook Muriz. 'You've not told me what you do here?'

'I seek the footprints of a worm,' Leto said, using the religious

291

phrase which said he was on hajj for his own *umma*, his personal revelation.

'One so young?' Muriz asked. He shook his head. 'I don't know what to do with you. You have seen us.'

'What have I seen?' Leto asked. 'I speak of Jacurutu and you make no response.'

'Riddle games,' Muriz said. 'What is that, then?' He nodded toward the distant butte.

Leto spoke from his vision: 'Only Shuloch.'

Muriz stiffened and Leto felt his own pulse quicken.

A long silence ensued and Leto could see the man debating and discarding various responses. *Shuloch!* In the quiet story time after a sietch meal, stories of the Shuloch caravan-serie were often repeated. Listeners always assumed that Shuloch was a myth, a place for interesting things to happen and only for the sake of the story. Leto recalled a Shuloch story: A waif was found at the desert's edge and brought into the sietch. At first the waif refused to respond to his saviors, then when he spoke no one could understand his words. As days passed he continued unresponsive, refused to dress himself or cooperate in any way. Every time he was left alone he made odd motions with his hands. All the specialists in the sietch were called in to study this waif but arrived at no answer. Then a very old woman passed the doorway, saw the moving hands, and laughed. 'He only imitates his father who rolls the spice-fibers into rope,' she explained. 'It's the way they still do it at Shuloch. He's just trying to feel less lonely.' And the moral: *In the old days of Shuloch there is security and a sense of belonging to the golden thread of life.*

As Muriz remained silent, Leto said: 'I'm the waif from Shuloch who knows only to move his hands.'

In the quick movement of the man's head, Leto saw that Muriz knew the story. Muriz responded slowly, voice low and filled with menace. 'Are you human?'

'Human as yourself,' Leto said.

'You speak most strangely for a child. I remind you that I am a judge who can respond to the *taqwa.*'

*Ah, yes,* Leto thought. In the mouth of such a judge, the *taqwa* carried immediate threat. *Taqwa* was the fear invoked by the presence of a demon, a very real belief among older Fremen. The arifa knew the ways to slay a demon and was always chosen 'because he has the wisdom to be ruthless without being cruel, to know when kindness is in fact the way to greater cruelty.'

But this thing had come to the point which Leto sought, and he said: 'I can submit to the *Mashhad*.'

'I'll be the judge of any Spiritual Test,' Muriz said. 'Do you accept this?'

'Bi-lal-kaifa,' Leto said. *Without qualification.*

A sly look came over Muriz's face. He said: 'I don't know why I permit this. Best you were slain out of hand, but you're a small Batigh and I had a son who is dead. Come, we will go to Shuloch and I'll convene the Isnad for a decision about you.'

Leto, noting how the man's every mannerism betrayed deadly decision, wondered how anyone could be fooled by this. He said: 'I know Shuloch is the Ahl as-sunna wal-jamas.'

'What does a child know of the real world?' Muriz asked, motioning for Leto to precede him to the 'thopter.

Leo obeyed, but listened carefully to the sound of the Fremen's footsteps. 'The surest way to keep a secret is to make people believe they already know the answer,' Leto said. 'People don't ask questions then. It was clever of you who were cast out of Jacurutu. Who'd believe Shuloch, the story-myth place, is real? And how convenient for the smugglers or anyone else who desires access to Dune.'

Muriz's footsteps stopped. Leto turned with his back against the 'thopter's side, the wing on his left.

Muriz stood half a pace away with his maula pistol drawn and pointed directly at Leto. 'So you're not a child,' Muriz said. 'A cursed midget come to spy on us! I thought you spoke too wisely for a child, but you spoke too much too soon.'

'Not enough,' Leto said. 'I'm Leto, the child of Paul Muad'Dib. If you slay me, you and your people will sink into the sand. If you spare me, I'll lead you to greatness.'

'Don't play games with me, midget,' Muriz snarled. 'Leto is at the real Jacurutu from whence you say . . . ' He broke off. The gun hand dropped slightly as a puzzled frown made his eyes squint.

It was the hesitation Leto had expected. He made every muscle indication of a move to the left which, deflecting his body no more than a millimeter, brought the Fremen's gun swinging wildly against the wing edge. The maula pistol flew from his hand and, before he could recover, Leto was beside him with Muriz's own crysknife pressed against the man's back.

'The tip's poisoned,' Leto said. 'Tell your friend in the 'thopter that he's to remain exactly where he is without moving at all. Otherwise I'll be forced to kill you.'

Muriz, nursing his injured hand, shook his head at the figure in the 'thopter, said: 'My companion Behaleth has heard you. He will be as unmoving as the rock.'

Knowing he had very little time until the two worked out a plan of action or their friends came to investigate, Leto spoke swiftly: 'You need me, Muriz. Without me, the worms and their spice will vanish from Dune.' He felt the Fremen stiffen.

'But how do you know of Shuloch?' Muriz asked. 'I know they said nothing at Jacurutu.'

'So you admit I'm Leto Atreides?'

'Who else could you be? But how do you —'

'Because you are here,' Leto said. 'Shuloch exists, therefore the rest is utter simplicity. You are the Cast Out who escaped when Jacurutu was destroyed. I saw you signal with your wings, therefore you use no device which could be overheard at a distance. You collect spice, therefore you trade. You could only trade with the smugglers. You are a smuggler, yet you are Fremen. You must be of Shuloch.'

'Why did you tempt me to slay you out of hand?'

'Because you would've slain me anyway when we'd returned to Shuloch.'

A violent rigidity came over Muriz's body.

'Careful, Muriz,' Leto cautioned. 'I know about you. It was in your history that you took the water of unwary travelers. By now this would be common ritual with you. How else could you silence the ones who chanced upon you? How else keep your secret? Batigh! You'd seduce me with gentle epithets and kindly words. Why waste any of my water upon the sand? And if I were missed as were many of the others — well, the Tanzerouft got me.'

Muriz made the *Horns-of-the-Worm* sign with his right hand to ward off the Rihani which Leto's words called up. And Leto, knowing how older Fremen distrusted mentats or anything which smacked of them by a show of extended logic, suppressed a smile.

'Namri spoke of us at Jacurutu,' Muriz said. 'I will have his water when —'

'You'll have nothing but empty sand if you continue playing the fool,' Leto said. 'What will you do, Muriz, when all of Dune has become green grass, trees, and open water?'

'It will never happen!'

'It is happening before your eyes.'

Leto heard Muriz's teeth grinding in rage and frustration. Presently the man grated: 'How would you prevent this?'

'I know the entire plan of the transformation,' Leto said. 'I

294

know every weakness in it, every strength. Without me, Shai-Hulud will vanish forever.'

A sly note returning to his voice, Muriz asked: 'Well, why dispute it here? We're at a standoff. You have your knife. You could kill me, but Behaleth would shoot you.'

'Not before I recovered your pistol,' Leto said. 'Then I'd have your 'thopter. Yes. I can fly it.'

A scowl creased Muriz's forehead beneath the hood. 'What if you're not who you say?'

'Will my father not identify me?' Leto asked.

'Ahhhh,' Muriz said. 'There's how you learned, eh? But . . . ' He broke off, shook his head. 'My own son guides him. He says you two have never . . . How could . . . '

'So you don't believe Muad'Dib reads the future,' Leto said.

'Of course we believe! But he says of himself that . . . ' Again Muriz broke off.

'And you thought him unaware of your distrust,' Leto said. 'I came to this exact place in this exact time to meet you, Muriz. I know all about you because I've *seen* you . . . and your son. I know how secure you believe yourselves, how you sneer at Muad'Dib, how you plot to save your little patch of desert. But your little patch of desert is doomed without me, Muriz. Lost forever. It has gone too far here on Dune. My father has almost run out of vision, and you can only turn to me.'

'That blind . . . ' Muriz stopped, swallowed.

'He'll return soon from Arrakeen,' Leto said, 'and then we shall see how blind he is. How far have you gone from the old Fremen ways, Muriz?'

'What?'

'He is *Wadquiyas* with you. Your people found him alone in the desert and brought him to Shuloch. What a rich discovery he was! Richer than a spice-vein. *Wadquiyas!* He has lived with you; his water mingled with your tribe's water. He's part of your Spirit River.' Leto pressed the knife hard against Muriz's robe. 'Careful, Muriz.' Leto lifted his left hand, released the Fremen's face flap, dropped it.

Knowing what Leto planned, Muriz said: 'Where would you go if you killed us both?'

'Back to Jacurutu.'

Leto pressed the fleshy part of his own thumb against Muriz's mouth. 'Bite and drink, Muriz. That or die.'

Muriz hesitated, then bit viciously into Leto's flesh.

Leto watched the man's throat, saw the swallowing convulsion, withdrew the knife and returned it.

'*Wadquiyas*,' Leto said. 'I must offend the tribe before you can take my water.'

Muriz nodded.

'Your pistol is over there.' Leto gestured with his chin.

'You trust me now?' Muriz asked.

'How else can I live with the Cast Out?'

Again Leto saw the sly look in Muriz's eyes, but this time it was a measuring thing, a weighing of economics. The man turned away with an abruptness which told of secret decisions, recovered his maula pistol and returned to the wing step. 'Come,' he said. 'We tarry too long in a worm's lair.'

> *The future of prescience cannot always be locked into the rules of the past. The threads of existence tangle according to many unknown laws. Prescient future insists on its own rules. It will not conform to the ordering of the Zensunni nor to the ordering of science. Prescience builds a relative integrity. It demands the work of this instant, always warning that you cannot weave every thread into the fabric of the past.*
>
> — Kalima: The Words of Muad'Dib
> The Shuloch Commentary

Muriz brought the ornithopter in over Shuloch with a practiced ease. Leto, seated beside him, felt the armed presence of Behaleth behind them. Everything went on trust now and the narrow thread of his vision to which he clung. If that failed, *Allahu akbahr*. Sometimes one had to submit to a greater order.

The butte of Shuloch was impressive in this desert. Its unmarked presence here spoke of many bribes and many deaths, of many friends in high places. Leto could see at Shuloch's heart a cliff-walled pan with interfringing blind canyons leading down into it. A thick growth of shadescale and salt bushes lined the lower edges of these canyons with an inner ring of fan palms, indicating the water riches of this place. Crude buildings of greenbush and spice-fiber had been built out from the fan palms. The buildings were green buttons scattered on the sand. There would live the cast out of the Cast Out, those who could go no lower except into death.

Muriz landed in the pan near the base of one of the canyons. A single structure stood on the sand directly ahead of the 'thopter:

a patch of desert vines and bejato leaves, all lined with heat-fused spice-fabric. It was the living replica of the first crude stilltents and it spoke of degradation for some who lived in Shuloch. Leto knew the place would leak moisture and would be full of night-biters from the nearby growth. So this was how his father lived. And poor Sabiha. Here would be her punishment.

At Muriz's order Leto let himself out of the 'thopter, jumped down to the sand, and strode toward the hut. He could see many people working farther toward the canyon among the palms. They looked tattered, poor, and the fact that they barely glanced at him or at the 'thopter said much of the oppression here. Leto could see the rock lip of a qanat beyond the workers, and there was no mistaking the sense of moisture in this air: open water. Passing the hut, Leto saw it was as crude as he'd expected. He pressed on to the qanat, peered down and saw the swirl of preda-tor fish in the dark flow. The workers, avoiding his eyes, went on with clearing sand away from the line of rock openings.

Muriz came up behind Leto, said: 'You stand on the boundary between fish and worm. Each of these canyons has its worm. This qanat has been opened and we will remove the fish presently to attract sandtrout.'

'Of course,' Leto said. 'Holding pens. You sell sandtrout and worms off-planet.'

'It was Muad'Dib's suggestion!'

'I know. But none of your worms or sandtrout survive for long away from Dune.'

'Not yet,' Muriz said. 'But someday . . .'

'Not in ten thousand years,' Leto said. And he turned to watch the turmoil on Muriz's face. Questions flowed there like the water in the qanat. Could this son of Muad'Dib really read the future? Some still believed Muad'Dib had done it, but . . . How could a thing such as this be judged?

Presently Muriz turned away, led them back to the hut. He opened the crude doorseal, motioned for Leto to enter. There was a spice-oil lamp burning against the far wall and a small figure squatted beneath it, back to the door. The burning oil gave off a heavy fragrance of cinnamon.

'They've sent down a new captive to care for Muad'Dib's sietch,' Muriz sneered. 'If she serves well, she may keep her water for a time.' He confronted Leto. 'Some think it evil to take such water. Those lace-shirt Fremen now make rubbish heaps in their new towns! Rubbish heaps! When has Dune ever before seen rubbish heaps? When we get such as this one – ' He gestured

297

toward the figure by the lamp. " – they're usually half wild with fear, lost to their own kind and never accepted by true Fremen.' Do you understand me, Leto-Batigh?'

'I understand you.' The crouching figure had not moved.

'You speak of leading us,' Muriz said. 'Fremen are led by men who've been blooded. What could you lead us in?'

'Kralizec,' Leto said, keeping his attention on the crouched figure.

Muriz glared at him, brows contracted over his indigo eyes. Kralizec? That wasn't merely war or revolution; that was the Typhoon Struggle. It was a word from the furthermost Fremen legends: the battle at the end of the universe. Kralizec?

The tall Fremen swallowed convulsively. This sprat was as unpredictable as a city dandy! Muriz turned to the squatting figure. 'Woman! Liban wahid!' he commanded. '*Bring us the spice-drink!*'

She hesitated. 'Do as he says, Sabiha,' Leto said.

She jumped to her feet, whirling. She stared at him, unable to take her gaze from his face.

'You know this one?' Muriz asked.

'She is Namri's niece. She offended Jacurutu and they have sent her to you.'

'Namri? But . . .'

'Liban wahid,' Leto said.

She rushed past them, tore herself through the doorseal and they heard the sound of her running feet.

'She will not go far,' Muriz said. He touched a finger to the side of his nose. 'A kin of Namri, eh. Interesting. What did she do to offend?'

'She allowed me to escape.' Leto turned then and followed Sabiha. He found her standing at the edge of the qanat. Leto moved up beside her and looked down at the water. There were birds in the nearby fan palms and he heard their calls, their wings. The workers made scraping sounds as they moved sand. Still he did as Sabiha did, looking down, deep into the water and its reflections. The corners of his eyes saw blue parakeets in the palm fronds. One flew across the qanat and he saw it reflected in a silver swirl of fish, all run together as though birds and predators swam in the same firmament.

Sabiha cleared her throat.

'You hate me,' Leto said.

'You shamed me. You shamed me before my people. They held an Isnad and sent me here to lose my water. All because of you!'

298

Muriz laughed from close behind them. 'And now you see, Leto-Batigh, that our Spirit River has many tributaries.'

'But my water flows in your veins,' Leto said, turning. 'That is no tributary. Sabiha is the fate of my vision and I follow her. I fled across the desert to find my future here in Shuloch.'

'You and , , .' He pointed at Sabiha, threw his head back in laughter.

'It will not be as either of you might believe,' Leto said. 'Remember this, Muriz. I have found the footprints of my worm.' He felt tears swimming in his eyes then.

'He gives water to the dead,' Sabiha whispered.

Even Muriz stared at him in awe. Fremen never cried unless it was the most profound gift of the soul. Almost embarrassed, Muriz closed his mouthseal, pulled his djeballa hood low over his brows.

Leto peered beyond the man, said: 'Here in Shuloch they still pray for dew at the desert's edge. Go, Muriz, and pray for Kralizec. I promise you it will come.'

*Fremen speech implies great concision, a precise sense of expression. It is immersed in the illusion of absolutes. Its assumptions are a fertile ground for absolutist religions. Furthermore, Fremen are fond of moralizing. They confront the terrifying instability of all things with institutionalized statements. They say : 'We know there is no* summa *of all attainable knowledge ; that is the preserve of God. But whatever men can learn, men can contain.' Out of this knife-edged approach to the universe they carve a fantastic belief in signs and omens and in their own destiny. This is an origin of their Kralizec legend : the war at the end of the universe.*

**– Bene Gesserit Private Reports/folio 800881**

'They have him securely in a safe place,' Namri said, smiling across the square stone room at Gurney Halleck. 'You may report this to your friends.'

'Where is this safe place?' Halleck asked. He didn't like Namri's tone, felt constrained by Jessica's orders. Damn the witch! Her explanations made no sense except the warning about what could happen if Leto failed to master his terrible memories.

'It's a safe place,' Namri said. 'That's all I'm permitted to tell you.'

'How do you know this?'

'I've had a distrans. Sabiha is with him.'

'Sabiha! She'll just tell him —'

'Not this time.'

'Are you going to kill him?'

'That's no longer up to me.'

Halleck grimaced. *Distrans.* What was the range of those damned cave bats? He'd often seen them flitting across the desert with hidden messages imprinted upon their squeaking calls. But how far would they go on this hellhole planet?

'I must see him for myself,' Halleck said.

'That's not permitted.'

Halleck took a deep breath to quiet himself. He had spent two days and two nights waiting for search reports. Now it was another morning and he felt his role dissolving around him, leaving him naked. He had never liked command anyway. Command always waited while others did the interesting and dangerous things.

'Why isn't it permitted?' he asked. The smugglers who'd arranged this safe-sietch had left too many questions unanswered and he wanted no more of the same from Namri.

'Some believe you saw too much when you saw this sietch,' Namri said.

Halleck heard the menace, relaxed into the easy stance of the trained fighter, hand near but not on his knife. He longed for a shield, but that had been ruled out by its effect on the worms, its short life in the presence of storm-generated static charges.

'This secrecy isn't part of our agreement,' Halleck said.

'If I'd killed him, would that have been part of our agreement?'

Again Halleck felt the jockeying of unseen forces about which the Lady Jessica hadn't warned him. This damned plan of hers! Maybe it was right not to trust the Bene Gesserit. Immediately, he felt disloyal. She'd explained the problem, and he'd come into her plan with the expectation that it, like all plans, would need adjustments later. This wasn't *any* Bene Gesserit; this was Jessica of the Atreides who'd never been other than friend and supporter to him. Without her, he knew he'd have been adrift in a universe more dangerous than the one he now inhabited.

'You can't answer my question,' Namri said.

'You were to kill him only if he showed himself to be . . . possessed,' Halleck said. 'Abomination.'

Namri put his fist beside his right ear. 'Your Lady knew we had tests for such. Wise of her to leave that judgment in my hands.'

Halleck compressed his lips in frustration.

'You heard the Reverend Mother's words to me,' Namri said. 'We Fremen understand such women but you off-worlders never understand them. Fremen women often send their sons to death.'

Halleck spoke past stiff lips. 'Are you telling me you've killed him?'

'He lives. He is in a safe place. He'll continue to receive the spice.'

'But I'm to escort him back to his grandmother if he survives,' Halleck said.

Namri merely shrugged.

Halleck understood that this was all the answer he'd get. Damn! He couldn't go back to Jessica with such unanswered questions! He shook his head.

'Why question what you cannot change?' Namri asked. 'You're being well paid.'

Halleck scowled at the man. Fremen! They believed all foreigners were influenced primarily by money. But Namri was speaking more than Fremen prejudice. Other forces were at work here and that was obvious to one who'd been trained in observation by a Bene Gesserit. This whole thing had the smell of a feint within a feint within a feint . . .

Shifting to the insultingly familiar form, Halleck said: 'The Lady Jessica will be wrathful. She could send cohorts against – '

'Zanadiq!' Namri cursed. 'You office messenger! You stand outside the Mohalata! I take pleasure in possessing your water for the Noble People!'

Halleck rested a hand on his knife, readied his left sleeve where he'd prepared a small surprise for attackers. 'I see no water spilled here,' he said. 'Perhaps you're blinded by your pride.'

'You live because I wished you to learn before dying that your Lady Jessica will not send cohorts against anyone. You are not to be lured quietly into the Huanui, off-world scum. I am of the Noble People, and you – '

'And I'm just a servant of the Atreides,' Halleck said, voice mild. 'We're the scum who lifted the Harkonnen yoke from your smelly neck.'

Namri showed white teeth in a grimace. 'Your Lady is prisoner on Salusa Secundus. The notes you thought were from her came from her daughter!'

By extreme effort, Halleck managed to keep his voice even. 'No matter. Alia will . . .'

Namri drew his crysknife. 'What do you know of the Womb

of Heaven? I am her servant, you male whore. I do her bidding when I take your water!' And he lunged across the room with foolhardy directness.

Halleck, not allowing himself to be tricked by such seeming clumsiness, flicked up the left arm of his robe, releasing the extra length of heavy fabric he'd had sewn there, letting that take Namri's knife. In the same movement, Halleck swept the folds of cloth over Namri's head, came in under and through the cloth with his own knife aimed directly for the face. He felt the point bite home as Namri's body hit him with a hard surface of metal armor beneath the robe. The Fremen emitted one outraged squeal, jerked backward, and fell. He lay there, blood gushing from his mouth as his eyes glared at Halleck then slowly dulled.

Halleck blew air through his lips. How could that fool Namri have expected anyone to miss the presence of armor beneath a robe? Halleck addressed the corpse as he recovered the trick sleeve, wiped his knife and sheathed it. 'How did you think we Atreides *servants* were trained, fool?'

He took a deep breath thinking: *Well, now. Whose feint am I?* There'd been the ring of truth in Namri's words. Jessica a prisoner of the Corrinos and Alia working her own devious schemes. Jessica herself had warned of many contingencies with Alia as enemy, but had not predicted herself as prisoner. He had his orders to obey, though. First there was the necessity of getting away from this place. Luckily one robed Fremen looked much like another. He rolled Namri's body into a corner, threw cushions over it, moved a rug to cover the blood. When it was done, Halleck adjusted the nose and mouth tubes of his stillsuit, brought up the mask as one would in preparing for the desert, pulled the hood of his robe forward and went out into the long passage.

*The innocent move without care* he thought, setting his pace at an easy saunter. He felt curiously free, as though he'd moved out of danger, not into it.

*I never did like her plan for the boy*, he thought. *And I'll tell her so if I see her. If.* Because if Namri spoke the truth, the most dangerous alternate plan went into effect. Alia wouldn't let him live long if she caught him, but there was always Stilgar – a good Fremen with a good Fremen's superstitions.

Jessica had explained it: 'There's a very thin layer of civilized behavior over Stilgar's original nature. And here's how you take that layer off him . . .'

*The spirit of Muad'Dib is more than words, more than the
letter of the Law which arises in his name. Muad'Dib must always
be that inner outrage against the complacently powerful,
against the charlatans and the dogmatic fanatics. It is that inner
outrage which must have its say because Muad'Dib taught us one
thing above all others : that humans can endure only in a fratern-
ity of social justice.*

— The Fedaykin Compact

Leto sat with his back against the wall of the hut, his attention
on Sabiha, watching the threads of his vision unroll. She had
prepared the coffee and set it aside. Now she squatted across
from him stirring his evening meal. It was a gruel redolent with
melange. Her hands moved quickly with the ladle and liquid
indigo stained the sides of his bowl. She bent her thin face over
the bowl, blending in the concentrate. The crude membrane
which made a stilltent of the hut had been patched with lighter
material directly behind her, and this formed a gray halo against
which her shadow danced in the flickering light of the cooking
flame and the single lamp.

That lamp intrigued Leto. These people of Shuloch were
profligate with spice-oil: a lamp, not a glowglobe. They kept
slave outcasts within their walls in the fashion told by the most
ancient Fremen traditions. Yet they employed ornithopters and
the latest spice harvesters. They were a crude mixture of ancient
and modern.

Sabiha pushed the bowl of gruel toward him, extinguished
the cooking flame.

Leto ignored the bowl.

'I will be punished if you do not eat this,' she said.

He stared at her, thinking: *If I kill her, that'll shatter one
vision. If I tell her Muriz's plans, that'll shatter another vision.
If I wait here for my father, this vision-thread will become a
mighty rope.*

His mind sorted the threads. Some held a sweetness which
haunted him. One future with Sabiha carried alluring reality
within his prescient awareness. It threatened to block out all
others until he followed it out to its ending agonies.

'Why do you stare at me that way?' she asked.

Still he did not answer.

She pushed the bowl closer to him.

Leto tried to swallow in a dry throat. The impulse to kill Sabiha welled in him. He found himself trembling with it. How easy it would be to shatter one vision and let the wildness run free!

'Muriz commands this,' she said, touching the bowl.

Yes, Muriz commanded it. Superstition conquered everything. Muriz wanted a vision cast for him to read. He was an ancient savage asking the witch doctor to throw the ox bones and interpret their sprawl. Muriz had taken his captive's stillsuit 'as a simple precaution'. There'd been a sly jibe at Namri and Sabiha in that comment. *Only fools let a prisoner escape.*

Muriz had a deep emotional problem, though: the Spirit River. The captive's water flowed in Muriz's veins. Muriz sought a sign that would permit him to hold a threat of death over Leto.

*Like father, like son,* Leto thought.

'The spice will only give you visions,' Sabiha said. The long silences made her uneasy. 'I've had visions in the orgy many times. They don't mean anything.'

*That's it!* he thought, his body locking itself into a stillness which left his skin cold and clammy. The Bene Gesserit training took over his consciousness, a pinpoint illumination which fanned out beyond him to throw the blazoning light of vision upon Sabiha and all of her Cast Out fellows. The ancient Bene Gesserit learning was explicit:

'*Languages build up to reflect specializations in a way of life. Each specialization may be recognized by its words, by its assumptions and sentence structures. Look for stoppages. Specializations represent places where life is being stopped, where the movement is dammed up and frozen.*' He saw Sabiha then as a vision-maker in her own right, and every other human carried the same power. Yet she was disdainful of her spice-orgy visions. They caused disquiet and, therefore, must be put aside, forgotten deliberately. Her people prayed to Shai-Hulud because the worm dominated many of their visions. They prayed for dew at the desert's edge because moisture limited their lives. Yet they wallowed in spice wealth and lured sandtrout to open qanats. Sabiha fed him prescient visions with a casual callousness, yet within her words he saw the illuminated signals: she depended upon absolutes, sought finite limits, and all because she couldn't handle the rigors of terrible decisions which touched her own flesh. She clung to her one-eyed vision of the universe, englobing and time-freezing as it might be, because the alternatives terrified her.

In contrast, Leto felt the pure movement of himself. He was a membrane collecting infinite dimensions and, because he saw those dimensions, he could make the terrible decisions.

*As my father did.*

'You must eat this!' Sabiha said, her voice petulant.

Leto saw the whole pattern of the visions now and knew the thread he must follow. *My skin is not my own.* He stood, pulling his robe around him. It felt strange against his flesh with no stillsuit protecting his body. His feet were bare upon the fused spice-fabric of the floor, feeling the sand tracked in there.

'What're you doing?' Sabiha demanded.

'The air is bad in here. I'm going outside.'

'You can't escape,' she said. 'Every canyon has its worm. If you go beyond the qanat, the worms will sense you by your moisture. These captive worms are very alert — not like the ones in the desert at all. Besides — ' how gloating her voice became! ' — you've no stillsuit.'

'Then why do you worry?' he asked, wondering if he might yet provoke a real reaction from her.

'Because you've not eaten.'

'And you'll be punished.'

'Yes!'

'But I'm already saturated with spice,' he said. 'Every moment is a vision.' He gestured with a bare foot at the bowl. 'Pour that onto the sand. Who'll know?'

'They watch,' she whispered.

He shook his head, shedding her from his visions, feeling new freedom envelop him. No need to kill this poor pawn. She danced to other music, not even knowing the steps, believing that she might yet share the power which lured the hungry pirates of Shuloch and Jacurutu. Leto went to the doorseal, put a hand upon it.

'When Muriz comes,' she said, 'he'll be very angry with — '

'Muriz is a merchant of emptiness,' Leto said. 'My aunt has drained him.'

She got to her feet. 'I'm going out with you.'

And he thought: *She remembers how I escaped her. Now she feels the fragility of her hold upon me. Her visions stir within her.* But she would not listen to those visions. She had but to reflect: How could he outwit a captive worm in its narrow canyon? How could he live in the Tanzerouft without stillsuit or Fremkit?

'I must be alone to consult my visions,' he said. 'You'll remain here.'

'Where will you go?'

'To the qanat.'

'The sandtrout come out in swarms at night.'

'They won't eat me.'

'Sometimes the worm comes down to just beyond the water,' she said. 'If you cross the qanat . . . ' She broke off, trying to edge her words with menace.

'How could I mount a worm without hooks?' he asked, wondering if she still could salvage some bit of her visions.

'Will you eat when you return?' she asked, squatting once more by the bowl recovering the ladle and stirring the indigo broth.

'Everything in its own time,' he said, knowing she'd be unable to detect his delicate use of Voice, the way he insinuated his own desires into her decision-making.

'Muriz will come and see if you've had a vision,' she warned.

'I will deal with Muriz in my own way,' he said, noting how heavy and slow her movements had become. The pattern of all Fremen lent itself naturally into the way he guided her now. Fremen were people of extraordinary energy at sunrise but a deep and lethargic melancholy often overcame them at nightfall. Already she wanted to sink into sleep and dreams.

Leto let himself out into the night alone.

The sky glittered with stars and he could make out the bulk of surrounding butte against their pattern. He went up under the palms to the qanat.

For a long time Leto squatted at the qanat's edge, listening to the restless hiss of sand within the canyon beyond. A small worm by the sound of it; chosen for that reason, no doubt. A small worm would be easier to transport. He thought about the worm's capture: the hunters would dull it with a water mist, using the traditional Fremen method of taking a worm for the orgy/transformation rite. But this worm would not be killed by immersion. This one would go out on a Guild heighliner to some hopeful buyer whose desert probably would be too moist. Few off-worlders realized the basic desiccation which the sandtrout had maintained on Arrakis. *Had maintained*. Because even here in the Tanzerouft there would be many times more airborne moisture than any worm had ever before known short of its death in a Fremen cistern.

He heard Sabiha stirring in the hut behind him. She was restless, prodded by her own suppressed visions. He wondered how it would be to live outside a vision with her, sharing each moment just as it came, of itself. The thought attracted him far more strongly than had any spice vision. There was a certain cleanliness about facing an unknown future.

'*A kiss in the sietch is worth two in the city.*'

The old Fremen maxim said it all. The traditional sietch had held a recognizable wildness mingled with shyness. There were traces of that shyness in the people of Jacurutu/Shuloch, but only traces. This saddened him by revealing what had been lost.

Slowly, so slowly that the knowledge was fully upon him before he recognized its beginnings, Leto grew aware of the soft rustling of many creatures all around him.

*Sandtrout.*

Soon it would be time to shift from one vision to another. He felt the movement of sandtrout as a movement within himself. Fremen had lived with the strange creatures for generations, knowing that if you risked a bit of water as bait, you could lure them into reach. Many a Fremen dying of thirst had risked his last few drops of water in this gamble, knowing that the sweet green syrup teased from a sandtrout might yield a small profit in energy. But the sandtrout were mostly the game of children who caught them for the Huanui. And for play.

Leto shuddered at the thought of what that *play* meant to him now.

He felt one of the creatures slither across his bare foot. It hesitated, then went on, attracted by the greater amount of water in the qanat.

For a moment, though, he'd felt the reality of his terrible decision. *The sandtrout glove.* It was the play of children. If one held a sandtrout in the hand, smoothing it over your skin, it formed a living glove. Traces of blood in the skin's capillaries could be sensed by the creatures, but something mingled with the blood's water repelled them. Sooner or later, the glove would slip off into the sand, there to be lifted into a spice-fiber basket. The spice soothed them until they were dumped into the death-still.

He could hear sandtrout dropping into the qanat, the swirl of predators eating them. Water softened the sandtrout, made it pliable. Children learned this early. A bit of saliva teased out the sweet syrup. Leto listened to the splashing. This was a migration of sandtrout come up to the open water, but they could not contain a flowing qanat patrolled by predator fish.

Still they came; still they splashed.

Leto groped on the sand with his right hand until his fingers encountered the leathery skin of a sandtrout. It was the large one he had expected. The creature didn't try to evade him, but moved eagerly onto his flesh. He explored its outline with his free hand – roughly diamond-shaped. It had no head, no extremities, no eyes, yet it could find water unerringly. With its fellows it could join body to body, locking one on another by the coarse interlacings of extruded cilia until the whole became one large sack-organism enclosing the water, walling off the 'poison' from the giant which the sandtrout would become: Shai-Hulud.

The sandtrout squirmed on his hand, elongating, stretching. As it moved, he felt a counterpart elongating and stretching of the vision he had chosen. *This thread, not that one.* He felt the sandtrout becoming thin, covering more and more of his hand. No sandtrout had ever before encountered a hand such as this one, every cell supersaturated with spice. No other human had ever before lived and reasoned in such a condition. Delicately Leto adjusted his enzyme balance, drawing on the illuminated sureness he'd gained in spice trance. The knowledge from those uncounted lifetimes which blended themselves with him provided the certainty through which he chose the precise adjustments, staving off the death from an overdose which would engulf him if he relaxed his watchfulness for only a heartbeat. And at the same time he blended himself with the sandtrout, feeding on it, feeding it, learning it. His trance vision provided the template and he followed it precisely.

Leto felt the sandtrout grow thin, spreading itself over more and more of his hand, reaching up his arm. He located another, placed it over the first one. Contact ignited a frenzied squirming in the creatures. Their cilia locked and they became a single membrane which enclosed him to the elbow. The sandtrout adjusted to the living glove of childhood play, but thinner and more sensitive as he lured it into the role of a skin symbiote. He reached down with the living glove, felt sand, each grain distinct to his senses. This was no longer sandtrout; it was tougher, stronger. And it would grow stronger and stronger . . . His groping hand encountered another sandtrout which whipped itself into union with the first two and adapted itself to the new role. Leathery softness insinuated itself up his arm to his shoulder.

With a terrible singleness of concentration he achieved the union of this new skin with his body, preventing rejection. No corner of his attention was left to dwell upon the terrifying consequences of what he did here. Only the necessities of his trance vision mattered. Only the Golden Path could come from this ordeal.

Leto shed his robe and lay naked upon the sand, his gloved arm outstretched into the path of migrating sandtrout. He remembered that once he and Ghanima had caught a sandtrout, abraded it against the sand until it contracted into the *child-worm*, a stiff tube, its interior pregnant with the green syrup. One bit gently upon the end and sucked swiftly before the wound was healed, gaining the few drops of sweetness.

They were all over his body now. He could feel the pulse of his blood against the living membrane. One tried to cover his face, but he moved it roughly until it elongated into a thin roll. The thing grew much longer than the child-worm, remaining flexible. Leto bit the end of it, tasted a thin stream of sweetness which continued far longer than any Fremen had ever before experienced. He could feel energy from the sweetness flow through him. A curious excitement suffused his body. He was kept busy for a time rolling the membrane away from his face until he'd built up a stiff ridge circling from jaw to forehead and leaving his ears exposed.

Now the vision must be tested.

He got to his feet, turned to run back toward the hut and, as he moved, found his feet moving too fast for him to balance. He plunged into the sand, rolled and leaped to his feet. The leap took him two meters off the sand and, when he fell back, trying to walk, he again moved too fast.

*Stop!* he commanded himself. He fell into the *prana-bindu* forced relaxation, gathering his senses into the pool of consciousness. This focused the inward ripples of the *constant-now* through which he experienced Time, and he allowed the vision-elation to warm him. The membrane worked precisely as the vision had predicted.

*My skin is not my own.*

But his muscles took some training to live with this amplified movement. When he walked, he fell, rolling. Presently he sat. In the quiet, the ridge below his jaw tried to become a membrane covering his mouth. He spat against it and bit, tasting the sweet syrup. It rolled downward to the pressure of his hand.

Enough time had passed to form the union with his body. Leto stretched flat and turned onto his face. He began to crawl, rasping the membrane against the sand. He could feel the sand distinctly, but nothing abraded his own flesh. With only a few swimming movements he traversed fifty meters of sand. The physical reaction was a friction-induced warming sensation.

The membrane no longer tried to cover his nose and mouth, but now he faced the second major step onto his Golden Path. His exertions had taken him beyond the qanat into the canyon where the trapped worm stayed. He heard it hissing toward him, attracted by his movements.

Leto leaped to his feet, intending to stand and wait, but the amplified movement sent him sprawling twenty meters farther into the canyon. Controlling his reactions with terrible effort, he sat back onto his haunches, straightened. Now the sand began to swell directly in front of him, rising up in a monstrous starlit curve. Sand opened only two body lengths from him. Crystal teeth flashed in the dim light. He saw the yawning mouth-cavern with, far back, the ambient movement of dim flame. The overpowering redolence of the spice swept over him. But the worm had stopped. It remained in front of him as First Moon lifted over the butte. The light reflected off the worm's teeth outlining the faery glow of chemical fires deep within the creature.

So deep was the inbred Fremen fear that Leto found himself torn by a desire to flee. But his vision held him motionless, fascinated by this prolonged moment. No one had ever before stood this close to the mouth of a living worm and survived. Gently Leto moved his right foot, met a sand ridge and, reacting too quickly, was propelled toward the worm's mouth. He came to a stop on his knees.

Still the worm did not move.

It sensed only the sandtrout and would not attack the deep-sand vector of its own kind. The worm would attack another worm in its territory and would come to exposed spice. Only a water barrier stopped it – and sandtrout, encapsulating water, were a water barrier.

Experimentally, Leto moved a hand toward that awesome mouth. The worm drew back a full meter.

Confidence restored, Leto turned away from the worm and began teaching his muscles to live with their new power. Cautiously he walked back toward the qanat. The worm remained motionless behind him. When Leto was beyond the water barrier he leaped with joy, went sailing ten meters across the sand, sprawled, rolled, laughed.

Light flared on the sand as the hut's doorseal was breached. Sabiha stood outlined in the yellow and purple glow of the lamp, staring out at him.

Laughing, Leto ran back across the qanat, stopped in front of the worm, turned and faced her with his hands outstretched.

'Look!' he called. 'The worm does my bidding!'

As she stood in frozen shock, he whirled, went racing around the worm and into the canyon. Gaining experience with his new skin, he found he could run with only the lightest flexing of muscles. It was almost effortless. When he put effort into running, he raced over the sand with the wind burning the exposed circle of his face. At the canyon's dead end instead of stopping, he leaped up a full fifteen meters, clawed at the cliff, scrabbled, climbing like an insect, and came out on the crest above the Tanzerouft.

The desert stretched before him, a vast silvery undulance in the moonlight.

Leto's manic exhilaration receded.

He squatted, sensing how light his body felt. Exertion had produced a slick film of perspiration which a stillsuit would have absorbed and routed into the transfer tissue which removed the salts. Even as he relaxed, the film disappeared now, absorbed by the membrane faster than a stillsuit could have done it. Thoughtfully Leto rolled a length of the membrane beneath his lips, pulled it into his mouth, and drank the sweetness.

His mouth was not masked, though. Fremen-wise, he sensed his body's moisture being wasted with every breath. Leto brought a section of the membrane over his mouth, rolled it back when it tried to seal his nostrils, kept at this until the rolled barrier remained in place. In the desert way, he fell into the automatic breathing pattern: in through his nose, out through his mouth. The membrane over his mouth protruded in a small bubble, but remained in place. No moisture collected on his lips and his nostrils remained open. The adaptation proceeded, then.

A 'thopter flew between Leto and the moon, banked, and came in for a spread-wing landing on the butte perhaps a hundred meters to his left. Leto glanced at it, turned, and looked back the way he had come up the canyon. Many lights could be seen down there beyond the qanat, a stirring of a multitude. He heard faint outcries, sensed hysteria in the sounds. Two men approached him from the 'thopter. Moonlight glinted on their weapons.

*The Mashhad*, Leto thought, and it was a sad thought. Here was the great leap onto the Golden Path. He had put on the living, self-repairing stillsuit of a sandtrout membrane, a thing of unmeasurable value on Arrakis . . . until you understood the price. *I am no longer human. The legends about this night will grow and magnify it beyond anything recognizable by the par-*

*ticipants. But it will become truth, that legend.*

He peered down from the butte, estimated the desert floor lay two hundred meters below. The moon picked out ledges and cracks on the steep face but no connecting pathway. Leto stood, inhaled a deep breath, glanced back at the approaching men, then stepped to the cliff's edge and launched himself into space. Some thirty meters down his flexed legs encountered a narrow ledge. Amplified muscles absorbed the shock and rebounded in a leap sideways to another ledge, where he caught a narrow outcropping with his hands, dropped twenty meters, leaped to another hand-hold and once more went down, bouncing, leaping, grasping tiny ledges. He took the final forty meters in one jump, landing in a bent-knee roll which sent him plunging down the slipface of a dune in a shower of sand and dust. At the bottom he scrambled to his feet, launched himself to the next dunecrest in one jump. He could hear hoarse shouts from atop the cliff but ignored them to concentrate on the leaping strides from dunetop to dunetop.

As he grew more accustomed to amplified muscles he found a sensuous joy that he had not anticipated in this distance-gulping movement. It was a ballet on the desert, defiance of the Tanzer-ouft which no other had ever experienced.

When he judged that the ornithopter's occupants had overcome their shock enough to mount pursuit once more, he dove for the moon-shadowed face of a dune, burrowed into it. The sand was like heavy liquid to his new strength, but the temperature mounted dangerously when he moved too fast. He broke free on the far face of the dune, found that the membrane had covered his nostrils. He removed it, sensed the new skin pulsing over his body in its labor to absorb his perspiration.

Leto fashioned a tube at his mouth, drank the syrup while he peered upward at the starry sky. He estimated he had come fifteen kilometers from Shuloch. Presently a 'thopter drew its pattern across the stars, a great bird shape followed by another and another. He heard the soft swishing of their wings, the whisper of their muted jets.

Sipping at the living tube, he waited. First Moon passed through its tracks, then Second Moon.

An hour before dawn Leto crept out and up to the dunecrest, examined the sky. No hunters. Now he knew himself to be embarked upon a path of no return. Ahead lay the trap in Time and Space which had been prepared as an unforgettable lesson for himself and all of mankind.

Leto turned northeast and loped another fifty kilometers before burrowing into the sand for the day, leaving only a tiny hole to the surface which he kept open with a sandtrout tube. The membrane was learning how to live with him as he learned how to live with it. He tried not to think of the other things it was doing to his flesh.

*Tomorrow I'll raid Gara Rulen*, he thought. *I'll smash their qanat and loose its water into the sand. Then I'll go on to Windsack, Old Gap, and Harg. In a month the ecological transformation will have been set back a full generation. That'll give us space to develop the new timetable.*

And the wildness of the rebel tribes would be blamed, of course. Some would revive memories of Jacurutu. Alia would have her hands full. As for Ghanima ... Silently to himself, Leto mouthed the words which would restore her memory. Time for that later ... if they survived this terrible mixing of threads.

The Golden Path lured him out there on the desert, almost a physical thing which he could see with his open eyes. And he thought how it was: as animals must move across the land, their existence dependent upon that movement the soul of humankind, blocked for eons, needed a track upon which it could move.

He thought of his father then, telling himself: '*Soon we'll dispute as man to man, and only one vision will emerge.*'

> *Limits of survival are set by climate, those long drifts of change which a generation may fail to notice. And it is the extremes of climate which set the pattern. Lonely, finite humans may observe climatic provinces, fluctuations of annual weather and, occasionally may observe such things as 'This is a colder year than I've ever known.' Such things are sensible. But humans are seldom alerted to the shifting average through a great span of years. And it is precisely in this alerting that humans learn how to survive on any planet. They must learn climate.*
>
> – Arrakis, the Transformation
> After Harq al-Ada

Alia sat cross-legged on her bed, trying to compose herself by reciting the Litany Against Fear, but chuckling derision echoed in her skull to block every effort. She could hear the voice; it controlled her ears, her mind.

'What nonsense is this? What have you to fear?'

The muscles of her calves twitched as her feet tried to make running motions. There was nowhere to run.

313

She wore only a golden gown of the sheerest Palian silk and it revealed the plumpness which had begun to bulge her body. The Hour of Assassins had just passed; dawn was near. Reports covering the past three months lay before her on the red coverlet. She could hear the humming of the air conditioner and a small breeze stirred the labels on the shigawire spools.

Aides had awakened her fearfully two hours earlier, bringing news of the latest outrage, and Alia had called for the report spools, seeking an intelligible pattern.

She gave up on the Litany.

These attacks had to be the work of rebels. Obviously. More and more of them turned against Muad'Dib's religion.

'And what's wrong with that?' the derisive voice asked within her.

Alia shook her head savagely. Namri had failed her. She'd been a fool to trust such a dangerous double instrument. Her aides whispered that Stilgar was to blame, that he was a secret rebel. And what had become of Halleck? Gone to ground among his smuggler friends? Possibly.

She picked up one of the report spools. *And Muriz!* The man was hysterical. That was the only possible explanation. Otherwise she'd have to believe in miracles. No human, let alone a child (even a child such as Leto) could leap from the butte at Shuloch and survive to flee across the desert in leaps that took him from dunecrest to dunecrest.

Alia felt the coldness of the shigawire under her hand.

Where was Leto, then? Ghanima refused to believe him other than dead. A Truthsayer had confirmed her story: Leto slain by a Laza tiger. Then who was the child reported by Namri and Muriz?

She shuddered.

Forty qanats had been breached, their waters loosed into the sand. The loyal Fremen and even the rebels, superstitious louts, all! Her reports were flooded with stories of mysterious occurrences. Sandtrout leaped into qanats and shattered to become hosts of small replicas. Worms deliberately drowned themselves. Blood dripped from Second Moon and fell to Arrakis, where it stirred up great storms. And the storm frequency *was* increasing!

She thought of Duncan incommunicado at Tabr, fretting under the restraints she'd exacted from Stilgar. He and Irulan talked of little else than the *real* meaning behind these omens. Fools! Even her spies betrayed the influence of these outrageous stories!

Why did Ghanima insist on her story of the Laza tiger?

Alia sighed. Only one of the reports on the shigawire spools reassured her. Farad'n had sent a contingent of his household guard 'to help you in your troubles and to prepare the way for the Official Rite of Betrothal.' Alia smiled to herself and shared the chuckle which rumbled in her skull. That plan, at least, remained intact. Logical explanations would be found to dispel all of this other superstitious nonsense.

Meanwhile she'd used Farad'n's men to help close down Shuloch and to arrest the known dissidents, especially among the Naibs: She debated moving against Stilgar, but the inner voice cautioned against this.

'Not yet.'

'My mother and the Sisterhood still have some plan of their own,' Alia whispered. 'Why is she training Farad'n?'

'Perhaps he excites her,' the Old Baron said.

'Not that cold one.'

'You're not thinking of asking Farad'n to return her?'

'I know the dangers in that!'

'Good. Meanwhile, that young aide Zia recently brought in, I believe his name's Agarves – Buer Agarves. If you'd invite him here tonight...'

'No!'

'Alia...'

'It's almost dawn, you insatiable old fool! There's a Military Council meeting this morning, the Priests will have –'

'Don't trust them, darling Alia.'

'Of course not!'

'Very well. Now, this Buer Agarves...'

'I said no!'

The Old Baron remained silent within her, but she began to feel a headache. A slow pain crept upward from her left cheek into her skull. Once he'd sent her raging down the corridors with this trick. Now, she resolved to resist him.

'If you persist, I'll take a sedative,' she said.

He could see she meant it. The headache began to recede.

'Very well.' Petulant. 'Another time, then.'

'Another time,' she agreed.

*Thou didst divide the sand by thy strength; Thou breakest the heads of the dragons in the desert. Yea, I behold thee as a beast coming up from the dunes; thou hast the two horns of the lamb, but thou speakest as the dragon.*

– Revised Orange Catholic Bible
Arran II:4

It was the immutable prophecy, the threads become rope, a thing Leto now seemed to have known all of his life. He looked out across the evening shadows on the Tanzerouft. One hundred and seventy kilometers due north lay Old Gap, the deep and twisting crevasse through the Shield Wall by which the first Fremen had migrated into the desert.

No doubts remained in Leto. He knew why he stood here alone in the desert, yet filled with a sense that he owned this entire land, that it must do his bidding. He felt the chord which connected him with all of humankind and that profound need for a universe of experiences which made logical sense, a universe of recognizable regularities within its perpetual changes.

*I know this universe.*

The worm which had brought him here had come to the stamping of his foot and, rising up in front of him, had stopped like an obedient beast. He'd leaped atop it and, with only his membrane-amplified hands, had exposed the leading lip of the worm's rings to keep it on the surface. The worm had exhausted itself in the nightlong dash northward. Its silicon-sulfur internal 'factory' had worked at capacity, exhaling lavish gusts of oxygen which a following wind had sent in enveloping eddies around Leto. At times the warm gusts had made him dizzy, filled his mind with strange perceptions. The reflexive and circular subjectivity of his visions had turned inward upon his ancestry, forcing him to relive portions of his Terranic past, then comparing those portions with his changing self.

Already he could feel how far he'd drifted from something recognizably human. Seduced by the spice which he gulped from every trace he found, the membrane which covered him no longer was sandtrout, just as he was no longer human. Cilia had crept into his flesh, forming a new creature which would seek its own metamorphosis in the eons ahead.

*You saw this, father, and rejected it,* he thought. *It was a thing too terrible to face.*

Leto knew what was believed of his father, and why.

*Muad'Dib died of prescience.*

But Paul Atreides had passed from the universe of reality into the *alam al-mythal* while still alive, fleeing from this thing which his son had dared.

Now there was only The Preacher.

Leto squatted on the sand and kept his attention northward. The worm would come from that direction, and on its back would ride two people: a young Fremen and a blind man.

A flight of pallid bats passed over Leto's head, bending their course southeast. They were random specks in the darkening sky, and a knowledgeable Fremen eye could mark their back-course to learn where shelter lay that way. The Preacher would avoid that shelter, though. His destination was Shuloch, where no wild bats were permitted lest they guide strangers to a secret place.

The worm appeared first as a dark movement between the desert and the northern sky. *Matar*, the rain of sand dropped from high altitudes by a dying stormwind, obscured the view for a few minutes, then it returned clearer and closer.

The cold-line at the base of the dune where Leto crouched began to produce its nightly moisture. He tasted the fragile dampness in his nostrils, adjusted the bubble cap of the membrane over his mouth. There no longer was any need for him to find soaks and sip-wells. From his mother's genes he had that longer, larger Fremen large intestine to take back water from everything which came its way. The living stillsuit grasped and retained every bit of moisture it encountered. And even while he sat here the membrane which touched sand extruded pseudopod-cilia to hunt for bits of energy which it could store.

Leto studied the approaching worm. He knew the youthful guide had seen him this time, noting the spot atop the dune. The worm rider would discern no principle in this object seen from a distance, but that was a problem Fremen had learned how to handle. Any unknown object was dangerous. The young guide's reactions would be quite predictable, even without the vision.

True to that prediction, the worm's course shifted slightly and aimed directly at Leto. Giant worms were a weapon which Fremen had employed many times. Worms had helped beat Shaddam at Arrakeen. This worm, however, failed to do its rider's bidding. It came to a halt ten meters away and no manner of goading would send it across another grain of sand.

Leto arose, feeling the cilia snap back into the membrane behind him. He freed his mouth and called out: 'Achlan, wasachlan!' *Welcome, twice welcome!*

The blind man stood behind his guide atop the worm, one hand on the youth's shoulder. The man held his face high, nose pointed over Leto's head as though trying to sniff out this interruption. Sunset painted orange on his forehead.

'Who is that?' the blind man asked, shaking his guide's shoulder. 'Why have we stopped?' His voice was nasal through the stillsuit plugs.

The youth stared fearfully down at Leto, said: 'It is only someone alone in the desert. A child by his looks. I tried to send the worm over him, but the worm won't go.'

'Why didn't you say?' the blind man demanded.

'I thought it was only someone alone in the desert!' the youth protested. 'But it's a demon.'

'Spoken like a true son of Jacurutu,' Leto said. 'And you, sire, you are The Preacher.'

'I am that one, yes.' And there was fear in The Preacher's voice because, at last, he had met his own past.

'This is no garden,' Leto said, 'but you are welcome to share this place with me tonight.'

'Who are you?' The Preacher demanded. 'How have you stopped our worm?' There was an ominous note of recognition in The Preacher's voice. Now he called up the memories of this alternate vision . . . knowing he could reach an end here.

'It's a demon!' the young guide protested. 'We must flee this place or our souls –'

'Silence!' The Preacher roared.

'I am Leto Atreides,' Leto said. 'Your worm stopped because I commanded it.'

The Preacher stood in frozen silence.

'Come, father,' Leto said. 'Alight and spend the night with me. I'll give you sweet syrup to sip. I see you've Fremkits with food and water jars. We'll share our riches here upon the sand.'

'Leto's yet a child,' The Preacher protested. 'And they say he's dead of Corrino treachery. There's no childhood in your voice.'

'You know me, sire,' Leto said. 'I'm small for my age as you were, but my experience is ancient and my voice has learned.'

'What do you here in the Inner Desert?' The Preacher asked.

'Bu ji,' Leto said. *Nothing from nothing.* It was the answer of a Zensunni wanderer, one who acted only from a position of rest, without effort and in harmony with his surroundings.

The Preacher shook his guide's shoulder. 'Is it a child, truly a child?'

'Aiya,' the youth said, keeping a fearful attention on Leto.

A great shuddering sigh shook The Preacher. 'No,' he said.

'It is a demon in child form,' the guide said.

'You will spend the night here,' Leto said.

'We will do as he says,' The Preacher said. He released his grip on the guide, slipped off the worm's side and slid down a ring to the sand, leaping clear when his feet touched. Turning, he said: 'Take the worm off and send it back into the sand. It is tired and will not bother us.'

'The worm will not go!' the youth protested.

'It will go,' Leto said. 'But if you try to flee on it, I'll let it eat you.' He moved to one side out of the worm's sensory range, pointed in the direction they had come. 'Go that way.'

The youth tapped a goad against the ring behind him, wiggled a hook where it held a ring open. Slowly the worm began to slide over the sand, turning as the youth shifted his hook down a side.

The Preacher, following the sound of Leto's voice, clambered up the duneslope and stood two paces away. It was done with a swift sureness which told Leto this would be no easy contest.

Here the visions parted.

Leto said: 'Remove your suit mask, father.'

The Preacher obeyed, dropping the fold of his hood and withdrawing the mouth cover.

Knowing his own appearance, Leto studied this face, seeing the lines of likeness as though they'd been outlined in light. The lines formed an indefinable reconciliation, a pathway of genes without sharp boundaries, and there was no mistaking them. Those lines came down to Leto from the humming days, from the water-dripping days, from the miracle seas of Caladan. But now they stood at a dividing point on Arrakis as night waited to fold itself into the dunes.

'So, father,' Leto said, glancing to the left where he could see the youthful guide trudging back to them from where the worm had been abandoned.

'Mu zein!' The Preacher said, waving his right hand in a cutting gesture. *This is no good!*

'Koolish zein,' Leto said, voice soft. *This is all the good we may ever have.* And he added, speaking in Chakobsa, the Atreides battle language: 'Here I am; here I remain! We cannot forget that, father.'

319

The Preacher's shoulders sagged. He put both hands to his empty sockets in a long-unused gesture.

'I gave you the sight of my eyes once and took your memories,' Leto said. 'I know your decisions and I've been to that place where you hid yourself.'

'I know.' The Preacher lowered his hands. 'You will remain?'

'You named me for the man who put that on his coat of arms,' Leto said. 'J'y suis, j'y reste!'

The Preacher sighed deeply. 'How far has it gone, this thing you've done to yourself?'

'My skin is not my own, father.'

The Preacher shuddered. 'Then I know how you found me here.'

'Yes, I fastened my memory to a place my flesh had never known,' Leto said. 'I need an evening with my father.'

'I'm not your father, I'm only a poor copy, a relic.' He turned his head toward the sound of the approaching guide. 'I no longer go to the visions for my future.'

As he spoke, darkness covered the desert. Stars leaped out above them and Leto, too, turned toward the approaching guide. 'Wabakh ul kuhar!' Leto called to the youth. *'Greetings!'*

Back came the response: 'Subakh un nar!'

Speaking in a hoarse whisper, The Preacher said: 'That young Assan Tariq is a dangerous one.'

'All of the Cast Out are dangerous,' Leto said. 'But not to me.' He spoke in a low, conversational tone.

'If that's your vision, I will not share it,' The Preacher said.

'Perhaps you have no choice,' Leto said. 'You are the *fil-haquiqa*, The Reality. You are Abu Dhur, Father of the Indefinite Roads of Time.'

'I'm no more than bait in a trap,' The Preacher said, and his voice was bitter.

'And Alia already has eaten that bait,' Leto said. 'But I don't like its taste.'

'You cannot do this!' The Preacher hissed.

'I've already done it. My skin is not my own.'

'Perhaps it's not too late for you to –'

'It is too late.' Leto bent his head to one side. He could hear Assan Tariq trudging up the duneslope toward them, coming to the sound of their voices. 'Greetings, Assan Tariq of Shuloch,' Leto said.

The youth stopped just below Leto on the slope, a dark shadow there in the starlight. There was indecision in the set of his shoulders, the way he tipped his head.

'Yes,' Leto said, 'I'm the one who escaped from Shuloch.'

'When I heard . . . ' The Preacher began. And again: 'You cannot do this!'

'I am doing it. What matter if you're made blind once more?'

'You think I fear that?' The Preacher asked. 'Do you not see the fine guide they have provided for me?'

'I see him.' Again Leto faced Tariq. 'Didn't you hear me, Assan? I'm the one who escaped from Shuloch.'

'You're a demon,' the youth quavered.

'Your demon,' Leto said. 'But you are my demon.' And Leto felt the tension grow between himself and his father. It was a shadowy play all around them, a projection of unconscious forms. And Leto felt the memories of his father, a form of backward prophecy which sorted visions from the familiar reality of this moment.

Tariq sensed it, this battle of the visions. He slid several paces backward down the slope.

'You cannot control the future,' The Preacher whispered, and the sound of his voice was filled with effort as though he lifted a great weight.

Leto felt the dissonance between them then. It was an element of the universe with which his entire life grappled. Either he or his father would be forced to act soon, making a decision by that act, choosing a vision. And his father was right: trying for some ultimate control of the universe, you only built weapons with which the universe eventually defeated you. To choose and manage a vision required you to balance on a single, thin thread – playing God on a high tightwire with cosmic solitude on both sides. Neither contestant could retreat into death-as-surcease-from-paradox. Each knew the visions and the rules. All of the old illusions were dying. And when one contestant moved, the other might countermove. The only real truth that mattered to them now was that which separated them from the vision background. There was no place of safety, only a transitory shifting of relationships, marked out within the limits which they now imposed and bound for inevitable changes. Each of them had only a desperate and lonely courage upon which to rely, but Leto possessed two advantages: he had committed himself upon a path from which there was no turning back, and he had accepted the terrible consequences to himself. His father still hoped there was a way back and had made no final commitment.

'You must not! You must not!' The Preacher rasped.

*He sees my advantage*, Leto thought.

Leto spoke in a conversational tone, masking his own tensions, the balancing effort this other-level contest required. 'I have no passionate belief in truth, no faith other than what I create,' he said. And he felt then a movement between himself and his father, something with granular characteristics which touched only Leto's own passionately subjective belief in himself. By such belief he knew that he posted the markers of the Golden Path. Someday such markers could tell others how to be human, a strange gift from a creature who no longer would be human on that day. But these markers were always set in place by gamblers. Leto felt them scattered throughout the landscape of his inner lives and, feeling this, poised himself for the ultimate gamble.

Softly he sniffed the air, seeking the signal which both he and his father knew must come. One question remained: Would his father warn the terrified young guide who waited below them?

Presently Leto sensed ozone in his nostrils, the betraying odor of a shield. True to his orders from the Cast Out, young Tariq was trying to kill both of these dangerous Atreides, not knowing the horrors which this would precipitate.

'Don't,' The Preacher whispered.

But Leto knew the signal was a true one. He sensed ozone, but there was no tingling in the air around them. Tariq used a pseudo-shield in the desert, a weapon developed exclusively for Arrakis. The Holtzmann Effect would summon a worm while it maddened that worm. Nothing would stop such a worm – not water, not the presence of sandtrout . . . nothing. Yes, the youth had planted the device in the duneslope and was beginning to edge away from the danger zone.

Leto launched himself off the duneslope, hearing his father scream in protest. But the awful impetus of Leto's amplified muscles threw his body like a missile. One outflung hand caught the neck of Tariq's stillsuit, the other slapped around to grip the doomed youth's robe at the waist. There came a single snap as the neck broke. Leto rolled, lifting his body like a finely balanced instrument which dove directly into the sand where the pseudo-shield had been hidden. Fingers found the thing and he had it out of the sand, throwing it in a looping arc far out to the south of them.

Presently there came a great hissing-thrashing din out on the desert where the pseudo-shield had gone. It subsided, and silence returned.

Leto looked up to the top of the dune where his father stood, still defiant, but defeated. That was Paul Muad'Dib up there, blind, angry, near despair as a consequence of his flight from the vision which Leto had accepted. Paul's mind would be reflecting now upon the Zensunni Long Koan: *In the one act of predicting an accurate future, Muad'Dib introduced an element of development and growth into the very prescience through which he saw human existence. By this, he brought uncertainty onto himself. Seeking the absolute of orderly prediction, he amplified disorder, distorted prediction.*

Returning to the dunetop in a single leap, Leto said: 'Now I'm your guide.'

'Never!'

'Would you go back to Shuloch? Even if they'd welcome you when you arrived without Tariq, where has Shuloch gone now? Do your *eyes* see it?'

Paul confronted his son then, aiming the eyeless sockets at Leto. 'Do you really know the universe you have created here?'

Leto heard the particular emphasis. The vision which both of them knew had been set into terrible motion here had required an act of creation at a certain *point* in time. For that moment, the entire sentient universe shared a linear view of time which possessed characteristics of orderly progression. They entered this time as they might step onto a moving vehicle, and they could only leave it the same way.

Against this, Leto held the multi-thread reins, balanced in his own vision-lighted view of time as multilinear and multilooped. He was the sighted man in the universe of the blind. Only he could scatter the orderly rationale because his father no longer held the reins. In Leto's view, a son had altered the past. And a thought as yet undreamed in the farthest future could reflect upon the *now* and move his hand.

Only *his* hand.

Paul knew this because he no longer could see how Leto might manipulate the reins, could only recognize the inhuman consequences which Leto had accepted. And he thought: *Here is the change for which I prayed. Why do I fear it? Because it's the Golden Path!*

'I'm here to give purpose to evolution and, therefore, to give purpose to our lives,' Leto said.

'Do you *wish* to live those thousands of years, changing as you now know you will change?'

Leto recognized that his father was not speaking about physical changes. Both of them knew the physical consequences: Leto would adapt and adapt; the skin-which-was-not-his-own would adapt and adapt. The evolutionary thrust of each part would melt into the other and a single transformation would emerge. When metamorphosis came, *if* it came, a thinking creature of awesome dimensions would emerge upon the universe – and that universe would worship him.

No . . . Paul was referring to the inner changes, the thoughts and decisions which would inflict themselves upon the worshippers

'Those who think you dead,' Leto said, 'you know what they say about your last words.'

'Of course.'

'*Now I do what all life must do in the service of life,*' Leto said. 'You never said that, but a Priest who thought you could never return and call him liar put those words into your mouth.'

'I'd not call him liar.' Paul took in a deep breath. 'Those are good last words.'

'Would you stay here or return to that hut in the basin of Shuloch?' Leto asked.

'This is your universe now,' Paul said.

The words filled with defeat cut through Leto. Paul had tried to guide the last strands of a personal vision, a choice he'd made years before in Sietch Tabr. For that, he'd accepted his role as an instrument of revenge for the Cast Out, the remnants of Jacurutu. They had contaminated him, but he'd accepted this rather than his view of this universe which Leto had chosen.

The sadness in Leto was so great he could not speak for several minutes. When he could manage his voice, Leto said: 'So you baited Alia, tempted her and confused her into inaction and the wrong decision. And now she knows who you are.'

'She knows . . . Yes, she knows.'

Paul's voice was old then and filled with hidden protests. There was a reserve of defiance in him, though. He said: 'I'll take the vision away from you if I can.'

'Thousands of peaceful years,' Leto said. 'That's what I'll give them.'

'Dormancy! Stagnation!'

'Of course. And those forms of violence which I permit. It'll be a lesson which humankind will never forget.'

'I spit on your lesson!' Paul said. 'You think I've not seen a thing similar to what you choose?'

'You saw it,' Leto agreed.

'Is your vision any better than mine?'

'Not one whit better. Worse, perhaps,' Leto said.

'Then what can I do but resist you?' Paul demanded.

'Kill me, perhaps?'

'I'm not that innocent. I know what you've set in motion. I know about the broken qanats and the unrest.'

'And now Assan Tariq will never return to Shuloch. You must go back with me or not at all because this is my vision now.'

'I choose not to go back.'

*How old his voice sounds,* Leto thought, and the thought was a wrenching pain. He said: 'I've the hawk ring of the Atreides concealed in my *dishdasha.* Do you wish me to return it to you?'

'If I'd only died,' Paul whispered. 'I truly wanted to die when I went into the desert that night, but I knew I could not leave this world. I had to come back and —'

'Restore the legend,' Leto said. 'I know. And the jackals of Jacurutu were waiting for you that night as you knew they would be. They wanted your visions! You knew that.'

'I refused. I never gave them one vision.'

'But they contaminated you. They fed you spice essence and plied you with women and dreams. And you *did* have visions.'

'Sometimes.' How sly his voice sounded.

'Will you take back your hawk ring?' Leto asked.

Paul sat down suddenly on the sand, a dark blotch in the starlight. 'No!'

*So he knows the futility of that path,* Leto thought. This revealed much, but not enough. The contest of the visions had moved from its delicate plane of choices down to a gross discarding of alternates. Paul knew he could not win, but he hoped yet to nullify that single vision to which Leto clung.

Presently Paul said: 'Yes, I was contaminated by the Jacurutu. But you contaminate yourself.'

'That's true,' Leto admitted. 'I am your son.'

'And are you a good Fremen?'

'Yes.'

'Will you permit a blind man to go into the desert finally? Will you let me find peace on my own terms?' He pounded the sand beside him.

'No, I'll not permit that,' Leto said. 'But it's your right to fall upon your knife if you insist upon it.'

'And you would have my body!'

'True.'

'No!'

*And so he knows that path,* Leto thought. The enshrining of Muad'Dib's body by his son could be contrived as a form of cement for Leto's vision.

'You never told them, did you, father?' Leto asked.

'I never told them.'

'But I told them,' Leto said. 'I told Muriz. Kralizec, the Typhoon Struggle.'

Paul's shoulders sagged. 'You cannot,' he whispered. 'You cannot.'

'I am a creature of this desert now, father,' Leto said. 'Would you speak thus to a Coriolis storm?'

'You think me coward for refusing that path,' Paul said, his voice husky and trembling. 'Oh, I understand you well, son. Augury and haruspication have always been their own torments. But I was never lost in the possible futures because this one is unspeakable!'

'Your Jihad will be a summer picnic on Caladan by comparison,' Leto agreed. 'I'll take you to Gurney Halleck now.'

'Gurney! He serves the Sisterhood through my mother.'

And now Leto understood the extent of his father's vision. 'No, father. Gurney no longer serves anyone. I know the place to find him and I can take you there. It's time for the new legend to be created.'

'I see that I cannot sway you. Let me touch you, then, for you are my son.'

Leto held out his right hand to meet the groping fingers, felt their strength, matched it, and resisted every shift of Paul's arm. 'Not even a poisoned knife will harm me now,' Leto said. 'I'm already a different chemistry.'

Tears slipped from the sightless eyes and Paul released his grip, dropped his hand to his side. 'If I'd chosen your way, I'd have become the *bicouros of shaitan.* What will you become?'

'For a time they'll call me the missionary of *shaitan,* too,' Leto said. 'Then they'll begin to wonder and, finally, they'll understand. You didn't take your vision far enough, father. Your hands did good things and evil.'

'But the evil was known after the event!'

'Which is the way of many great evils,' Leto said. 'You crossed over only into a part of my vision. Was your strength not enough?'

'You know I couldn't stay there. I could never do an evil act which was known before the act. I'm not Jacurutu.' He clambered to his feet. 'Do you think me one of those who laughs alone at night?'

'It is sad that you were never really Fremen,' Leto said. 'We Fremen know how to commission the arifa. Our judges can choose between evils. It's always been that way for us.'

'Fremen, is it? Slaves of the fate you helped to make?' Paul stepped toward Leto, reached out in an oddly shy movement, touched Leto's sheathed arm, explored up it to where the membrane exposed an ear, then the cheek and, finally, the mouth. 'Ahhhh, that is your own flesh yet,' he said. 'Where will that flesh take you?' He dropped his hand.

'Into a place where humans may create their futures from instant to instant.'

'So you say. An Abomination might say the same.'

'I'm not Abomination, though I might've been,' Leto said. 'I saw how it goes with Alia. A demon lives in her, father. Ghani and I know that demon: it's the Baron, your grandfather.'

Paul buried his face in his hands. His shoulders shook for a moment, then he lowered his hands and his mouth was set in a harsh line. 'There is a curse upon our House. I prayed that you would throw that ring into the sand, that you'd deny me and run away to make . . . another life. It was there for you.'

'At what price?'

After a long silence, Paul said: 'The end adjusts the path behind it. Just once I failed to fight for my principles. Just once. I accepted the Mahdinate. I did it for Chani, but it made me a bad leader.'

Leto found he couldn't answer this. The memory of that decision was there within him.

'I cannot lie to you any more than I could lie to myself,' Paul said. 'I know this. Every man should have such an auditor. I will only ask this one thing: is the Typhoon Struggle necessary?'

'It's that or humans will be extinguished.'

Paul heard the truth in Leto's words, spoke in a low voice which acknowledged the greater breadth of his son's vision. 'I did not see that among the choices.'

'I believe the Sisterhood suspects it,' Leto said. 'I cannot accept any other explanation of my grandmother's decision.'

The night wind blew coldly around them then. It whipped Paul's robe around his legs: He trembled. Seeing this, Leto said: 'You've a kit, father. I'll inflate the tent and we can spend this night in comfort.'

But Paul could only shake his head, knowing he would have

no comfort from this night or any other. Muad'Dib, The Hero, must be destroyed. He'd said it himself. Only The Preacher could go on now.

*Fremen were the first humans to develop a conscious/unconscious symbology through which to experience the movements and relationships of their planetary system. They were the first people anywhere to express climate in terms of a semi-mathematic language whose written symbols embody (and internalize) the external relationships. The language itself was part of the system it described. Its written form carried the shape of what it described. The intimate local knowledge of what was available to support life was implicit in this development. One can measure the extent of this language/system interaction by the fact that Fremen accepted themselves as foraging and browsing animals.*

– The Story of Liet-Kynes
by Harq al-Ada

'Kaveh wahid,' Stilgar said. *Bring coffee.* He signaled with a raised hand to an aide who stood at one side near the single door to the austere rock-walled room where he had spent this wakeful night. This was the place where the old Fremen Naib usually took his spartan breakfast, and it was almost breakfast time, but after such a night he did not feel hungry. He stood, stretching his muscles.

Duncan Idaho sat on a low cushion near the door, trying to suppress a yawn. He had just realized that, while they talked, he and Stilgar had gone through an entire night.

'Forgive me, Stil,' he said. 'I've kept you up all night.'

'To stay awake all night adds a day to your life,' Stilgar said, accepting the tray with coffee as it was passed in the door. He pushed a low bench in front of Idaho, placed the tray on it and sat across from his guest.

Both men wore the yellow robes of mourning, but Idaho's was a borrowed garment worn because the people of Tabr had resented the Atreides green of his working uniform.

Stilgar poured the dark brew from the fat copper carafe, sipped first, and lifted his cup as a signal to Idaho – the ancient Fremen custom: *'It is safe; I have taken some of it.'*

The coffee was Harah's work, done just as Stilgar preferred it: the beans roasted to a rose-brown, ground to a fine powder in a stone mortar while still hot, and boiled immediately; a pinch of melange added.

Idaho inhaled the spice-rich aroma, sipped carefully but noisily. He still did not know if he had convinced Stilgar. His mentat faculties had begun to work sluggishly in the early hours of the morning, all of his computations confronted at last by the inescapable datum supplied in the message from Gurney Halleck.

Alia had known about Leto! She'd known.

And Javid had to be a part of that knowing.

'I must be freed of your restraints,' Idaho said at last, taking up the arguments once more.

Stilgar stood his ground. 'The agreement of neutrality requires me to make hard judgments. Ghani is safe here. You and Irulan are safe here. But you may not send messages. Receive messages, yes, but you may not send them. I've given my word.'

'This is not the treatment usually accorded a guest and an old friend who has shared your dangers,' Idaho said, knowing he'd used this argument before.

Stilgar put down his cup, setting it carefully into its place on the tray and keeping his attention on it as he spoke. 'We Fremen don't feel guilt for the same things that arouse such feelings in others,' he said. He raised his attention to Idaho's face.

*He must be made to take Ghani and flee this place,* Idaho thought. He said: 'It was not my intention to raise a storm of guilt.'

'I understand that,' Stilgar said. 'I raise the question to impress upon you our Fremen attitude, because that is what we are dealing with: Fremen. Even Alia thinks Fremen.'

'And the Priests?'

'They are another matter,' Stilgar said. 'They want the people to swallow the gray wind of sin, taking *that* into the everlasting. This is a great blotch by which they seek to know their own piety.' He spoke in a level voice, but Idaho heard the bitterness and wondered why that bitterness could not sway Stilgar.

'It's an old, old trick of autocratic rule,' Idaho said. 'Alia knows it well. Good subjects must feel guilty. The guilt begins as a feeling of failure. The good autocrat provides many opportunities for failure in the populace.'

'I've noticed.' Stilgar spoke dryly. 'But you must forgive me if I mention to you once more that this is your wife of whom you speak. It is the sister of Muad'Dib.'

'She's possessed, I tell you!'

'Many say it. She will have to undergo the test one day. Meanwhile there are other considerations more important.'

Idaho shook his head sadly. 'Everything I've told you can be verified. The communications with Jacurutu was always through Alia's Temple. The plot against the twins had accomplices there. Money for the sale of worms off-planet goes there. All of the strings lead to Alia's office, to the Regency.'

Stilgar shook his head, drew in a deep breath. 'This is neutral territory. I've given my word.'

'Things can't go on this way!' Idaho protested.

'I agree.' Stilgar nodded. 'Alia's caught inside the circle and every day the circle grows smaller. It's like our old custom of having many wives. This pinpoints male sterility.' He bent a questioning gaze on Idaho. 'You say she deceives you with other men – "using her sex as a weapon" is the way I believe you've expressed it. Then you have a perfectly legal avenue available to you. Javid's here in Tabr with messages from Alia. You have only to –'

'On your neutral territory?'

'No, but outside in the desert . . .'

'And if I took that opportunity to escape?'

'You'll not be given such an opportunity.'

'Still, I swear to you, Alia's possessed. What do I have to do to convince you of –'

'A difficult thing to prove,' Stilgar said. It was the argument he'd used many times during the night.

Idaho recalled Jessica's words, said: 'But you've ways of proving it.'

'A way, yes,' Stilgar said. Again he shook his head. 'Painful, irrevocable. That is why I remind you about our attitude toward guilt. We can free ourselves from guilts which might destroy us in everything except the Trial of Possession. For that, the tribunal, which is all of the people, accepts complete responsibility.'

'You've done it before, haven't you?'

'I'm sure the Reverend Mother didn't omit our history in her recital,' Stilgar said. 'You well know we've done it before.'

Idaho responded to the irritation in Stilgar's voice. 'I wasn't trying to trap you in a falsehood. It's just –'

'It's the long night and the questions without answers,' Stilgar said. 'And now it's morning.'

'I must be allowed to send a message to Jessica,' Idaho said.

'That would be a message to Salusa,' Stilgar said. 'I don't make evening promises. My word is meant to be kept: that is why Tabr's neutral territory. I will hold you in silence. I have pledged this for my entire household.'

'Alia must be brought to your Trial!'

'Perhaps. First, we must find out if there are extenuating circumstances. A failure of authority, possibly. Or even bad luck. It could be a case of that natural bad tendency which all humans share, and not possession at all.'

'You want to be sure I'm not just the husband wronged, seeking others to execute his revenge,' Idaho said.

'The thought has occurred to others, not to me,' Stilgar said. He smiled to take the sting out of his words. 'We Fremen have our science of tradition, our *hadith*. When we fear a mentat or a Reverend Mother, we revert to the *hadith*. It is said that the only fear we cannot correct is the fear of our mistakes.'

'The Lady Jessica must be told,' Idaho said. 'Gurney says – '

'That message may not come from Gurney Halleck.'

'It comes from no other. We Atreides have our ways of verifying messages. Stil, won't you at least explore some of – '

'Jacurutu is no more,' Stilgar said. 'It was destroyed many generations ago.' He touched Idaho's sleeve. 'In any event, I cannot spare the fighting men. These are troubled times, the threat to the qanat . . . you understand?' He sat back. 'Now, when Alia – '

'There is no more Alia,' Idaho said. .

'So you say.' Stilgar took another sip of coffee, replaced the cup. 'Let it rest there, friend Idaho. Often there's no need to tear off an arm to remove a splinter.'

'Then let's talk about Ghanima.'

'There's no need. She has my countenance, my bond. No one can harm her here.'

*He cannot be that naïve*, Idaho thought.

But Stilgar was rising to indicate that the interview was ended.

Idaho levered himself to his feet, feeling the stiffness in his knees. His calves felt numb. As Idaho stood, an aide entered and stood aside. Javid came into the room behind him. Idaho turned. Stilgar stood four paces away. Without hesitation, Idaho drew his knife in one swift motion and drove its point into the breast of the unsuspecting Javid. The man staggered backward, pulling himself off the knife. He turned, fell onto his face. His legs kicked and he was dead.

'That was to silence the gossip,' Idaho said.

The aide stood with drawn knife, undecided how to react. Idaho had already sheathed his own knife, leaving a trace of blood on the edge of his yellow robe.

'You have defiled my honor!' Stilgar cried. 'This is neutral – '

331

'Shut up!' Idaho glared at the shocked Naib. 'You wear a collar, Stilgar!'

It was one of the three most deadly insults which could be directed at a Fremen. Stilgar's face went pale.

'You are a servant,' Idaho said. 'You've sold Fremen for their water.'

This was the second most deadly insult, the one which had destroyed the original Jacurutu.

Stilgar ground his teeth, put a hand on his crysknife. The aide stepped back away from the body in the doorway.

Turning his back on the Naib, Idaho stepped into the door, taking the narrow opening beside Javid's body and speaking without turning, delivered the third insult. 'You have no immortality, Stilgar. None of your descendants carry your blood!'

'Where do you go now, mentat?' Stilgar called as Idaho continued leaving the room. Stilgar's voice was as cold as a wind from the poles.

'To find Jacurutu,' Idaho said, still not turning.

Stilgar drew his knife. 'Perhaps I can help you.'

Idaho was at the outer lip of the passage now. Without stopping, he said: 'If you'd help me with your knife, water-thief, please do it in my back. That's the fitting way for one who wears the collar of a demon.'

With two leaping strides Stilgar crossed the room, stepped on Javid's body and caught Idaho in the outer passage. One gnarled hand jerked Idaho around and to a stop. Stilgar confronted Idaho with bared teeth and a drawn knife. Such was his rage that Stilgar did not even see the curious smile on Idaho's face.

'Draw your knife, mentat scum!' Stilgar roared.

Idaho laughed. He cuffed Stilgar sharply — left hand, right hand — two stinging slaps to the head.

With an incoherent screech, Stilgar drove his knife into Idaho's abdomen, striking upward through the diaphragm into the heart.

Idaho sagged onto the blade, grinned up at Stilgar, whose rage dissolved into sudden icy shock.

'Two deaths for the Atreides,' Idaho husked. 'The second for no better reason than the first.' He lurched sideways, collapsed to the stone floor on his face. Blood spread out from his wound.

Stilgar stared down past his dripping knife at the body of Idaho, took a deep, trembling breath. Javid lay dead behind him: And the consort of Alia, the Womb of Heaven, lay dead at Stilgar's own hands. It might be argued that a Naib had but protected the honor of his name, avenging the threat to his

332

promised neutrality. But this dead man was Duncan Idaho. No matter the arguments available, no matter the 'extenuating circumstances', nothing could erase such an act. Even were Alia to approve privately, she would be forced to respond publicly in revenge. She was, after all, Fremen. To rule Fremen, she could be nothing else, not even to the smallest degree.

Only then did it occur to Stilgar that this situation was precisely what Idaho had intended to buy with his 'second death'.

Stilgar looked up, saw the shocked face of Harah, his second wife, peering at him in an enclosing throng. Everywhere Stilgar turned there were faces with identical expressions: shock and an understanding of the consequences.

Slowly Stilgar drew himself erect, wiped the blade on his sleeve and sheathed it. Speaking to the faces, his tone casual, he said: 'Those who'll go with me should pack at once. Send men to summon worms.'

'Where will you go, Stilgar?' Harah asked.

'Into the desert.'

'I will go with you,' she said.

'Of course you'll go with me. All of my wives will go with me. And Ghanima. Get her, Harah. At once.'

'Yes, Stilgar . . . at once.' She hesitated. 'And Irulan?'

'If she wishes.'

'Yes, husband.' Still she hesitated. 'You take Ghani as hostage?'

'Hostage?' He was genuinely startled by the thought. 'Woman . . . ' He touched Idaho's body softly with a toe. 'If this mentat was right, I'm Ghani's only hope.' And he remembered then Leto's warning: *'Beware of Alia. You must take Ghani and flee.'*

---

*After the Fremen, all Planetologists see life as expressions of energy and look for the overriding relationships. In small pieces, bits and parcels which grow into general understanding, the Fremen racial wisdom is translated into a new certainty. The thing Fremen have as a people, any people can have. They need but develop a sense for energy relationships. They need but observe that energy soaks up the patterns of things and builds with those patterns.*

— The Arrakeen Catastrophe
After Harq al-Ada

It was Tuek's Sietch on the inner lip of False Wall. Halleck stood in the shadow of the rock buttress which shielded the high entrance to the sietch, waiting for those inside to decide whether they would shelter him. He turned his gaze outward to the northern desert and then upward to the gray-blue morning sky. The smugglers here had been astonished to learn that he, an off-worlder, had captured a worm and ridden it. But Halleck had been equally astonished at their reaction. The thing was simple for an agile man who'd seen it done many times.

Halleck returned his attention to the desert, the silver desert of shining rocks and gray-green fields where water had worked its magic. All of this struck him suddenly as an enormously fragile containment of energy, of life -- everything threatened by an abrupt shift in the pattern of change.

He knew the source of this reaction. It was the bustling scene on the desert floor below him. Containers of dead sandtrout were being trundled into the sietch for distillation and recovery of their water. There were thousands of the creatures. They had come to an outpouring of water. And it was this outpouring which had set Halleck's mind racing.

Halleck stared downward across the sietch fields and the qanat boundary which no longer flowed with precious water. He had seen the holes in the qanat's stone walls, the rending of the rock liner which had spilled water into the sand. What had made those holes? Some stretched along twenty meters of the qanat's most vulnerable sections, in places where soft sand led outward into water-absorbing depressions. It was those depressions which had swarmed with sandtrout. The children of the sietch were killing them and capturing them.

Repair teams worked on the shattered walls of the qanat. Others carried minims of irrigation water to the most needy plants. The water source in the gigantic cistern beneath Tuek's windtrap had been closed off, preventing the flow into the shattered qanat. The sun-powered pumps had been disconnected. The irrigation water came from dwindling pools at the bottom of the qanat and, laboriously, from the cistern within the sietch.

The metal frame of the doorseal behind Halleck crackled in the growing warmth of the day. As though the sound moved his eyes, Halleck found his gaze drawn to the farthest curve of the qanat, to the place where water had reached most impudently into the desert. The garden-hopeful planners of the sietch had planted a special tree there and it was doomed unless the water flow could be restored soon. Halleck stared at the silly, trailing plumage of a willow tree there shredded by sand and wind. For him, that tree symbolized the new reality for himself and for Arrakis.

*Both of us are alien here.*

They were taking a long time over their decision within the sietch, but they could use good fighting men. Smugglers always needed good men. Halleck had no illusions about them, though. The smugglers of this age were not the smugglers who'd sheltered him so many years ago when he'd fled the dissolution of his Duke's fief. No, these were a new breed, quick to seek profit.

Again he focused on the silly willow. It came to Halleck then that the stormwinds of his new reality might destroy these smugglers and all of their friends. It might destroy Stilgar with his fragile neutrality and take with him all of the tribes who remained loyal to Alia. They'd all become colonial peoples. Halleck had seen it happen before, knowing the bitter taste of it on his own homeworld. He saw it clearly, recalling the mannerisms of the city. Fremen, the pattern of the suburbs, and the unmistakable ways of the rural sietch which rubbed off even on this smugglers' hideaway. The rural districts were colonies of the urban centers. They'd learned how to wear a padded yoke, led into it by their greed if not their superstitions. Even here, especially here, the people had the attitude of a subject population, not the attitude of free men. They were defensive, concealing, evasive. Any manifestation of authority was subject to resentment -- any authority: the Regency's, Stilgar's, their own Council . . .

*I can't trust them,* Halleck thought. He could only use them and nurture their distrust of others. It was sad. Gone was the old give and take of free men. The old ways had been reduced to ritual words, their origins lost to memory.

Alia had done her work well, punishing opposition and rewarding assistance, shifting the Imperial forces in random fashion, concealing the major elements of her Imperial power. The spies! Gods below, the spies she must have!

Halleck could almost see the deadly rhythm of movement and countermovement by which Alia hoped to keep her opposition off balance.

*If the Fremen remain dormant, she'll win,* he thought.

The doorseal behind him crackled as it was opened. A sietch attendant named Melides emerged. He was a short man with a gourd-like body which dwindled into spindly legs whose ugliness was only accented by a stillsuit.

'You have been accepted,' Melides said.

And Halleck heard the sly dissimulation in the man's voice. What that voice revealed told Halleck there was sanctuary here for only a limited time.

*Just until I can steal one of their 'thopters*, he thought.

'My gratitude to your Council,' he said. And he thought of Esmar Tuek, for whom this sietch had been named. Esmar, long dead of someone's treachery, would have slit the throat of this Melides on sight.

> *Any path which narrows future possibilities may become a lethal trap. Humans are not threading their way through a maze; they scan a vast horizon filled with unique opportunities. The narrowing viewpoint of the maze should appeal only to creatures with their noses buried in sand. Sexually produced uniqueness and differences are the life-protection of the species.*
>
> – The Spacing Guild Handbook

'Why do I not feel grief?' Alia directed the question at the ceiling of her small audience chamber, a room she could cross in ten paces one way and fifteen the other. It had two tall and narrow windows which looked out across the Arrakeen rooftops at the Shield Wall.

It was almost noon. The sun burned down into the pan upon which the city had been built.

Alia lowered her gaze to Buer Agarves, the former Tabrite and now aide to Zia who directed the Temple guards. Agarves had brought the news that Javid and Idaho were dead. A mob of sycophants, aides and guards had come in with him and more crowded the areaway outside, revealing that they already knew Agarves's message.

Bad news traveled fast on Arrakis.

He was a small man, this Agarves, with a round face for a Fremen, almost infantile in its roundness. He was one of the new breed who had gone to water-fatness. Alia saw him as though he had been split into two images: one with a serious face and opaque indigo eyes, a worried expression around the mouth, the other image sensuous and vulnerable, excitingly vulnerable. She especially liked the thickness of his lips.

Although it was not yet noon, Alia felt something in the shocked silence around her that spoke of sunset.

*Idaho should've died at sunset*, she told herself.

'How is it, Buer, that you're the bearer of this news?' she

336

asked, noting the watchful quickness which came into his expression.

Agarves tried to swallow, spoke in a hoarse voice hardly more than a whisper. 'I went with Javid, you recall? And when . . . Stilgar sent me to you, he said for me to tell you that I carried his final obedience.'

'Final obedience,' she echoed. 'What'd he mean by that?'

'I don't know, Lady Alia,' he pleaded.

'Explain to me again what you saw,' she ordered, and she wondered at how cold her skin felt.

'I saw . . . ' He bobbed his head nervously, looked at the floor in front of Alia. 'I saw the Holy Consort dead upon the floor of the central passage, and Javid lay dead nearby in a side passage. The women already were preparing them for Huanui.'

'And Stilgar summoned you to this scene?'

'That is true, My Lady. Stilgar summoned me. He sent Modibo, the Bent One, his messenger in sietch. Modibo gave me no warning. He merely told me Stilgar wanted me.'

'And you saw my husband's body there on the floor?'

He met her eyes with a darting glance, returned his attention once more to the floor in front of her before nodding. 'Yes, My Lady. And Javid dead nearby. Stilgar told me . . . told me that the Holy Consort had slain Javid.'

'And my husband, you say Stilgar –'

'He said it to me with his own mouth, My Lady. Stilgar said he had done this. He said the Holy Consort provoked him to rage.'

'Rage,' Alia repeated. 'How was that done?'

'He didn't say. No one said. I asked and no one said.'

'And that's when you were sent to me with this news?'

'Yes, My Lady.'

'Was there nothing you could do?'

Agarves wet his lips with his tongue, then: 'Stilgar commanded, My Lady. It was his sietch.'

'I see. And you always obeyed Stilgar.'

'I always did, My Lady, until he freed me from my bond.'

'When you were sent to my service, you mean?'

'I obey only you now, My Lady.'

'Is that right? Tell me, Buer, if I commanded you to slay Stilgar, your old Naib, would you do it?'

He met her gaze with a growing firmness. 'If you commanded it, My Lady.'

'I do command it. Have you any idea where he's gone?'

'Into the desert; that's all I know, My Lady.'

'How many men did he take?'

'Perhaps half the effectives.'

'And Ghanima and Irulan with him!'

'Yes, My Lady. Those who left are burdened with their women, their children and their baggage. Stilgar gave everyone a choice – go with him or be freed of their bond. Many chose to be freed. They will select a new Naib.'

'I'll select their new Naib! And it'll be you, Buer Agarves, on the day you bring me Stilgar's head.'

Agarves could accept selection by battle. It was a Fremen way. He said: 'As you command, My Lady. What forces may I –'

'See Zia. I can't give you many 'thopters for the search. They're needed elsewhere. But you'll have enough fighting men. Stilgar has defamed his honor. Many will serve with you gladly.'

'I'll get about it, then, My Lady.'

'Wait!' She studied him a moment, reviewing whom she could send to watch over this vulnerable infant. He would need close watching until he'd proved himself. Zia would know whom to send.

'Am I not dismissed, My Lady?'

'You are not dismissed. I must consult you privately and at length on your plans to take Stilgar.' She put a hand to her face. 'I'll not grieve until you've exacted my revenge. Give me a few minutes to compose myself.' She lowered her hand. 'One of my attendants will show you the way.' She gave a subtle hand signal to one of her attendants, whispered to Shalus, her new Dame of Chamber: 'Have him washed and perfumed before you bring him. He smells of worm.'

'Yes, mistress.'

Alia turned then, feigning the grief she did not feel, and fled to her private chambers. There, in her bedroom, she slammed the door into its tracks, cursed and stamped her foot.

*Damn that Duncan! Why? Why? Why?*

She sensed a deliberate provocation from Idaho. He'd slain Javid and provoked Stilgar. It said he knew about Javid. The whole thing must be taken as a message from Duncan Idaho, a final gesture.

Again she stamped her foot and again, raging across the bedchamber.

*Damn him! Damn him! Damn him!*

Stilgar gone over to the rebels and Ghanima with him. Irulan, too.

*Damn them all!*

Her stamping foot encountered a painful obstacle, descending onto metal. Pain brought a cry from her and she peered down, finding that she'd bruised her foot on a metal buckle. She snatched it up, stood frozen at the sight of it in her hand. It was an old buckle, one of the silver-and-platinum originals from Caladan awarded originally by the Duke Leto Atreides I to his swordmaster, Duncan Idaho. She'd seen Duncan wear it many times. And he'd discarded it here.

Alia's fingers clutched convulsively on the buckle. Idaho had left it here when ... when ...

Tears sprang from her eyes, forced out against the great Fremen conditioning. Her mouth drew down into a frozen grimace and she sensed the old battle begin within her skull, reaching out to her fingertips, to her toes. She felt that she had become two people. One looked upon these fleshly contortions with astonishment. The other sought submission to an enormous pain spreading in her chest. The tears flowed freely from her eyes now, and the Astonished One within her demanded querulously: 'Who cries? Who is it that cries? Who is crying now?'

But nothing stopped the tears, and she felt the painfulness which flamed through her breast as it moved her flesh and hurled her onto the bed.

Still someone demanded out of that profound astonishment: 'Who cries? Who is that ...'

> By these acts Leto II removed himself from the evolutionary succession. He did it with a deliberate cutting action, saying: 'To be independent is to be removed.' Both twins saw beyond the needs of memory as a measuring process, that is, a way of determining their distance from their human origins. But it was left to Leto II to do the audacious thing, recognizing that a real creation is independent of its creator. He refused to reenact the evolutionary sequence, saying, 'That, too, takes me farther and farther from humanity.' He saw the implications in this: that there can be no truly closed systems in life.
>
> — The Holy Metamorphosis
> by Harq al-Ada

There were birds thriving on the insect life which teemed in the damp sand beyond the broken qanat: parrots, magpies, jays. This had been a djedida, the last of the new towns, built on a foundation of exposed basalt. It was abandoned now. Ghanima, using the morning hours to study the area beyond the original plantings of the abandoned sietch, detected movement and saw a banded gecko lizard. There'd been a gila woodpecker earlier, nesting in a mud wall of the djedida.

She thought of it as a sietch, but it was really a collection of low walls made of stabilized mud brick surrounded by plantings to hold back the dunes. It lay within the Tanzerouft, six hundred kilometers south of Sihaya Ridge. Without human hands to maintain it, the sietch already was beginning to melt back into the desert, its walls eroded by sandblast winds, its plants dying, its plantation area cracked by the burning sun.

Yet the sand beyond the shattered qanat remained damp, attesting to the fact that the squat bulk of the windtrap still functioned.

In the months since their flight from Tabr the fugitives had sampled the protection of several such places made uninhabitable by the Desert Demon. Ghanima didn't believe in the Desert Demon, although there was no denying the visible evidence of the qanat's destruction.

Occasionally they had word from the northern settlements through encounters with rebel spice-hunters. A few 'thopters – some said no more than six – carried out search flights seeking Stilgar, but Arrakis was large and its desert was friendly to the fugitives. Reportedly there was a search-and-destroy force charged with finding Stilgar's band, but the force which was led by the former Tabrite Buer Agarves had other duties and often returned to Arrakeen.

The rebels said there was little fighting between their men and the troops of Alia. Random depredations of the Desert Demon made Home Guard duty the first concern of Alia and the Naibs. Even the smugglers had been hit, but they were said to be scouring the desert for Stilgar, wanting the price on his head.

Stilgar had brought his band into the djedida just before dark the previous day, following the unerring moisture sense of his old Fremen nose. He'd promised they would head south for the palmyries soon, but refused to put a date on the move. Although he carried a price on his head which once would have bought a planet, Stilgar seemed the happiest and most carefree of men.

'This is a good place for us,' he'd said, pointing out that the windtrap still functioned. 'Our friends have left us some water.'

They were a small band now, sixty people in all. The old, the sick, and the very young had been filtered south into the palmyries, absorbed there by trusted families. Only the toughest remained, and they had many friends to the north and the south.

Ghanima wondered why Stilgar refused to discuss what was happening to the planet. Couldn't he see it? As qanats were shattered, Fremen pulled back to the northern and southern lines which once had marked the extent of their holdings. This movement could only signal what must be happening to the Empire. One condition was the mirror of the other.

Ghanima ran a hand under the collar of her stillsuit and resealed it. Despite her worries she felt remarkably free here. The inner lives no longer plagued her, although she sometimes felt their memories inserted into her consciousness. She knew from those memories what this desert had been once, before the work of the ecological transformation. It had been drier, for one thing. That unrepaired windtrap still functioned because it processed moist air.

Many creatures which once had shunned this desert ventured to live here now. Many in the band remarked how the daylight owls proliferated. Even now, Ghanima could see antbirds. They jigged and danced along the insect lines which swarmed in the damp sand at the end of the shattered qanat. Few badgers were to be seen out here, but there were kangaroo mice in uncounted numbers.

Superstitious fear ruled the new Fremen, and Stilgar was no better than the rest. This djedida had been given back to the desert after its qanat had been shattered a fifth time in eleven months. Four times they'd repaired the ravages of the Desert Demon, then they'd no longer had the surplus water to risk another loss.

It was the same all through the djedidas and in many of the old sietches. Eight out of nine new settlements had been abandoned. Many of the old sietch communities were more crowded than they had ever been before. And while the desert entered this new phase, Fremen reverted to their old ways. They saw omens in everything. Were worms increasingly scarce except in the Tanzerouft? It was the judgment of Shai-Hulud! And dead worms had been seen with nothing to say why they died. They went back to desert dust swiftly after death, but those crumbling hulks which Fremen chanced upon filled the observers with terror.

Stilgar's band had encountered such a hulk the previous month and it had taken four days for them to shake off the feeling of evil. The thing had reeked of sour and poisonous putrefaction.

341

Its moldering hulk had been found sitting on top of a giant spiceblow, the spice mostly ruined.

Ghanima turned from observing the qanat and looked back at the djedida. Directly in front of her lay a broken wall which once had protected a *mushtamal*, a small garden annex. She'd explored the place with a firm dependence upon her own curiosity and had found a store of flat, unleavened spice-bread in a stone box.

Stilgar had destroyed it, saying: 'Fremen would never leave good food behind them.'

Ghanima had suspected he was mistaken, but it hadn't been worth the argument or the risk. Fremen were changing. Once they'd moved freely across the *bled*, drawn by natural needs: water, spice, trade. Animal activities had been their alarm clocks. But animals moved to strange new rhythms now while most Fremen huddled close in their old cave-warrens within the shadow of the northern Shield Wall. Spice-hunters in the Tanzerouft were rare, and only Stilgar's band moved in the old ways.

She trusted Stilgar and his fear of Alia. Irulan reinforced his arguments now, reverting to odd Bene Gesserit musings. But on faraway Salusa, Farad'n still lived. Someday there would have to be a reckoning.

Ghanima looked up at the gray-silver morning sky, questing in her mind. Where was help to be found? Where was there someone to listen when she revealed what she saw happening all around them? The Lady Jessica stayed on Salusa, if the reports were to be believed. And Alia was a creature on a pedestal, involved only in being colossal while she drifted farther and farther from reality. Gurney Halleck was nowhere to be found, although he was reported seen everywhere. The Preacher had gone into hiding, his heretical rantings only a fading memory.

And Stilgar.

She looked across the broken wall to where Stilgar was helping repair the cistern. Stilgar reveled in his role as the will-o'-the-desert, the price upon his head growing monthly.

Nothing made sense anymore. Nothing.

Who was this Desert Demon, this creature able to destroy qanats as though they were false idols to be toppled into the sand? Was it a rogue worm? Was it a third force in rebellion – many people? No one believed it was a worm. The water would kill any worm venturing against a qanat. Many Fremen believed the Desert Demon was actually a revolutionary band bent on overthrowing Alia's Mahdinate and restoring Arrakis to its old ways. Those who believed this said it would be a good thing. Get rid of that greedy apostolic succession which did little else than uphold its own mediocrity. Get back to the true religion which Muad'Dib had espoused.

A deep sigh shook Ghanima. *Oh, Leto,* she thought, *I'm almost glad you didn't live to see these days. I'd join you myself, but I've a knife yet unblooded. Alia and Farad'n. Farad'n and Alia. The Old Baron's her demon, and that can't be permitted.*

Harah came out of the djedida, approaching Ghanima with a steady sand-swallowing pace. Harah stopped in front of Ghanima, demanded, 'What do you alone out here?'

'This is a strange place, Harah. We should leave.'

'Stilgar waits to meet someone here.'

'Oh? He didn't tell me that.'

'Why should he tell you everything? *Maku?*' Harah slapped the water pouch which bulged the front of Ghanima's robe. 'Are you a grown woman to be pregnant?'

'I've been pregnant so many times there's no counting them,' Ghanima said. 'Don't play those adult-child games with me!'

Harah took a backward step at the venom in Ghanima's voice.

'You're a band of stupids,' Ghanima said, waving her hand to encompass the djedida and the activities of Stilgar and his people. 'I should never have come with you.'

'You'd be dead by now if you hadn't.'

'Perhaps. But you don't see what's right in front of your faces! Who is it that Stilgar waits to meet here?'

'Buer Agarves.'

Ghanima stared at her.

'He is being brought here secretly by friends from Red Chasm Sietch,' Harah explained.

'Alia's little plaything?'

'He is being brought here under blindfold.'

'Does Stilgar believe that?'

'Buer asked for the parley. He agreed to all of our terms.'

'Why wasn't I told about this?'

'Stilgar knew you would argue against it.'

'Argue against . . . This is madness!'

Harah scowled. 'Don't forget that Buer is . . .'

'He's *Family!*' Ghanima snapped. 'He's the grandson of Stilgar's cousin. I know. And the Farad'n whose blood I'll draw one day is as close a relative to me. Do you think that'll stay my knife?'

343

'We've had a distrans. No one follows his party.'

Ghanima spoke in a low voice: 'Nothing good will come of this, Harah. We should leave at once.'

'Have you read an omen?' Harah asked. 'That dead worm we saw! Was that –'

'Stuff that into your womb and give birth to it elsewhere!' Ghanima raged. 'I don't like this meeting nor his place. Isn't that enough?'

'I'll tell Stilgar what you –'

'I'll tell him myself!' Ghanima strode past Harah, who made the sign of the worm horns at her back to ward off evil.

But Stilgar only laughed at Ghanima's fears and ordered her to look for sandtrout as though she were one of the children. She fled into one of the djedida's abandoned houses and crouched in a corner to nurse her anger. The emotion passed quickly, though; she felt the stirring of the inner lives and remembered someone saying: 'If we can immobilize them, things will go as we plan.'

*What an odd thought.*

But she couldn't recall who'd said those words.

> *Muad'Dib was disinherited and he spoke for the disinherited of all time. He cried out against that profound injustice which alienates the individual from that which he was taught to believe, from that which seemed to come to him as a right.*
>
> – The Mahdinate, An Analysis
> by Harq al-Ada

Gurney Halleck sat on the butte at Shuloch with his baliset beside him on a spice-fiber rug. Below him the enclosed basin swarmed with workers planting crops. The sand ramp up which the Cast Out had lured worms on a spice trail had been blocked off with a new qanat. Plantings moved down the slope to hold it.

It was almost time for the noon meal and Halleck had been on the butte for more than an hour, seeking privacy in which to think. Humans did the labor below him, but everything he saw was the work of melange. Leto's personal estimate was that spice production would fall soon to a stabilized one-tenth of its peak in the Harkonnen years. Stockpiles throughout the empire doubled in value at every new posting. Three hundred and twenty-one liters were said to have bought half of Novebruns Planet from the Metulli Family.

The Cast Out worked like men driven by a devil, and perhaps they were. Before every meal, they faced the Tanzerouft and prayed to Shai-Hulud personified. That was how they saw Leto and, through their eyes, Halleck saw a future where most of humankind shared that view. Halleck wasn't sure he liked the prospect.

Leto had set the pattern when he'd brought Halleck and The Preacher here in Halleck's stolen 'thopter. With his bare hands Leto had breached the Shuloch qanat, hurling large stones more than fifty meters. When the Cast Out had tried to intervene, Leto had decapitated the first to reach him, using no more than a blurred sweep of his arm. He'd hurled others back into their companions and had laughed at their weapons. In a demon-voice he'd roared at them: 'Fire will not touch me! Your knives will not harm me! I wear the skin of Shai-Hulud!'

The Cast Out had recognized him then and recalled his escape, leaping from the butte 'directly to the desert'. They'd prostrated themselves before him and Leto had issued his orders. 'I bring you two guests. You will guard them and honor them. You will rebuild your qanat and begin planting an oasis garden. One day I'll make my home here. You will prepare my home. You will sell no more spice, but you will store every bit you collect.'

On and on he'd gone with his instructions, and the Cast Out had heard every word, seeing him through fear-glazed eyes, through a terrifying awe.

Here was Shai-Hulud come up from the sand at last!

There'd been no intimation of this metamorphosis when Leto had found Halleck with Ghadhean al-Fali in one of the small rebel sietches at Gare Ruden. With his blind companion, Leto had come up from the desert along the old spice route, traveling by worm through an area where worms were now a rarity. He'd spoken of several detours forced upon him by the presence of moisture in the sand, enough water to poison a worm. They'd arrived shortly after noon and had been brought into the stone-walled common room by guards.

The memory haunted Halleck now.

'So this is The Preacher,' he'd said.

Striding around the blind man, studying him, Halleck recalled the stories about him. No stillsuit mask hid the old face in sietch, and the features were there for memory to make its comparisons. Yes, the man did look like the old Duke for whom Leto had been named. Was it a chance likeness?

'You know the stories about this one?' Halleck asked, speaking

345

in an aside to Leto. 'That he's your father come back from the desert?'

'I've heard the stories.'

Halleck turned to examine the boy. Leto wore an odd stillsuit with rolled edges around his face and ears. A black robe covered it and sandboots sheathed his feet. There was much to be explained about his presence here – how he'd managed to escape once more.

'Why do you bring The Preacher here?' Halleck asked. 'In Jacurutu they said he works for them.'

'No more. I bring him because Alia wants him dead.'

'So? You think this is a sanctuary?'

'You are his sanctuary.'

All this time The Preacher stood near them, listening but giving no sign that he cared which turn their discussion took.

'He has served me well, Gurney,' Leto said. 'House Atreides has not lost all sense of obligation to those who serve us.'

'House Atreides?'

'I am House Atreides.'

'You fled Jacurutu before I could complete the testing which your grandmother ordered,' Halleck said, his voice cold. 'How can you assume – '

'This man's life is to be guarded as though it were your own.' Leto spoke as though there were no argument and he met Halleck's stare without flinching.

Jessica had trained Halleck in many of the Bene Gesserit refinements of observation and he'd detected nothing in Leto which spoke of other than calm assurance. Jessica's orders remained, though. 'Your grandmother charged me to complete your education and be sure you're not possessed.'

'I'm not possessed.' Just a flat statement.

'Why did you run away?'

'Namri had orders to kill me-no matter what I did. His orders were from Alia.'

'Are you a Truthsayer, then?'

'I am.' Another flat statement filled with self-assurance.

'And Ghanima as well?'

'No.'

The Preacher broke his silence then, turning his blind sockets toward Halleck but pointing at Leto. 'You think *you* can test him?'

'Don't interfere when you know nothing of the problem or its consequences,' Halleck ordered, not looking at the man.

'Oh, I know its consequences well enough,' The Preacher said. 'I was tested once by an old woman who thought she knew what she was doing. She didn't know, as it turned out.'

Halleck looked at him then. 'You're another Truthsayer?'

'Anyone can be a Truthsayer, even you,' The Preacher said. 'It's a matter of self-honesty about the nature of your own feelings. It requires that you have an inner agreement with truth which allows ready recognition.'

'Why do you interfere?' Halleck asked, putting hand to crysknife. Who was this Preacher?

'I'm responsive to these events,' The Preacher said. 'My mother could put her own blood upon the altar, but I have other motives. And I do see your problem.'

'Oh?' Halleck was actually curious now.

'The Lady Jessica ordered you to differentiate between the wolf and the dog, between *ze'eb* and *ke'leb*. By her definition a wolf is someone with power who misuses that power. However, between wolf and dog there is a dawn period when you cannot distinguish between them.'

'That's close to the mark,' Halleck said, noting how more and more of the sietch had entered the common room to listen. 'How do you know this?'

'Because I know this planet. You don't understand? Think how it is. Beneath the surface there are rocks, dirt, sediment, sand. That's the planet's memory, the picture of its history. It's the same with humans. The dog remembers the wolf. Each universe revolves around a core of *being*, and outward from that core go all of the memories, right out to the surface.'

'Very interesting,' Halleck said. 'How does that help me carry out my orders?'

'Review the picture of your history which is within you. Communicate as animals would communicate.'

Halleck shook his head. There was a compelling directness about this Preacher, a quality which he'd recognized many times in the Atreides, and there was more than a little hint that the man was employing the powers of Voice. Halleck felt his heart begin to hammer. Was it possible?

'Jessica wanted an ultimate test, a stress by which the underlying fabric of her grandson exposed itself,' The Preacher said. 'But the fabric's always there, open to your gaze.'

Halleck turned to stare at Leto. The movement came of itself, compelled by irresistible forces.

The Preacher continued as though lecturing an obstinate

pupil. 'This young person confuses you because he's not a singular being. He's a community. As with any community under stress, any member of that community may assume command. This command isn't always benign, and we get our stories of Abomination. But you've already wounded this community enough, Gurney Halleck. Can't you see that the transformation already has taken place? This youth has achieved an inner co-operation which is enormously powerful, that cannot be subverted. Without eyes I see this. Once I opposed him, but now I do his bidding. He is the Healer.'

'Who are you?' Halleck demanded.

'I'm no more than what you see. Don't look at me, look at this person you were ordered to teach and test. He has been formed by crisis. He survived a lethal environment. He is here.'

'Who are you?' Halleck insisted.

'I tell you only to look at this Atreides youth! He is the ultimate feedback upon which our species depends. He'll reinsert into the system the results of its past performance. No other human could know that past performance as he knows it. And you consider destroying such a one!'

'I was ordered to test him and I've not – '

'But you have!'

'Is he Abomination?'

A weary laugh shook The Preacher. 'You persist in Bene Gesserit nonsense. How they create the myths by which men sleep!'

'Are you Paul Atreides?' Halleck asked.

'Paul Atreides is no more. He tried to stand as a supreme moral symbol while he renounced all moral pretensions. He became a saint without a god, every word a blasphemy. How can you think – '

'Because you speak with his voice.'

'Would you test me, now? Beware, Gurney Halleck.'

Halleck swallowed, forced his attention back to the impassive Leto who still stood calmly observant. 'Who's being tested?' The Preacher asked. 'Is it, perhaps, that the Lady Jessica tests you, Gurney Halleck?'

Halleck found this thought deeply disturbing, wondering why he let this Preacher's words move him. But it was a deep thing in Atreides servants to obey that autocratic mystique. Jessica, explaining this, had made it even more mysterious. Halleck now felt something changing within himself, a *something* whose edges had only been touched by the Bene Gesserit training

348

Jessica had pressed upon him. Inarticulate fury arose in him. He did not want to change!

'Which of you plays God and to what end?' The Preacher asked. 'You cannot rely on reason alone to answer that question.'

Slowly, deliberately, Halleck raised his attention from Leto to the blind man. Jessica kept saying he should achieve the balance of *kairits* – 'thou shalt-thou shalt not.' She called it a discipline without words and phrases, no rules or arguments. It was the sharpened edge of his own internal truth, all-engrossing. Something in the blind man's voice, his tone, his manner, ignited a fury which burned itself into blinding calmness within Halleck.

'Answer my question,' The Preacher said.

Halleck felt the words deepen his concentration upon this place, this one moment and its demands. His position in the universe was defined only by his concentration. No doubt remained in him. This was Paul Atreides, not dead, but returned. And this non-child, Leto. Halleck looked once more at Leto, really saw him. He saw the signs of stress around the eyes, the sense of balance in the stance, the passive mouth with its quirking sense of humor. Leto stood out from his background as though at the focus of a blinding light. He had achieved harmony simply by accepting it.

'Tell me, Paul,' Halleck said. 'Does your mother know?'

The Preacher sighed. 'To the Sisterhood, all of it, I am dead. Do not try to revive me.'

Still not looking at him, Halleck asked: 'But why does she – '

'She does what she must. She makes her own life, thinking she rules many lives. Thus we all play god.'

'But you're alive,' Halleck whispered, overcome now by his realization, turning at last to stare at this man, younger than himself, but so aged by the desert that he appeared to carry twice Halleck's years.

'What is that?' Paul demanded. 'Alive?'

Halleck peered around at the watching Fremen, their faces caught between doubt and awe.

'My mother never had to learn my lesson.' It was Paul's voice! 'To be a god can ultimately become boring and degrading. There'd be reason enough for the invention of free will! A god might wish to escape into sleep and be alive only in the unconscious projections of his dream-creatures.'

'But you're alive!' Halleck spoke louder now.

Paul ignored the excitement in his old companion's voice, asked: 'Would you really have pitted this lad against his sister in the test-Mashhad? What deadly nonsense! Each would have said: "No! Kill me! Let the other live!" Where would such a test lead? What is it then to be alive, Gurney?'

'That was not the test,' Halleck protested. He did not like the way the Fremen pressed closer around them, studying Paul, ignoring Leto.

But Leto intruded now. 'Look at the fabric, father.'

'Yes . . . yes . . . ' Paul held his head high as though sniffing the air. 'It's Farad'n, then!'

'How easy it is to follow our thoughts instead of our senses,' Leto said.

Halleck had been unable to follow this thought and, about to ask, was interrupted by Leto's hand upon his arm. 'Don't ask, Gurney. You might return to suspecting that I'm Abomination. No! Let it happen, Gurney. If you try to force it, you'll only destroy yourself.'

But Halleck felt himself overcome by doubts. Jessica had warned him. *'They can be very beguiling, these pre-born. They have tricks you've never even dreamed.'* Halleck shook his head slowly. And Paul! God's below! Paul alive and in league with this question mark he'd fathered!

The Fremen around them could no longer be held back. They pressed between Halleck and Paul, between Leto and Paul, shoving the two to the background. The air was showered with hoarse questions. 'Are you Muad'Dib? Are you truly Muad'Dib? Is it true what he says? Tell us!'

'You must think of me only as The Preacher,' Paul said, pushing against them. 'I cannot be Paul Atreides or Muad'Dib, never again. I'm not Chani's mate or Emperor.'

Halleck, fearing what might happen if these frustrated questions found no logical answer, was about to act when Leto moved ahead of him. It was there Halleck first saw an element of the terrible change which had been wrought in Leto. A bull voice roared, 'Stand aside!' – and Leto moved forward, thrusting adult Fremen right and left, knocking them down, clubbing them with his hands, wrenching knives from their hands by grasping the blades.

In less than a minute those Fremen still standing were pressed back against the walls in silent consternation. Leto stood beside his father. 'When Shai-Hulud speaks, you obey,' Leto said.

And when a few of the Fremen had started to argue, Leto had torn a corner of rock from the passage wall beside the room's exit and crumbled it in his bare hands, smiling all the while.

'I will tear your sietch down around your faces,' he said.

'The Desert Demon,' someone whispered.

'And your qanats,' Leto agreed. 'I will rip them apart. We have not been here, do you hear me?'

Heads shook from side to side in terrified submission.

'No one here has seen us,' Leto said. 'One whisper from you and I will return to drive you into the desert without water.'

Halleck saw hands being raised in the warding gesture, the sign of the worm.

'We will go now, my father and I, accompanied by our old friend,' Leto said. 'Make our 'thopter ready.'

And Leto had guided them to Shuloch then, explaining enroute that they must move swiftly because 'Farad'n will be here on Arrakis very soon. And, as my father has said, then you'll see the real test, Gurney.'

Looking down from the Shuloch butte, Halleck asked himself once more, as he asked every day: 'What test? What does he mean?'

But Leto was no longer in Shuloch, and Paul refused to answer.

> *Church and State, scientific reason and faith, the individual and his community, even progress and tradition – all of these can be reconciled in the teachings of Muad'Dib. He taught us that there exist no intransigent opposites except in the beliefs of men. Anyone can rip aside the veil of Time. You can discover the future in the past or in your own imagination. Doing this, you win back your consciousness in your inner being. You know then that the universe is a coherent whole and you are indivisible from it.*
>
> > – The Preacher at Arrakeen
> > After Harq al-Ada

Ghanima sat far back outside the circle of light from the spice lamps and watched this Buer Agarves. She didn't like his round face and agitated eyebrows, his way of moving his feet when he spoke, as though his words were a hidden music to which he danced.

*He's not here to parley with Stil,* Ghanima told herself, seeing this confirmed in every word and movement from this man. She moved farther back away from the Council circle.

Every sietch had a room such as this one, but the meeting hall of the abandoned djedida struck Ghanima as a cramped place because it was so low. Sixty people from Stilgar's band plus the nine who'd come with Agarves filled only one end of the hall. Spice-oil lamps reflected against low beams which supported the ceiling. The light cast wavering shadows which danced on the walls, and the pungent smoke filled the place with the smell of cinnamon.

The meeting had started at dusk after the moisture prayers and evening meal. It had been going on for more than an hour now, and Ghanima couldn't fathom the hidden currents in Agarves' performance. His words appeared clear enough, but his motions and eye movements didn't agree.

Agarves was speaking now, responding to a question from one of Stilgar's lieutenants, a niece of Harah's named Rajia. She was a darkly ascetic young woman whose mouth turned down at the corners, giving her an air of perpetual distrust. Ghanima found the expression satisfying in the circumstances.

'Certainly I believe Alia will grant a full and complete pardon to all of you,' Agarves said. 'I'd not be here with this message otherwise.'

Stilgar intervened as Rajia made to speak once more. 'I'm not so much worried about our trusting her as I am about whether she trusts you.' Stilgar's voice carried growling undertones. He was uncomfortable with this suggestion that he return to his old status.

'It doesn't matter whether she trusts me,' Agarves said. 'To be candid about it, I don't believe she does. I've been too long searching for you without finding you. But I've always felt she didn't really want you captured. She was —'

'She was the wife of the man I slew,' Stilgar said. 'I grant you that he asked for it. Might as well've fallen on his own knife. But this new attitude smells of —'

Agarves danced to his feet, anger plain on his face. 'She forgives you! How many times must I say it? She had the Priests make a great show of asking divine guidance from —'

'You've only raised another issue.' It was Irulan, leaning forward past Rajia, blonde head set off against Rajia's darkness. 'She has convinced you, but she may have other plans.'

'The Priesthood has —'

'But there are all these stories,' Irulan said. 'That you're more than just a military advisor, that you're her —'

'Enough!' Agarves was beside himself with rage. His hand hovered near his knife. Warring emotions moved just below the surface of his skin, twisting his features. 'Believe what you will, but I cannot go on with that woman! She fouls me! She dirties everything she touches! I am used. I am soiled. But I have not lifted my knife against my skin. Now – no more!'

Ghanima, observing this, thought: *That, 'at least, was truth coming from him.*

Surprisingly Stilgar broke into laughter. 'Ahhhh, cousin,' he said. 'Forgive me, but there's truth in anger.'

'Then you agree?'

'I've not said that.' He raised a hand as Agarves threatened another outburst. 'It's not for my sake, Buer, but there are these others.' He gestured around him. 'They are my responsibility. Let us consider for a moment what reparations Alia offers.'

'Reparations? There's no word of reparations. Pardon, but no –'

'Then what does she offer as surety of her word?'

'Sietch Tabr and you as Naib, full autonomy as a neutral. She understands now how –'

'I'll not go back to her entourage or provide her with fighting men,' Stilgar warned. 'Is that understood?'

Ghanima could hear Stilgar beginning to weaken and thought: *No, Stil! No!*

'No need for that,' Agarves said. 'Alia wants only Ghanima returned to her and the carrying out of the betrothal promise which she –'

'So now it comes out!' Stilgar said, his brows drawing down. 'Ghanima's the price of my pardon. Does she think me –'

'She thinks you sensible,' Agarves argued, resuming his seat.

Gleefully, Ghanima thought: *He won't do it. Save your breath. He won't do it.*

As she thought this, Ghanima heard a soft rustling behind and to her left. She started to turn, felt powerful hands grab her. A heavy rag reeking of sleep-drugs covered her face before she could cry out. As consciousness faded, she felt herself being carried toward a door in the hall's darkest reaches. And she thought: *I should have guessed! I should've been prepared!* But the hands that held her were adult and strong. She could not squirm away from them.

Ghanima's last sensory impressions were of cold night air, a glimpse of stars, and a hooded face which looked down at her, then asked: 'She wasn't injured, was she?'

The answer was lost as the stars wheeled and streaked across her gaze, losing themselves in a blaze of light which was the inner core of her selfdom.

*Muad'Dib gave us a particular kind of knowledge about prophetic insight, about the behavior which surrounds such insight and its influence upon events which are seen to be 'on line'. (That is, events which are set to occur in a related system which the prophet reveals and interprets.) As has been noted elsewhere, such insight operates as a peculiar trap for the prophet himself. He can become the victim of what he knows – which is a relatively common human failing. The danger is that those who predict real events may overlook the polarizing effect brought about by over-dulgence in their own truth. They tend to forget that nothing in a polarized universe can exist without its opposite being present.*

– The Prescient Vision
by Harq al-Ada

Blowing sand hung like fog on the horizon, obscuring the rising sun. The sand was cold in the dune shadows. Leto stood outside the ring of the palmyrie looking into the desert. He smelled dust and the aroma of spiny plants, heard the morning sounds of people and animals. The Fremen maintained no qanat in this place. They had only a bare minimum of hand planting irrigated by the women, who carried water in skin bags. Their windtrap was a fragile thing, easily destroyed by the stormwinds but easily rebuilt. Hardship, the rigors of the spice trade, and adventure were a way of life here. These Fremen still believed heaven was the sound of running water, but they cherished an ancient concept of Freedom which Leto shared.

*Freedom is a lonely state*, he thought.

Leto adjusted the folds of the white robe which covered his living stillsuit. He could feel how the sandtrout membrane had changed him and, as always with this feeling, he was forced to overcome a deep sense of loss. He no longer was completely human. Odd things swam in his blood. Sandtrout cilia had penetrated every organ, adjusting, changing. The sandtrout itself was changing, adapting. But Leto, knowing this, felt himself torn by the old threads of his lost humanity, his life caught in primal anguish with its ancient continuity shattered. He knew the trap in indulging in such emotion, though. He knew it well.

*Let the future happen of itself*, he thought. *The only rule governing creativity is the act of creation itself.*

It was difficult to take his gaze away from the sands, the dunes – the great emptiness. Here at the edge of the sand lay a few rocks, but they led the imagination outward into the winds,

354

the dust, the sparse and lonely plants and animals, dune emerging into dune, desert into desert.

Behind him came the sound of a flute playing for the morning prayer, the chant for moisture which now was a subtly altered serenade to the new Shai-Hulud. This knowledge in Leto's mind gave the music a sense of eternal loneliness.

*I could just walk away into that desert,* he thought.

Everything would change then. One direction would be as good as another. He had already learned to live a life free of possessions. He had refined the Fremen mystique to a terrible edge: everything he took with him was necessary, and that was all he took. But he carried nothing except the robe on his back, the Atreides hawk ring hidden in its folds, and the skin-which-was-not-his-own.

It would be easy to walk away from here.

Movement high in the sky caught his attention: the splayed-gap wingtips identified a vulture. The sight filled his chest with aching. Like the wild Fremen, vultures lived in this land because this was where they were born. They knew nothing better. The desert made them what they were.

Another Fremen breed was coming up in the wake of Muad-'Dib and Alia, though. They were the reason he could not let himself walk away into the desert as his father had done. Leto recalled Idaho's words from the early days: 'These Fremen! They're magnificently alive. I've never met a greedy Fremen.'

There were plenty of greedy Fremen now.

A wave of sadness passed over Leto. He was committed to a course which could change all of that, but at a terrible price. And the management of that course became increasingly difficult as they neared the vortex.

Kralizec, the Typhoon Struggle, lay ahead . . . but Kralizec or worse would be the price of a misstep.

Voices sounded behind Leto, then the clear piping sound of a child speaking: 'Here he is.'

Leto turned.

The Preacher had come out of the palmyrie, led by a child.

*Why do I still think of him as The Preacher?* Leto wondered.

The answer lay there on the clean tablet of Leto's mind: *Because this is no longer Muad'Dib, no longer Paul Atreides.* The desert had made him what he was. The desert and the jackals of Jacurutu with their overdoses of melange and their constant betrayals. The Preacher was old before his time, old not despite the spice but because of it.

'They said you wanted to see me now,' The Preacher said, speaking as his child guide stopped.

Leto looked at the child of the palmyrie, a person almost as tall as himself, with awe tempered by an avaricious curiosity. The young eyes glinted darkly above the child-sized stillsuit mask.

Leto waved a hand. 'Leave us.'

For a moment there was rebellion in the child's shoulders, then the awe and native Fremen respect for privacy took over. The child left them.

'You know Farad'n is here on Arrakis?' Leto asked.

'Gurney told me when he flew me down last night.'

And The Preacher thought: *How coldly measured his words are. He's like I was in the old days.*

'I face a difficult choice,' Leto said.

'I thought you'd already made all the choices.'

'We know *that* trap, father.'

The Preacher cleared his throat. The tensions told him how near they were to the shattering crisis. Now Leto would not be relying on pure vision, but on vision management.

'You need my help?' The Preacher asked.

'Yes. I'm returning to Arrakeen and I wish to go as your guide.'

'To what end?'

'Would you preach once more in Arrakeen?'

'Perhaps. There are things I've not said to them.'

'You will not come back to the desert, father.'

'If I go with you?'

'Yes.'

'I'll do whatever you decide.'

'Have you considered? With Farad'n there, your mother will be with him.'

'Undoubtedly.'

Once more, The Preacher cleared his throat. It was a betrayal of nervousness which Muad'Dib would never have permitted. This flesh had been too long away from the old regimen of self-discipline, his mind too often betrayed into madness by the Jacurutu. And The Preacher thought that perhaps it wouldn't be wise to return to Arrakeen.

'You don't have to go back there with me,' Leto said. 'But my sister is there and I must return. You could go with Gurney.'

'And you'd go to Arrakeen alone?'

'Yes. I must meet Farad'n.'

'I will go with you,' The Preacher sighed.

And Leto sensed a touch of the old vision madness in The Preacher's manner, wondered: *Has he been playing the prescience game?* No. He'd never go that way again. He knew the trap of a partial commitment. The Preacher's every word confirmed that he had handed over the visions to his son, knowing that everything in this universe had been anticipated.

It was the old polarities which taunted The Preacher now. He had fled from paradox into paradox.

'We'll be leaving in a few minutes, then,' Leto said. 'Will you tell Gurney?'

'Gurney's not going with us?'

'I want Gurney to survive.'

The Preacher opened himself to the tensions then. They were in the air around him, in the ground under his feet, a motile thing which focused onto the non-child who was his son. The blunt scream of his old visions waited in The Preacher's throat.

*This cursed holiness!*

The sandy juice of his fears could not be avoided. He knew what faced them in Arrakeen. They would play a game once more with terrifying and deadly forces which could never bring them peace.

> *The child who refuses to travel in the father's harness, this is the symbol of man's most unique capability. 'I do not have to be what my father was. I do not have to obey my father's rules or even believe everything he believed. It is my strength as a human that I can make my own choices of what to believe and what not to believe, of what to be and what not to be.'*
>
> – Leto Atreides II
> The Harq al-Ada Biography

Pilgrim women were dancing to drum and flute in the Temple plaza, no coverings on their heads, bangles at their necks, their dresses thin and revealing. Their long black hair was thrown straight out, then straggled across their faces as they whirled.

Alia looked down at the scene from her Temple aerie, both attracted and repelled. It was mid-morning, the hour when the aroma of spice-coffee began to waft across the plaza from the vendors beneath the shaded arches. Soon she would have to go out and greet Farad'n, present the formal gifts and supervise his first meeting with Ghanima.

It was all working out according to plan. Ghani would kill

him and, in the shattering aftermath, only one person would be prepared to pick up the pieces. The puppets danced when the strings were pulled. Stilgar had killed Agarves just as she'd hoped. And Agarves had led the kidnappers to the djedida without knowing it, a secret signal transmitter hidden in the new boots she'd given him. Now Stilgar and Irulan waited in the Temple dungeons. Perhaps they would die, but there might be other uses for them. There was no harm in waiting.

She noted that town Fremen were watching the pilgrim dancers below her, their eyes intense and unwavering. A basic sexual equality had come out of the desert to persist in Fremen town and city, but social differences between male and female already were making themselves felt. That, too, went according to plan. Divide and weaken. Alia could sense the subtle change in the way the two Fremen watched those off-planet women and their exotic dance.

*Let them watch. Let them fill their minds with ghafla.*

The louvers of Alia's window had been opened and she could feel a sharp increase in the heat which began about sunrise in this season and would peak in mid-afternoon. The temperature on the stone floor of the plaza would be much higher. It would be uncomfortable for those dancers, but still they whirled and bent, swung their arms and their hair in the frenzy of their dedication. They had dedicated their dance to Alia, the Womb of Heaven. An aide had come to whisper this to Alia, sneering at the off-world women and their peculiar ways. The aide had explained that the women were from Ix, where remnants of the forbidden science and technology remained.

Alia sniffed. Those women were as ignorant, as superstitious and backward as the desert Fremen . . . just as that sneering aide had said, trying to curry favor by reporting the dedication of the dance. And neither the aide nor the Ixians even knew that Ix was merely a number in a forgotten language.

Laughing lightly to herself, Alia thought: *Let them dance.* The dancing wasted energy which might be put to more destructive uses. And the music was pleasant, a thin wailing played against flat tympani from gourd drums and clapped hands.

Abruptly the music was drowned beneath a roaring of many voices from the plaza's far side. The dancers missed a step, recovered in a brief confusion, but they had lost their sensuous singleness, and even their attention wandered to the far gate of the plaza, where a mob could be seen spreading onto the stones like water rushing through the opened valve of a qanat.

Alia stared at that oncoming wave.

She heard words now, and one above all others: 'Preacher! Preacher!'

Then she saw him, striding with his first spread of the wave, one hand on the shoulder of his young guide.

The pilgrim dancers gave up their whirling, retired to the terraced steps below Alia. They were joined by their audience, and Alia sensed awe in the watchers. Her own emotion was fear.

*How dare he!*

She half turned to summon guards, but second thoughts stopped her. The mob already filled the plaza. They could turn ugly if thwarted in their obvious desire to hear the blind visionary.

Alia clenched her fists.

*The Preacher!* Why was Paul doing this? To half the population he was a 'desert madman' and, therefore, sacred. Others whispered in the bazaars and shops that it must be Muad'Dib. Why else did the Mahdinate let him speak such angry heresy?

Alia could see refugees among the mob, remnants from the abandoned sietches, their robes in tatters. That would be a dangerous place down there, a place where mistakes could be made.

'Mistress?'

The voice came from behind Alia. She turned, saw Zia standing in the arched doorway to the outer chamber. Armed House Guards were close behind her.

'Yes, Zia?'

'My Lady, Farad'n is out here requesting audience.'

'Here? In my chambers?'

'Yes, My Lady.'

'Is he alone?'

'Two bodyguards and the Lady Jessica.'

Alia put a hand to her throat, remembering her last encounter with her mother. Times had changed, though. New conditions ruled their relationship.

'How impetuous he is,' Alia said. 'What reason does he give?'

'He has heard about . . .' Zia pointed to the window over the plaza. 'He says he was told you have the best vantage.'

Alia frowned. 'Do you believe this, Zia?'

'No, My Lady. I think he has heard the rumors. He wants to watch your reaction.'

'My mother put him up to this!'

'Quite possibly, My Lady.'

'Zia, my dear, I want you to carry out a specific set of very important orders for me. Come here.'

Zia approached to within a pace. 'My Lady?'

'Have Farad'n, his guards, *and* my mother admitted. Then prepare to bring Ghanima. She is to be accoutered as a Fremen bride in every detail – *complete*.'

'With knife, My Lady?'

'With knife.'

'My Lady, that's – '

'Ghanima poses no threat to me.'

'My Lady, there's reason to believe she fled with Stilgar more to protect him than for any other – '

'Zia!'

'My Lady?'

'Ghanima already has made her plea for Stilgar's life and Stilgar remains alive.'

'But she's the heir presumptive!'

'Just carry out my orders. Have Ghanima prepared. While you're seeing to that, send five attendants from the Temple Priesthood out into the plaza. They're to invite The Preacher up here. Have them wait their opportunity and speak to him, nothing more. They are to use no force. I want them to issue a polite invitation. Absolutely no force. And Zia . . .'

'My Lady?' How sullen she sounded.

'The Preacher and Ghanima are to be brought before me simultaneously. They are to enter together upon my signal. Do you understand?'

'I know the plan, My Lady, but – '

'Just do it! Together.' And Alia nodded dismissal to the amazon aide. As Zia turned and left, Alia said: 'On your way out, send in Farad'n's party, but see that they're preceded by ten of your most trustworthy people.'

Zia glanced back but continued leaving the room. 'It will be done as you command, My Lady.'

Alia turned away to peer out the window. In just a few minutes the *plan* would bear its bloody fruit. And Paul would be here when his daughter delivered the *coup de grace* to his holy pretensions. Alia heard Zia's guard detachment entering. It would be over soon. All over. She looked down with a swelling sense of triumph as The Preacher took his stance on the first step. His youthful guide squatted beside him. Alia saw the yellow robes of Temple Priests waiting on the left, held back by the press of the crowd. They were experienced with crowds, however. They'd find a way to approach their target. The Preacher's voice boomed out over the plaza, and the mob waited upon his words with rapt attention. Let them listen! Soon his words would be made to mean other things than he intended. And there'd be no *Preacher* around to protest.

She heard Farad'n's party enter, Jessica's voice. 'Alia?'

Without turning Alia said: 'Welcome, Prince Farad'n, mother. Come and enjoy the show.' She glanced back then, saw the big Sardaukar, Tyekanik, scowling at her guards who were blocking the way. 'But this isn't hospitable,' Alia said. 'Let them approach.' Two of her guards, obviously acting on Zia's orders, came up to her and stood between her and the others. The other guards moved aside. Alia backed to the right side of the window, motioned to it. 'This is truly the best vantage point.'

Jessica, wearing her traditional black aba robe, glared at Alia, escorted Farad'n to the window, but stood between him and Alia's guards.

'This is very kind of you, Lady Alia,' Farad'n said. 'I've heard so much about this Preacher.'

'And there he is in the flesh,' Alia said. She saw that Farad'n wore the dress gray of a Sardaukar commander without decorations. He moved with a lean grace which Alia admired. Perhaps there would be more than idle amusement in this Corrino Prince.

The Preacher's voice boomed into the room over the amplifier pickups beside the window. Alia felt the tremors of it in her bones, began to listen to his words with growing fascination.

'I found myself in the Desert of Zan,' The Preacher shouted, 'in that waste of howling wilderness. And God commanded me to make that place clean. For we were provoked in the desert, and grieved in the desert, and we were tempted in that wilderness to forsake our ways.'

*Desert of Zan*, Alia thought. That was the name given to the place of the first trial of the Zensunni Wanderers from whom the Fremen sprang. But his words! Was he taking credit for the destruction wrought against the sietch strongholds of the loyal tribes?

'Wild beasts lie upon your lands,' The Preacher said, his voice booming across the plaza. 'Doleful creatures fill your houses. You who fled your homes no longer multiply your days upon the sand. Yea, you who have forsaken our ways, you will die in a fouled nest if you continue on this path. But if you heed my warning, the Lord shall lead you through a land of pits into the Mountains of God. Yea, Shai-Hulud shall lead you.'

Soft moans arose from the crowd. The Preacher paused, swinging his eyeless sockets from side to side at the sound. Then he raised his arms, spreading them wide, called out: 'O God, my flesh longeth for Thy way in a dry and thirsty land!'

An old woman in front of The Preacher, an obvious refugee by the patched and worn look of her garments, held up her hands to him, pleaded: 'Help us, Muad'Dib. Help us!'

In a sudden fearful constriction of her breast, Alia asked herself if that old woman really knew the truth. Alia glanced at her mother, but Jessica remained unmoving, dividing her attention between Alia's guards, Farad'n and the view from the window. Farad'n stood rooted in fascinated attention.

Alia glanced out the window, trying to see her Temple Priests. They were not in view and she suspected they had worked their way around below her near the Temple doors, seeking a direct route down the steps.

The Preacher pointed his right hand over the old woman's head, shouted: 'You are the only help remaining! You were rebellious. You brought the dry wind which does not cleanse, nor does it cool. You bear the burden of our desert, and the whirlwind cometh from that place, from that terrible land. I have been in that wilderness. Water runs upon the sand from shattered qanats. Streams cross the ground. Water has fallen from the sky in the Belt of Dune! O my friends, God has commanded me. Make straight in the desert a highway for our Lord, for I am the voice that cometh to thee from the wilderness.'

He pointed to the steps beneath his feet, a stiff and quivering finger. 'This is no lost djedida which is no more inhabited forever! Here have we eaten the bread of heaven. And here the noise of strangers drives us from our homes! Thy breed for us a desolātion, a land wherein no man dwelleth, nor any man pass thereby.'

The crowd stirred uncomfortably, refugees and town Fremen peering about, looking at the pilgrims of the Hajj who stood among them.

*He could start a bloody riot!* Alia thought. *Well, let him. My Priests can grab him in the confusion.*

She saw the five Priests then, a tight knot of yellow robes working down the steps behind The Preacher.

'The waters which we spread upon the desert have become blood,' The Preacher said, waving his arms wide. 'Blood upon our land! Behold our desert which could rejoice and blossom; it has lured the stranger and seduced him in our midst. They come

362

for violence! Their faces are closed up as for the last wind of Kralizec! They gather the captivity of the sand. They suck up the abundance of the sand, the treasure hidden in the depths. Behold them as they go forth to their evil work. It is written: "And I stood upon the sand, and I saw a beast rise up out of that sand, and upon the head of that beast was the name of God!"'

Angry mutterings arose from the crowd. Fists were raised, shaken.

'What is he doing?' Farad'n whispered.

'I wish I knew,' Alia said. She put a hand to her breast, feeling the fearful excitement of this moment. The crowd would turn upon the pilgrims if he kept this up!

But The Preacher half turned, aimed his dead sockets toward the Temple and raised a hand to point at the high windows of Alia's aerie. 'One blasphemy remains!' he screamed. 'Blasphemy! And the name of that blasphemy is Alia!'

Shocked silence gripped the plaza.

Alia stood in unmoving consternation. She knew the mob could not see her, but she felt overcome by a sense of exposure, of vulnerability. The echoes of calming words within her skull competed with the pounding of her heart. She could only stare down at that incredible tableau. The Preacher remained with a hand pointing at her windows.

His words had been too much for the Priests, though. They broke the silence with angry shouts, stormed down the steps, thrusting people aside. As they moved the crowd reacted, breaking like a wave upon the steps, sweeping over the first lines of onlookers, carrying The Preacher before them. He stumbled blindly, separated from his young guide. Then a yellow-clad arm arose from the press of people; a crysknife was brandished in its hand. She saw the knife strike downward, bury itself in The Preacher's chest.

The thunderous clang of the Temple's giant doors being closed broke Alia from her shock. Guards obviously had closed the doors against the mob. But people already were drawing back, making an open space around a crumpled figure on the steps. An eerie quiet fell over the plaza. Alia saw many bodies, but only this one lay by itself.

Then a voice screeched from the mob: 'Muad'Dib! They've killed Muad'Dib!'

'Gods below,' Alia quavered. 'Gods below.'

'A little late for that, don't you think?' Jessica asked.

Alia whirled, noting the sudden startled reaction of Farad'n as he saw the rage on her face. 'That was Paul they killed!' Alia screamed. 'That was your son! When they confirm it, do you know what'll happen?'

Jessica stood rooted for a long moment, thinking that she had just been told something already known to her. Farad'n's hand upon her arm shattered the moment. 'My Lady,' he said, and there was such compassion in his voice that Jessica thought she might die of it right there. She looked from the cold, glaring anger on Alia's face to the sympathetic misery on Farad'n's features, and thought: *Perhaps I did my job too well.*

There could be no doubting Alia's words. Jessica remembered every intonation of The Preacher's voice, hearing her own tricks in it, the long years of instruction she'd spent there upon a young man meant to be Emperor, but who now lay a shattered mound of bloody rags upon the Temple steps.

*Ghafla blinded me,* Jessica thought.

Alia gestured to one of her aides, called: 'Bring Ghanima now.'

Jessica forced herself into recognizing these words. *Ghanima? Why Ghanima now?*

The aide had turned toward the outer door, motioning for it to be unbarred, but before a word could be uttered the door bulged. Hinges popped. The bar snapped and the door, a thick plasteel construction meant to withstand terrible energies, toppled into the room. Guards leaped to avoid it, drawing their weapons. Jessica and Farad'n's bodyguards closed in around the Corrino Prince.

But the opening revealed only two children: Ghanima on the left, clad in her black betrothal robe, and Leto on the right, the gray slickness of a stillsuit beneath a desert-stained white robe.

Alia stared from the fallen door to the children, found she was trembling uncontrollably.

'The family here to greet us,' Leto said. 'Grandmother.' He nodded to Jessica, shifted his attention to the Corrino Prince. 'And this must be Prince Farad'n. Welcome to Arrakis, Prince.'

Ghanima's eyes appeared empty. She held her right hand on a ceremonial crysknife at her waist, and she appeared to be trying to escape from Leto's grip on her arm. Leto shook her arm and her whole body shook with it.

'Behold me, family,' Leto said. 'I am Ari, the Lion of the Atreides. And here – ' Again he shook Ghanima's arm with that powerful ease which set her whole body jerking. ' – here is Aryeh, the Atreides Lioness. We come to set you onto Secher Nbiw, the Golden Path.'

Ghanima, absorbing the trigger words, *Secher Nbiw*, felt the locked-away consciousness flow into her mind. It flowed with a linear nicety, the inner awareness of her mother hovering there behind it, a guardian at a gate. And Ghanima knew in that instant that she had conquered the clamorous past. She possessed a gate through which she could peer when she needed that past. The months of self-hypnotic suppression had built for her a safe place from which to manage her own flesh. She started to turn toward Leto with the need to explain this when she became aware of where she stood and with whom.

Leto released her arm.

'Did our plan work?' Ghanima whispered.

'Well enough,' Leto said.

Recovering from her shock, Alia shouted at a clump of guards on her left: 'Seize them!'

But Leto bent, took the fallen door with one hand, skidded it across the room into the guards. Two were pinned against the wall. The others fell back in terror. That door weighed half a metric ton and this child had thrown it.

Alia, growing aware that the corridor beyond the doorway contained fallen guards, realized that Leto must have dealt with them, that this child had shattered her impregnable door.

Jessica, too, had seen the bodies, seen the awesome power in Leto and had made similar assumptions, but Ghanima's words touched a core of Bene Gesserit discipline which forced Jessica to maintain her composure. This grandchild spoke of a plan.

'What plan?' Jessica asked.

'The Golden Path, our Imperial plan for our Imperium,' Leto said. He nodded to Farad'n. 'Don't think harshly of me, cousin. I act for you as well. Alia hoped to have Ghanima slay you. I'd rather you lived out your life in some degree of happiness.'

Alia screamed at her guards cowering in the passage: 'I command you to seize them!'

But the guards refused to enter the room.

'Wait for me here, sister,' Leto said. 'I have a disagreeable task to perform.' He moved across the room toward Alia.

She backed away from him into a corner, crouched and drew her knife. The green jewels of its handle flashed in the light from the window.

Leto merely continued his advance, hands empty, but spread and ready.

Alia lunged with the knife.

Leto leaped almost to the ceiling, struck with his left foot. It caught Alia's head a glancing blow and sent her sprawling with a bloody mark on her forehead. She lost her grip on the knife and it skidded across the floor. Alia scrambled after the knife, but found Leto standing in front of her.

Alia hesitated, called up everything she knew of Bene Gesserit training. She came off the floor, body loose and poised.

Once more Leto advanced upon her.

Alia feinted to the left but her right shoulder came up and her right foot shot out in a toe-pointing kick which could disembowel a man if it struck precisely.

Leto caught the blow on his arm, grabbed the foot, and picked her up by it, swinging her around his head. The speed with which he swung her sent a flapping, hissing sound through the room as her robe beat against her body.

The others ducked away.

Alia screamed and screamed, but still she continued to swing around and around and around. Presently she fell silent.

Slowly Leto reduced the speed of her whirling, dropped her gently to the floor. She lay in a panting bundle.

Leto bent over her. 'I could've thrown you through a wall,' he said. 'Perhaps that would've been best, but we're now at the center of the struggle. You deserve your chance.'

Alia's eyes darted wildly from side to side.

'I have conquered those inner lives,' Leto said. 'Look at Ghani. She, too, can – '

Ghanima interrupted: 'Alia, I can show you – '

'No!' The word was wrenched from Alia. Her chest heaved and voices began to pour from her mouth. They were disconnected, cursing, pleading. 'You see! Why didn't you listen?' And again: 'Why're you doing this? What's happening?' And another voice: 'Stop them! Make them stop!'

Jessica covered her eyes, felt Farad'n's hands steady her.

Still Alia raved: 'I'll kill you!' Hideous curses erupted from her. 'I'll drink your blood!' The sounds of many languages began to pour from her, all jumbled and confused.

The huddled guards in the outer passage made the sign of the worm, then held clenched fists beside their ears. She was possessed!

Leto stood, shaking his head. He stepped to the window and with three swift blows shattered the supposedly unbreakable crystal-reinforced glass from its frame.

366

A sly look came over Alia's face. Jessica heard something like her own voice come from that twisting mouth, a parody of Bene Gesserit control. 'All of you! Stay where you are!'

Jessica lowering her hands, found them damp with tears.

Alia rolled to her knees, lurched to her feet.

'Don't you know who I am?' she demanded. It was her old voice, the sweet and lilting voice of the youthful Alia who was no more. 'Why're you all looking at me that way?' She turned pleading eyes to Jessica. 'Mother, make them stop it.'

Jessica could only shake her head from side to side, consumed by ultimate horror. All of the old Bene Gesserit warnings were true. She looked at Leto and Ghani standing side by side near Alia. What did those warnings mean for these poor twins?

'Grandmother,' Leto said, and there was pleading in his voice. 'Must we have a Trial of Possession?'

'Who are you to speak of trial?' Alia asked, and her voice was that of a querulous man, an autocratic and sensual man far gone in self-indulgence.

Both Leto and Ghanima recognized the voice. The Old Baron Harkonnen. Ghanima heard the same voice begin to echo in her own head, but the inner gate closed and she sensed her mother standing there.

Jessica remained silent.

'Then the decision is mine,' Leto said. 'And the choice is yours, Alia. Trial of Possession, or . . . ' He nodded toward the open window.

'Who're you to give me a choice?' Alia demanded, and it was still the voice of the Old Baron.

'Demon!' Ghanima screamed. 'Let her make her own choice!'

'Mother,' Alia pleaded in her little-girl tones. 'Mother, what're they doing? What do you want me to do? Help me.'

'Help yourself,' Leto ordered and, for just an instant, he saw the shattered presence of his aunt in her eyes, a glaring hopelessness which peered out at him and was gone. But her body moved, a sticklike, thrusting walk. She wavered, stumbled, veered from her path but returned to it, nearer and nearer the open window.

Now the voice of the Old Baron raged from her lips: 'Stop! Stop it, I say! I command you! Stop it! Feel this!' Alia clutched her head, stumbled closer to the window. She had the sill against her thighs then, but the voice still raved. 'Don't do this! Stop it and I'll help you. I have a plan. Listen to me. Stop it, I say. Wait!' But Alia pulled her hands away from her head, clutched the broken casement. In one jerking motion, she pulled herself over the sill and was gone. Not even a screech came from her as she fell.

In the room they heard the crowd shout, the sodden thump as Alia struck the steps far below.

Leto looked at Jessica. 'We told you to pity her.'

Jessica turned and buried her face in Farad'n's tunic.

> *The assumption that a whole system can be made to work better through an assault on its conscious elements betrays a dangerous ignorance. This has often been the ignorant approach of those who call themselves scientists and technologists.*
>
> — The Butlerian Jihad
> by Harq al-Ada

'He runs at night, cousin,' Ghanima said. 'He runs. Have you seen him run?'

'No,' Farad'n said.

He waited with Ghanima outside the small audience hall of the keep where Leto had called them to attend. Tyekanik stood at one side, uncomfortable with the Lady Jessica, who appeared withdrawn, as though her mind lived in another place. It was hardly an hour past the morning meal, but already many things had been set moving – a summons to the Guild, messages to CHOAM and the Landsraad.

Farad'n found it difficult to understand these Atreides. The Lady Jessica had warned him, but still the reality of them puzzled him. They still talked of the betrothal, although most political reasons for it seemed to have dissolved. Leto would assume the throne; there appeared little doubt of that. His odd *living skin* would have to be removed, of course ... but, in time ...

'He runs to tire himself,' Ghanima said. 'He's Kralizec embodied. No wind ever ran as he runs. He's a blur atop the dunes. I've seen him. He runs and runs. And when he has exhausted himself at last, he returns and rests his head in my lap. "Ask our mother within to find a way for me to die," he pleads.'

Farad'n stared at her. In the week since the riot in the plaza, the Keep had moved to strange rhythms, mysterious comings and goings; stories of bitter fighting beyond the Shield Wall came to him through Tyekanik, whose military advice had been asked.

'I don't understand you,' Farad'n said. 'Find a way for him to die?'

'He asked me to prepare you,' Ghanima said. Not for the first time, she was struck by the curious innocence of this Corrino Prince. Was that Jessica's doing, or something born in him?

'For what?'

'He's no longer human,' Ghanima said. 'Yesterday you asked when he was going to remove the *living skin*? Never. It's part of him now and he's part of it. Leto estimates he has perhaps four thousand years before metamorphosis destroys him.'

Farad'n tried to swallow in a dry throat.

'You see why he runs?' Ghanima asked.

'But if he'll live so long and be so —'

'Because the memory of being human is so rich in him. Think of all those lives, cousin. No. You can't imagine what that is because you've no experience of it. But I know. I can imagine his pain. He gives more than anyone ever gave before. Our father walked into the desert trying to escape it. Alia became Abomination in fear of it. Our grandmother has only the blurred infancy of this condition, yet must use every Bene Gesserit wile to live with it — which is what Reverend Mother training amounts to anyway. But Leto! He's all alone, never to be duplicated.'

Farad'n felt stunned by her words. Emperor for four thousand years?

'Jessica knows,' Ghanima said, looking across at her grandmother. 'He told her last night. He called himself the first truly long-range planner in human history.'

'What . . . does he plan?'

'The Golden Path. He'll explain it to you later.'

'And he has a role for me in this . . . plan?'

'As my mate,' Ghanima said. 'He's taking over the Sisterhood's breeding program. I'm sure my grandmother told you about the Bene Gesserit dream for a male Reverend with extraordinary powers. He's —'

'You mean we're just to be —'

'Not *just*.' She took his arm, squeezed it with a warm familiarity. 'He'll have many very responsible tasks for both of us. When we're not producing children, that is.'

'Well, you're a little young yet,' Farad'n said, disengaging his arm.

'Don't ever make that mistake again,' she said. There was ice in her tone.

Jessica came up to them with Tyekanik.

'Tyek tells me the fighting has spread off-planet,' Jessica said. 'The Central Temple on Biarek is under siege.'

Farad'n thought her oddly calm in this statement. He'd reviewed the reports with Tyekanik during the night. A wildfire of rebellion was spreading through the Empire. It would be put down, of course, but Leto would have a sorry Empire to restore.

'Here's Stilgar now,' Ghanima said. 'They've been waiting for him.' And once more she took Farad'n's arm.

The old Fremen Naib had entered by the far door escorted by two former Death Commando companions from the desert days. All were dressed in formal black robes with white piping and yellow headbands for mourning. They approached with steady strides, but Stilgar kept his attention on Jessica. He stopped in front of her, nodded warily.

'You still worry about the death of Duncan Idaho,' Jessica said. She didn't like this caution in her old friend.

'Reverend Mother,' he said.

*So it's going to be that way!* Jessica thought. *All formal and according to the Fremen code, with blood difficult to expunge.*

She said: 'By our view, you but played a part which Duncan assigned you. Not the first time a man has given his life for the Atreides. Why do they do it, Stil? You've been ready for it more than once. Why? Is it that you know how much the Atreides give in return?'

'I'm happy you seek no excuse for revenge,' he said. 'But there are matters I must discuss with your grandson. These matters may separate us from you forever.'

'You mean Tabr will not pay him homage?' Ghanima asked.

'I mean I reserve my judgment.' He looked coldly at Ghanima. 'I don't like what my Fremen have become,' he growled. 'We will go back to the old ways. Without you if necessary.'

'For a time, perhaps,' Ghanima said. 'But the desert is dying, Stil. What'll you do when there are no more worms, no more desert?'

'I don't believe it!'

'Within one hundred years,' Ghanima said, 'there'll be fewer than fifty worms, and those will be sick ones kept in a carefully managed reservation. Their spice will be for the Spacing Guild only, and the price . . . ' She shook her head. 'I've seen Leto's figures. He's been all over the planet. He knows.'

'Is this another trick to keep the Fremen as your vassals?'

'When were you ever my vassal?' Ghanima asked.

Stilgar scowled. No matter what he said or did, these twins always made it his fault!

'Last night he told me about this Golden Path,' Stilgar blurted. 'I don't like it!'

'That's odd,' Ghanima said, glancing at her grandmother. 'Most of the Empire will welcome it.'

'Destruction of us all,' Stilgar muttered.

'But everyone longs for the Golden Age,' Ghanima said. 'Isn't that so, grandmother?'

'Everyone,' Jessica agreed.

'They long for the Pharaonic Empire which Leto will give them,' Ghanima said. 'They long for a rich peace with abundant harvests, plentiful trade, a leveling of all except the Golden Ruler.'

'It'll be the death of the Fremen!' Stilgar protested.

'How can you say that? Will we not need soldiers and brave men to remove the occasional dissatisfaction? Why, Stil, you and Tyek's brave companions will be hard pressed to do the job.'

Stilgar looked at the Sardaukar officer and a strange light of understanding passed between them.

'And Leto will control the spice,' Jessica reminded them.

'He'll control it absolutely,' Ghanima said.

Farad'n, listening with the new awareness which Jessica had taught him, heard a set piece, a prepared performance between Ghanima and her grandmother.

'Peace will endure and endure and endure,' Ghanima said. 'Memory of war will all but vanish. Leto will lead humankind through that garden for at least four thousand years.'

Tyekanik glanced questioningly at Farad'n, cleared his throat.

'Yes, Tyek?' Farad'n said.

'I'd speak privately with you, My Prince.'

Farad'n smiled, knowing the question in Tyekanik's military mind, knowing that at least two others present also recognized this question. 'I'll not sell the Sardaukar,' Farad'n said.

'No need,' Ghanima said.

'Do you listen to this child?' Tyekanik demanded. He was outraged. The old Naib there understood the problems being raised by all of this plotting, but nobody else knew a damned thing about the situation!

Ghanima smiled grimly, said: 'Tell him, Farad'n.'

Farad'n sighed. It was easy to forget the strangeness of this child who was not a child. He could imagine a lifetime married to her, the hidden reservations on every intimacy. It was not a totally pleasant prospect, but he was beginning to recognize its inevit-

371

ability. Absolute control of dwindling spice supplies! Nothing would move in the universe without the spice.

'Later, Tyek,' Farad'n said.

'But –'

'*Later, I said!*' For the first time, he used Voice on Tyekanik, saw the man blink with surprise and remain silent.

A tight smile touched Jessica's mouth.

'He talks of peace and death in the same breath,' Stilgar muttered. 'Golden Age!'

Ghanima said: 'He'll lead humans through the cult of death into the free air of exuberant life! He speaks of death because that's necessary, Stil. It's a tension by which the living know they're alive. When his Empire falls . . . Oh, yes, it'll fall. You think this is Kralizec now, but Kralizec is yet to come. And when it comes, humans will have renewed their memory of what it's like to be alive. The memory will persist as long as there's a single human living. We'll go through the crucible once more, Stil. And we'll come out of it. We always arise from our own ashes. Always.'

Farad'n, hearing her words, understood now what she'd meant in telling him about Leto running. *He'll not be human.*

Stilgar was not yet convinced. 'No more worms,' he growled.

'Oh, the worms will come back,' Ghanima assured him. 'All will be dead within two hundred years, but they'll come back.'

'How . . .' Stilgar broke off.

Farad'n felt his mind awash in revelation. He knew what Ghanima would say before she spoke.

'The Guild will barely make it through the lean years, and only then because of its stockpiles and ours,' Ghanima said. 'But there'll be an abundance after Kralizec. The worms will return after my brother goes into the sand.'

*As with so many other religions, Muad'Dib's Golden Elixir of Life degenerated into external wizardry. Its mystical signs became mere symbols for deeper psychological processes, and those processes, of course, ran wild. What they needed was a living god, and they didn't have one, a situation which Muad'Dib's son has corrected.*

— Saying attributed to Lu Tung-pin
(Lu, The Guest of the Cavern)

Leto sat on the Lion Throne to accept the homage of the tribes. Ghanima stood beside him, one step down. The ceremony in the Great Hall went on for hours. Tribe after Fremen tribe passed before him through their delegates and their Naibs. Each group bore gifts fitting for a god of terrifying powers, a god of vengeance who promised them peace.

He'd cowed them into submission the previous week, performing for the assembled arifa of all the tribes. The Judges had seen him walk through a pit of fire, emerging unscathed to demonstrate that his skin bore no marks by asking them to study him closely. He'd ordered them to strike him with knives, and the impenetrable skin had sealed his face while they struck at him to no avail. Acids ran off him with only the lightest mist of smoke. He'd eaten their poisons and laughed at them.

At the end he'd summoned a worm and stood facing them at its mouth. He'd moved from that to the landing field at Arrakeen, where he'd brazenly toppled a Guild frigate by lifting one of its landing fins.

The arifa had reported all of this with a fearful awe, and now the tribal delegates had come to seal their submission.

The vaulted space of the Great Hall with its acoustical dampening systems tended to absorb sharp noises, but a constant rustling of moving feet insinuated itself into the senses, riding on dust and the flint odors brought in from the open.

Jessica, who'd refused to attend, watched from a high spy hole behind the throne. Her attention was caught by Farad'n and the realization that both she and Farad'n had been outmaneuvered. Of course Leto and Ghanima had anticipated the Sisterhood! The twins could consult within themselves a host of Bene Gesserits greater than all now living in the Empire.

She was particularly bitter at the way the Sisterhood's mythology had trapped Alia. *Fear built on fear!* The habits of generations had imprinted the fate of Abomination upon her. Alia had known no hope. Of course she'd succumbed. Her fate made the accomplishment of Leto and Ghanima even more difficult to face. Not one way out of the trap, but two. Ghanima's victory over the inner lives and her insistence that Alia deserved only pity were the bitterest things of all. Hypnotic suppression under stress linked to the wooing of a benign ancestor had saved Ghanima. They might have saved Alia. But without hope, nothing had been attempted until it was too late. Alia's water had been poured upon the sand.

Jessica sighed, shifted her attention to Leto on the throne. A giant canopic jar containing the water of Muad'Dib occupied a place of honor at his right elbow. He'd boasted to Jessica that his father-within laughed at this gesture even while admiring it.

That jar and the boasting had firmed her resolve not to participate in this ritual. As long as she lived, she knew she could never accept Paul speaking through Leto's mouth. She rejoiced that House Atreides had survived, but the things-that-might-have-been were beyond bearing.

Farad'n sat cross-legged beside the jar of Muad'Dib's water. It was the position of the Royal Scribe, an honor newly conferred and newly accepted.

Farad'n felt that he was adjusting nicely to these new realities, although Tyekanik still raged and promised dire consequences. Tyekanik and Stilgar had formed a partnership of distrust which seemed to amuse Leto.

In the hours of the homage ceremony, Farad'n had gone from awe to boredom to awe. They were an endless stream of humanity, these peerless fighting men. Their loyalty renewed to the Atreides on the throne could not be questioned. They stood in submissive terror before him, completely daunted by what the arifa had reported.

At last it drew to a close. The final Naib stood before Leto – Stilgar in the 'rearguard position of honor'. Instead of panniers heavy with spice, fire jewels, or any of the other costly gifts which lay in mounds around the throne, Stilgar bore a headband of braided spice-fiber. The Atreides Hawk had been worked in gold and green into its design.

Ghanima recognized it and shot a sidewise glance at Leto.

Stilgar placed the headband on the second step below the throne, bowed low. 'I give you the headband worn by your sister when I took her into the desert to protect her,' he said.

Leto suppressed a smile.

'I know you've fallen on hard times, Stilgar,' Leto said. 'Is there something here you would have in return?' He gestured at the piles of costly gifts.

'No, My Lord.'

'I accept your gift then,' Leto said. He rocked forward, brought up the hem of Ghanima's robe, ripped a thin strip from it. 'In return, I give you this bit of Ghanima's robe, the robe she wore when she was stolen from your desert camp, forcing me to save her.'

Stilgar accepted the cloth in a trembling hand. 'Do you mock me, My Lord?'

'Mock you? By my name, Stilgar, never would I mock you. I have given you a gift without price. I command you to carry it always next to your heart as a reminder that all humans are prone to error and all leaders are human.'

A thin chuckle escaped Stilgar. 'What a Naib you would have made!'

'What a Naib I am! Naib of Naibs. Never forget that!'

'As you say, My Lord.' Stilgar swallowed, remembering the reports of his arifa. And he thought: *Once I thought of slaying him. Now it's too late.* His glance fell on the jar, a graceful opaque gold capped with green. 'That is water of my tribe.'

'And mine,' Leto said. 'I command you to read the inscription upon its side. Read it aloud that all may hear it.'

Stilgar cast a questioning glance at Ghanima, but she returned it with a lift of her chin, a cold response which sent a chill through him. Were these Atreides imps bent on holding him to answer for his impetuosity and his mistakes?

'Read it,' Leto said, pointing.

Slowly Stilgar mounted the steps, bent to look at the jar. Presently he read aloud: 'This water is the ultimate essence, a source of outward streaming creativity. Though motionless, this water is the means of all movement.'

'What does it mean, My Lord?' Stilgar whispered. He felt awed by the words, touched within himself in a place he could not understand.

'The body of Muad'Dib is a dry shell like that abandoned by an insect,' Leto said. 'He mastered the inner world while holding the outer in contempt, and this led to catastrophe. He mastered the outer world while excluding the inner world, and this delivered his descendants to the demons. The Golden Elixir will vanish from Dune, yet Muad'Dib's seed goes on, and his water moves our universe.'

Stilgar bowed his head. Mystical things always left him in turmoil.

'The beginning and the end are one,' Leto said. 'You live in air but do not see it. A phase has closed. Out of that closing grows the beginning of its opposite. Thus, we will have Kralizec. Everything returns later in changed form. You have felt thoughts in your head; your descendants will feel thoughts in their bellies. Return to Sietch Tabr, Stilgar, Gurney Halleck will join you there as my advisor in your Council.'

'Don't you trust me, My Lord?' Stilgar's voice was low.

'Completely, else I'd not send Gurney to you. He'll begin recruiting the new force we'll need soon. I accept your pledge of fealty, Stilgar. You are dismissed.'

Stilgar bowed low, backed off the steps, turned and left the hall. The other Naibs fell into step behind him according to the Fremen principle that 'the last shall be first'. But some of their queries could be heard on the throne as they departed.

'What were you talking about up there, Stil? What does that mean, those words on Muad'Dib's water?'

Leto spoke to Farad'n. 'Did you get all of that, Scribe?'

'Yes, My Lord.'

'My grandmother tells me she trained you well in the mnemonic processes of the Bene Gesserit. That's good. I don't want you scribbling beside me.'

'As you command, My Lord.'

'Come and stand before me,' Leto said.

Farad'n obeyed, more than ever thankful for Jessica's training. When you accepted the fact that Leto no longer was human, no longer could think as humans thought, the course of his Golden Path became ever more frightening.

Leto looked up at Farad'n. The guards stood well back out of earshot. Only the counselors of the Inner Presence remained on the floor of the Great Hall, and they stood in subservient groups well beyond the first step. Ghanima had moved closer to rest an arm on the back of the throne.

'You've not yet agreed to give me your Sardaukar,' Leto said. 'But you will.'

'I owe you much, but not that,' Farad'n said.

'You think they'd not mate well with my Fremen?'

'As well as those new friends, Stilgar and Tyekanik.'

'Yet you refuse?'

'I await your offer.'

'Then I must make the offer, knowing you will never repeat it.

I pray my grandmother has done her part well, that you are prepared to understand.'

'What must I understand?'

'There's always a prevailing mystique in any civilization,' Leto said. 'It builds itself as a barrier against change, and that always leaves future generations unprepared for the universe's treachery. All mystiques are the same in building these barriers – the religious mystique, the hero-leader mystique, the messiah mystique, the mystique of science/technology, and the mystique of nature itself. We live in an Imperium which such a mystique has shaped, and now that Imperium is falling apart because most people don't distinguish between mystique and their universe. You see, the mystique is like demon possession; it tends to take over the consciousness, becoming all things to the observer.'

'I recognize your grandmother's wisdom in these words,' Farad'n said.

'Well and good, cousin. She asked me if I were Abomination. I answered in the negative. That was my first treachery. You see, Ghanima escaped this, but I did not. I was forced to balance the inner lives under the pressure of excessive melange. I had to seek the active cooperation of those aroused lives within me. Doing this, I avoided the most malignant and chose a dominant helper thrust upon me by the inner awareness which was my father. I am not, in truth, my father or this helper. Then again, I am not the Second Leto.'

'Explain.'

'You have an admirable directness,' Leto said. 'I'm a community dominated by one who was ancient and surpassingly powerful. He fathered a dynasty which endured for three thousand of our years. His name was Harum and, until his line trailed out in the congenital weaknesses and superstitions of a descendant, his subjects lived in a rhythmic sublimity. They moved unconsciously with the changes of the seasons. They bred individuals who tended to be short-lived, superstitious, and easily led by a god-king. Taken as a whole, they were a powerful people. Their survival as a species became habit.'

'I don't like the sound of that,' Farad'n said.

'Nor do I, really,' Leto said. 'But it's the universe I'll create.'

'Why?'

'It's a lesson I learned on Dune. We kept the presence of death a dominant specter among the living here. By that presence, the dead changed the living. The people of such a society sink down into their bellies. But when the time comes for the opposite, when they arise, they are great and beautiful.'

'That doesn't answer my question,' Farad'n protested.

'You don't trust me, cousin.'

'Nor does your own grandmother.'

'And with good reason,' Leto said. 'But she acquiesces because she must. Bene Gesserits are pragmatists in the end. I share their view of our universe, you know. You wear the marks of that universe. You retain the habits of rule, cataloguing all around you in terms of their possible threat or value.'

'I agreed to be your scribe.'

'It amused you and flattered your real talent, which is that of historian. You've a definite genius for reading the present in terms of the past. You've anticipated me on several occasions.'

'I don't like your veiled insinuations,' Farad'n said.

'Good. You come from infinite ambition to your present lowered estate. Didn't my grandmother warn you about infinity? It attracts us like a floodlight in the night, blinding us to the excesses it can inflict upon the finite.'

'Bene Gesserit aphorisms!' Farad'n protested.

'But much more precise,' Leto said. 'The Bene Gesserit believed they could predict the course of evolution. But they overlooked their own changes in the course of that evolution. They assumed they would stand still while their breeding plan evolved. I have no such reflexive blindness. Look carefully at me, Farad'n, for I am no longer human.'

'So your sister assures me.' Farad'n hesitated. Then: 'Abomination?'

'By the Sisterhood's definition, perhaps. Harum is cruel and autocratic. I partake of his cruelty. Mark me well: I have the cruelty of the husbandman, and this human universe is my farm. Fremen once kept tame eagles as pets, but I'll keep a tame Farad'n.'

Farad'n's face darkened. 'Beware my claws, cousin. I well know my Sardaukar would fall in time before your Fremen. But we'd wound you sorely, and there are jackals waiting to pick off the weak.'

'I will use you well, that I promise,' Leto said. He leaned forward. 'Did I not say I'm no longer human? Believe me, cousin. No children will spring from my loins, for I no longer have loins. And this forces my second treachery.'

Farad'n waited in silence, seeing at last the direction of Leto's argument.

'I shall go against every Fremen precept,' Leto said. 'They

will accept because they can do nothing else. I kept you here under the lure of a betrothal, but there will be no betrothal of you and Ghanima. My sister will marry me!'

'But you –'

'Marry, I said. Ghanima must continue the Atreides line. There's also the matter of the Bene Gesserit breeding program, which is now my breeding program.'

'I refuse,' Farad'n said.

'You refuse to father an Atreides dynasty?'

'What dynasty? You'll occupy the throne for thousands of years.'

'And mold your descendants in my image. It will be the most intensive, the most inclusive training program in all of history. We'll be an ecosystem in miniature. You see, whatever system animals choose to survive by must be based on the pattern of interlocking communities, interdependence, working together in the common design which is the system. And this system will produce the most knowledgeable rulers ever seen.'

'You put fancy words on a most distasteful –'

'Who will survive Kralizec?' Leto asked. 'I promise you, Kralizec will come.'

'You're a madman! You will shatter the Empire.'

'Of course I will ... and I'm not a man. But I'll create a new consciousness in all men. I tell you that below the desert of Dune there's a secret place with the greatest treasure of all time. I do not lie. When the last worm dies and the last melange is harvested upon our sands, these deep treasures will spring up throughout our universe. As the power of the spice monopoly fades and the hidden stockpiles make their mark, new powers will appear throughout our realm. It is time humans learned once more to live in their instincts.'

Ghanima took her arm from the back of the throne, crossed to Farad'n's side, took his hand.

'As my mother was not wife, you will not be husband,' Leto said. 'But perhaps there will be love, and that will be enough.'

'Each day, each moment brings its change,' Ghanima said. 'One learns by recognizing the moments.'

Farad'n felt the warmth of Ghanima's tiny hand as an insistent presence. He recognized the ebb and flow of Leto's arguments, but not once had Voice been used. It was an appeal to the guts, not to the mind.

'Is this what you offer for my Sardaukar?' he asked.

'Much, much more, cousin. I offer your descendants the Imperium. I offer you peace.'

'What will be the outcome of your peace?'

'Its opposite,' Leto said, his voice calmly mocking.

Farad'n shook his head. 'I find the price for my Sardaukar very high. Must I remain Scribe, the secret father of your royal line?'

'You must.'

'Will you try to force me into your habit of peace?'

'I will.'

'I'll resist you every day of my life.'

'But that's the function I expect of you, cousin. It's why I chose you. I'll make it official. I will give you a new name. From this moment, you'll be called Breaking of the Habit, which in our tongue is Harq al-Ada. Come, cousin, don't be obtuse. My mother taught you well. Give me your Sardaukar.'

'Give them,' Ghanima echoed. 'He'll have them one way or another.'

Farad'n heard fear for himself in her voice. Love, then? Leto asked not for reason, but for an intuitive leap. 'Take them,' Farad'n said.

'Indeed,' Leto said. He lifted himself from the throne, a curiously fluid motion as though he kept his terrible powers under most delicate control. Leto stepped down then to Ghanima's level, moved her gently until she faced away from him, turned and placed his back against hers. 'Note this, cousin Harq al-Ada. This is the way it will always be with us. We'll stand thus when we are married. Back to back, each looking outward from the other to protect the one thing which we have always been.' He turned, looked mockingly at Farad'n, lowered his voice: 'Remember that, cousin, when you're face to face with my Ghanima. Remember that when you whisper of love and soft things, when you are most tempted by the habits of my peace and my contentment. Your back will remain exposed.'

Turning from them, he strode down the steps into the waiting courtiers, picked them up in his wake like satellites, and left the hall.

Ghanima once more took Farad'n's hand, but her gaze looked beyond the far end of the hall long after Leto had left it. 'One of us had to accept the agony,' she said, 'and he was always the stronger.'

# DUNE
## by Frank Herbert

DUNE is the finest, most widely acclaimed science fiction novel of this century. Huge in scope, towering in concept, it is a work which will live in the reader's imagination for the rest of his life.

'DUNE seems to me unique among science fiction novels in the depth of its characterisation and the extraordinary detail of the world it creates. I know nothing comparable to it except THE LORD OF THE RINGS.'                      – Arthur C. Clarke

'Certainly one of the landmarks of modern science fiction . . . an amazing feat of creation.'                      – Analog

NEW ENGLISH LIBRARY

# DUNE MESSIAH
## by Frank Herbert

A holy war has made Paul Atreides the religious and political leader of a thousand planets. The malign sisterhood of the Bene Gesserit, unable to dominate the man they have made a god, set out to destroy him.

Paul, who is able to foresee the plans of his enemies, resolves to adapt and shape them to a goal that is as shocking as it is unexpected.

*Dune Messiah* – long-awaited successor to double award winner *Dune* – is an epic of imperial intrigue that spans the universe, rich and strange in its evocation of the history, institutions and people of a far future age.

**NEW ENGLISH LIBRARY**

# FRANK HERBERT

| | |
|---|---|
| Dune | £2.50 |
| Dune Messiah | £1.95 |
| God Emperor of Dune | £2.50 |
| Heretics of Dune | £2.50 |
| Direct Descent | £2.25 |
| The Dragon in the Sea | £1.25 |
| The Eyes of Heisenberg | £1.50 |
| The Godmakers | £1.95 |
| The Green Brain | £1.50 |
| The Heaven Makers | £1.25 |
| The Santaroga Barrier | £1.25 |
| Whipping Star | £1.25 |
| The White Plague | £2.50 |
| The Worlds of Frank Herbert | £0.40 |
| The Home Computer Handbook | £3.95 |